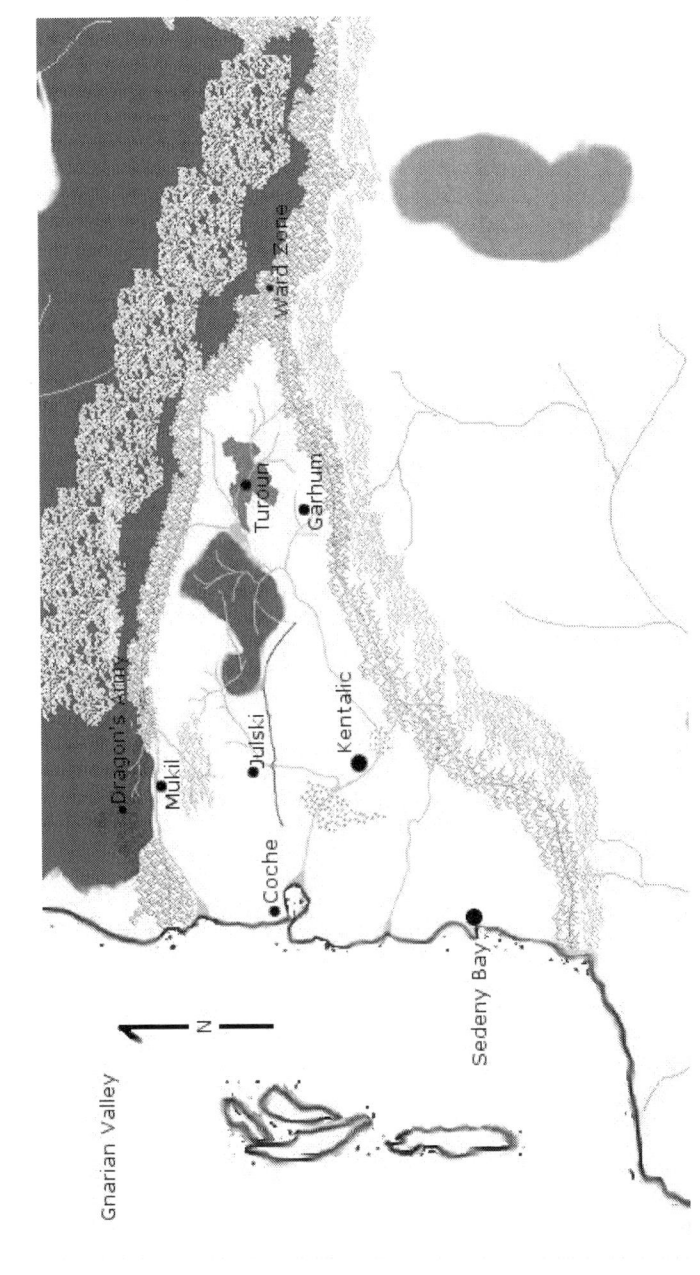

Restoration Of Numar

Merry Christmas!

Crystalyn Emerald Dragon

Restoration Of Numar

A Dragon's Army Novel

Crystalyn Emerald Dragon

This Dragon's Army novel is a work of fiction. All events and characters are fictitious.

Restoration Of Numar
A Dragon's Army Novel

Copyright © 2010 Crystalyn Emerald Dragon
All Rights Reserved

Cover art by Amanda Carroll
Cover design by Crystalyn Emerald Dragon

ISBN 978-1449955916
EAN-13 9781449955915

Restoration Of Numar

Acknowledgements

Great and many thanks to everyone who helped me get this book ready for publishing. To my parents and siblings who tirelessly read and reread these pages to make sure that there were no errors, and to all of my cousins and aunts who also put in their efforts to proofing. To my friends for rooting for me, and keeping me encouraged, telling me to never give up.

I love you all.

And great thanks to my sister, who worked so hard to create the lovely cover art!

Chapter One

A New Home

Smoke billowed up out of the burned ruins of the city of Yelm, darkening the sky for miles around. Yelm had been a fairly large city, before it had become the main target of King Cerin's enemies. The surrounding land was war torn and burned, sending refugees in all directions – those that survived the initial attack and plundering.

Only when the last soldiers vanished over the horizon did a charred metal plate flip over, behind one of the outer shops that had been partially burnt down. A small face smeared with soot peeked out of the exposed hole, turning as hands were rubbed after the handling of the still-hot metal. Ducking down again, the boy crawled through a tunnel too small for any soldier to get into, whether he wore armor or not.

"Looks all clear, now. But the place is a mess." He said, to a collection of other young creatures. Not all were of his race, though, many having pinfeathers or stubby leather limbs that would later in life sport leather wings. Several were scaly, others were furry, and many were the wrinkled and strangely colored children of the store's previous owners, Goblins.

Only a few of the faces that looked at him weren't streaked by dust, soot, and tears. And those were the ones that had no capacity for tears. They were still covered in soot and dust, but it wasn't nearly as prominent in the dark interior of the hidey-hole.

"Is the other way open? There's no way I can get out of here by that route." Said one of the larger members – an equine type creature known as a Centaurii. He was still spindly as a foal, mane and tail still very short. Coat blue as a sapphire, his skin was a deep blood red before fading back into blue where his equine head joined his humanoid torso. Long legs folded up, he was crammed back into the farthest corner, out of the way of all the other occupants. His mother, whom he already knew was dead, had unceremoniously stuffed him down the narrow hole. She had perished mere moments after poking him in the hole, and her high scream still haunted his waking hours as well as his dreams. But he knew that without his mother's strength to haul him out again, he was stuck in the tiny cave.

"I'll have to go see." The boy said, turning around to scramble back up the narrow hole. Clambering out onto the surface, he trotted to the smoldering building's corner. He peeked into the alley before running down that as well, ducking a burning beam. Looking out into the streets, he stared aghast at the wreckage and death strewn haphazardly everywhere. Closing his eyes, he made his way to the front entrance to the store, and pushed his way inside. The door took a great deal of shoving on his part to get it to move enough for him to slip past. Skirting the still-burning oils counter, he made his way to the back of the store where the hatch in the floor was, concealed by a heavy rug. Straining to pull the rug away, the boy saw that the rug was not entirely removable for the crates sitting on it, and that the crates also were on the hatch. "There's no way I can clear this… " he said, sitting down where he was, in the soot and ash. A smoke darkened sky could be seen above him, and he stared at it for a length of time, before contemplating the iron crate that blocked the hatch. "If I only had some majick …" he mumbled, remembering some of the spells his father had taught him.

Getting up, he started searching the ruins for a bottle of majick, though he knew that if there had been any, the soldiers would have taken it all. Finding yet another floor-hatch behind the main counter, he pulled on the ring. Instead of the hatch lifting, the ring pulled away from the hatch. "Well, that's useless!" he exclaimed, squatting to look at the rod that the ring was now suspended on. As he watched on amazement, the hatch grumbled, and sank into the floor before sliding aside, revealing a brightly lit room below. Climbing down into it, he found shelves of goods, including yokes for man and beast, axles for wagons, wheels, boxes of dried goods, bags of beans, cans of oils of all sorts, and a myriad of things he had no idea what they were. A storehouse for the store up above was what it was – all untouched by the armies. Finding a tiny box stashed on a bottom shelf, he pulled it out and lifted the latch to open the top. Inside was a set of vials, each of a different color. Different shades of the colors swirled gently around and around inside the vials as if they were alive.

"Majick!" he breathed, astounded, never having seen more than a drop of majick at one time before. Closing the box and clutching it to his chest, he made his way back up to the store and to the other hatch. Setting the box down on the floor, he carefully opened the box and selected the first vial. Twisting the top just enough to let a tiny drop escape onto his fingers, he quickly tightened the top again, and put the vial down as the majick on his fingers pooled slowly. Moving to the crate, he mumbled words in a language that he didn't know what it was, spreading the majick along the edges of the crate. Stepping back he said the final word of the spell, and waited.

Nothing happened.

"Curse you, you dumb crate!" he kicked it violently, in frustration. To his utter horror, it sailed away and smashed into the only remaining upright in the back room. As he stood and stared, what was left of the building came crashing down around him. Only at the last instant did he have the sense to flee, barely missing getting crushed by the falling structure.

Standing out in the street, he sighed. "That did me a lot of good." He said, realizing that the hatch was even more buried – along with the box of majick, and the hatch to the stores. Looking at the heap for a while, he plopped down in the dirt to ponder his new problems. Eventually, he got up and went into the wreckage to see if there was anything he could do.

Scrambling in and under various suspended bits, he pushed and shoved until he managed to find the hatch again – this time more than only partly held shut. Searching around, he looked for the tiny box of majick, hoping that it had not been smashed in the structure's falling throes. Tipping a short chunk of roofing over, he found the little box entirely unharmed, saved by a pocket in the bottom of the rubble he'd moved.

"At last. A piece of luck!" Scooping the box up he left the ruins to sit in the street again, inspecting the contents of the little box once again. Leaving the building, he returned to the hole that he'd crawled out of and sat near its mouth.

"Find it yet?" a small voice called out, to him. "What was all that noise?"

"Ya, I found it. But the building fell down." He said, leaning towards the hole to be better heard.

"Oh. So we can't get out that way?"

"No."

"We're trapped!" came the wailing cries of several children.

"No, no! I have a box of majick!" he said. "Does any one down there know how to use it?"

Silence echoed loudly from the hole, and he sighed, hopelessly.

Eventually, a tiny goblin came crawling up into the light. "I – I know ... a little bit."

"That's all I know, too. I hope you know a different bit from what I know." He offered the box to the goblin.

The goblin took it, squatting on its haunches to set the box on its knobby knees. Lifting the lid, it peered at the contents. "I don't know these kinds. What are they?"

"Um." The boy leaned forward again, to look into the box. "That ..." He frowned, pointing at a vial, then sighed. "I don't know. It's just majick. I have no idea what kind it is."

"Oh. I only know earth majick."

"Well ... earth is generally brown ..." He pointed at a vial that swirled in soft hues of brown and grey.

The goblin took it out, handling it gingerly. "That's a lot of majick."

"I know. Don't waste it." The boy said. "We may need it later."

"Ok." The goblin set the box down gently, closing the lid carefully before turning to face the opening. Cracking the top slightly, the goblin dribbled a touch on the mouth of the hole, before stepping back and muttering in an obscure Goblin dialect. The earth heaved, making the trapped occupants scream wildly. After an uncertain moment when the earth didn't know what it was supposed to be, the hole widened before settling down to its normal routine – just being dirt.

The boy carefully edged over the newly stirred earth, and looked down into the hole. "Everybody ok?"

"I think so!" Came the reply.

"No! Mutsgae puked on me!" Came another distressed voice.

"Ew." He backed up, knowing that since Mutsgae was a carrion-eating variety of Lizard, that particular puke was especially putrid.

Within moments, young of all sorts of different races were scrambling out of the hole that was now filled with stench of the worst kind. Even the young Centaurii found a way to squeeze out – all the others desperately pushing on his rump helped a great deal in aiding his escape.

When all were finally out, including Mutsgae, there were some two-dozen newly orphaned members standing about in the rubble. The largest by far was the Centaurii foal, the smallest being a gnome that could make an entire bedchamber out of the foal's hand. The others ranged wildly from species to species, every one a sentient being. All were soot streaked and filthy beyond recognition, some cut and bleeding varying colors of blood. Moments after having gotten out, most scattered in all directions to what was left of their original homes. The boy stayed put – he knew his home was gone. It had been in the upper stories of this very building where his parents had been renting the space from the shop owner. There was nothing left but the burnt out husk that had managed to stay erect after his adventure with the box. Nearby stood the Centaurii, also unmoving. He had nowhere to go – he too knew that all he'd had was gone. Beside him stood Mutsgae – too sick to move, the Lizard merely hunkered at the Centaurii's feet. Mutsgae was a Lizard of the low sort – he wasn't a Lizard-man, being more akin to a small crocodile. He could travel at a high rate of speed, should it suit him. But it rarely suited a Lizard to move faster than a creep. His kind were fairly rare, amongst the more 'civilized' races. Most assumed them stupid, or worse, a source of meat and hide.

    Mutsgae's family had been in the town because, among other things, Lizards were fearsome warriors, and his brood mother had been a mercenary. The rest of his clutch had died enroute to various other hiding places. Mutsgae and his siblings were still too small to be of any use in a fight, other than to get themselves killed. Currently, he was no bigger than a puppy. But when fully grown, he would be longer than a man was tall, and four times as deadly.

    Smoke wafted across the small area where the three hunkered, obscuring everything from sight and causing them all to choke and cough. When it cleared, the boy stood and started to walk away. "Might as well find somewhere else to be." He stopped at the box of majick, and selected a vial of swirling purples. The rest he left for the other young creatures to divide or use. Tucking it into his shirt, he continued on.

    "Certainly." The Centaurii followed. "You don't mind if I follow?"

    "Well ... we'll probably be safer together, in a group."

    "Most certainly." The Centaurii twisted, to look back at the miserable lump that was Mutsgae. "And him?"

    "Probably ought to get him out of there."

    "Ok." Turning, the Centaurii trotted back to Mutsgae, scooped him up and trotted back to where the boy was walking, trying to not trip on the bits and pieces of town.

    "What a mess. What's the point, in all this, I wonder?" the boy mused.

"No idea. Mother never even mentioned that such a thing could ever happen. I wish I could hide in her tail, back in the stables."

The boy choked on a laugh. "Ok."

"If she were here, she'd know what to do."

"Wishful thinking won't get us very far, you know."

"Ever tried it?"

"All the time, and every time my Da would give me a lecture about how if I ever wanted to be something worth while, to stop wishing and start doing."

"Your Da sounds like he never had any fun at all. He ought to have had a few brisk gallops."

The boy laughed. "The only gallops Da got were the kind that had him running for the pot."

"What kind is that?"

"Never mind."

"Where are we going?" The Centaurii asked.

"No idea. Got any ideas?"

"No. Well ... we could head towards the Homelands."

"Where's that?" the boy asked.

"No idea. Mother always spoke of them."

"That does us a fat lot of good."

"Excellent! Which way?"

"Ever hear of sarcasm?"

"No. What is it? Does it taste good?"

"Hardly. Usually bitter."

"Bitter's ok, I guess, since I haven't had anything to eat in ... I don't know how long."

The boy sighed. "Never mind."

"But I'm hungry."

"Sarcasm isn't edible."

"Oh." He dropped Mutsgae when he started to writhe too much to hang on to. The Lizard started sniffing about in the rubble, trailing along behind the Centaurii, sniffing out things that only a Lizard would eat. The other two made a point of not paying him any mind, lest they lose what little they still had in their stomachs. Belly full, Mutsgae followed after the other two at a fast scrabble, for his short legs.

"Where are you going?" he asked, in a high nasal voice.

"Nowhere, anywhere, away from here." The boy replied.

"Oh. Are you sure that's a good idea?"

"Why wouldn't it be?" the boy asked, gesturing around. "All this wreckage, dead bodies. We'd catch our death here."

"But this is where there's food, and this is where the armies won't come. Because they've already been here."

"Muts has a point on that last bit." The Centauri said. "Though I doubt I could find any unsoiled hay here."
"True. But I'd still rather not stay."
"Nor I." The Centaurii agreed.
"Well..." Mutsgae looked about at all the potential dinners he would be leaving behind, sighed, and scrambled after the other two. He was used to being in amongst many others – being on his own was as much a shock to him as any thing else that had happened. He felt more at ease when with the other two, and didn't want to be left behind.

By the time the three made it to the edge of the ruined town, they'd picked up one more companion – the little gnome. She sat atop the Centaurii's head, pillowed in his forelock as he trotted along behind the boy. Somewhere, she'd found a new set of clothes that hadn't been burnt or soiled, and had changed. She also bore a small travel sack that measured about as big as a pea. This she tied to one hair of the forelock, to make sure it wouldn't get lost.

At the edge of the town, they stopped to look out across the land, past columns of smoke from the burning fields. The ravaging armies hadn't left anything at all for their enemies to possibly come behind and take. Which meant there was nothing left for anyone else, either.

Finding a patch of withered yet green grass, the Centaurii started pulling up fistfuls of it, stuffing some of it into his long mouth, wadding the rest up to carry with him.

The boy, too, was feeling hunger pains, but he wasn't going to eat grass. He wasn't that hungry. Yet.

But the Centaurii seemed to enjoy the little snack of a meal, leaving no blade longer than a single inch. As the Centaurii ate and gathered, the boy poked about in the rubble some more to try and find something he could eat. He discovered that one shell of a house had the unusual feature of a cellar inside the house, and he was able to make his own carry sack of food, after adequately filling his belly on canned fruits and salted meats. Picking up an unbroken loaf of bread and another of hard cheese, he added those to his sack of meat and fruits.

Tying the bundle securely, he picked it up and carried it out to where the others were. It was a heavy bundle, and wasn't nearly as big as he could have wished. But he knew that it would grow light all too soon.

Finding a seat, he waited until the others were all done with whatever collecting they were doing.

"Do you like bread?" The boy asked of the Centaurii.
"Sure. I like bread. Why?"

"There's some in that house there." He indicated the husk he'd found the pantry in.

"Really?"

"Sure."

"Ok." The Centauri trotted that way to go investigate. Soon, he too emerged with a bundle slightly larger than the boy's. He had also stuffed his grass ball into it, to keep from losing the precious blades.

The two then set out, the gnome riding on the Centaurii's head, and Mutsgae trailing along behind at his own pace. At times, they weren't even sure he was following he was so far behind. Other times, he led the odd party, tail swishing back and forth as he trotted on short legs.

The first day's travel was easy – they merely wanted to get away from the burnt out town. But the second, they were plainly lost. They didn't even know which way they'd come from. The day before, they had elected to avoid the open road, because that was how the armies had come, and then left. But on the second day, they knew that without some knowledge of the surrounding lands, they had been fools to not follow it.

Tall trees towered above them all, the trunks wider than a full-grown Centaurii was long. The forest floor was open and covered with leaves, but that didn't aid in their direction.

Mutsgae warned that he could smell an animal had been there – a large one. But then, to him, the boy was large. The boy interpreted this as meaning that the woods were wolf infested.

High above their heads, birds and flying things that weren't birds called out, mocked, and chided them in wordless tones.

"Can you smell which way we came from?" the Centaurii asked.

"No. The winds last night stirred the leaves too well." Mutsgae said, swinging his short head from side to side in a slow arc.

"Well – let's pick a direction. Odds are that we won't leave the way we came here by." The boy said, seated on a root with his pack by his feet.

"Maybe. But how can we be certain?" The Centaurii asked.

"Can't. But would you rather sit here and gripe all day while a wolf could be contemplating us for breakfast?"

"Wolf?" the Centaurii asked, in a high pitched tone, glancing all around. "Where?"

"Who knows?" The boy picked up a pack and set out in the first direction that came to hand.

"That way. Follow him." The Gnome said, pulling on a strand of the Centaurii's forelock to get his attention.

The Centaurii turned and leaped over a root to follow the boy. Mutsgae toddled around the root, and then followed. He walked along with his nose just barely above the ground, sniffing out all sorts of interesting smells in the wake of the others.

Three days passed without any sort of problems, and on the fourth, they came across a hugely tall stone wall. They traveled along it for half a day, until they came across a tall, broad, wooden door with iron banding. The boy tried to open it, but it wouldn't budge. It was either locked, or so long unused that it was stuck.

"I wonder what's on the other side?" He mused, contemplating the door. "Why is there a wall here in the middle of a forest?"

"It's not. Look – there are no trees on that side of the wall." The Centaurii said, pointing up. "Lots of sun, only."

"Oh. So it's a wall protecting the forest, or a wall protecting something *from* the forest?"

"I guess."

The boy tried the door again, but it still wouldn't budge. "Too bad we can't climb the trees and see what's over there."

"Who says we can't?" Mutsgae asked.

The others regarded each other for a moment, then all looked down at the little Lizard.

Mutsgae soon found himself clawing his way up a trunk so broad it could have been a road, pulling himself up to the lowest branch. That lowest branch was a lot higher than he'd thought, and it had looked pretty far. He had to stop and just hang three times before he reached it. When he looked down, the others looked like colored dots, and the wall merely a twig.

"Well? What's over there?" The Centaurii bellowed up to him.

Mutsgae, having plumb forgot why in the world he was up in a tree, remembered why he'd made that grueling climb. Turing his snout out over the wall, he trotted along the branch to get a look past the foliage.

Pushing his head past the leaves, he sank claws into the bark to keep from falling as he peered out. What greeted his eyes was a wide-open plain, perfectly flat, and checker boarded with growing crops. Farther off, beyond the crops was a ring of trees akin to the one he was in, surrounding a city of tall structures. "Wow." He murmured, hypnotized by a sight he had never imagined even existed.

"What's out there?" the Centaurii bellowed again.

The sound made him let go, and he realized with fright that there was no longer anything but a ferocious wind from below. He grabbed at anything that might be there, but there was nothing – he was falling.

The others watched in horror as the little puppy sized Lizard plummeted from the tree for apparently no reason. They could do nothing but watch, as he fell for a few timeless seconds before making a horrid, heavy 'thud' in the leaves.

A few leaves slowly drifted back down to where they had been before Mutsgae had cast them up, as the others stared at the spot Mutsgae now occupied, unmoving.

"Muts?" The Gnome asked, standing on the Centaurii's nose, bare toes grasping the hairs there.

"Is he dead?" The Centaurii asked, causing the gnome to nearly lose her balance and fall.

"I hope not!" The boy edged over, and nudged the Lizard with a gentle hand. "He's not breathing."

The Gnome sent up a wail that nearly deafened the poor Centaurii. He clapped a hand over his snout where she stood, effectively cutting off her cry.

Mutsgae then inhaled a long deep breath, and choked up a leaf.

"He's alive!" the boy said, bending to scoop up the stunned Lizard. "Are you ok?"

Mutsgae groaned, and flopped loosely in the boy's arms, before passing out again.

"This can't be good." The Centaurii said, releasing the Gnome girl.

"Do you think something on the other side attacked him?" The Gnome asked.

The other two considered that idea. They had no way of knowing either way. So they elected to not give danger an opportunity to strike twice. Better safe than sorry. The boy carried Mutsgae, while the Centaurii carried both packs, the Gnome still riding his nose, feet braced against the edges of his nostrils. He really didn't like her being there, but otherwise, there was no way for her to keep up with the group.

Traveling along the wall, they only stopped after nightfall, and well away from the wall's forbidding face. During the night, the boy sat up straight from where he had been sleeping when a long howl tore the night in two. He uneasily edged over towards the Centaurii, and only then realized he had no idea what the Centaurii's name was. There had been no need to use it, so he had never asked.

Now he sorely wished he knew. He also wished the Centaurii was awake. Though what the leggy foal of a creature could do, he had no idea. The Centaurii was actually younger than he, but he seemed to unconsciously turn to him for reassurance, due to his being bigger.

Stretching out a foot, he pushed on the Centaurii's outstretched hoof. "Hey! Psst!" he pushed again, trying to wake him up. "Wake up! I hear something!"

The Centaurii stubbornly remained asleep, however, moving the disturbed hoof closer to his body. Silently looking around, the boy got to his hands and knees to crawl over to where he could grab the Centaurii's ear and blow in it.

At the first try, he only flicked the ear away, continuing to slumber. The boy gave up on that idea, grabbed the ear and stuck a wet finger down in it.

The Centaurii jumped upright, though still lying down. "Wha -?"

"Shh! I heard something."

He looked around, unconsciously rubbing the wet ear with a hand. "Where's Muts?"

"Over by the root, where we left him last night."

"Are you sure it wasn't him?"

"Quite sure." The boy replied. "Look, what is your name?"

"My name? There's noises out there and you're concerned with my name?" the Centaurii asked.

"How else will I call you if you get separated, without sounding like a fool?"

"Oh, now you're concerned about sounding like a fool. Look, you already sound like a fool, so shut up." The Centaurii got to his feet, and listened, tall ears swiveling slowly. "I don't hear anything."

"I did. It was loud."

"Horus."

"Hoarse? Who's hoarse?" The boy asked.

"No, my name. You asked. My name is Horus." The Centaurii said, quietly. The dark, chill, and near complete silence was starting to scare him again. Once again he wished his mother was there.

"Oh. I'm Deilo." The boy said.

All the talk woke Mutsgae, and the Lizard rolled to his feet and trundled over to where the other two were. "What's going on?" he asked, setting down on his belly to hold his aching head.

"We heard something." Deilo replied.

"We? You heard something." Horus corrected.

"Oh." Mutsgae got back to his feet, and looked around. "Where are we?"

"The wall is that way about a hundred paces." Deilo pointed.

Mutsgae looked that way, and after a moment, started off in that direction.

"Hey! Wh ... where is he going?" Deilo asked.

"To the wall, obviously. Might be a good idea. Where's the Gnome?" Horus asked, looking around.

"Still in your forelock." Deilo scrambled after Mutsgae. After a moment of feeling his forehead, Horus followed them.

The three piled up against the wall, drawing warmth from each other as they waited the night out. Deilo had dozed off again after a few hours, and Horus was nearly asleep when another long howl echoed through the woods. Horus jumped to his feet, knocking both Deilo and Mutsgae to either side.

"Ohh." Deilo groaned, as Mutsgae rolled back upright.

"I heard it!" Horus hissed.

Mutsgae trundled along the wall, before arcing out away from it, walking in a big half circle around his companions. Reaching the wall again, he walked back toward them. "I only smell the same things that I told you about earlier."

"Something big." Deilo said, softly, imagining a wolf as big as an ox, big teeth dripping as it stalked them in the darkness. He shivered, and tried to think of something else, but he'd done too good a job frightening himself.

"What's on the other side of the wall, Muts?" Horus asked.

"Nothing."

"What do you mean, nothing?" Deilo asked, distracted.

"Just lots of big gardens. And way in the distance, a row of trees around a town."

"A town!" Deilo jumped to his feet. "We have to get that door open!" He took off running back along the wall, towards the iron bound door.

Horus looked at Mutsgae. "He's crazy, right?"

"He's scared." Mutsgae replied. "You left your packs out there."

Horus looked at the darkness under the trees, and sighed. After a moment of indecision, he took off at a quick trot into the trees. Finding the campsite, he snatched up the two food satchels. Then he turned tail and raced as fast as he could back to the wall, imagining every scary thing he'd ever dreamed off chasing him. By the time he reached the wall, he was terrified of every little shadow.

When he returned to the wall, Mutsgae got to his feet and headed after Deilo. Completely spooked, Horus followed him.

The two found Deilo tugging and pulling at the door, trying to make it open.
"I don't think that will work." Horus said, coming to a stop after turning to face the scary woods. "It's probably locked on the other side."
"At least I'm trying!" Deilo grunted.
Unnoticed by the other two, Mutsgae looked up the wall. After a moment's contemplation, he started up it, sharp little claws catching on the stony texture of the wall. Once he reached the top, he sat there and rested for a long moment. Below, Deilo had started cussing the door, though he tried to keep his voice down in the process.
Who knew what lurked out there in the darkness?
Turning to peek over the other edge of the wall, Mutsgae gauged how far down it was. The wall was very tall, and only a foot thick at the top. At the bottom he guessed it to be closer to twelve feet thick. Turning tail, he backed over the edge, scrabbling his hind claws to find purchase. Not finding any, he repositioned his front feet, and tried again, rump and tail dangling over the edge. Still not finding any purchase, he started to pull himself back up when his front feet lost their hold. With a startled yelp and a lot of grabbing, Mutsgae slipped right off the edge of the wall, sliding down the steeply sloped wall. His claws dragging on the stone slowed him, but only a little. He still landed with a solid thump on the ground, spraining his tail. Rolling away from the wall groaning, Mutsgae held his tail in all four feet. After several minutes, he heaved a resigned sigh and rolled upright again.
On the other side of the wall, Horus noticed Mutsgae was missing.
"Where's Muts?"
"How should I know? I thought you were watching him." Deilo said, getting rather short of temper despite being scared.
They both jumped away from the door when it groaned, staring at it. Shortly thereafter there was a heavy thud, and the groaning stopped. A small click, and the door swung open towards them smoothly on heavy, well-oiled hinges.
Mutsgae looked up at them both, standing on top of a wooden bar thicker than he was long.
"It was barred? How'd you get over there?" Deilo asked.
"I climbed, and yes ... I opened the door for you. Let's go."
Horus stepped through, scooping Mutsgae up as he went. Deilo followed, pausing long enough to pull the door shut behind him, and latch it. The latch was heavy, but well maintained and easily operated. The bar, however, he left that laying on the

ground. How Mutsgae had moved it, he had no idea, but he knew he couldn't move something that big.

They walked out into vast croplands, the feathery grassy crop only coming up to Deilo and Horus' knees. As they walked, Horus snatched up a few handfuls to eat.

"I don't know what this is, but it tastes wonderful." Horus said, around a mouthful.

"You know, some people grow some crops that aren't edible. They're medicinal or majickal." Deilo said. "That, and some people don't like strangers walking through and eating their crops. Do you want to be shot?"

Horus stopped chewing, and after a moment, spat the mouthful out and cleaned his tongue. "Now you tell me."

Deilo ignored the comment, looking for a path that led to the town even as he headed in that general direction. One of the things that were striking about this town – beyond the wall itself – was that the town literally glowed. The foursome could see every detail of the visible buildings. The glow was a soft blue, and Deilo assumed it had something to do with water majick. It was a very unusual color to see on a town that wasn't on a seacoast.

The glow also told them another thing – the town contained a very accomplished majickan, and probably wouldn't get attacked by the marauding soldiers. Between the wall, spooky forest, and a majickan, Deilo considered the town nearly invincible. Only the Wizard himself could beat that – and he was all the way in the majickal land of Gnaria. And there were rumors that he had finally perished ... at the hands of something as mundane as a storm. One of Deilo's favorite stories was that of the great Wizards ... of whom only the one still lived, if he lived.

These days all that remained were feuding kings, and the Queen.

Finding a path finally, Deilo followed it, glancing back to see if Horus followed. Horus looked like he was going to be ill, but it was entirely in his head. His fears that the plants he had eaten would kill him or worse were making him queasy.

"Are you going to be ok?" Deilo asked, eventually.

"I think I'm going to die." Horus croaked.

"What? Why?"

"My stomach is cramping." Horus put Mutsgae down, and laid down there in the path.

"This isn't a good place to take a nap." The Gnome said, directly into his ear. "Get up."

"I'm gonna die." Horus moaned.

"Are you sure it's not just gas?" Deilo asked, walking over to where the Centaurii lay.

"Just gas?" Horus exclaimed. "I ate majickal weeds!"

"You don't know that for sure." Deilo pointed out.

"Majickal weeds?" The Gnome asked, incredulously.

"Are you aware that if you ate any of the genus that contain those plants, you'd BE DEAD BY NOW?" she shouted into his ear, startling him to his feet.

"I would?" he asked, uncertainly.

"Of course. As for medicinal plants, those are not grown in large fields of nothing but, and are often used as spices, too. So there. Stop being a pansy." She told him. "Let's get going, shall we?"

Grumbling about his stomach, Horus followed Deilo up the path. Mutsgae trundled out of the crop beside the path and followed them, nose barely a half inch off the ground. Deciding that he was definitely falling behind his long-legged companions, he hurried his pace some, and the faster gait made his tail swing back and forth in a comical manner. Once he'd caught up again, he slowed down once more – only to fall behind again. This went on time and again until they reached the trees, whereupon they all slowed to a creep. The trees were taller than those of the forest, but also much thinner. They swayed gently in the light breeze, their leaves singing softly to any who cared to listen. Instead of having just a few branches and leaves far overhead, they had branches from just over an adult's head level all the way up to the very top, giant round leaves creating an intensely black shadow. They walked beneath those boughs, and it was as if the trees came to life, swaying faster and sounding as if they were talking excitedly.

"Do you think they're enchanted trees?" Mutsgae whispered.

"Don't be ridiculous." Deilo replied, trying to sound brave and failing utterly. "Enchanted trees would have eaten us by now ... right?" He looked to Horus, who merely shrugged.

They continued on in silence, listening to the whispering of the trees, until they reached the first building. The structures were unlike anything they had seen before. From a distance they had looked like normal, square buildings. But here, up close, they were obviously round, some of them oval. A few towered to great heights before ending in a mushroom-like cap, others sitting quite low with their conical tops. A few had angular, pyramidal roofs that looked rather silly atop a round structure. Entrances were arches with curling decorations. Rather than being a mundane group of weathered buildings, these all looked freshly painted with great artistic flair. There appeared to be a fascination for arches, circles, curls, and anything else turning gracefully. Past a few outer rings of buildings, there was a great circular courtyard paved with diamond-shaped stones of varying color. The blue hue of the town's light gave the place a very mystical air ... they all got the feeling that important events took place there. In the very center of the courtyard rose a circular pavilion with a conical top. Each pillar was carved to resemble some fantastic creature holding up the roof on their up-lifted limbs. Atop the very point of the roof reared the legendary Malici – a great winged equine that sported dual forward-pointing horns on his forehead. They weren't very long, as far as horns went, but they were very strong, and very sharp. They were intended for stabbing, and in the legends, Malici used them often in battle. His kind were called Pegacorns, and they were the stuff of legends ... no one recalled ever actually seeing one. But there were plenty of widespread tales of them, even in the far-flung lands.

"Wow." Horus breathed. "What is this place?"

"I don't know." Deilo replied, dumbstruck by the magnificence of the place.

Parked between Horus' front hooves, Mutsgae just stared at the pavilion in awe. But unlike the others, he was soon on to other attractions ... like the smells on the courtyard floor. He trundled forward, sniffing here and there as he went.

"What do you smell?" The Gnome asked, leaning forward out of her nest in Horus' forelock.

"Shoes." Mutsgae replied. "Lots and lots of shoes. Someone has a bad case of a foot infection ... but other than that, just shoes. There aren't any animals at all, here, other than the birds. Not even any Races that wouldn't be wearing shoes."

"I'd be wearing shoes, if I was big enough." Horus said.

Deilo looked down at his own bare feet – his parents had never been well enough off to get him any shoes. And he'd been so used to not having any that it had never occurred to him to look for some before leaving Yelm.

The lighting changed there on the ground – it couldn't quite be called a shadow, as there was no way for an actual shadow to be there – and Deilo looked up to his side. Not four feet away stood a tall, slender man in leather warrior's garb, dual sword hilts showing over his shoulders. Deilo yelped, and jumped away, colliding with Horus. Horus went down as if he didn't have a leg to stand on, never mind that he had four. Deilo landed on top of him, and the Gnome was thrown free to roll across the stone paving.

Hearing Deilo's yell, Mutsgae turned around, and just stared at the tall warrior there. And at his shoes. Those were the shoes he smelled. Soft leather that wouldn't make a single sound, and they were knee-high.

The warrior never moved, even as Deilo and Horus scrambled back to their feet, turning to face the warrior. Only by then, there were a lot more than just the one. They were all over the place, even on the rooftops. And more than half of them were women, just as tall, and identically clad in warrior's leather.

"Um." Deilo looked around, terrified.

Horus didn't know what to do with himself. Run? Fold up? Cry?

Unnoticed and nearly invisible on the stones, the Gnome laid perfectly still. She knew that if she moved, she'd be spotted.

Mutsgae, terrified of being out there by himself, turned and raced back to where Horus and Deilo were, to squat between their feet.

The first warrior spoke, but it was no language any of them knew, so they remained silent. After a long, tense moment, the Warrior spoke again – this time in the common language.

"Who are you?"

"Deilo." Deilo said, timidly. "I'm Deilo."

"Why are you here?"

"We ... we were in the woods ... and we ... the wall ... there are things out there, sir. We came in. We ..." Deilo trailed off, as the warrior held up a hand.

"You were in the forest? Why?"

"We ... our home was burnt down by the soldiers, sir. So we left. We were lost."

The warrior turned and looked at another, who turned and vanished, along with a dozen others.

"Where was your home?"

"Yelm." Deilo said.

The warrior was silent, and after a moment the threesome realized that all but the one had vanished again, just as suddenly as they had come.

"Um ... where are we?" Deilo ventured.

"Come this way." The warrior turned, and walked away. The three followed him, and Horus made a quick side-step to scoop up the Gnome. The warrior led them into one of the buildings, and when they stepped into the front room, they were greeted with brilliant white lighting. When their eyes adjusted, they saw that the light came from a hanging chandelier that was covered in majickally glowing spheres, suspended from the very center of the room. There, they could see that the warrior was not, after all, a man. But rather something quite different. His skin was a shade of grey, hair soot black, eyes blacker than coal, and his ears were pointed. His hair was pulled back into a small knot at the back of his neck, and the details of his garments were more visible. His shoulder-guards sported metallic knobs, and his gauntlets were decorated in nearly invisible lines.

All those features meant only one thing – from his Race to his clothing, all four companions immediately knew what he was – and that unless they pissed someone off, they were safe here with them.

He was a SwordDancer – one of the most elite fighters the lands had ever known. They weren't prone to wars, however, opting more to smaller skirmishes. SwordDancers rarely ever were seen as more than pairs, and generally were only seen one at a time. They were usually hired as assassins, and caravan guards – but while they were renowned for their fighting prowess, they were even further known for their honesty and morals.

The group relaxed somewhat, though still uneasy – having seen so many around, it could only mean one of two things – they had stumbled either onto a training facility, or a town of these people. Something that no one ever knew was there, or where.

The SwordDancer gestured to the lone occupant of the room, then turned and left, back outside.

She was one of the SwordDancer's Race, but apparently was not a SwordDancer herself, as she wore nothing even remotely similar to SwordDancer garb. Rising from her pillow seat, she walked over to where the three stood, and looked them over.

"You're awfully young to be out on your own. With whom did you travel?"

"Just us, ma'am." Deilo replied.

"Just you four?" she asked.

"Yes, ma'am." Deilo said.

She looked at Horus. "Do you speak?"

"Yes, ma'am." Horus said.

"And the lizard at your feet? Is that a pet of yours? Or a familiar?"

"Mutsgae?" Horus asked, shocked. "Mutsgae is neither, he's a Lizard."

She looked down at the little Lizard, who was glaring up at her. "Don't look like that, Mutsgae. I suspected what you were."

That comment seemed to satisfy him, and he sniffed the floor, noting that she wore leather slippers – equally as silent as the boots.

She turned and walked back to her pillow, and sat down on it, before rearranging some strange items on a low table next to her. "Are you three aware that you could have died, out there in the enchanted wood?"

"Enchanted wood? Those trees are enchanted, after all?"

"The forest, child. Not our trees. Though, yes, those are enchanted, too. The Forest could have easily slain you all. The mnarag are quite numerous, especially at this time of year."

"Mnarag?" Deilo asked, pasty white. "Wolves?"

"The Great Wolf, yes. Very little ever crosses the forest, for them. I am surprised you four made it as far as our wall."

"Is that why the wall is there?" Horus asked.

"Precisely. Even we can fall prey to the likes of them." She said.

"Are you a SwordDancer, too?" Horus asked.

"No. I'm not." She said. "I imagine you are hungry? Even after snacking on our crops." She gestured at another low table that suddenly held four plates ... one of them incredibly tiny. "Eat."

The four looked at it longingly, but did not move.

"What is going to happen to us, now?" Deilo asked.

"Tomorrow morning, you will be taken out of the forest, and to a town. There you will be given lodging until you see fit to leave."

"We can't stay here?" Horus asked.

"No – you cannot stay here. This is a very special place, and you have already disrupted many things just by showing up." She said, gesturing at the table again. "Eat. In the morning, you will eat again."

The three moved obediently, and Horus set the Gnome down on the table. She straightened her clothing, and went to where her tiny plate waited. Each plate held items specific to each of their diets – it was not hard to tell whose was whose. Mutsgae's plate was downright putrid looking, but thankfully they couldn't smell it. Horus' plate was piled deep with various layers of green things, and Deilo's plate was deep with meats and stewed vegetables. The Gnome's plate was similar to Deilo's, only on a smaller scale. Meat gleaned from large insects, and mushroom bits instead of tubers. Grass seed was also part of her meal, cooked to a soft mash.

They each ate with gusto, delighted at having real food again, and the meals didn't last long. Soon all four plates were licked clean, and they were ushered to a room where pallets were made for each of them. There they slept, entirely oblivious to the world around them. It was only a few hours until morning, when they were roused by a SwordDancer and led back out into the main room. There, on the same table, breakfast waited. By the wall was stacked carry-sacks of varying sizes. These were given little attention as long as there was food on the table, however. Once the morning meal was done, the three were taken to yet another room, where they were cleaned up and given fresh clothing to wear, suitable for journeying. Deilo was delighted to stomp around in his new shoes. They didn't lend themselves very well to stomping, however, as they were made of the same soft leather that the SwordDancer's boots were. Horus also had shoes, but of a different sort. They were wooden on bottom, to hold up against his hooves, and had leather tops that tied to his pasterns. Not the traditional shoes of someone like him, but they would do the job of getting him places without going lame.

The group was entirely surprised at how they looked afterwards ... nothing like what they thought. Horus turned out to be a richer color than expected, now that all the mud, soot, and grime was washed out of his fur, and Mutsgae was colored like fall leaves. They had thought he was merely grey, before.

Properly presentable, they were fed once again, a light snack, and then the bundles by the wall were handed out.

"These are travel sacks – tend them well and they will serve you well." They were told. There was even one specially tailored for Mutsgae to carry on his own little back. He was proud to carry his own, and strutted about in it, showing it to the others. The Gnome was given one, as well, hers being suitably small. The SwordDancer from the night before shouldered the one remaining pack – the largest by far – and led them outside.

The courtyard looked entirely different during the morning's sun, but it was still deserted. The majickal aura was gone, looking more like a simple, decorated pavilion and paved yard. Even the legendary Malici looked more like a simple winged horse, his horns nearly invisible against the sky.

The SwordDancer led them across the courtyard, between several of the buildings, under the shadow of a very tall tower, and out into the fields. There was a path, however, and no crops were trampled as they made their way to the wall. During the day, the wall looked a lot closer to the town than it had during the night. But it still looked just as huge. When they reached the wall, the SwordDancer opened one of the two massive doors there, and then closed it again after they had all moved through. The four just looked around, rather confused. They had been expecting a road to be there, but instead there was merely more forest. And not even a path. They didn't get a chance to ask any questions, however, as the SwordDancer struck out into the woods, expecting them to follow. The three doing the walking had to hurry to keep up with his long strides. It used up all their breath, leaving none for talking or asking questions. The Gnome simply sat quietly, riding in Horus' forelock again, watching the world go by a lot faster than she ever could have traveled it on her own.

After a half day, the SwordDancer suddenly stopped in a small glen. As soon as he did, the other three collapsed to the ground, panting. He looked at them for a moment, and then crouched. "Eat. Be quick and silent. This is not a safe place to linger." He warned, before following his own advice. Removing a small cloth-wrapped package from his pack, he proceeded to eat without another word. The others followed the example, eyeing the woods as they rested their weary limbs. No sooner had they finished the last bite of the small lunch, the SwordDancer had them moving out again, at the same pace.

The ground started to slope, making walking a little easier for a while, and then it simply didn't matter any more. They were tired and weary, aching all over. The only things keeping them silent were the lack of breath, and the fear of what was in the woods that spurred the SwordDancer to such speed.

The SwordDancer, on the other hand, wished they were going faster. To him, they were traveling merely at a brisk walk. Not nearly fast enough to cover the territory they had to cover that day.

The sun had long since started its journey down out of the sky when the ground suddenly went soft and mushy. This startled the children enough that they stopped entirely to stare at the ground.

"Come. Quickly." The SwordDancer said, not stopping.

They scrambled to catch up with him again, picking their feet up quickly from the strange ground. Mutsgae started to lag behind, having been at a dead run the whole way. Deilo noticed, and scooped the little lizard up, cradling him in his arms.

Mutsgae breathed a sigh of relief, limbs sprawled limply every which way. Deilo's arms got tired quickly, though, and he had to shift Mutsgae to over his shoulder. Mutsgae was agreeable with this, watching the world recede from his backward-facing view.

Then the mushy ground eventually changed to murky looking water. When it did, the SwordDancer stopped, and looked either way up and down the irregular shore of the swamp. Then he turned and went up the shore. The others followed in his steps, watching the still water warily.

The SwordDancer stopped at a bush, and pushed his way into it, leaving the others outside.

"What -?" Deilo asked, puffing. He didn't dare sit down on the soggy ground, however much he wanted to get off his feet.

The SwordDancer ignored the comment, as he pushed his way deeper into the bush. In the very heart of the bush, he found what he was looking for – a hollowed out place that the water filled, and in it was tethered a small canoe like boat. He quickly untied the tether, and pushed the boat out of the bush into the waters of the swamp. Jumping lightly into it, he rode it out of the big bush, and when he was clear he steered it back to the shore where the wide-eyed children stood. Pushing the boat up into the mud, he stepped out, and assisted each into the boat.

"Sit low, and don't move." He instructed them all, as he showed Horus how to fold up in the bottom of the boat.

Then he climbed in, himself, and put paddle to water, pushing them away from the shore. Only once they were well away from the shore and traveling across the vast expanse of swamp did he relax. Once he did the atmosphere calmed, and the children relaxed as well. It wasn't long before they were all sound asleep, draped here and there in the boat as it smoothly slid along the water's mirror-smooth surface under the high boughs of the swamp trees. When the sun started setting, they had covered more ground since acquiring the boat than they had the whole rest of the day. By nightfall, they were a very long ways away, gliding through grassy marshes.

When Deilo woke up, he was greeted by an inky sky that was speckled with stars like he had never seen before. Sitting up, he looked around at the marsh.

"Where are we?" he asked quietly, listening to the night songs of the marsh creatures.

"Passing through the Anturian marsh." The SwordDancer replied. We will be to solid ground again by morning. Go back to sleep – you'll need it."

Deilo nodded, and laid down again, pillowing his head on Horus' soft shoulder.

Through the night they passed out of the marshes and onto a small river. There the SwordDancer set his paddle across the boat, letting the current carry them. Only occasionally did he put his paddle to the water to correct their direction. The river joined with another one after an hour, becoming larger. There, the SwordDancer steered the boat to one shore to coast along there, well away from the swirling vortex that blended the two rivers into one. Once past the dangers there, the boat coasted back to the faster current in the middle of the river. Here, however, the SwordDancer had to avoid other, larger boats. They had come into a well-used waterway. Most of the boats were tied off for the night, only a few traveling through the darkness. Those that were traveling bore large lights of one form or another. The SwordDancer's boat, on the other hand, slid past with no lights whatsoever, entirely unnoticed by the other boats. Like a ghost on the water, the SwordDancer escorted his charges past all the boats, on to where a city's glow lit the night sky. The sun was peeking over the horizon before they had quite reached the city, however.

The growing light woke the children, and they spent a deal of time staring at their new surroundings. It was a far cry from the swamp they had gone to sleep in. Rolling hills and stony knolls, interchanging pastures and forests, all busy with people of many Races. Soon pastures and forests turned to loose communities, then to the closer buildings of the city proper. Teeming roads rose to huge bridges that spanned the river, carrying the traffic of wagons, carriages, riding beasts, and foot traffic over the river. The city looked like it went on forever, as they glided down the waterway. But soon the SwordDancer turned to the shore, and tied off to a dock. There, he helped them out of the boat. Once they were all solidly on the dock boards, the SwordDancer left the boat, tossing a coin to the dock master, who nodded and made a note on a freestanding panel.

The SwordDancer led them through packed streets to a low-fronted Inn that rose taller than it first appeared to. Walking into the building, the SwordDancer called the innkeeper's attention.

The innkeeper, a large troll of a creature, lumbered over. "Aye?"

The SwordDancer gestured at the four children. "Rooms for them. Long term."

The innkeeper looked down at the group, and grunted. "Ok. How long, long term?"

"Until you are notified otherwise, long term." The SwordDancer said.

"And you?"

"I will not be staying."

"Is someone coming to get them?"

"No."

The innkeeper frowned. "I don't run an orphanage, sir."

"I didn't say you did." The SwordDancer replied coolly. "They need a place to stay until a better place is found. Their own homes have been burned flat and their families slaughtered."

"I don't keep a refugee camp, either." The innkeeper grunted.

The SwordDancer just looked at him quietly.

The troll looked right back for a split second, then nodded. "Aye, rooms for three."

"Four." The SwordDancer corrected. "Close together, if possible."

"A suite, then?"

"It will do."

"Who will be paying for this? You?"

"You can go to the Guild for your pay, as long as you can show they still reside here." The SwordDancer replied. "Reasonable rates – if you over charge, you'll be answering to the Guild."

"Just rooms?" The innkeeper asked.

"And meals."

"And do I get to complain when they start driving away my other customers?"

The SwordDancer was silent a moment, then looked at the four. Turning back to the innkeeper, he said: "Any good inn can use a few helpers. Put them to work – but don't over work them, we will be watching. That should pay for their meals and half the room."

The innkeeper frowned, but knew better than to try and protest – he didn't know just how irritable this particular SwordDancer was, and how open to banter.

After a moment of trying to figure out what to do next, the innkeeper finally nodded. "This way." He turned and lumbered away, to the back of the tavern that occupied the entire main floor. At the back was a huge staircase, and though it was heavily built it groaned under the weight of the innkeeper. The upper stories of rooms were much nicer than the tavern had been, and the innkeeper took them all the way to the top floor, where there was an unoccupied suite of rooms.

"Give the girls some time, and they'll have it set up for ye right proper." The innkeeper said, as they stepped in and looked around. The SwordDancer checked it out, and was apparently satisfied with what he saw.

"This will do." He said.

"Good." the innkeeper replied, before the SwordDancer turned and left.

Horus walked over to one of the large windows, and looked down at the bustling city. "Nothing like home." He commented.

Deilo nodded, looking around at the nearly barren rooms. There were the basic toiletry items, but no beds, no chairs, nothing. Just a few rugs and curtains. A few of the walls had tapestries or paintings hung on them.

Mutsgae hunkered in the middle of the room, staring up at the innkeeper, who was still standing there.

After a long moment, the innkeeper said: "What?"

Mutsgae didn't answer, merely turning and following Deilo.

Shortly thereafter, a crowd of maids arrived, took one good look at the occupants of the room, and left again. They were soon back, however, toting all sorts of things into the room. There was soon a bed for each of them, cabinets for their clothes – those that wore them – and chairs to suit each. The rooms were suddenly a lot smaller looking than they were before, full of furniture to suit the children's respective Races. There was one room for each of them – the Gnome's room being a cupboard type contraption set against one wall of the fourth room. The fourth room doubled as a common room, since the Gnome was too small to use it all herself.

And then the maids were gone again, just as abruptly as they had come. The innkeeper looked everything over once, grunted, and lumbered out again, leaving the four in their new home.

"Now what do we do? We've gone from one wilderness to another." Deilo despaired.

Mutsgae looked around, as silent as before.

"We can explore. Surely the innkeeper won't expect us to go to work right away." Horus said.

Before any could reply, the door opened again, and a maid came in, balancing a large, heavily laden tray on one shoulder, nearly bent double under it. She pushed the door shut with one slippered foot, and made her way to the table occupying the middle of the fourth room, nodding to the three she could see.

"I reckon you'll be wanting your breakfasts, now, hm? Here you go, then." She somehow managed to get the huge tray off her shoulder and onto the table in one swift move, without dumping over any of the glasses or bowls that were perched on it. She then swiftly unloaded the whole thing onto the table, setting it up nicely. "Come on. Eat up – you'll be needing it, if the boss gives you much of anything to do." She said, cheerily, removing the tray and propping it against one wall.

Deilo had no problem with his chair, and the maid lifted Mutsgae into his tall chair, giving him an affectionate pat on the head.

"Aren't you a cute little fella?" she cooed, before noticing that Horus simply stood at the table, shoving the bench there out of the way. "Oh, no, good sir. You must sit at the table, like this." She showed him how to sit on the bench that was designed for a Centaurii to sit on.

Horus simply sat there for a moment, marveling at the very idea, his front legs poking off the front end of the bench and dangling down. His rump and rear legs were supported by the rear end of the bench, and he found it fairly comfortable. Then he turned his attention back to the table full of food.

"Now where is the wee miss?" The maid asked, looking around for the Gnome. Finding her half way up Delio's chair back, the maid plucked the Gnome from her climb, and set her on the table, at a tiny table and chair sitting there. "There you go, miss."

"Thank you." The Gnome did a slight curtsey, before taking her seat.

"As soon as you are all finished, come down to the kitchens. I'll take you to the back room, and we'll see about getting you some clothes worth wearing." The maid performed her own curtsey, swept up the tray, and was gone.

Though there was a great deal of food and drink on the table, not a speck of it remained when the foursome finished with it. Deilo picked up the Gnome, and Horus scooped Mutsgae out of his chair, and the foursome went back down the stairs to the tavern. Going across the already crowded room, they pushed through a set of doors into the kitchen. Once they were spotted, a pair of maids took them out a back door, into a huge storeroom. There were heaps of supplies, heaps of furniture for the various Races, and tall stacks of nothing but boxes in the extreme rear of the massive room. There was another exit that led to a broad stair, allowing the furniture to be moved to the rooms without having to go through the kitchens and tavern.

The two maids took them to the very back, where all the boxes were, and proceeded to pull boxes open. The boxes they opened contained vast amounts of cloth, in many colors and patterns. The two were chattering away, holding various samples up to the children to see what they looked like. Twice the Gnome had to be rescued from having a piece of cloth dropped on her.

"So sorry, miss. You really are hard to see, like that." One maid apologized.

Once a selection of regular weight material was made, the maids refolded and stored the rest of the material, before pulling out a flatter box. Inside that box were carefully folded expanses of incredibly fine material.

"What are you going to do with that?" Horus asked.

"The little miss needs new clothes, too, and she can't wear something this heavy – not in this weather!" a maid responded, indicating the normal weight material. She then laid out a fold of each color and print, so the Gnome could make a choice.

"I like the green, and the brown." She said, pointing, standing on the materials.

"Green it is, then." The other maid said, scooping up the material.

"What about the brown?" the Gnome asked.

"We can't have you tromping around in brown, miss. You'd blend right into the floor, and never see you before we stepped on you." The other maid said. "Pick another color – one we can all see."

She considered the remaining materials, pinching her bottom lip. After long deliberations, she pointed at a light blue. "That one."

"Ok, then! Off we go to see the mistress." The material was re-boxed, and the maids escorted the foursome back through the kitchens and into yet another room, both of them carrying an armload of folded fabrics.

In the room was a myriad of tools and tables – all pertaining to the making and mending of clothing. There were machines built to sew fabric as light as gossamer, or as heavy as saddle leather. There were many cutting tables, and baskets heaped with things like scissors, bobbins, spools of thread, yarns, puffs poked full of pins, laces, and knotted string. Seated at a machine at the far end of the room, an elderly looking Dtri worked on mending a pair of riding breeches, while the owner of the article stood in the doorway that led to the side street.

When she finished, the feathered and scaled Dtri shook out the pants and handed them to the customer, who dropped a pair of coins into her hand. She turned, dropping them into a pocket in her apron. "What have ye got here?" she asked, without a trace of the funny accent the lizard-avian Dtri Race usually had.

"Just some children needing new clothes, mistress." One maid said, dropping her heap of materials on a table, and taking the Gnome out of her own apron pocket. "There you go, miss." She said, setting her on the table next to the material.

The second maid deposited her load of cloth on the other side of the first stack, nodded to the Dtri, and left again.

"How many, and how big?" The Dtri asked, eyeing first the Gnome, and then Horus. Currently only the Centaurii's head stood above the table top, but that would change quickly as he grew into his legs.

"There's four, mistress." The maid said, pointing to each.

The Dtri bent over and peeked under the table to see where the maid pointed, and made a strange noise at the sight of Mutsgae. "Where did you dig up this assortment?" She asked, standing upright again.

"They came in just this morning, mistress. They're to be staying here for a long while, and be working their way, too. The boss said they'll be needing some new clothes before they'll be presentable around here."

"That they will." The Dtri agreed, eyeing Deilo's strange clothing. "And shoes, too, I'll warrant."

"Might be a good idea, mistress." The maid agreed, before leaving.

The Dtri stuck a row of pins in her wide beak, and pulled out a length of knotted string. "And what will your name be?" she asked of the Gnome.

"Lillia." She replied.

"Lillia. I need you to stand up straight, and hold your arms out."

Lillia obeyed, holding her arms out to either side.

The Dtri began measuring the little Gnome with her knotted string, every now and then making a little noise to herself. "What do you prefer, Lillia, skirts or breeches?"

"Skirts, if I may."

"Excellent. Those are easier to make, in this small a size. Long skirts, or short?"

"Medium, if I may, mistress." Lillia said.

The Dtri smiled slightly, the softer tissues at the edges of her beak performing the entire expression. "You needn't call me that, Lillia. You children can just call me Piofei. Those maids are sticklers about their ma'am's and sir's."

"Piofei." Lillia said, trying the unusual name out.

"Yes." Piofei encouraged. "Are you going to want sleeves?"

"If I may."

"Long or short?"

"Medium." Lillia said.

"You're just a medium sort of gal, aren't you?" Piofei laughed.

"Not really. I'd have a lot of growing to do, to be that." Lillia said, with a smile.

"Are you going to want shirts and skirts, or dresses?" Piofei asked.

"Dresses, Piofei."

"Good. At least you know what you want. Some people come in here, and don't even know what it is they want me to sew, and then expect me to churn out the 'perfect' piece. Hmph!" Piofei straightened, and checked the knotted string against a board. "Ok, that covers you." She sorted through the materials, and lifted the lighter ones out. "These'll be yours, I reckon?"

"Yes, Piofei." Lillia said.

"Green and blue, aye? That will make a pretty dress."

"Piofei?"

"Yes?" the Dtri looked at her, from inspecting the material and measuring it in arm-lengths.

"If I may, could I have one in each color?" Lillia asked.

Piofei laughed. "My dear, you can have three in each color, and one of both!"

"Thank you, Piofei." Lillia bowed in the custom of the Gnomes.

Piofei laughed. "Darling girl. Ok, stand aside." She picked up a charcoal bit, and made a quick note on a white board, the scratch marks she made entirely mysterious to the four children.

Lillia moved to the basket that sat on that table, and took a seat on its braided rim.

"Now, for you, young man. What is your name?" Piofei asked, drawing Deilo out to a clear area of floor.

"Deilo." Deilo said.

"Deilo, hm? I need you to stand just like pretty Lillia did, ok? Good boy." She said, as Deilo obeyed. She then started measuring him with the long, knotted string. Once she had measured him over, she consulted the stack of heavier cloth. "Which of these is for you?" she asked.

Deilo only shrugged.

"If I may, those are for him." Lillia said, pointing to the dark blue, brown, and black materials.

"Alright, thank you, Lillia." Piofei said, smiling at Deilo and ruffling his hair. "Some one will be needing a haircut, too, hm?"

"No." Deilo said, tolerating the treatment.

"No? Will you be preferring your pants fitted, or loose?"

"Loose." Deilo said.

"And your shirts, do you want sleeves?"

"No."

"Fitted, or loose?"

"Loose."

"Ok. Good choices, considering you'll be growing like a weed, hm?"

"They're comfier that way." Deilo said.

Piofei laughed, and made a note on her board with the charcoal. Then she turned her attention to Horus. "And what is your name?" she asked, escorting Deilo out of the way and putting Horus in the clear floor space.

"Do I really need clothes?" Horus asked.

"That's a really long name, is there something shorter that people call you?"

Deilo grinned, as Horus frowned.

"Horus." Horus said.

"Good! Much easier to remember." She said. "Horus, I'll be needing you to stand with your heels back, and your arms up, ok?"

He understood the arms up – the others had done that much. But 'heels back' confused him. Eventually, Piofei bent over his back, and pulled his rear hooves back until he was standing like a show horse.

"Why do I have to stand like this?" Horus asked.

"It puts more of your spine at a greater length, meaning your clothes will fit not only while you stand, but while you walk, as well." She said, measuring him.

"Do I really need clothes?" Horus asked again.

"Yes." Piofei replied. "Every creature, unless it's drowning in heaps of thick wool, needs clothes. See? Even I wear clothes, and I have feathers." She said, pulling more of the string out of her apron pocket.

"But that's just an apron." Horus objected.

Piofei smiled. "Don't worry, young fellow. Your clothes won't be that bad. You wait and see."

Horus heaved a sigh.

"Wait. Do that again."

"Do what again?" Horus asked.

"Breathe deep, and hold it."

Horus sucked in a breath.

"Good. I thought so. You have grown a whole eight knots, just by breathing!" she said, inspecting her string again after removing it from his equine ribs.

"Is that bad?" Horus asked.

Piofei laughed. "No. It just means you breathe deep. And that's good, for your Race. Some never use their larger lungs, and as such, don't have the stamina they ought to."

"Oh. Mother always taught me to breathe with all my lung." Horus said.

"Your mother was wise." Piofei said. "Where is she?"

At Horus' complete silence, she looked over at his face. It didn't take a genius to determine that what she saw meant that something terrible had to have happened. "I'm sorry."

Horus looked down at his toes.

"Well, now it's your turn, little fellow. Are you a fellow?" Piofei said, lifting Mutsgae onto the table.

"Yes." Mutsgae said, rather indignant.

"Oh, don't look like that. It really is hard to tell, with you so young." Piofei said. "What is your name?"

"Mutsgae."

"Mutsgae. Ok. I may have to ask you that again, later on." She admitted, running a length of string down his spine.

Mutsgae edged away. "No self-respecting Lizard warrior wears clothes."

"I shall keep that in mind, should I meet one." Piofei said, dragging him back over by his tail. "Now hold still."

Mutsgae protested, but was no match for the swift-fingered Dtri. Soon, whether he liked it or not, she had his measurements. She let him go after that, and he shot right off the table before he could stop himself. Horus just barely managed to catch him by his tail, stopping him from plowing nose-first into a knobby machine. He still yelled at the top of his lungs, before Horus quickly set him down. Seated on the floor, Mutsgae kneaded his tail with both hands, whining.

Piofei shook her head, and looked the foursome over. "When you come back, tomorrow, I will have your clothes ready. Then we will see about getting you some foot wear."

As if summoned by majick, a maid showed up again, and took them all back to their rooms.

"You'll be wanting to stay here, out of the way. You don't want to be making the boss angry. If you'll be needing anything, pull the rope." She told them, indicating the rope by the door, before leaving.

Deilo plopped on the floor. "Oh brother. Now we're grounded."

Horus walked over to the window again, and looked out, down at the crowded street below. As the noon hours approached, the street only filled with more people, the traffic getting thicker than before. "Do you think what they said was true? That the soldiers won't come here?"

"Who knows if it's true." Deilo said, sprawling on the floor haphazardly.

"We are a very long way away." Lillia pointed out. "We might not even be in King Cerin's land anymore."

"So?"

"So, King Cerin's enemies won't come and pillage here." Lillia said, walking over to her room.

"What if this is the land of King Cerin's enemy?" Horus asked.

"I don't think so. No body here is killing and pillaging." Deilo said.

"Why would they burn their own homes down?" Mutsgae asked.

"Cause they're barbarians." Deilo stated.

"I don't think so." Horus disagreed. "Even barbarians need homes."

"Whatever." Deilo got to his feet, and opened the door, peeking out. "Do we have to stay in here, or can we go outside, do you think?"

"You'd better stay here." Lillia said, seated in the doorway to her tiny room.

Deilo made a face at her, sticking out his tongue.

"You'd better stay here." Mutgae said, before promptly walking out of the room, between Deilo's feet.

"Hey! Where are you going?" Deilo asked.

Mutsgae looked back at him. "People here seem to think I'm a pet. Maybe I can get something to eat from somebody." He said, before heading on down the hall.

Deilo sighed. Nobody would mistake *him* for a pet. Mutsgae, maybe. But not him. So, he was trapped, while Mutsgae got to tramp around.

"What? Where's he going?" Horus asked, having walked over to the door and peeked out over Deilo's shoulder.

"Who knows. Might get himself eaten, instead of fed." Deilo said, shutting the door.

Mutsgae moved to the stair leading down into the tavern, and began the awkward process of negotiating a way down them. Mostly that meant falling one step at a time, and more often than not, he landed on his nose. By the time he reached the ground floor, his nose hurt worse than his stomach had.

Rubbing his nose with both paws, Mutsgae surveyed the tavern. Just like the streets outside, the tavern was filling as the day progressed. Some were there for a drink, some for a meal, and some there simply to talk to the others. Mutsgae bumped down the last step, and began negotiating his way between stomping feet to a table where he had seen a cluster that looked like a family group. Finding a foot big enough, he sat down on it. The reaction was instant – the owner scooted back away from the table and looked down at him. Mutsgae picked himself up, shook, and looked back.

The creature that owned the foot said something in a language Mutsgae didn't know, and everyone else at the table also scooted back to look down at him. Mutsgae looked from face to face, suddenly worried. They didn't look like they were going to feed him.

Eventually, he was picked up and inspected, turned over and over until he thought he was going to puke again. Then he was handed to the next, who did the same. When the third person started inspecting him, his guts rebelled and he spewed half-digested rotted matter all over three of the occupants at the table.

Half the tavern cleared out in a matter of moments, most covering their noses and gagging. The group who had been at the table fled the general area, and the ones covered in stomach matter made it out to the street before they, too, started retching.

Stumbling around under the deserted table, Mutsgae groaned and tried to find the stairs. He never made it that far, before he was swatted into a can with a broom, and the can emptied out into the street. Mutsgae tumbled head over tail until he came to rest against the far building. There, he simply slumped with a sigh, entirely limp.

Three stories up and peering out the window, Horus saw Mutsgae go tumbling across the street, nearly getting trampled on several occasions by passing beasts of burden.

"Muts is down there! In the street! Looks like he got thrown out." Horus said, pointing.

"Where?" Deilo asked, running to the window and peering out. "I can't see anything but the sill."

"Somebody should go get him." Horus said.

"I'll go get him!" Deilo said, rushing for the door.

"Stop!" Lillia cried.

Deilo stopped. "Why?"

"Pull the rope – the maid will go get him. Don't go out there, yourself." Lillia said. "You might get kidnapped."

"No I won't." Deilo scoffed. "Kidnapping is illegal."

"Where you used to live. Who knows what the law here is? And laws never stop anybody." Lillia said. "Pull the rope."

Heaving a dejected sigh, Deilo pulled the rope. When nothing happened, he pulled again, then again and again and again.

"It's not working. I'll have to go get him, myself." Deilo said, rather disappointed in the rope – he'd been hoping for a big gonging bell or something. But even as he reached for the door, it opened.

"Ye only have to pull the rope *once*." The maid said. "What is it, that's so urgent?"

"Muts is down in the road." Horus said, pointing out the window again.

"Muts?" The maid asked, walking over to the window to look.

"Our lizard. He's down there. See?" Horus pointed again, past the maid.

Without a word, the maid hurried out. Shortly, Horus saw her cross the busy street, dodging the traffic to get there. She scooped Mutsgae up in her apron, and carried him back, one hand pinching her nose and the other holding the folds of her apron.

It was some time before the maid returned – with a washed Mutsgae.

"Stay here." She told him sternly, before leaving again.

Mutsgae only slumped where she'd put him, in his little bed.

"*I* should stay here, huh?" Deilo asked. "What'd you do??"

Mutsgae only groaned.

They were fed supper at the end of the day, and breakfast again the next day, before they were taken back down to see Piofei. On the table where Lillia was set down were several outfits of clothes for both Lillia and Deilo. Lillia was very pleased with the dresses she found, while Deilo tried on the shirts. They fit him as if a well-known tailor had been hired to make him clothes, and given him some room to grow, as well.

Horus was fitted out in a sleeveless tunic that flared at his waist to allow it to hang flat in front, while riding smoothly over his back. A second tunic was given to him, this one obviously formal wear. The tunic spread away over his back to cover the whole thing, and drape down around his hocks. The small tunic was made of a light, soft, dyed leather, while the larger tunic was made of a medium-weight material.

Mutsgae found himself dressed in a strange looking piece of clothing, which when he was in it, didn't look too strange at all. More like a short shirt adapted for his build.

"I'm not going to wear this." Mutsgae protested.

"Sure you will." Piofei assured him. "It'll keep you from getting the street treatment again." She said, with a small smile.

Mutsgae grumbled, but didn't reply, hunkering down where he stood.

"Thank you, ma'am. These are wonderful." Lillia said, holding up one of her dresses.

"You're quite welcome, Lillia." Piofei said, with a slight nod and smile.

"This is itchy." Horus said, scratching under his tunic.

"You'll get used to it." Piofei assured him.

"How can you get used to being itchy?" Horus asked.

"Now – about your shoes." Piofei said, opening the door to the street. "Now that you all have decent clothes – put some on, and let's go." She nodded to both Deilo and Lillia.

Both of them stepped into provided shrouds, and changed from their own, travel-worn clothing, into the new ones. And then the four of them followed Piofei out into the street, Lillia riding on Horus' forelock.

Piofei took them up the street for a long ways, before turning onto another street that was lined with street vendors squatting against the front walls of shops. She led them past many stalls, calling greetings in return to those she received from the vendors. Finding the place she was looking for, she led the foursome between two stalls and into a small store.

"Nikul! I have some hunting for you to do!" She called, waiting in the front of the crowded storefront. There were tables everywhere, holding racks and shelves lined with foot wear for everything. Tiny folk, large folk, flying folk, running folk, hoofed

Restoration of Numar

folk, those with claws, those with soft feet, every shoe imaginable was there on display, and many that were entirely too strange to figure out.

A slim, silk-skinned creature with fuzzy antennae glided out of the back, walking along on a dozen different legs, making it look like he floated from place to place when he moved. "Mkio nimk, Piofei?"

Piofei nodded to the creature. "I have four who need shoes, Nikul."

Nikul looked the four children over, and moved into a strange, smooth bow. "Juin, paue qm. Tionetche?"

"We'll start with Horus, here." Piofei gestured to the young Centaurii.

Nikul bent, and lifted Horus' front hoof, removed the wooden-and leather shoe, and made a rapid tikking noise. It set his foot down, turned in one smooth motion, and left again, into the back. Soon he was back, wearing a many-pocketed apron, handles of tools poking out of it in every direction, including down. How the tools stayed in, there was no telling. Nikul then proceeded to pick up each of Horus' feet in turn, remove the makeshift shoes, and trim his hooves. Horus protested at first, but Piofei reassured him that it was perfectly alright.

Once all his feet were trimmed neatly, Nikul measured Horus' feet in every way, from height, depth, width, and thickness. Then he left again, only to return shortly with a wooden box that looked like it weighed quite a bit. Nikul set it down on the floor with a sigh. "Huinji, biouner guit nackentuchet. Foi/turg/pag/niclentchenmperama."

"What?" Horus asked.

"That will do." Piofei said.

Nikul pried the box open with the handle to one of his tools, revealing a box full of steel shoes for the Centaurii kind – all of them about the right size for Horus.

"Oh, gods." Horus said, looking at them.

Nikul proceeded to go through the box one shoe at a time, four times – once for each of Horus' feet, trying each shoe on until he found one that fit to his satisfaction. Then he fastened the shoes to Horus' feet in the oddest way – the shoes appeared to clamp themselves onto his feet and hold themselves on, while never looking like they were anything more than shoes to be nailed on.

"Niy." Nikul said.

"Walk around, see how they work." Piofei prompted.

Horus walked around, making banging noises every time his feet touched the stone floor. "My feet weigh a ton!"

"You'll get used to it." Piofei assured him.

Crystalyn Dragon

Nikul watched Horus walk, closely, and eventually nodded with satisfaction. "Nu." He banged the lid back down on the box, and looked at Piofei. "De?"

"Deilo." Piofei gestured to the boy.

Nikul nodded, and carried the box of steel shoes away. Then he came back, scrubbed Deilo's feet cleaner than they'd been since he was born, and measured his feet. Nikul then fetched out another box, this time prying it open and setting it on a table for Piofei to sort through. She came out with two pair – and had Deilo try them on. He walked around in them, and Piofei shook her head, making him take them off again. She handed him a third set, and watched him walk in those.

"These'll do. I'll make him some socks to wear with them." Piofei said, tucking Deilo's leather slippers into her apron pocket.

Nikul nodded, and packed up the box, to carry it back.

"De?"

"Lillia." Piofei took the Gnome down off Horus' head, and set her on the table.

Nikul reached up onto a shelf, and took a small box down. This, he set on the table next to Lillia, and lifted the lid off. Inside were hundreds of pairs of shoes for Gnomes. They left the selection of shoes to Lillia, as she was the only one who could successfully lift out just one pair of shoes, and not crush them to oblivion. It didn't take her long to find a pair that fit remarkably well, and Nikul put the box away again.

"De?"

"Mutsgae." Piofei lifted the lizard off the floor, and set him on the table.

Nikul looked at the little lizard, and shook his head. "Herp, netevs. Xentreampolmrlm."

"What'd he say?" Deilo asked, knowing he couldn't repeat those sounds.

"None at all?" Piofei asked.

"Hnuips." Nikul said, with certainty

"Well, Mutsgae. It seems you're out of luck. Nikul says your kind don't wear shoes. At all." Piofei said.

"I could have told you that." Mutsgae said. "Mother never wore shoes."

"Oh well. How much, Nikul?"

"Juinksd. Deunmse, Piofei; wesrtnme."

Piofei lifted a pouch out of one of her own apron pockets, and counted out a collection of coins onto the table.

Nikul nodded, and picked them up.

"Have a nice day, Nikul." Piofei escorted the four back out into the street, and all the way back to the inn. Horus made an incredible racket the whole way, his new shoes banging off the stone pavement. It took him a while to figure out how to walk in the shoes, and tripped many times over when the shoes caught on a ledge. By the time they reached the inn, both he and Deilo were tired of lifting their shoes for every step, their leg muscles burning.

    Maids took them back up to their rooms, where they were fed lunch and allowed to rest. For dinner, however, they were shown to their daily chores first. Horus was assigned to help in the courtyard, where people's mounts were kept, as the animals were familiar with the sight of another four-legged creature. Deilo was set to helping in the kitchens, and Lillia made sure all the majick lamps stayed full, along the tavern's back wall, behind the bar. Mutsgae was allowed to roam the courtyard, to chase whatever lurked there. He found a thriving population of rats and other varmits, and he found it especially tasty when he stashed his kills for three days before eating them. The smell that created was distasteful to most, however, and he was soon moved to a different place to do other things.

    The inn didn't really know what to do with him, though, and he ended up being a messenger from one part of the inn to another, spending most of his time in Piofei's workshop. He enjoyed scaring the hair off the cats that hung around the door to the street the most, but sometimes Piofei employed him to the task of running off the annoying flying lizards that liked to perch in her windows.

Chapter Two

Gnaria

Horus yelled in surprise as his back legs tripped up instead of stepping backwards, and the frightened pack beast he had been trying to lead only freaked out further at the sound. Gripping the rope in his hands even harder as the beast tried to yank free, Horus dumped backwards on his rump, completely unable to get his feet back under him.

"Mutsgae! Get OUT OF THE WAY!" He yelled, kicking backwards with both rear hooves. They connected solidly with what had tripped him – Mutsgae's scaly side.

Grunting, Mutsgae lifted his head off the cobblestones and yawned sleepily. "Huh?" he asked.

"Get out of the way!" Horus repeated. "Why must you always sleep in the walkways?" he demanded, pulling the smaller pack animal back to all six of its feet.

"Ih." Mutsgae pushed to his feet, and ambled to one side, tilting his head to watch Horus fight with the beast. Completely grown at fifteen years of age, Horus was no small creature. But neither was he a very muscular sort of creature. Even though he was larger than the pack animal, the animal was considerably stronger, and giving Horus a hard time of it. "What's wrong with it?" Muts asked.

"You! You resemble a voracious predator, remember?!" Horus snapped, frustrated.

"Huh." Mutsgae reached upwards with his giant, toothy maw, and took hold of the dangling rope behind Horus' heels.

Turning, he ambled into the barns, towing the startled animal along behind. Not quite fully grown, Mutsgae was still a formidable creature. Five and a half feet long and weighing more than anyone would want to lift, he was very muscular, and nigh unmovable without Mutsgae's consent. His mere presence made the inn a very safe place to be, as no one dared cause mischief with a 'guard dog' like him laying in the door way. He spent a great deal of time sleeping – usually in the way of Horus' work – or watching the going-ons of the place.

Horus stumbled to the side, and watched as Muts made the creature walk all the way to the doors and through. Shaking his long head, he followed after. Between the two of them, they managed to get it into a stall, and Horus proceeded to unburden the creature of its load.

Muts watched for a moment, then wandered back outside to frighten the newest arrival to the inn.

"Gods above! What is that?!" they screeched, loosing a few feathers.

Muts only grinned, long past caring that everyone that saw him thought he was a beast. Rows of long, pointy teeth showed in his grin, startlingly white in contrast to his green and grey skin.

"That's just Mutsgae." A hand said, taking the arrival's mount. "He won't bite."

"You keep a predator like that in your stables?" the horrified guest asked, staying well clear of the Lizard.

"Sure. Why not? Would you rather he stay in your room?"

"No! But I'll not have it stay in the same place as my beasts!"

"Apologies, sir. Feel free to tell him to leave." The hand said, before walking away with the animal.

The feathered creature stared at Muts for a moment, and then fled into the inn. Muts only laughed, stretching out right there across the entrance to the barn and resting his head on his front feet.

"Muts! Move!" Horus said, for the umpteenth time that day, coming out of the stall and attempting to step over Mutsgae's broad back.

"OK." Muts moved, sideways, tripping Horus again.

Horus crashed to the stones, yelled, and kicked out. One hoof caught Muts on the shoulder, but did not do any damage. Muts only laughed, and moved off, towards the inn's front door. There he stretched out in the shade and watched the street. Horus rolled to his feet, yelled something Muts didn't catch after the retreating Lizard, and then returned to his duties.

Deilo stepped out the front door, looked around, and then down at Muts. "What is Horus yelling about, now?" He asked. Now twenty three, Deilo had grown out completely and was a strapping young man. Though he still worked mostly in the kitchens, he got about the inn quite a bit, checking on things.

"The usual." Muts mumbled in reply, snout resting on his fingers.

Deilo heaved a sigh and shook his head. "You really ought not provoke him like that, Muts." He then grinned despite himself, and toed Muts' shoulder. "Naughty Lizard."

"Hey!" Muts twisted around faster than Deilo could blink, but he didn't bite. Instead Deilo's boot was merely bumped away by Mutsgae's snout.

Deilo only laughed, and went back inside again.

Heaving a sigh, Mutsgae laid down again, eyes rolling. Spotting something in his left eye, he stopped rolling it to focus in on it.

Still barely big enough to not get inhaled, Lillia was standing there, smiling at him.

"What?" Mutsgae asked.

"Could you open the door for me?" She asked, holding a basket on one arm that was covered. The basket was sized to match her, and Mutsgae couldn't fathom what could possibly fit in it. But he did push to his feet and amble over to the door. As big as he was, it was still fairly hard for him to reach the door latch. The inn had made provisions for him, however, and there was a lower device designed so that Mutsgae could open the door from nose level. Shoving the door open, he waited as Lillia walked under him and into the inn. "Thank you." She said, dropping a curtsey on the way past.

Mutsgae only grunted in reply, before shutting the door once more and returning to the veranda.

In her bright pink dress, Lillia could hardly be missed, as she walked across the floor, headed for the back stair. Into one side of the stair was set what looked like a gear track, to most. But it was indeed only a long, miniature stair specifically set there for Lillia to ascend and descend the stair on her own.

Deilo scooped her up before she had gotten half way across the room, though, and carried her up. "What's that you've got?" He asked.

"Material for a couple new dresses." She replied, setting the basket on her lap.

"You went all the way to the market by yourself?" Deilo asked.

"No, silly. I went with Mila." She said, referring to one of the maids. "She got word of an ill aunt, so I caught a ride back on a wagon."

"A wagon? That's a tad dangerous, don't you think? You could have gotten squished." Deilo said, setting her down in front of her little cupboard room.

"Not at all. I was perfectly safe." Lillia said. "How go things today? Any better yet?" she asked, setting the basket down by her feet.

"Yes, actually. We have had two people come in, today. Both of them with trains of pack beasts." Deilo said.

"Good, good. But that's not going to make up for this past week's doldrums. We need far more business than that." Lillia said.

"I know. But there is not much we can do about that, is there? The war is getting worse, and less people are traveling or trading through here. Did you know that there are rumors that *we* might get attacked?"

Lillia *tsk*ed. "You spend far too much time listening to folk gossip. This city is walled. We can't get attacked."

"What makes you say that?" Deilo asked. "Walls didn't stop Kiliso Bay from getting burnt to the ground."

Lillia was silent a moment. "Don't dwell on it, Deilo. You could attract desolation with thoughts like that."

"What if we are, though? What then?"

"Life goes on, Deilo. Don't worry about it. It's not as if Elves are going to come in and steal everyone's souls." She said, patting Deilo's finger. "Thank you for the lift."

"Any time. What brought up Elves?" Deilo asked.

"I heard someone mention having seen one." She said. "In the market. There's no truth to it, though – everyone knows Elves no longer dwell in the lands. Evil creatures such as that would have a very hard time simply hiding for so long. The only proof that there ever were Elves at all, are all the Helves running around. And they are a testament to the darkness of such creatures."

"Helves are solid, though. Elves aren't, are they?"

"Helves are also only *half* Elf, Deilo. Of course they're solid." Lillia said. "Thank goodness they're all caged as soon as they're found."

"Well ... yes." Deilo said, standing.

Lillia waved, before turning and walking into her room, taking her basket with her.

Deilo shrugged, and walked back down the stairs, behind the counter and through the doors into the kitchen where he resumed his previous tasks.

That evening Horus came inside, to plunk down on a stone bench and lean on the table there by it. Deilo showed up shortly with a mug of ale for each of them, and sat down across from him. "And?"

"And what?" Horus asked, after taking a pull off the mug. The froth remained on his furred lip until he stuck out a wide tongue to lick it clean.

"How are the creatures?" Deilo asked.

"Alright, I suppose. That feathered one ... is it a Dtri? I don't know ... it keeps coming back out to make sure its animals are 'happy'. Drives me nuts. Never happy. So I told it to take care of the animals itself. I'll probably hear it from the Keeper, in a few hours, huh?"

"Probably." Deilo agreed. "Don't blame you, though. Mutsgae didn't have anything to do with it, did he?"

"I bet you he's the whole reason. He terrified that Dtri when it arrived. So now the Dtri thinks that its animals might get eaten. Or something like that. I don't know."

"Try not to get so mad at him, ok?" Deilo said.

"Who's mad?" Horus asked. "What's for dinner, anyway?"

"Who's mad? The whole inn heard you yelling earlier, Horus!" Deilo said.

"Ah, well ... getting dumped on my ass will tend to do that. Muts was sleeping in the gateway again." Horus said. "What's for dinner?"

"Don't you have eyes? He's not exactly easy to miss." Deilo said.

"Of course I do. Just not on my ass." Horus said. "I was going backwards, trying to coax a terrified burden beast through to the back yard, where I could put it in the only stall we had left for a creature of that mass. What's for dinner?"

Deilo opened his mouth to speak, but Horus interrupted him with a gesture.

"Ah – ah! What's for dinner?" he repeated.

"Stew, why? You keep asking that." Deilo said.

"Maybe because I wanted an answer? Yes? Why stew? Stew again? Oh, lord of Mercy, take me now!" he beseeched the ceiling.

"What? You don't like my stew?" Deilo asked, poking out his bottom lip.

"Of course I do. But the same dish gets old, after awhile, you know?" Horus said. "How come we can't have salad?"

"You want salad? Ok, go find something green out there in that drought-besot garden, and we'll have salad." Deilo said, before draining his mug.

"Huh. We can't afford green stuffs anymore?"

"No." Deilo said. "In case you haven't noticed, business is a little dry of late..." Deilo gestured loosely. "This hall used to always be packed, even when not meal times. Now look at it."

Horus looked around, at the sea of tables and benches, every one empty barring the one they occupied themselves. "You have a point."

"The Keeper is talking about shutting up shop until trade picks up again." Deilo said. "Others talk of the war coming here."

"You know that's just talk. No army in its right mind would attack here."

Deilo looked over at him. "That's what Lillia said."

"She's right, and you know it." Horus said, inspecting the inside of his mug.

"Huh. Well, a body still has to wonder. I heard once that there's a new device that King Trinatte is trying out ... a wall breacher."

Horus snorted. "A plain old mangonel would do that much."

"Not against a majicked wall, it wouldn't." Deilo pointed out. "Which is why walled cities are considered safe. Except one thing. Did you hear about Kiliso Bay?"

"Yup. Burnt flat. What's new?"

"Kiliso Bay had majicked walls, Horus."

Horus looked up at him. "They did?"

Deilo nodded. "Why do you think the news made such a stir?"

"Huh." Horus grunted. "Don't believe everything you hear, Deilo."

Mutsgae came in the front door, singing at the top of his lungs. Both Deilo and Horus clapped hands over their ears to block out the wretched noise. Lizard voices and singing simply did not go together, even when it was Lizard Song being put to voice. But Mutsgae was singing a Dtri ditty, and that was even worse.

"Hey! Cut that out!" One of the maids popped out the kitchen, and threw a pan of water out on Mutsgae. The Lizard shook his head vigorously, then laughed and ambled over to where the other two were.

Deilo put his hands down as Muts maneuvered up into a slanted posture. Back feet still on the floor and belly resting on the bench, Muts could only just barely prop his elbows on the table. To stay there, he dropped his chin on the tabletop.

"Hi, guys. What're you doing?" he asked.

"Huh?" Horus asked, taking his hands off his ears.

"You're all wet." Deilo said, sluicing water off the table with a hand.

"Hm. Yes." Mutsgae said, the corners of his long mouth turning upwards. "Helps keep the bugs off."

"What bugs?" Horus asked.

"Has anyone seen the Keeper lately?" Mutsgae asked.

"No, not lately." Horus said. "I prefer not to see him."

"With you there, buddy." Deilo said. "Why?"

"Well, he usually comes outside fairly often. But I haven't seen him in four days." Mutsgae said. "Do you think he's taken ill?"

"I'll ask." Deilo said. "One of the maids ... maybe the cook will know something."

"Now that you mention it, yes. I haven't seen him in some days ..." Horus said. "I wonder what is going on?"

Deilo shrugged. "Do you want to eat now or later?"

"Stew? Later. I think if I have any more stew, I'm going to blow up." Horus said.

Deilo laughed, and returned to the kitchens.

"What's wrong with stew?" Mutsgae asked. "Besides all the vegetables in it?"

Horus wrinkled his long face at Mutsgae. "What's wrong with the vegetables?"

In the kitchens, Deilo looked up from washing out a pot when he spotted Lillia walking across the counter top. Her face was creased by a deep frown, and her eyes were downcast.

"What's wrong, Lillia?" Deilo asked, setting the pot down on the counter.

"I don't know, D. I don't know. I have a really bad feeling ... it's been getting worse as time goes by." She sat down on an upturned cup, propping her tiny feet up on the handle.

"Bad feeling?" Deilo asked. "What sort of bad feelings?" he asked, opening a cabinet and retrieving a towel to dry the pot out with. Fluffing it out of its folds, he poked it into the pot and swabbed it around.

"Bad feelings ... in general. Like I had before our old home got torn apart."

"That's not good. You're not having these feelings cause I told you about the war, are you?" He asked, tipping the pot up to dry the bottom.

"No, of course not. I've had them for awhile. And then you said something ... I blew you off. Like I have been to my own instincts. But I think I was wrong ... something terrible is going to happen ... I don't know when. I don't know what. But something is bad. Very bad."

"Huh." Deilo grunted, heaving the heavy iron pot over to the stove where it would finish drying. Returning to the counter, he leaned his elbows on it and looked down at her, towel still in one hand. "What should we do, then?" he asked.

"I don't know. But I think we might ought to tell the others. See what they think. Before we take it to the Keeper and get laughed at for our troubles." Lillia said.

"Hm. Right, then. Well ... no time like the present." Deilo said, setting down the half-soaked towel and offering her a hand. She pushed to her feet, and stepped up onto his hand, one hand on the tip of his raised thumb for balance. Deilo lifted her up to his shoulder, where she stepped off and sat down next to his shirt collar. Gripping the collar edge, she watched as Deilo went out into the dining area where he had left their friends. The room was deserted already, however, and the door out to the yard was standing ajar.

Deilo expertly made his way between the tables, and looked out the door. There in the cobblestone yard the two witnessed Horus chasing Mutsgae all over the place, the one yelling and the other laughing.

Being how they were designed, Horus eventually won out, and caught the tiring Lizard. Over very short distances, Mutsgae was faster, but he could only go a short ways. Horus, on the other hand, could gallop for hours. The yard wasn't quite big enough to get going that fast, but the two nearly managed it anyway. When Horus caught Mutsgae, he gave him a thrashing with his front hooves, only half the blows even managing to nick the squirming Lizard.

"Hey! Hey! Cut it out, guys! You can play later. Lillia has something to say." Deilo yelled over the racket, walking over. He stopped a few paces short, and crossed his arms across his chest.

Horus landed on all four feet, hooves landing either side of Mutsgae's head, and he looked over at Deilo and Lillia. Mutsgae was still for a long moment, staring at those feet that would have got him good had he moved just then, in either direction. Then he squirmed out from under Horus, and looked up at the others.

"What news?" Mutsgae asked.

"I think something bad is going to happen." Lillia said.

"Like what?" Horus asked, adjusting his stance so his feet were closer to actually being under him.

"I don't know, yet. I only know the last time I felt like this, it was before our home was burnt down." Lillia said.

"Home?" Mutsgae asked, being the only one who didn't associate a specific place as 'home'.

"Yes. The town? Yelm?" Lillia asked.

"Where's Yelm?" Mutsgae asked.

Horus whacked him. "The town where we all met each other, duh!"

"Oh!" Mutsgae asked. "That town." He was quiet a moment. "That's bad. What do we do about it?"

"How do we know your feelings have anything to do with events such as that?" Horus asked.

"She's a Gnome, Horus." Deilo said. "Related to faerie folk. They know these things." He pointed out.

"Oh. Right. Ok. So, like Muts said. What do we do about it?"

"That's what we're hoping you two will help us decide." Deilo said. "What do we do, who do we tell? And will they listen?"

"Heck if I know." Muts said. "Everyone thinks I'm a carnivorous pet."

"That's cuz you are, Muts." Horus patted the Lizard affectionately on the head.

"Cut it out!" Muts said, moving away. "I am not, either."

"Enough!" Lillia said. "Focus, people. Focus."

"And? Any ideas?" Deilo said.

"Why not just tell the Keeper, and let him figure it out? He probably has more information on such topics than we do. He talks to folk." Horus said.

The group was silent, looking at each other expectantly.

"Well?" Horus asked.

"Who's going to do the telling?" Deilo asked. "You?"

"Heck no. Not me. Why not you?"

"It wasn't my idea!" Deilo protested.

"I'll tell him." Muts volunteered. "But don't expect him to do much."

"Why?" Lillia asked, looking down at the Lizard.

"I always tell him wacky stuff. He laughs at me." Mutsgae said, shrugging.

"This is hardly wacky, Muts." Deilo said.

"Yeah, but he won't know that." Muts said.

Again, they were all silent, eyeing each other on varying levels.

"Alright. I'll go tell him." Deilo said, turning to walk toward the inn again.

"What's that noise?" Mutsgae asked, lifting his head.

"Your belly. Shut up." Horus said.

"No, I mean it. What's that noise?" Mutsgae asked, as a high whine became audible to the others. Deilo stopped, one foot

almost to the stones. He set his foot down as the whine grew in intensity.
"What's that noise?" Deilo asked.
Horus looked around, then up. "D! Move!" He turned tail and leapt into a run towards the barn. Deilo turned around, just as the inn exploded into a massive fireball, shards of wood flying in all directions. Deilo was sent flying, to crash heavily into the paved ground, Lillia tumbling away. Frightened but still possessing his wits, Deilo rolled over and sprang to his feet as things began plummeting to the ground around him. He lit out for the barn, bending to scoop up Lillia on the way. Mutsgae remained where he had been, too short to have been knocked over by the blast. He just stared at the raging inferno that had been the inn, until Horus' yell broke him out of his trance. He turned and fled to the barn, after the others.
Deilo dropped at Horus' feet with a heavy groan, setting Lillia down.
"Are you ok?" Horus asked, bending to look at his friend as Mutsgae arrived.
"I don't think so. Did the inn just blow up?" Deilo asked, as the high whine started up again. This time there was more than one of them. Great flaming balls fell out of the sky, obliterating any building they fell on, be they wood, stone, or earthen structures. The area was soon a screaming mass of frightened people fleeing in all directions.
"More than the inn, I think." Horus said, pushing the doors to the barn closed.
"I think my arm is dislocated." Deilo said, holding his shoulder.
"You're covered in lacerations." Lillia said, standing on his thigh and looking up at him. "Thank you for picking me up." Her own clothing torn, she didn't look like she was actually wounded.
"Let me see that." Horus said, moving to inspect Deilo's shoulder. "There's certainly something wrong with it." He confirmed. "Here." He took a lightweight blanket out of a cubby, and tore it into strips. Then he fashioned a sling for Deilo's arm. "I don't know if we can find a doctor, so this will have to do."
Deilo winced as the arm was manipulated into the sling. "Hurts."
"I'm sure it does." Horus said.
A crashing noise that drowned out all the raging sounds from outside drew their attention, in time to see Mutsgae come running back out of the back of the barn. "RUN! GET OUT! RUN!" He bellowed, four legs forcing his bulk ever faster,

hurtling toward the closed barn doors. Right behind him came a hurtling mass of frightened pack animals, all blinded by their fear.

Horus yelled, and lunged for the doors, while Deilo snatched up Lillia and rolled to one side, under a stall door and into the uninhabited stall. Horus managed to get the doors open, and skidded around to the side, hanging onto the heavy swinging doors for balance. Mutsgae shot out of the barn, all the animals hot on his tail. Once they were all gone, Horus looked in the barn again, to see a scene of mass chaos. The barn had been wrecked by the stampede. All the stalls were splinters, bits of wood and other items strewn everywhere.

"D?" Horus asked, stepping over and under bits of the barn interior.

"Over here." Deilo could be heard gasping, under a fallen section of wall. Lillia crawled out of the gap at Deilo's side, still for the most part unhurt.

"Hurry ... this thing is crushing him." She said, getting to her feet.

Horus jumped over and around obstacles, hurrying to where Deilo was trapped. Grabbing the section of stall wall, he heaved upwards. "Can you get free?" He asked, grunting.

"No – my foot is still pinned ... AH!" Deilo yelled in pain, as part of the debris shifted. "My leg! My leg! Get it off!"

Horus heaved up on the wall, and threw it aside, to reveal a beam that had Deilo pinned down. Removing the wall had shifted another beam that lay on the one pinning Deilo, and the extra weight was working on breaking bones.

"Hurry!" Lillia cried.

Horus stepped over Deilo, placing his big feet carefully. He shifted the top most beam to the side, and then attempted to lift the lower one. "Augh!"

"I'm free!" Deilo said, scooting back, out from under the beam.

Horus released the beam, and it fell with a crash, sending up a plume of dust and grit. Grunting, he stepped back to regain his balance, only to get startled forward again when Deilo yelled.

"What now?" Horus asked, turning.

"You stood on me!" Deilo gasped, leaning back on a piece of wood.

"Apologies."

"Where's Muts?" Deilo asked, over the din coming in from the outside.

"I don't know." Horus said, moving to help Deilo up. Once Deilo was on his feet, Horus lifted him up and placed him over his own back. "Hang on." He bent, picked up Lillia, and made his way out of the rubble.

A sphere of fire impacted the barn just as they left it, and it erupted in a massive explosion. Horus braced as the gust of hot air washed out over them, barely keeping his feet under him as he hung onto Deilo and Lillia. Standing in the doorway of the already wrecked barn had saved them any more pains, as there was nothing there but air to blast at them. The bits of barn went in every other direction, and then the roof started to come down. Recovered, Horus jumped forward, fleeing the falling wreckage. He galloped out of the yard and around to the street, in front of what had been the inn mere moments ago.

"Muts!" Horus yelled, having problems negotiating the rubble-strewn streets with a load on his back. He had never before had to carry anything on his back before, much less a person. "Muts!"

"Mutsgae!" Lillia called out, her high voice piercing through even the shrills and noise of the carnage about them.

Around the far side of what was left of what had been a bank, Mutsgae showed up, swiftly negotiating the obstacle-strewn street.

"Let's go!" Horus called, turning and heading for the city walls. Mutsgae stayed close on his tail, keeping up by sheer will with Horus' trot. Horus could only maintain the pace for a short time, with his load, and was reduce to a fast walk, huffing and puffing. "I'm glad I wasn't born a riding beast." He grumped.

"Catch him!" Lillia cried, as Deilo started tipping off Horus' back, unconscious.

Horus barely managed the catch, and propped him back up again. "Just a while longer, D, OK? Hang in there."

"I think he passed out from the pain." Lillia said, hanging onto Horus' mane.

"Most probably."

"Do we have any idea where we are going?" Mutsgae asked, better able to keep up with the slower pace.

"Out of the city? I don't know. We'll cross that bridge when we get there. Right now we just concentrate on not getting smashed to pieces." Horus said, as they approached one of the many gates into the city.

"Horus – wait ..." Mutsgae said, slowing to a stop, sniffing the air.

"What?" Horus asked, slowing and turning to look back.

"I smell ... fire." Mutsgae said, slowly.

"So do I, Muts. This whole city is on fire!" Horus said, starting to lose his temper at the delay.

"Wait, listen to him." Lillia said.

Mutsgae didn't reply, still smelling the air. And then he backed up quickly, looking rather alarmed. Spooked by Mutsgae's reaction, Horus followed, hopping over a freshly fallen bit of building. Another building exploded a short ways off, filling the air with debris before crumbling in on itself.

"Muts!" Horus called. "Where are you going? Out is the other way!"

Behind Horus, the gates exploded in a terrific pyrotechnic display, bits of twisted metal and wood flying everywhere. Horus yelled, and jumped forward into a full gallop, dodging and jumping obstacles as he fled up the street.

Through the flames of what had been the gate, hundreds of soldiers poured through, wielding spears and shields. Behind them came swordsmen, with shields, and behind them came a larger sort of creature that only remotely resembled a man, carrying a large two-handed sword and no shield. In amongst them ran more men, armed only with partial shields and bows. These made their way to the walls on either side, and up, where they could fire in on the city.

Mutsgae hid, not able to flee like Horus had, slithering under a partially suspended section of wall. He looked around, rather frightened, but at a loss for what to do. Horus had long ago disappeared from sight, down a side street. So he did what he did best ... he sat still and waited, hidden in the shadow.

Horus on the other hand, kept running and running, until he heard Lillia's shouts, finally.

"What has gotten into you?" She shrieked. "You dropped Deilo!"

Horus slid to a complete halt, and looked back, and then all around.

"That way! Hurry!" Lillia pointed.

Horus turned, and took off once again, afraid for his friend. Deilo wasn't too far back, but certainly looked more banged up for the event. Horus scooped him up again, and this time held him in his arms.

"I am not built for this." He complained, turning to run on, again. He soon found he was near another gate, but it too was blown to splinters. Through it he could see the siege engines lobbing the firebombs into the city, and amid them, scores upon scores of soldiers of every caliber. "Oh, good Gods above." He said, turning to run back deeper into the city, only to find himself cut off by more of the same invading soldiers. They had ranged across the street, and had spears leveled at him. Horus groaned, and jumped to the side, tearing off down a side street. Behind him, the soldiers broke into a run, after him, yelling at the top of their lungs to be heard over the racket of the invasion. Fortunately, Horus knew the streets fairly well, and quickly lost the soldiers in the maze of narrow streets, ducking through some darker passages that were normally packed, but were now devoid of any citizens.

"Where is Muts?" Horus asked, pausing in a dark spot that seemed safe for the moment, blowing heavily from the exertion. He rested Deilo on top of a large box he found there, and leaned on the wall.

"I don't know. We lost him really quickly." Lillia said, hopping from Horus to the box nimbly.

By that point, the city had managed to muster a few soldiers of its own, mostly the law enforcement numbers, but there were a few militia mixed in. They hardly had a chance against the invading force, but they tried, rushing out towards the walls to try and slow the tide. Mostly so as to give time to the others fleeing the city by way of the river.

Where they met the invading soldiers, bloody fights broke out, swords and shields clashing wildly, nearly drowning out the yells of the men. But loudest of all were the screams of the wounded and dieing. One such encounter erupted directly on top of the piece of wall under which Mutsgae was hiding. The wall rocked and creaked, entirely unstable under all the feet pounding around on it. Mutsgae sat still even so, until a body crashed off the edge right in front of his snout. Shocked, he drew back away from the corpse. But then he grew angry, and slipped out from under the far side of the wall. Rushing in a short burst he rose off the ground slightly, impacting a soldier with open jaws. He clamped down on the man's side as they fell, tumbling. The soldier screamed, mostly out of shock. The armor he wore on his torso protected him from Mutsgae's teeth for the moment. The soldier then thrashed, flailing at the Lizard with his sword. He caught Muts a solid blow to the brow with the hilt of the blade. To any other creature, it would have stunned or even knocked them unconscious. But it only enraged the Lizard, who clamped down harder on the soldier. His teeth punctured through the armor, piercing through layers of clothing and down through the man's ribs. The soldier screamed in pain, then, trying to fight Mutsgae off with a new vigor.

Having a solid hold, Mutsgae thrashed the soldier to the side, ripping the rib cage completely open, killing the man. The scent and taste of his blood tripped a trigger in Mutsgae's brain, whereupon he went berserk attacking the others nearby almost without discretion. He stopped only when there were no more foes within sight, all dead. Turning, he moved off down the road, stalking towards where he could smell another fight happening.

Half way down the nearby rubble-strewn road, however, he encountered a new smell. He could smell the sweat off Horus' flanks, and the fear therein. He could also smell Deilo, there with. The trigger in Mutsgae's brain flipped back, and he altered course to follow the trail to find his missing friends.

He found them where they were hiding in the dark, all of them so still as to be dead. Mutsgae knew they weren't however – they smelled alive even yet.

"Muts, is that you?" Horus asked, almost inaudibly.

"'Tis me." Mutsgae rumbled, in reply.

"Oh, good. We'd thought we'd lost you." Horus said, as Lillia stared at the Lizard as if she knew what he'd been doing. After a moment, Horus noticed her expression. "Lil? What is it?"

"Mutsgae. His voice. It's different." She said. "Deeper."

"Yes? So? What of it?" Horus asked.

"Horus, don't be an idiot. That means he's blooded – he's killed." Lillia hissed.

Horus stared at her for a moment, then at Mutsgae. "Eh?"

Mutsgae didn't respond to any of it, merely sitting up closer to the road than his friends were, to keep and eye out. "What are we going to do from here?" He asked.

"Hide, for the moment." Horus said. "Hiding worked last time."

"We were also a lot smaller, then, if you recall." Mutsgae pointed out. "A lot easier to hide, and of little value to the invading force."

"So?" Horus asked, worried.

"So, now we're bigger, harder to hide. And we are more of value, as well. As prisoners, as feed for the beasts of war ... or as recruits." Mutsgae said.

"Who could find us here?" Horus asked.

Mutsgae twisted just enough to look back and up at the Centaurii. "I did."

" ...oh." Horus said, soberly. He looked over at Deilo's battered, unconscious form. "Oh."

Deilo was covered in shallow, seeping wounds, the sling had fallen off his dislocated shoulder, his leg was bruising deeply – if it wasn't slightly fractured, too. On top of all that he had several rich bruises from when he'd toppled off of Horus' back. Lillia was standing on Deilo, inspecting the deeper of the surface wounds, looking for splinters to remove.

"Will he be ok?" Mutsgae asked. "He looks worse than the city does, almost."

"I don't know. I'm not a doctor." Lillia said. "Any of these by themselves, sure. Wouldn't even slow him down. But all of it at once? I really don't know. He's lucky he's unconscious and can't feel anything right now."

"He looks terrible." Horus agreed.

Restoration of Numar

"We need to figure out how to get out of the city." Lillia said.

"But where will we go when we get out there? How far do we have to get, to be away from the invaders?" Horus asked.

"Far." Mutsgae said. "There are lots of them. The city will be filled to over flowing whenever they finish trickling through the gates."

"Trickling?!" Horus gasped. "That horde was a trickle?!"

Mutsgae nodded, then looked out again. "Trickling. There won't be anywhere to hide."

"Ok – while we figure out how to get out, we also need to figure out where we're going to head to." Lillia said. "First set the destination, then figure out how to get there."

"We've never been anywhere but here." Horus pointed out. "Here, Yelm, and in between."

"There's a whole wide world out there." Lillia assured him. "I've read about all sorts of Kingdoms."

"Are any of them better than this one?" Horus asked, dejectedly.

Lillia considered that for a moment. "Some of them are more powerful than others, but it's always in a state of flux. All the Kingdoms are at war with one or more neighbors."

"I was afraid of that." Horus said.

"However, there is a Queendom, and there is relative peace. Other than that, there's only Gnaria." Lillia said. "The Wizard's land."

"Are you joking? Gnaria is a made up story of wishful thinking!" Horus said. "There are no Wizards, any more, and there certainly isn't any isolated valley that knows eternal peace!"

"Actually, yes there is." Mutsgae said, quietly. "My mother was from there."

Both the Gnome and the Centaurii stared at him. "What?"

"My mother was hatched in Gnaria." He said, looking back at them.

"What makes you so certain of that?" Lillia asked.

"She told me so." Mutsgae said.

"A lot of people claim things, Muts!" Horus grumped.

"Shhhh!" Lillia warned. "Muts, can you be certain of that?"

"Yes."

"Ok, so we'll assume for now that Gnaria is a real place. Do we try to go there?" Lillia asked.

"Oh, why not? The whole rest of the world is crazy, why not us?" Horus said.

53

"I'd love to see the land where my mother was hatched." Mutsgae said.

"Ok, so now we've got a destination. Now ... who knows how to get there?" Lillia asked.

The question was met by a silence broken only by the sounds of the battles strewn throughout the city and the crumbling of burning buildings. The three friends just looked at each other for a minute, until a falling piece of roof tiling smashed on the ground nearby, startling them all. Jumping, they looked up as one, to see a pair of armed figures on the rooftop looking down at them, swords glinting with the wetness of blood.

Mutsgae crouched, hissing threateningly as Horus jumped for where Deilo was strewn on a box. Lillia screamed, and Horus had to pull up short when one of the figures landed on the box, one foot on either side of Deilo's inert form. The figure straightened, twin blades lowered to either side.

"How injured are you?" Asked a shadow-soft voice.

Horus looked up, at the form, then blinked. "A SwordDancer?"

"Answer the question." The SwordDancer stated.

"We aren't, except for Deilo. He's hurt pretty badly." Horus said.

The second form moved, towards the street atop the building, and crouched there. Mutsgae turned, watching warily as he left Horus to deal with the lower one.

"Can you carry him and move swiftly?" The SwordDancer asked.

"What do you want with us?" Lillia asked, crouched still on Deilo's chest, under the SwordDancer.

The SwordDancer looked down at her. "You do not honestly think we would rescue you from the Forest, only to have you die in the city we brought you to, do you?"

Lillia gasped. "Are you the one who brought us here?" She asked, squinting up at the shadowed figure. "You haven't aged a day!"

After a moment, the SwordDancer laughed softly. "I am the same. Now come, hurry. We do not have the luxury of time to tarry."

Horus stepped forward and scooped up Deilo and Lillia when the SwordDancer stepped aside. Mutsgae looked back at him when the SwordDancer lightly hopped down from the box.

"Come." The SwordDancer said, moving to the end of the little dark alley. He paused there, and looked out in all directions before moving off across the street into another alley. He moved just as lightly, swiftly, and silently as he had when he'd escorted them to the city. Horus hurried after, but the steel on his feet made an awful clattering on the cobblestones. Mutsgae followed him, as the second SwordDancer leapt from the top of the building.

She landed lightly, as if it had been a much smaller drop, and sprinted after the group, doing a quick spin before entering the new alleyway.

The lead SwordDancer stopped, and took Deilo from Horus. "Take those off your feet, or we'll never get out of here alive." He instructed the Centaurii.

Horus looked at the SwordDancer blankly for a moment, and then started fighting with the shoes on his feet. When it became apparent that Horus couldn't really remove them himself, the other SwordDancer moved forward and helped untie the shaped shoes, and pry them off. She set each down gently, to make as little noise as possible. When all four were off, she returned to the rear as the other SwordDancer handed Deilo back to Horus.

"What is your name?" Lillia asked, hanging onto what was left of Deilo's shirt.

The SwordDancer glanced at her. "You may call me Roan." He replied.

Lillia nodded. "Roan."

"Silence is a must. Speak only if you must. Your life resides on this." Roan then turned and moved off, deeper into the shadow. Horus followed him, glancing back to see Mutsgae eyeing the other SwordDancer. In the end Mutsgae followed Horus, with the SwordDancer bringing up the rear.

The group traveled in near silence through shadowed passages, hurrying across open places when there was no way around. Once they were ambushed by a group of six soldiers. Three died almost instantly, before the group realized their error. They retreated hastily, giving Roan lots of room.

Most all Races knew of SwordDancers, and just how fast and deadly they were.

Roan faced the remaining three, both swords low and dripping their comrade's blood. The standoff lasted only a mere moment. The remaining three fled the area, one of them yelling in a foreign tongue.

Roan waved Horus forward, pointing with a sword at what appeared to be a heap of refuse. "Go there. Around the side, you will find a net. Lift it and go under." He instructed.

Horus did as he was instructed, Mutsgae following at his heels. The female SwordDancer followed still, both her swords still in her hands. Horus approached the heap warily, watching for any sign of a net. He found it, but if he hadn't been told it was there, he never would have seen it at all. He hissed at Mutsgae, and gestured with a forefoot.

"There."

Mutsgae moved forward, tasting the air as he approached the heap and the net. It smelled of old trash, but when he moved the net aside, he found a narrow tunnel that Horus could walk down standing erect. Moving aside, he held the net back with one taloned hand. However, before Horus could move to enter the tunnel, the SwordDancer jumped forward, and entered first. Horus followed her in, though warily. Behind him, Mutsgae glanced back at Roan before entering.

Roan was still across the street, standing quite visibly at the corner of a building. He still looked very dangerous and intimidating, though, and Mutsgae was glad the SwordDancer was on their side.

Or so he hoped. There was no telling what the warriors wanted with them.

The trio traveled through the tunnel as it grew increasingly close and rank, harder to squeeze through. It became impossible for Mutsgae to navigate, as the lower portion of the tunnel became only as wide as a booted foot. He was forced to tip up on one side and ooch his way through the tunnel that way, claws digging into the soil and rock. Every great now and then there would be a wooden or stone support beam that he had to squeeze past.

The tunnel seemed to go on and on forever, time unending, as they followed the SwordDancer. She kept a swift pace at first, but as time wore on, she slowed to the pace the others were forced to. Horus could place his feet easily enough, but he had to physically shove both sets of shoulders past the sides. Carrying Deilo increasingly became a more impossible task, long before the hide scraped off Horus' shoulders.

Finally, the tunnel suddenly widened into a low room. There was clearer air in the room, and more room to move in, even if the taller members had to now duck.

The moment the SwordDancer halted, both Horus and Mutsgae collapsed to the mossy floor with groans of pain and exhaustion. Horus laid his burden down, then, arranging Deilo carefully. He then just lay there in misery, both sets of shoulders scrubbed bloody. His hindquarters were also in bad shape, though not quite as bad. Mutsgae on the other hand, had a thoroughly scoured belly and back, with all four legs worn completely out. His skin was still more or less intact however, being made of tougher stuff than Horus'.

The SwordDancer moved about in the darkness, before they heard the scraping of flint on rock, and there was a flame.

Though a faint spark, it blinded all who saw it. After a moment of soft breaths, the SwordDancer had a very small flame going in some dried moss. She picked the small bundle of flame up and moved it closer to Horus. She inspected his sides, and applied a cool cream to his wounds. Moving to inspect Mutsgae, she left him as he was. Moving the fire again and adding a little moss to it to make it keep burning, she inspected Deilo.

She cleaned all his wounds, bandaged the worst of them, applied a pungent cream to the bruises, and relocated his shoulder with a swift motion. The loud snap it made caused Horus to jump, and the pain from it woke Deilo up.

He screamed bloody murder.

The SwordDancer poked a rag in his mouth, and covered it with a hand. "Shh." When his voice faded, she applied more cream to his shoulder. Deilo pulled the rag out of his mouth with his good arm.

He hissed in pain, and laid back limply. "Where are we, and who are you?"

"You may call me Till, and we are in an underground tunnel. War rages overhead. If you value your life, you will stay quiet." She said, giving him the small can that held the cream. "Apply this wherever you feel pain."

Deilo pushed himself up, and Horus offered an arm to support him. "How are you feeling?" Horus asked, holding the can so Deilo could use his good arm to apply it.

"Awful. Like a stampeding horde ran me over."

"Um. One did." Lillia said, scooping out a double-handful of the soft cream. She sniffed it, then inspected it by the fire. "Hm. It's a numbing cream, as well as one to speed healing. Interesting!"

"You are very quick." Till said.

"No – I'm small. The cream has completely numbed out my hands and wrists, and my own bruises are already fading." Lillia pointed out. She walked the comparably long distance to Mutsgae and applied her handfuls to his belly. He closed his eyes and let her work, also noticing the relief right away.

"There isn't more tunnel like that, ahead, is there?" Horus asked.

"There is, but not for a long ways." Till replied. "You should be healed by the time we get there."

"Where does this tunnel go?" Deilo asked.

"To the Forest." Till said, simply.

"Yikes. Who decided to dig a tunnel that far?" Horus asked. "And why?"

"It's a smuggling tunnel." Till said. "It goes from the edge of the forest to the inside of the city ... those who dug it dealt in contraband, and wished to not get caught at the gates. The portion of the Forest it goes to is not all that far away. It still has its risks, but those who built it decided it preferable to chance the Mnarag."

"Yikes." Deilo agreed. "The great wolf, is preferable?" he shook his head, placing the lid on the cream. Horus then handed it back to the SwordDancer.

"How did you know the city was under attack so fast?" Horus asked.

"We knew it was going to happen ahead of time. We always know. All our people in the area left before the siege began. Roan and I had to travel here, after hearing of it. Thus we arrived a bit late to be getting you out. It is still possible, however. He should be rejoining us shortly."

"Roan?" Deilo asked, squinting at Till. The little fire was dieing, and in the dim glow, he could not tell even what Race she was, beyond bipedal.

"He stopped behind to seal the tunnel against any pursuit." Till said.

"Oh."

"You all need to rest – get what sleep you can. You will be awakened when the time comes." Till put the little fire out, and all went pitch black once more.

In the deep darkness, it was all too easy for sore and weary bodies to pass out. They were reawakened by a bright light that left them all a bit stunned for a moment. When their eyes cleared, they saw it was a sword that was glowing, and it was Roan who held the sword.

"Good afternoon." Roan said. "Are you able to continue on?"

"To where?" Deilo asked, blearily.

Roan lowered the glowing sword, to look at Deilo. "Ah. You are awake? Good. It will make things easier on your friend. We are leaving the city. We shall escort you as far as we must."

"I don't wanna move." Horus grumped.

"You will, when they find the opening to this tunnel. And you can be assured they will. It is inevitable." Roan said, as Till drew one of her own swords. A muttered word and a brief spark of majick, and her blade glowed in the darkness, as well.

"That's a neat trick." Mutsgae mentioned.

"Come. Let us be on our way." Roan said, urging everyone to their feet.

When Deilo got up, he looked around until he saw Lillia walking across the mossy floor as if it were a chest-deep pasture to wade through. He stooped, and picked her up gently.

"It's good to see you survived." Deilo said, setting her on his shoulder.

She grinned at him. "You think I wouldn't? It was you we worried over."

Deilo nodded, and followed Roan down another tunnel way. Behind him came Horus, and then Mutsgae. Bringing up the rear once more was Till, with her glowing blade. The tunnel was wider and easier to pass than the first one had been, and all walked down it in relative comfort. There were a few places where there was low stones to be ducked by the taller members, but they were easily seen and avoided in the light of the glowing swords. The journey seemed unending all over again, by the darkness beyond the light, and the little-changing tunnel.

The tunnel dipped low, rose up once more, and swerved to either side in seemingly random intervals. However, the changes seemed to indicate to Roan and Till where they were in their travels. They made low comments to each other that didn't make much sense to the others of the group. But it made little difference. The younger members were long past wanting to fold up and crash when Roan decided to finally stop. They were still in the tunnel, with little room to do anything except collapse where they stood.

Roan hooked the hilt of his glowing sword on his chest armor, and drew the other blade. This one he stabbed into the wall, and pried a large chunk of wet soil out. A second chunk, and there was a trickle of water draining into the tunnel. Cleaning his muddy sword, Roan watched the water until it ran clearer. Sheathing his second blade, he produced a small bowl, and filled it from the trickle. It was a slow business, and Deilo passed out from exhaustion before the bowl filled with water. When the bowl filled, Roan set it aside, and caught the small bowl that Till tossed to him over everyone's heads. He set that one under the trickle, and by the time it filled, the first bowl of water had settled out. Roan picked that one up, and passed it around. Everyone took a sip from it, but no more. The water was distasteful, but to a parched throat it was wonderful. Horus roused Deilo to sip, and then passed it back to Till. She took a sip of it, then set it down for Mutsgae. He emptied it of what water was left, even sucking up the settled bits in the bottom. Till took the bowl, and tossed it back up to Roan, who set it to refilling once more. The group dozed off and on, taking little sips of water as it became available. After all were sufficiently rested and watered, Roan distributed a handful of dried breads and meats. Afterwards they all sipped once more. The bowls were stashed, and they moved on.

It seemed as if another eternity had passed, just in the time they had spent resting, and there was no way for the group to tell how much time had exactly passed.

They continued on in the same fashion for seeming ages, until the tunnel suddenly shrank down again, becoming stone. Horus became thoroughly wedged, and yelped when Mutsgae stumbled into his hocks.

"I'm ... stuck!" Horus grunted, shoving Mutsgae back again with his heels.

"Is it wider ahead of where you're stuck?" Mutsgae asked, as Till moved forward over Mutsgae's head.

"I dunno – maybe." Horus said.

Deilo watched as Till climbed up onto Horus' back, and took a look at the situation. Lillia, on Deilo's shoulder still, noticed Deilo's strange expression, and poked his ear.

"Deilo? What is it?" She asked.

"Huh? Oh, nothing. Just a bit of Deja vu. Him. Stuck. In a tunnel."

Horus made a wretched face at Deilo. "Very funny."

Till inspected the rocks to either side. "If you aren't averse to it, I think we can pop you free with enough force. You just have to stay relaxed, so you slip rather than tear." Till said.

"Pop me?!" Horus squeaked. "That's going to hurt, isn't it?"

"Would you rather stay stuck?" Till asked, slipping off his round rump.

"Of course not. I'd die in here."

"Precisely." Till said, planting a spike-armored shoulder on Horus' rump to shove on him.

"OUW!" Horus shoved her back with a sharp kick. "Don't put that spiked thing on my ass!"

"Oh, for crying out loud. Get out of the way." Mutsgae pulled Till farther back.

"Oh, no. What are you going to do now?" Horus asked, trying to twist to see.

Mutsgae surged up and forward, slamming his shoulders into Horus' rear hard enough to throw them both forward to the ground.

"OUWGH!" Horus yelled as he toppled forwards, the Lizard tangled into his hind legs. Mutsgae grunted, and then pulled himself free.

"There. Let's go."

Deilo stood back far enough to give Horus plenty of room to get up again. When he was up again, he asked, "Are you ok?"

"Other than a bent tail and scrubbed sides? I suppose." Horus grumped.

"Good, let us proceed, then." Roan said, before resuming the trek through the tunnel.

"There aren't anymore narrow places, I hope." Horus said, as he proceeded to follow Deilo in the gloom.

"There shouldn't be." Roan replied. "You may wish to resume silence ... we draw near to the surface once more."

Horus heaved a sigh. "Finally."

There were several more narrow places in the tunnel, but none so tight that Horus would become wedged again. The tunnel began to slope upwards suddenly, and Roan stopped just shy of where fresh air wafted into the dank air of the tunnel. Gesturing for silence to the others, he quenched the light of his blade, as he drew the other. Roan crept forward slowly and cautiously. Pushing aside the limbs of the bush that hid the narrow entrance, he peered outside. Seeing nothing, he ventured farther out, still slow and silent. The tunnel's entrance was positioned in the side of a low rise that had bushes dotted all over it, and very little could be seen of outside from the tunnel itself.

Roan crept forward once more, leaning to one side to see what there was to be seen. He still saw and heard nothing, and stepped out, close to the edge of the bush. He spun on one foot when a harsh voice rang out;

"Halt! Who goes there?!"

Roan stepped free of the bush, and spotted the owner of the voice – a large furred creature that normally spent time underground ... it was probably the one that had dug the long tunnel, and now guarded it.

The creature looked Roan up and down, its small eyes narrowed. "A SwordDancer, eh?" it grunted. "What are you doing in my tunnel? Did that lousy scum send you to dispatch me to avoid the fees?"

"Nay. I know not of whom you speak. I am here only to escort others – be it through your tunnel." Roan replied.

"Ah. That is not so bad. But you still have to pay the fees for using my tunnel, no matter what you used it for."

"What fees?" Roan asked.

"Well, seeing how you are escorting people rather than goods, I can't very well ask for a percentage, now can I? Hm... let me think. How many others?"

"Four." Roan said. "And my own companion."

"Ah. Six, eh? That is not so many. What sort of coin do you carry?"

"None." Roan said.

"That is too bad, then. You will have to give me one of your swords, then."

Roan frowned at the creature. "How about I let you keep your head, instead?"

It opened its mouth, closed it, and then nodded. "That will do."

Roan stepped back, sheathed one blade, and pulled the brush aside. "Come."

The others filed out of the tunnel, and Horus shook the first chance he got, shedding a huge cloud of fine dust. The creature watched the group curiously, but held his tongue. It knew it could not hope to take on one SwordDancer, much less two ... *and* a Lizard.

Mutsgae looked the creature up and down, and then ignored it. Roan nodded to it, and then led the party off into the woods. The Forest there was far different than it had been where the foursome had been before ... here the trees were shorter, tighter together, and the ground was choked with brush. There were but few places one taller than Mutsgae could walk unimpeded. A few times Roan's blade was reduced to machete work so that they might pass at all, much less with any comfort. Another whole day was spent trudging through the woods, until they reached a stream, where Roan stopped.

"We will stop here for the night. Drink your fill." He said, before following his own advice. Till leaned on a tree, looking back the way they had come. After a moment, Roan joined her, and they spoke in low tones.

"I am not certain, but I believe we are being followed." Till remarked.

Roan looked off through the brush. "It would be too easy for someone to follow our trail. How many, do you think?"

Till shrugged slightly. "I can't tell. About ten. No more than fifteen."

"That is a lot of warriors."

"They probably don't want to chance all of us being warriors, too." Till said. "Though, we aren't."

"With that many, the others may be in some danger." Roan said. "We will have to lose them, before we pause to rest."

Till nodded, looking over at the collapsed heaps that were their charges. "I don't think they can go very far, though, much less at any kind of speed. Thus we cannot outrun them. What do you suggest?"

Roan considered it, glancing over at the others. "The Lizard can probably hide incredibly well, especially out here. As can the Gnome. The other two, however, pose something of a problem."

"Can the boy climb?" Till asked. "Maybe he could become concealed in the trees."

"We shall see. You and I will have to continue on with the Centaurii, and after a short ways one of us will circle back through the limbs, to keep and eye on things here – we don't want to chance them being found." Roan said. "Hopefully, the Centaurii can run well."

Till nodded. "Go tell them." She looked back down their own trail, watching for movement.

Roan moved over to where the others were. "Change of plans. You and you, hide yourselves as well as you can. We are being followed." He pointed to each Mutsgae and Lillia. Then he pointed at Deilo. "Can you climb?"

"After a fashion." Deilo said. "Though I had buildings to climb, not trees."

"Good. Hide yourself up in the trees. Do not draw attention to yourself, lest you lose your life."

"What about Horus?" Lillia asked. "He can't very well hide."

"He will have to continue on, with us. I trust you can still run, though tired?" Roan asked.

"I don't know for how far." Horus said. "But I can try."

"When we have gone some distance, one of us will circle back, to keep an eye on things here." Roan said. "The other will stay with Horus, and continue on. Maybe there will be someplace farther along where you will not leave an obvious trail."

"This doesn't sound good." Deilo said. "Why would someone be following us?"

"Either they are soldiers from through the tunnel, or the smugglers. Both would want you, for varying reasons."

"Oh dear." Lillia said.

"Go. Hide." Roan said, before waving Horus over.

Lillia vanished almost instantly, able to hide a lot of places most would never even think of to look for someone. Deilo was given an assist up the tree by Mutsgae, and he climbed all the way to the top, to put as much foliage between himself and the ground.

Mutsgae wormed under a bush and down into the leaf litter, becoming nearly invisible.

"Remember, the key to hiding is being still. Movement will give you away." Roan said. "And be silent." Then he led Horus away at a quick pace, Till following right behind.

Deilo heaved a small sigh, and made himself as comfortable as he could – it might be some time before things happened and safety returned. Nearly an hour passed, before anyone else entered the small area. First came a large dog-like creature, sniffing the trail out. It was held in check by a harness, a lead running from its shoulders to the hand of a tall reptilian fellow. Striding along on powerful rear legs, he seemed to see everything as he turned his head. Pulling the creature to a stop, he crouched and inspected the ground.

"They paused here." He hissed, evidently pleased. "Apparently still unaware of us."

A small crowd of goblins, and a few men, all armed to the teeth joined him shortly.

"Good. That will make them easier to take down." One of the men said.

"What if the yoil was telling the truth when it said there were two SwordDancers?" one of the goblins asked.

"No matter. They must still be dealt with. No one must know of our tunnel ... no one! And it is no consequence if the city burns ... it will be rebuilt. We will still need our tunnel. The SwordDancers too must die."

"That will not be an easy thing to accomplish." A goblin said.

"Why do you think we brought him along?" the man gestured at the reptilian, who only grinned toothily.

"Ach."

"Water the beast, and refill the water bags. They are obviously in a hurry to get somewhere ... I would have thought they would have stayed here longer." The man ordered.

The whole group moved to the water, some of them within inches of Mutsgae's snout and completely unaware of it.

The reptile, once done watering the beast and himself, looked around, the beast at his side.

"This does not look right." He said, once having found the exit trail.

"What do you mean by not right?"

"There are some tracks missing ... there is still the horse/Centaurii, and two sets of man feet. There is the Lizard track and a man track missing."

"Are you sure?"

"Yes – they also left here at a run. They know we are here."

"Lizards don't run very well. It probably took to the stream and swam away – indeed there are its tracks on the bank. What of the other man?" A goblin said.

"Might he be on the horse?" another goblin asked. "There is no one here."

"It is possible." The other man said, uttering his first words since entering the area.

The group stood there for a moment, trying to decide on whether or not to take off after the tracks they had, or to try and search the area for someone who might not be there. In the end, they decided to leave two goblins and a man to search, while the others continued on. Just as they came to that decision, they came under attack from a group of soldiers. All were men, all were armored, and swift with their surprise attack. The battle was short and bloody ... in a matter of moments all the soldiers were dead, as well as all the goblins, the men, and the beast. The only one left standing was the reptilian, and he was wounded badly.

Snarling as his last foe toppled headless, the reptilian roared his victory to the sky. Afterwards, he remained looking up, frowning. Tilting his head to one side, he limped over to the tree Deilo was hiding in, and sniffed the bark.

"Ah, there you are." He hissed. The reptilian prepared to climb the tree, talons sinking into the bark as he pulled himself upwards.

Two things happened immediately, dividing his attention as well as bewildering him.

Till launched out of a nearby tree with a blood-curdling yell, both swords free and ready to kill, and the bush on the ground exploded with snarling fury.

Mutsgae got to the reptilian first, having propelled himself upwards and through the air with incredible speed. His jaws closed on the reptilian's spine, just above his hips. When he fell backwards, his weight yanked them both back down off the tree's trunk.

The reptilian uttered a pain-filled yell upon being bitten, and had the wind knocked out of him upon landing on the ground. Till impacted the tree where he had been a moment before, and she immediately redirected herself, launching directly down at the reptilian.

Having a raging Lizard under his back and a SwordDancer attacking from above was more than the reptilian had bargained on, but he fought back desperately. Despite his best efforts, though, Mutsgae had already permanently crippled him from the waist down, and was working on chewing his head off. A swift thrust from Till's sword ended his life abruptly, and he went limp, twitching here and there as nerves fired.

Till hopped off of the heap, and turned.

Mutsgae, upon realizing his foe was dead, shoved the carcass off and rolled over. Once belly-down again, he looked around.

"You will make a formidable foe, one day." Till said, to him. "With the proper training, of course."

Mutsgae only grunted, searching the dead for any that were merely pretending. Finding none alive, he simply sat. "What now? We have seen both smugglers and soldiers."

"If we are lucky? No more soldiers will follow through. The smugglers, however, are certainly going to come find out what happened when these do not return. If we are lucky, they will think that it was merely a conflict with the invading soldiers and nothing more. Let us move on, and rejoin the others." Till said. "Come, let us depart." She called.

Lillia appeared from inside a cluster of delicate mushrooms, and waited there until Deilo had descended the tree. When he reached the ground, he picked her up and set her on his shoulder.

"Thank you." Lillia said, as he followed Till into the trees.

Till attempted to set a swift pace, despite the weariness in the group. It did not last long, however, as she soon started leaving the others behind. She slowed up, and let them set their own pace, though she did try to urge them on.

Half way through the night Roan joined them, and he guided them to where Horus was hidden, crashed completely out flat out on his side in a cavern made of tumbled boulders.

"Where did these come from?" Deilo asked, sitting down tiredly. "There is no mountain here." He lifted Lillia down, and she moved off to one side.

"No one knows. Some speculate that one of the Wizards was planning on building something here, before their demise happened." Roan said. "Rest. We move out in the morning."

"Where are we going?" Mutsgae asked.

"To another town, one we believe to be out of the line of fire for the time being." Roan said. "It is some ways yet."

"Oh." Deilo leaned over, pillowing his head on Horus' side. Mutsgae settled in nearby, Lillia finding a bed between his shoulder blades – a place where she wouldn't get stepped on in the night.

Morning came bright and early, with breakfast waiting for them. One of the SwordDancers had made a successful hunt, and an entire carcass was roasting on a flat rock a short ways off.

Even Mutsgae ate of it, though it wasn't tastefully rotted yet. They were all starving, and ate until they could hold no more. There was little left of the carcass when they were finished. After the meal, Till led them to the stream's banks again, to drink their fill.

"I have a question." Deilo said, after having had a meaningful look from Mutsgae.

"What is that?" Roan asked.

"Does Gnaria exist?" Deilo asked, looking over at the SwordDancer.

Roan lifted a brow. "Gnaria?"

"Yes. Does it exist? Or is it a fable?"

"Of course Gnaria exists." Roan said. "Why?"

"We were thinking on going there, before you found us, if we could determine if it existed. Tales have it that there is war free. Is that true?"

"Up to a point. Gnaria does not know war the way these lands do, but it has its own internal conflicts ... between the Wizard and the Scholars. And then there is a new faction making itself heard there, also. No one really knows what they are up to, yet."

"Do you know how to get there?" Deilo asked.

"No." Roan said.

"Oh." Deilo said. "I was hoping you could point us there."

Roan shook his head, with a slight grin. "We are going there."

"We are? How? If you do not know the way?"

"Till knows the way." Roan said. "She has been there."

"Oh. How far away is it?" Deilo asked.

"A long ways. We are far from the ranges, and they themselves are a thing to be reckoned with." Till said.

"Oh."

"How long will it take to get there?" Horus asked.

"Depends. If it were only Roan and I? We could be there very shortly. But at the pace you three keep? We could be at this journey for a long time." Till said.

"There is no way to shorten the trip?" Deilo asked.

"There are ways to speed the travel to the ranges, yes, but they require things we do not have. Through the ranges themselves, there is no way but on foot. No flying thing passes the ranges, no majick thing passes the ranges, and no great group, such as an army, passes the ranges." Roan said. "A small group such as we should make it alright, if we do not find any of the dragons that live there. Till and I are not equipped to battle a dragon – or a pair of them."

"Dragons?" Lillia asked.

"Yes. There are perils on the journey to Gnaria – that is why it is still a relatively safe place. Gnaria cannot be conquered by conventional means. Just getting there is a real trick." Till said. "Do you still want to go there?"

The group looked at one another, then they all nodded.

"If it means a place to live that won't get burnt down for us, yes."

"I presume you know that some consider the Wizard worse than any king?" Roan asked.

"I have heard that, yes. I have also heard that he is better than any king." Deilo said. "It waits to be seen."

"Ah."

"Will this help any?" Deilo asked, drawing a small, well-padded bundle from his clothing. He set it down and unwrapped it carefully, revealing the tiny tube of majick that he had picked up years ago in Yelm.

"You still have that?" Horus asked, astounded.

"How did you come to have it on you when all this mess started?" Mutsgae asked.

"I always carried it with me – just in case, and to keep it from getting stolen." Deilo said. "But I never really had a use for it."

Roan crouched, looking at the little vial sitting on the wrapping. Leaning forward, he picked it up and looked at it. The shades of purple within swirled with a life all their own, slowly and constantly moving. He looked at Deilo. "This is a lot of sky majick. How did you happen across it?"

"It was one vial of many, each one a different color, in a box in a shop in Yelm. The shop I lived at before we stumbled across the place where we found you the first time." Deilo said. "I picked it up just in case ... but I have never needed it. Not that I know how to use it."

"It is good that you did not try." Roan stood, and handed the vial to Till.

She took it gently, looking at it. "That is a lot."

"That was a long time to carry it, too. It has been many years since then." Roan said.

"And it never broke!" Lillia said. "After all the beatings and falls you took? Incredible!" she said. "Nice wrapping, though. Looks warm." She sat down in the middle of it.

After a moments consideration, Till spoke again. "This may even be enough to do exactly what he asked ... speed the trip."

"Are you sure that is an acceptable risk?" Roan asked. "If it runs out short, we could all catch our deaths."

"No, I think it will just do. Give me a moment to recall the finer details of the spell ..."

"What spell?" Deilo asked, but Roan only shrugged slightly.

The group sat in silence, resting and digesting their breakfast as Till thought, contemplating the tiny vial in her hand. It took many long minutes before she nodded to herself.

"I think I got it."

"Let me hear." Roan said, to be safe.

Till started speaking in what sounded to the younger members as the SwordDancer tongue, with a majickal lilt to it.

"Do you really only speak that, most times?" Deilo asked, when she finished.

"Yes." Roan replied, thinking.

"Why are we an exception?" Horus asked.

"There was no time for something as absurd as that. We knew you knew not the tongue." Till said. "There were things to be done. However, keep in mind, if you come to our kind again, you must be able to speak to us in our way."

"Oh."

"Why do you keep that rule?" Deilo asked.

"To keep business to a minimum. To prevent frivolous jobs. We are mercenaries... elite, but still mercenaries. Forcing others to learn our tongue before presenting us with a job ensures that it is not just a passing rage that has them hiring us. They must be serious, before we will take them seriously." Till said.

"Part of that didn't sound right." Roan said, before repeating part of the spell back to her, and then again, altered. Till thought on it, and then shook her head.

"No, it was closer, originally."

"Close isn't good enough, when dealing with majick." Lillia said. "Please be sure of what you are doing, before you try it. I would rather walk two months, than be vaporized or worse by a miss-represented word in a spell."

Till nodded to Lillia. "I won't attempt it until there is no doubt. Have no fear. I have the same preference."

"Why are you trying to do a spell in your own tongue?" Deilo asked. "Isn't it easier to do it in the original majick language?"

"Sure. If you know the majick language backwards and forwards." Roan said. "Most people only have a rudimentary understanding of the tongue, and as a result, many die. Others only know single phrases. Due to this, there is no sure way to learn the language, short of taking lessons straight from the Wizard himself."

"Oh."

"As such, it is far safer to modify our own to the task presented. Wherein we know exactly what meanings a said word has, and prevent any misconstrued meanings."

"I see."

Till spoke, repeating the spell yet again. Those who didn't know the tongue couldn't tell if she had changed part of it or not. After a moment's thought, Roan nodded.

"I believe that is it." He said, straightening as he folded both arms over his armored chest.

Till took a moment more to consider her words, before actually opening the vial of magic. Taking a belt knife, she scratched a design in the weathering of the rock beneath her, chanting the spell as she drew. She paused, counted everybody to be sure of the numbers. She then continued on, applying the majick heavily to both the rock, and the air around them. The group was soon surrounded in a thick purple mist that could have been a chunk of the sky itself, come to take them.

Everyone experienced a sudden inability to breathe, as if they were drowning with no water to be seen. Just before the blackout point, the mist suddenly cleared, and they were standing on a grassy knoll overlooking a small village.

Even the battle-hardened SwordDancers spent a moment sitting down and gasping for air, before anything was said or done.

When he caught his breath, Roan spoke in low tones. "Now I remember why I detest majick."

Till only grinned at him, getting to her feet. Roan stood, as Till helped Deilo to his feet. Horus rolled around a bit, before finally getting up. No one noticed when Mutsgae stood – he looked the same when prone and when standing.

"Which town is this?" Roan asked, noting the intimidating wall of high peaks that rose out of the open plain off to one side. They appeared to be in the right place.

"I believe it was called Normaj, that last time I came through. Depends on who owns it now." Till said. "I was here some eighteen months ago."

"Ah."

"I thought we'd stop in here for supplies, before we tackle the mountains." Till said. "They were nice enough folks."

"What all are we going to get?" Deilo asked, after taking a deep, reassuring breath.

Roan looked over at him, and then shrugged. "Depends – how much are you willing to carry over the mountains?" He strode down the knoll, towards the town. Till brought up the rear again, as the little group followed him in.

The various vendors gave the group a wary eye and a silent tongue as they passed through, the market-goers giving them a wide berth.

When Roan stopped at a vendor's booth, the vendor cleared his throat nervously. "I don't speak SwordDancer."

"You don't have to. You are not doing business with me. I am doing business with you. So I shall speak your tongue." Roan said.

Not having understood a single word of the exchange, Deilo asked, "How many languages do you know?"

Roan looked over at him. "Many." He then turned his attention back to the wares before him, inspecting each with an expert eye. In short order Roan had every member equipped with the necessities for crossing the mountains at that time of the year. Horus protested his load, but being what he was, he was stuck with a considerable bundle to carry on his equine back. To make things easier, Roan had even equipped him with a suitable harness to hold it all secure. It did little to quell Horus' grumbles, however.

The group stopped at a tavern for a hot meal, and then set out towards the formidable mountains. The day was already mostly gone by then, and they only made a few, but quick miles over the open land. They ate a cold meal and drank from a stream, refilling their water bags before turning in for the night. They slept in the open, on an assortment of thick blankets, with the exception of Mutsgae. It was altogether too warm to sleep under them. The second day was much longer, traveling over increasingly steeper hills, though the true mountains were still in the distance. During the day Roan shot a small sheep and field dressed it before rubbing it with coarse salt and slinging it over one shoulder. They ate cold meals again for lunch, but at dinner they roasted the sheep and ate most of it. The rest was packed away for other meals.

It took them six days just to reach the mountains, traveling for as long each day as could be squeezed out of the city-dwelling youths. Till regularly applied generous amounts of her numbing cream to them, so they could sleep well enough to be ready to go again the next morning.

The only one spared the harsh treatment of travel was Lillia, though she too had her discomforts.

When they reached the rugged mountains, they turned and went along their length for two days before coming to a spot that was marginally lower than the rest.

"We have to go up that?" Deilo despaired, sitting down on a boulder and looking up at the forbidding slope. Jagged rocks and gnarly shrubs protruded all over the slope, the rest covered by loose gravel. Every great now and then there was the occasional stringy tree, providing little to no shade, and a very prickly handhold.

"That is the pass, yes." Till said, propping a foot up on a large rock as she looked up it. "There is a lower one farther west."

"Why can't we go there?" Horus asked.

"Because it is some hundred and eighty miles away." Till said. "It is far easier to just cross here. If we are lucky, this stretch isn't being hunted at the moment."

"Hunted? By what?" Deilo asked.

"We told you there were dragons in the mountains." Roan said, almost inaudibly. "We meant it. Do not yell, you will only attract them from farther away."

Horus put a foot out to each corner, and rested that way, knowing that if he got down, not even a well-rested Mutsgae could get him up again. He was too tired. Gazing up at the treacherous slope, he sighed. "I'll never make it up that."

"Why not?" Till asked. "Mules do it all the time."

A bit rankled, Horus replied: "I'm not a mule, either, now am I?"

"We shall see, shan't we?" Till said, before starting up the slope. She made it look effortless, the gravel not even shifting under her boot soles.

"I wish I could walk on air the way you people do." Deilo said, before struggling up the slope after her. The gravel wouldn't stay put for him, shifting and crunching under the heavily treaded boots that Roan had bought for him in the village.

"It is merely a matter of training." Roan said, urging the others up the slope. Even Mutsgae didn't want to go, his short legs beyond exhausted from having to keep up with everybody. In a flash of irritability, he snarled at Roan's prodding, flashing jagged teeth dangerously.

"Unless you seriously care to pit your little teeth against my big ones, you'd best keep those inside your mouth." Roan said, giving the Lizard a warning look.

Grumpily, Mutsgae got up and started up the slope after the others. He handled it fairly well, not having to worry so much about balance, though he did have a small but heavy load to carry. Strength he had in plenty. Endurance he had but little.

A week into the mountains didn't seem to get them any closer to the other side, and nerves were beginning to fray amongst the youths, though the SwordDancers attempted to keep their morale up.

"Why is this trip so long? These mountains can't possibly be this big." Horus grumped, flopping down on a bed of gravel that happened to have some dirt in it, and a few soft ferns.

"It's the Wizard." Till answered, patiently. "It is majick that makes the short journey long, the easy path difficult, to weed out any army, or any who do not possess the will to get to the other side."

"Why?" Deilo despaired, sitting down in the shade of a leafier tree. Being still put a chill on him, though, and he pulled out a blanket to draped over his already coated torso.

"Think about it." Roan said. "What are you?"

"I don't understand the question." Deilo replied.

"You are refugees, fleeing a war torn land. If it were easy to get to Gnaria, everyone would flood there. Gnaria would become over crowded in short order. The quality of the land, of living, would suffer greatly. Too many people in too small an area would only breed more war. Gnaria is also the only unconquered land. It would be an easy target for some egotistical King, if he could get an army through the mountains. But the ward set on the mountains destroys all parties numbering too great – no one knows what exactly that number might be, either. It probably varies from one moment to the next. Gnaria has no army. It only has a powerful Wizard, and a handful of his enforcers. Sometimes those are cavalry, sometimes they are not. Do you want to get there, or not? If you don't, you can turn around and be back out of the mountains in under three days."

"What? That fast?" Deilo asked, surprised.

"The ward doesn't stop those going out of Gnaria – only those going in." Till said.

A brief trickle of pebbles stopped all talk instantly, and all eyes turned upwards, to the very top of a steep cliff nearby. At the top sat a gnarly beast with an angular head and stubby wings that might or might not carry it through the air. It looked right back at them, swinging its great head from side to side, blowing gently through giant nostrils.

"Hold perfectly still." Roan instructed, in a barely audible voice.

No one even blinked, staring up at the terrifying sight overhead. The dragon snuffed once, looking around as if it suddenly couldn't see them. After a moment it straightened, and roared at the top of its lungs, vibrating the very rock they stood on. Then it looked down again, as if searching.

A second head appeared over the edge of the cliff, and looked down, then around. After a moment, it nipped at the first dragon and moved off again. It took much longer for the other to decide there was nothing of interest, and follow, back out of sight again.

The pair of dragons were visible for some time, off and on, as they moved about the mountain, plainly hunting. Only when they were over the top of a nearby ridge did Roan relax, and sit down.

"Where did you learn that?" Till asked, also relaxing and leaning on a tree.

"By accident, actually." Roan said. "How do most people react to dragons?"

"They run. As fast and as far as they can." Till replied. "If they are lucky, they find a bolt hole that the dragon can't dig out."

"Right. And most get eaten, don't they?" Roan asked.

"Yes. Most." Till agreed.

"What other animal is prolific in these mountains?" Roan asked, still talking solely to Till, but speaking so all could hear and understand.

Till spent a moment thinking on it. "The ybexi?" She guessed.

"That's one name for them, yes." Roan said. "The golden fleeced mountain goat, particular to these mountains. What do they do when they spook?"

"They freeze." Till said. "It makes them too easy to hunt."

"For us, yes. I happened across a dragon once, and I ran, like most. Luckily, I found a bolt-hole ... but not before I ran right past an entire herd of ybexi. They all froze. I deliberately did it, hoping that the herd would distract the beast from me. But it never even noticed them. When it finally left, the goats started moving again. How do most things react to a dragon? It runs. If it doesn't run, it's not food, apparently. I think those dragons in particular key on movement. If it doesn't move, it's a tree or rock. They can't tell you're not rock. They can smell you, but it's the same to them as a rock you sat on. I tested the theory, not knowing if it was simply that ybexi don't taste good to dragons. First I drugged a ybexi so it couldn't freeze when frightened, and deliberately drew in a dragon. It ate it without a second thought. So I tried holding still when I next encountered one – I didn't have much of a choice at the time, I was in a spot where I couldn't run anywhere. A box canyon. It worked. It frustrates them, of course ... thus the roar to try and get you to run so they can see you. And ever since it has worked for me," Roan said.

"Fascinating." Till said. "Most things run, because most predators can see you anyway."

"However, there aren't many predators where dragons hunt – all is fair game. Thus the ybexi flourish here." Roan said. "But it's still a tad frightening to stare down a dragon."

"Yes." Till agreed.

Deilo carefully stored away all the information, even the bit that the supposedly fearless SwordDancers weren't fearless after all. They got frightened, too!

After a short while just sitting so the youths could rest after the climb, and then the fright right after, the SwordDancers urged them onward once more, to squeeze in a few more miles before dark. When asked, they pointed out the golden-fleeced mountain goats to the youths. The animals browsed happily on everything organic, be it dead leaf, twig, or something green. And they didn't frighten easily. They just watched the group walk on by, unperturbed at the sight of travelers. Only when they stumbled across one right in their path did it frighten and go stiff. It didn't even blink, as they inspected it up close. Its fleece was soft and downy, deeper than their fingers were long. Underneath the fleece it was heavily muscular, with a rounded out belly. Its head had only short spike horns, designed for clearing snow and ice from food or water. Its dished face was entirely funny looking, with bulging eyes set wide apart on either side of its face. However, as Roan took a moment to show them, the ybexi was not entirely defenseless. He lifted its lip and showed them the razor like canines it possessed. Solely for fighting, not for eating.

"How do they fight, if they freeze?" Deilo asked.

"They don't. It takes a dragon to scare one stiff. Or a party, like us, happening on one while it's alone. They fight each other with those, as well as lesser predators. Like the mountain cats."

"Mountain cats ... lesser predators ... hm. Interesting concept." Mutsgae mused.

The group moved on, leaving the ybexi to relax and hurry back to its little herd. They traveled on for a week more, before suddenly getting a glimpse of lower land between two mountainsides. The valley was dotted with heavy rain-bearing clouds, the sun rays shining down in between them for a really spectacular look. It made the magical valley look incredibly magical.

Far off in the distance, on the horizon, a tall spire twisted up out of the ground, giving off its own eerie glow. The SwordDancers explained that the tower was the Wizard's, and it was a great deal farther off than it looked – another aspect of the mountain enchantment. To give the effect of being easily spotted from the Wizard's abode.

It took them two more days to reach the edge of the mountains, and three more to cross the narrow strip of foothills at the mountains' feet.

When they reached the wooded flatland, Roan abruptly stopped, and looked around.

"What?" Deilo asked, cautiously.

Roan looked over at him, again, then around. "You should be safe here. Here is where we leave you. Continue on in that direction," Roan pointed straight into the heart of Gnaria. "and you will come upon a town." He lifted a small purse, and handed it to Deilo. "This is for a night's boarding, a map, and maybe even a guide. You might get a discount on the map and guide, due to Horus. But that is not guaranteed."

"Me?" Horus asked. "Why?"

"Because both in and out of Gnaria, the Cartography Guild is primarily comprised of members of your Race. And as with all, they are partial to their own kind." Roan said. "Good luck." He turned, and headed back towards the mountains, Till on his heels.

"Wait!" Deilo called, turning after them.

Roan stopped, and looked back.

"Will we see you again?"

"If you are lucky? No." Roan said. "Keep your noses clean. You don't want to attract the attention of the Wizard." He turned, and continued on again, in silence. The youths stood there for a long time, watching until the SwordDancers were out of sight.

Chapter Three

Floating H

    Deilo heaved a sigh, and looked at the small leather purse in his hand. "Well."
    "All of a sudden, I'm scared silly." Horus said.
    "I know what you mean." Deilo said. "Let's get going."
He led them into the trees, until it became apparent that he had no sense of direction in the woods.
    Mutsgae took over the job, then, having a better sense for it. It also had the additional perk of he got to set the pace for his long-legged friends, instead of the other way around. No one complained, however, glad to take it easy for a time. They were all in much better shape than they had been, though, and the going was easier. All of them had put on some considerable muscle tone, and could walk for a long ways before needing to stop and rest. They stopped to rest often anyway, simply because they could.
    As a result, it took them two days to reach the appointed town, rather than just one. When they got there, they found an inn and slept in real beds for the first time since losing their last home. The hot meals that came with it were also savored. The day was spent wandering the town almost aimlessly, before Deilo stumbled across an object that jogged his memory: a map.
    "Where can I get a map?" he asked, of the person who owned it.

"You can have that one, for the right price." The vendor chuckled, leaning on one of his tables as he sewed a pair of strips of leather together.

"What price is that?" Deilo asked, eyeing the map uncertainly. "Why does it have big blank spots in it?"

"Those are places no one goes, no one maps. I wouldn't go there, if I were you."

"Do maps come in other languages?" Deilo asked. "I can't read the writing on that one."

"Not from here, are you?"

"No, we just got here." Deilo admitted. "I don't know the first thing about Gnaria."

"Ah. Well, in that case, you have to learn to read it. Nothing here is written in anything but Gnarian. And lad, ye be lucky I know the tongue you speak. You would do well to learn the tongue, as well."

"That's going to take a lot of time. Time I don't have." Deilo said.

"Why don't you have it?"

"I need more than just air to live." Deilo said. "As do my friends. We need to find homes. Jobs. Something. And we can't do that if we can't communicate."

"Ah. I see." He said. "Well, I reckon you're in a spot, then."

"Do you know anything that might help us out?"

"Ah, well, there's your first problem. Here in Gnaria, even knowledge has to be bought. If you want someone to give you a straight answer to anything you ask, you gotta pay them a pretty chink."

"A ... what?" Deilo asked.

The vendor dug a coin out of his purse, and showed it to Deilo. "This is a chink."

"Oh."

"But, since you seem to be a nice lad, and you're new here, I'll try to help ye out a tad. First, you need the language. Both reading and understanding. Right?"

"Right."

"Well, normally, there's only two ways of learnin'. The long, hard, honest way, by listenin' and learnin'. Or, the expensive, fast, easy way. Ye get a hypnotist t' 'implant' the language in yer mind. Like so. See?"

"*What?*" Deilo asked, bewildered.

"An', it's risky, an' don't always work right." The vendor said.

"Good gods. I don't even want to ask what exactly you are talking about." Deilo said. "Are you saying we haven't got a chance at all, to make it here?"

"Nah. There's another way, while ye learns the language some. You get indentured."

"I ... *what?*"

"Y'know. Ye work for someone for room and board."

"That's not indentured, where I come from. Indentured is the same as slavery."

"Not true. Ye jest have to pay yer debts off before ye can leave." The vendor said.

"That's hardly an improvement, and not an option."

"Picky little lad, ain'tchee?" he said, resuming his stitching.

Deilo sighed. "Do you know anyone who would let us work for room and board?"

"Depends on yer skills, lad. What can you do?"

"Almost anything." Deilo said. "I used to work at an inn. I was a cook's help, as well as occasional help in the yard, and in the tavern."

"That's not a real common thing around here. Inns are scarce." The vendor said, cutting his thread with his teeth. He tied a knot in it, and then started re-threading his needle. "Those that are about, don't have yards."

"What else is there to do, here?" Deilo asked.

"Most folks run their own business, and they're all small timers. They don't need or can't afford help." The vendor said. "To be honest, lad, there's not really much you can do. I suppose you might be able to get a job on some farm somewhere, and work in exchange for room and feed. But you can't do that here. The land's too dry for a farm to have space for extra mouths. You'd have to head north, or west to find good land that will have real successful farms."

"North and west?"

"Or." The vendor said. "The ones to the north border the marshes and swamps. The ones to the west are more grassland farms. They deal more with livestock than with crops."

"Oh. Thanks. And how far north?" Deilo asked, pointing to the map. "There's a big blank spot to the north."

"You don't want to go that far north, lad. That blank spot is blank for a reason. No one goes there. It's inhabited by feral beasts that eat anyone who goes in there."

"Who got the word out about it, then?" Deilo asked.

"There's a *shezuit* that travels through that land. It took a lot of lives to install that line – and a lot of majick." The vendor pointed at a dotted line that crossed one edge of the blank area.

"A *shezuit*?" Deilo asked. "What is that?"

"A method of travel. You ride the *shezuit*, and you blast through that area so fast you almost can't see what's happening outside. Likewise, you cannot be attacked, or killed, by the locals." The vendor said.

"Oh." Deilo said, even more mystified. "And to the west?"

"Just follow the mountains. It will be obvious when you reach the ranch country. There will be fences, animals bearing brands in great herds, and every great now and then people tending to them."

"Oh."

"What do your friends do?"

"Well, Horus is good with animals – he worked in the yard with the stock that came and went with the boarders. Muts was usually out there with him, lending a hand now and then. Mostly he made sure the boarders behaved themselves. Lillia did various things. Usually with the maids."

"Ah. Well, sounds like an interesting group. You might make it out on a farm, then. Good luck."

"Thanks. Where can I get a map?"

"You can buy that one, if you want. Or look at the other stalls. Different maps are done to different detail, and the detail generally varies in where the cartographer knows best. Each map is hand drawn, by different people." The vendor said. "It's generally a better idea to just get a guide, if you're simply going from one spot to another. Only folk who do a lot of wandering around invest in maps."

"Maps are expensive?" Deilo asked.

"It's a form of information, lad. Of course they are." The vendor said.

"Where do I get a guide, and how much are they?"

"Guides are usually found in the square, or at the cartographer's guild. Most of the time they're Centaurii, too. But not always. Your best bet is to stick with a Centaurii. They're more liable to actually know where they're going. That's not a guarantee, but it's the best bet. Price usually varies from guide to guide, and how far you're going."

"Say I'm going from here to the west, about here? Is this where the farms are?" Deilo pointed at a spot on the map farther up the range.

"That's the near edge, yes." The vendor said. "From here to there, it could cost you anywhere from, oh, say about 90 silver, to nearly 300. That's low end, high end. If they're cheaper than 90, don't take it. And the high end is robbery." He said, running his fingers down the strip of leather, thinking. "Though, you'd really only need a guide if you're really bad at getting lost. The mountains will guide you the whole way. Just go until you find what you're looking for. Be sure to pack a good deal of supplies, though. There aren't many towns right along the mountains."

"Ok, thanks. And from here to the northern farms?"

"Now be careful, lad. Northern farms, to a guide, means all the way up here." The vendor pointed at the northern end of the country. "Along the Viget river. You probably don't want to go that far, do you? You be sure to specify where you want to go. From here to the marshes could cost somewhere between 190 silver, to 700. For going that direction, you need a guide. It's too easy to get lost."

"Thanks." Deilo said. "I guess we're stuck with going west, then. We can't afford to go north. Roan didn't give us that much coin."

"Who's this, now?"

"Roan?" Deilo asked. "He's a SwordDancer that escorted us into this country."

"A SwordDancer escorted you here, and then gave you money?"

" ... yes?" Deilo asked.

"Are you somebody important, or something?"

"No. Just repeated refugees, is all." Deilo said. "We stumbled into Roan at an awkward place, and he helped us out."

"Awkward place? What exactly would that be?"

"I really don't know, but they sure didn't want us there. And we were kids at the time, so they took us elsewhere. And then rescued us from where they took us, some fifteen years later."

"Hoppin' oysters, lad. That's some tale. If you hadn't been as sincere as you were, I wouldn'ta believed a word of it!"

"Well, that's your choice." Deilo said. "Thanks for the advice."

"It's alright, lad. You be careful, out there."

Deilo nodded, and walked on, looking for the square that the vendor had mentioned. When he found it, he headed back to the inn to talk to the others. He had to wait some hours before they turned up – and Mutsgae smelled awful.

"What did you get into?!" Deilo demanded, covering his nose and mouth in disgust.

"A feast." Mutsgae said, stretching out in the dirt in front of the inn. He knew already that he wasn't going to be allowed in until he bathed.

"Ick!"

"Amen to that." Horus said, nostrils pinched shut as he approached. "Ok, who found what?"

"Muts found dinner, it seems, and I found out a few things that might come in handy." Deilo said. "Information, mostly. You?"

"Not a thing. No one would talk to me unless I paid them, and there's no way I'm gonna pay someone to yak at me. Most of it prolly would have been bad info, anyway. Not to mention I didn't have any money. You have it all, right?"

"Yeah, I do. And I heard about that bit about payment. Seems folk here don't give away anything – up to and including knowledge. I did, however, manage to find someone who'd talk to me anyway. He says we need to learn the language ... but we knew that. He knew ours, so it was ok for then. He also presented some ideas for what we could do, until we get our feet under us. He said there isn't much work in the towns – all there is, is already filled. It's not like where we came from, where everybody needed help. However, he said there are places outside the towns that might put us to work. But not here. This place is too dry. He suggested to go north, to the marshes, or west, to the ranches."

Mutsgae grunted. "What could we do on a marsh?"

"Not much, I think. Lillia wouldn't do well there, either." Deilo said.

"And to the west? You said it was ranches that way?" Horus asked.

"That's what he said, yes. Ranch country. It's also the only way we can afford to go. We don't have enough money to pay for a guide to the north, and we can't read the map or its warnings. He said maps are only a good investment if you are going to do a lot of traveling. Maps are expensive. However, to the west, guides should be cheaper, if we want one, and the mountains will lead us the whole way."

"That sounds ok." Horus said. "Mountains are hard to miss."

"Yeah. I know. Especially these mountains." Deilo said, looking up at the peaks south of the town.

"Where's Lillia?" Mutsgae asked.

"I'm here." Lillia said, from Horus' forelock.

"Ok."

"So, what do you all think?" Deilo asked.

"Looks like we're going west." Mutsgae said. "We all can work out there, I think ... except maybe Lillia. And she doesn't eat much. We can feed her."

"I agree." Horus said.

"Ok. We'll go west. Do we invest in a guide?"

The group considered that for a moment.

"I don't see why we need one." Horus said.

"Nor do I." Mutsgae said.

"Don't get over confident." Lillia warned. "I think we ought to. Better to be safe than sorry."

"I agree with Lillia." Deilo said. "We should at least look into it – if they are more than we can afford, we'll try it on our own, or tag along with someone else who's going that way."

Horus shrugged. "Ok."

"Alright." Mutsgae said.

"The vendor also said to stock up real well, before we go." Deilo said. "But he didn't say exactly what we needed."

"All the more reason for a guide." Lillia said. "A guide would know exactly what we would need."

"Ok, it's decided then. We'll get a guide. And we'll talk to the guide about what we need. Hopefully we can afford what we need." Deilo said. "Who wants to do what?"

"Well, Roan said we might get a discount on a map or guide, if I did it." Horus said.

"No, he said we might, since you're with us." Lillia said. "Very different."

Horus rolled his eyes. "Whatever."

"We all go, then." Deilo said. "Mutsgae, go bathe. Now."

Mutsgae rose, and left, off to find some water to rinse off in.

"All of us?" Lillia asked. "No offense intended, but we may have better luck securing a guide without Mutsgae along."

"True, but we also want to be up front. We don't want to buy a guide, just to have them freak out at Mutsgae." Deilo said.

"Well, alright."

"Maybe folks here aren't as afraid of Lizards." Horus said.

"I wouldn't bet on it." Mutsgae said, coming back. "Everyone who saw me either tried to poke me to death with pitchforks, or ran screaming at the sight of me."

"Ah, well ... maybe Lillia is right, then." Deilo conceded.

"I'll wait for you outside town, to the west. On the road?"

"Sure, why not." Horus said. "Go around town, not through."

"Sure thing." Mutsgae then left again.

"Maybe we can prepare our guide before he encounters Muts." Deilo said.

"Let's go – I think the less time we waste, the better off we'll be." Lillia said.

"Ok." The group then headed off across town, towards the square.

83

Standing hip-shot in front of the Cartographer's Guild, M'lar was rather bored – and rather glad of it. After his last hair-raising trip through the mountains to the south, he was happy to be back in Gnaria again. He didn't suppose he'd ever accept a contract to guide folks across them again. He'd much rather stay within Gnaria. It was calmer, if not safer. No hungry dragons, no raging armies to dodge, and no cliffs to nearly fall off.

It was nice, being bored. And to have time to just soak up the sun ... His green fur and yellow skin didn't let him burn in the sunlight, and he was glad of it. He was odd colored – even for a Centaurii, but he was rather proud of his stunning looks. It made him very distinctive, and helped with his business. It was a good thing he was good at what he did. If he weren't, his striking colors would hurt his business rather than help.

Someone or something blocked the sun on his chest, but he waited patiently for it to move on, not bothering to open his eye.

"Excuse me, sir. Where can we find a guide?"

M'lar cracked one eye, then opened both, looking at the young human lad standing before him. "A guide?" He then noticed the even younger Centaurii standing behind him, in the typical blue and red Centaurii colors. Even stranger than that was the little miniature human girl standing on the Centaurii youth's head. "To where?"

"West. To the ranch lands." Deilo said.

"How far west?"

"I don't know. How far west are they?"

M'lar considered the lad. He was definitely not Gnarian ... he spoke the foreign tongue too well to have learned it in Gnaria – and he also apparently didn't know the Gnarian tongue. Which meant he also wouldn't have a clue where he was going. "Pretty far." M'lar said. "Almost half way to the sea."

"Sea?" Deilo asked.

Yup. A foreigner. "Never mind. I can take you there." At least it was inside Gnaria – and even a simple trip. Easy money. If they weren't going to be too much trouble by being ignorant.

"How much?"

"How many?" M'lar countered.

"Four."

"I only see three. Where's the other?"

"Waiting for us outside town, to the west." Deilo said.

"Ok. Fair enough. To the western ranches? About 150 silver chinks should cover it."

"150?" Deilo asked, as if that were exorbitant. "It's not that far! Will you take us there for, say, 100?"

Restoration of Numar

"No." M'lar said. "150 is my price. Not a chink less. If you want cheaper, you get cheaper. I don't do cheap. You pay my fee, or you find someone else to take you." He gestured at the Guild doors. He really didn't want to go anyway.

Deilo considered that for a moment, then said; "Show me your map."

M'lar narrowed his eyes at the lad. Show him his map? What kind of stunt was that? Was he an agent, sent by one of his rivals? He looked Deilo over, up and down. He didn't look like an agent – he looked like a travel worn boy who'd seen way too many miles lately. Miles he wasn't accustomed to. "Why?" He asked.

"How else am I to know you aren't cheap?" Deilo countered. "I want to know if you really know the way, and how well you know the way."

Or, M'lar thought, he could be one of those weirdos that could see something once, and then recall it perfectly in every detail later on – he just wanted the map to go there on his own. Maybe? Maybe not. He didn't look like one of those. Why would one of those want to go to ranch lands? Those types usually stayed in cities, where they could make a living off it. The request made sense, in a weird sort of way. "Alright." He pulled open a pouch on his harness, and lifted out a small piece of parchment. He started unfolding it, and it became larger than it originally had looked. He flipped it over to show the lad, and ran a finger along the said route. "I know the way quite well." And then he flipped it back over and refolded it, before the lad could look at it long enough to memorize anything.

But Deilo had seen what he had wanted to see. There was detail there, though he couldn't read it. It also showed him how far the journey was ... sort of. If he knew how far it was to anywhere, it would have. But his sense of scale wasn't there yet. He didn't know how far that was.

"Ok. You know the route. Very good. Now explain to me why the price is so high." Deilo said.

"One, I'm a very good guide. Two, I know the way very well. And three, I always travel well supplied. I don't like being thin when I get somewhere." M'lar said.

"Well supplied?" Deilo asked.

"Yes. If you skimp on what you pay me, I have less to buy supplies with. Do you like to eat light?"

"You will supply the items? All of them?" Deilo asked.

"Yes. Though you may add to them as you like – but you will be carrying it, not I." M'lar said. What planet had they just dropped off of?

"Ok. If this is the case, then 150 is a good price." Deilo said. "How long will it take to get supplied?"
"Not long. What does your other friend eat?"
"Meat. Preferably rancid meat, but meat." Deilo said.
"Disgusting. But, not my problem. I will not carry rancid meat, however. One of you must do it."
"We won't, either. He will eat it fresh."
"Fresh? What do you think this is, a *shezuit*? We carry dried foods, and water." M'lar said. "Jerked meat, dried fruit, dry bread, and lots of water. What kind of waybread do you prefer?"
"Waybread?"
M'lar sighed. What had he just got himself into? "Never mind."
"Do we pay you now, or later?"
"Now would be nice. I can't buy supplies if I've no money to do it with." M'lar said.
Deilo looked at Horus, who nodded. Deilo then fished out the said amount of money. Counting it a second time, he then counted it aloud a third time into M'lar's hand.
M'lar appreciated the honesty and careful precision demonstrated there, and made note of it. "If you do not have other plans, at least one of you should come with me."
"Wouldn't have it any other way." Deilo said, before looking at Horus, who nodded. Horus followed M'lar, while Deilo headed back across the square.
"What is your name?" M'lar asked.
"Horus."
M'lar's snout wrinkled. That was an odd name, for a Centaurii. "You may call me M'lar."
"I'm Lillia." Lillia said. "I don't think I can eat food dried to your standards – I need something softer."
"I am well aware of that, little Lillia. I know where we can get some preserved foods that are not dried. You are small enough, and will need little enough, that it will not matter that much. Most travel food is dried in consideration of weight to be carried."
"We'll be carrying everything we need for between here and there?" Lillia asked.
"Yes. Would you rather run out between here and there?" M'lar asked.
"No."
"Roan didn't travel like that." Horus said, speculatively.
"Each to his own." M'lar said, before stopping at a market stall. "How big is your meat eating friend, and how much will he need to consume?"
"Pretty big, and a lot." Horus said. "He's a Lizard."

"A riding beast?" M'lar asked, picking over the wares.
"Not even." Horus said. "His kind are more prone to mercenary work. Though he isn't one."
"Ah." M'lar said, unable to think of a reptilian species that was sentient. This would be interesting.
Horus watched with interest as M'lar picked out the supplies to go with them. Lots of dried foods, a few packages of not-dried foods for Lillia, a packet of spices, and a medium sized cook pot. They then went back to the Guild building, where M'lar picked up several empty water skins.
He then took a look at Horus' harness, and shook his head. "Who made this thing?"
"I have no idea." Horus said. "Roan bought it for me before we crossed the mountains.
"It's horrible." M'lar said. "Take it off. We'll get you one made for Centaurii kind. This is for mules."
Horus shucked the harness, and M'lar traded it for a different harness, though it took a few additional coins to make the trade. M'lar than showed Horus how to work it – it was designed so that the wearer could take it on and off at will, by himself. It also was designed to fit the Centaurii's peculiar build.
"It's nice." Horus said, moving about in it.
"Of course it is." M'lar said. "If you treat it right, that harness will serve you for years to come." He then looked Horus up and down. "How much weight are you accustomed to carrying?"
Horus balked at answering that question. It meant he was going to be used as a mule again! So he significantly lowered the answer from the truth, when he answered.
M'lar looked at him speculatively. "You ought to be able to carry far more than that. It'll be good practice, for later on." He gave Horus far more weight than Horus liked, but Horus held his tongue – it was less than Roan had saddled him with.
"Do you think you can carry that?" M'lar asked.
"I think so."
"Good." M'lar then went to the town water fountain, and filled all the water bags there. He hung each on his own harness as he filled them, until the harness was covered in water bags.
Horus just watched, amazed. M'lar was incredibly stronger than he would have guessed. And to be willing to carry it! Horus was inspired, to become more like that.
"I don't think that pack will stay." Horus said, pointing to one that was hanging loose on M'lar's side.
"It won't." M'lar said. "Your friend will carry it. It is his pack."
"Oh."

Lillia just watched it all, knowing full well that Horus had lied – but she understood why and didn't blame him.
When they were finished, M'lar said; "Ok, take us to your friend. Will the other know to meet us there?"
"He's smart enough to figure it out." Horus said.
"Ok."
Horus started west, out of town, ooching his harness around under the weight until he got it to where it was comfortable. Not too terribly far outside town, Horus slowed down, looking around.
"Muts?" He called. "Muts!"
Farther up the road, Mutsgae emerged from the tall grasses in the ditch. "Over here."
M'lar stared openly at Mutsgae, from nose to tail. Definitely a predator. Definitely a lizard. Definitely sentient – it spoke! "What kind of creature is he?" M'lar asked. "I've never seen the like."
"Just your average Lizard." Horus said. "Some people mistake them for dumb beasts, and hunt them ... but they really are people."
Mutsgae sat silently for a moment, before speaking, watching the two Centaurii approach. "You're the guide?"
"Yes." M'lar said. "You can call me M'lar. You are ...? Muts?"
"That's what they call me. The full name is Mutsgae." Mutsgae replied. "Where is Deilo? Did you have to sell him to afford all that mess?"
M'lar laughed.
"No – I don't know where Deilo went. I think he's going to meet us here." Horus replied.
"Oh." Mutsgae turned around and nosed back into the grasses, before an approaching party reached them.
M'lar stood silent, off to one side of the road as he waited.

Deilo rejoined the group after a few hours, wearing a few new items – among them being a stout little bow, three quivers of arrows, and two blades – one a skinning knife, the other a short sword.
M'lar eyed the assortment. "Expecting trouble?"
Deilo stopped dead, and just looked at him oddly. "What?"
M'lar indicated the weaponry. "Expecting trouble?"
Deilo frowned, then looked down as his assemblage. "Oh. No. We need something to hunt with." He said.

"Hunt?" M'lar asked, as if he'd never heard of the idea before.

"Yeah. For meat? A body can get awful hungry with no meat to eat. Especially Muts ... who is...? Where?" he asked, looking around curiously

"Over here." Mutsgae said, from the ditch.

"Oh."

"Well, ok. Here's your pack." M'lar handed Deilo the pack off his side.

Deilo took it without a word, and shouldered it. They started off, down the road without any further ado. Mutsgae traveled off the road for a long ways, preferring the softer ground there. When they came across a thick forest, M'lar led them off the road and into it, as Deilo told Horus all about his adventures finding a bow he could draw ... and then haggling the vendor down to a price he could afford. Then he told them about hunting all over the town before he could find a knife dealer that he could talk to, much less haggle with.

Lillia found it hilarious, while Mutsgae ignored it, sniffing the ground that passed under his nose.

Near nightfall, Mutsgae abruptly stopped. "Deilo. There's a goat nearby."

Deilo dropped his pack quickly, freeing up his bow and knocking an arrow. M'lar winced at the treatment to the pack, and also at the delay. But he stopped anyway, to see how this would turn out.

Deilo stalked through the trees just like Roan had taught him, watching for a goat. When he saw something, it wasn't a goat. It was a gazelle. But it was still edible. So he took a slow, careful aim as the gazelle just looked back at him, completely unafraid.

People traversed this track all the time ... and nobody ever hunted.

Deilo let fly, and the arrow flew straight and true. The gazelle sensed its danger too late, springing away just before the arrow hit its mark. Thus the arrow sunk into its lungs rather than its heart. It ran, but not far. Horus took off running, as soon as Deilo had let fly, expecting it to run. Lillia hung on – also ready for the maneuver. She watched as Horus chased the beast down, and catch it as it slowed down. Horus made quick work of it, snapping its head back hard enough to snap the neck. He then carried the dead animal back to the others in his arms. Deilo extracted the arrow first, cleaned it, and put it back in the quiver. Then he and Horus made quick work of skinning and gutting it out, throwing the skin and offal to Mutsgae – who ate them happily. The rest was spitted, and set up to roast whole, right then.

M'lar was impressed – not only at the idea, but that it had worked, and at the efficiency of the group's motions. They obviously knew what they were doing. Meaning there would be plenty of food, and rationing wouldn't be so strict. M'lar was always happy to eat.

The roasting meant that the day's travel was over, though M'lar never complained – he had just learned something very interesting, and there was fresh, free meat to be had. And a lot of it. M'lar set up the cook pot on the edge of the fire, and with some water and dried vegetables he soon had a nice stew bubbling away, to go with the meat.

It smelled absolutely delicious, and when it was ready, all ate until they were stuffed tight. There was nothing left of the little gazelle or the stew by the time they finished, and all slept with a full belly – even Mutsgae. Between the cast offs and the last bit of the carcass on top of the meal, he was happily full.

The next morning M'lar gave everyone some of the way bread, except Mutsgae, who was not only not interested, but still too full to eat. Horus broke off a corner of his bread, powdered it in the palm of his hand, and offered it to Lillia. She picked out the pieces she wanted, and Horus licked up the rest of it before munching on the rest of his bread. After eating and cleaning up the campsite, they all moved on, following M'lar, who had by then decided that this odd little group should be no problem at all.

They traveled at an easy pace, every third day gorging on the fresh meat of some unlucky small creature. They traveled through forests, through sparse forest, then through brush country before reaching a rolling grassland that was divided by fences. The fences blocked their passage, and M'lar led them along the fences back towards the mountains, until they reached a road – presumably the same one that they had originally started the trip on.

He then led them for three days through a land where he didn't let them do any hunting – all the animals belonged to somebody. On the fourth day they reached a small town that catered to the people that lived and worked on the ranches.

"Well, here we are. Three days late, but well fed." M'lar said.

"Three days late?" Deilo asked.

"Yes. It usually doesn't take that long to travel that far. Between your friend's short legs and the stops for hunting, it took extra time. But that is ok ... that was a very nice trip. Maybe we can do business again sometime." M'lar said. "Will you be wanting the leftover supplies?"

"Yes, if we may have them." Deilo said. "I don't know how long we'll be here before getting a job."

"Job hunting, eh? Well, let me tell you something. Don't go to work for the K-barr ranch. They'll do you wrong every time." M'lar said.

"Thanks." Deilo said.

"No problem." M'lar traded the leftover supplies to Deilo for his water skins that Deilo had. He then nodded to them all and walked away, deeper into the town.

"Well ... now what?" Deilo asked, giving the bundle of food over to Horus when he offered to take it.

"At home, a lot of hiring happened in the lobby. We need to find a tavern or lobby to check out." Lillia said. "Some place that the locals go to."

They looked around, but the little town didn't look like much at all.

"Well, that there looks like the only inn in town." Horus said, pointing at a low ramshackle building with a false second story.

"It's a far cry from home, isn't it?" Deilo said, before leading the little group towards the door.

They were stopped at the door, however. "No animals allowed inside."

"Animals?" Deilo asked. "We have no animals."

The doorman pointed at Mutsgae, who blinked. "I'm not an animal." Mutsgae replied, making a point of showing teeth, indicating that he might have taken it as an insult.

The doorman blinked, then frowned. "Apologies." He stepped back and let them enter.

Deilo looked around the dark interior, squinting. After the brightness of outdoors, it was nearly impossible to see anything. This made them stop just inside the door, which also gave everyone inside a chance to get a good look at them.

When his eyes adjusted, Deilo led his friends deeper inside.

He approached a huge Goblin, who looked to own the place. No wonder it was so dark inside!

"What be ye needing?" The goblin asked, leaning on the small counter there.

Deilo looked around. There were only two people in the miniature lobby ... and one looked like he had crashed there simply because he was too drunk to get anywhere else. The other was a mean-eyed fellow apparently watching over the other. Deilo looked back at the goblin. "I was wondering if you knew of anyone who needed help. We're looking for work."

"I don't need any help." The goblin replied.

"Do you know of anyone who does?" Deilo asked, again.

"I don't need any help." The goblin said.

Out on the road again, the friends grouped. "That was productive." Horus said, sarcastically.

"Don't I know it. That creature's track was stuck. And that fellow sitting there was creeping me out." Deilo said.

"There's only one other place to try, without having to go store to store asking." Mutsgae said, indicating the local tavern with his snout.

"I don't think I want to go in there. Not after what we saw at the Inn." Deilo said.

"Well, we don't have much choice, do we?" Horus headed towards the tavern. Deilo sighed, and followed. After a moment, Mutsgae followed them. He stayed outside, this time, to avoid creating a stir, stretching out in the powdered dirt in front of the building.

Inside, Deilo and Horus were forced to stop and wait for their eyes to adjust again – this time to too much light. The place was incredibly bright, probably to cut through the smoke that saturated the air up high.

Horus sniffed once. "Incense?"

"Probably to cover up the smell of liquor breath." Deilo whispered, before moving on. He stopped at the counter, glanced at it, and decided against leaning on it. It looked clean enough – it even shined, it was so well polished. But the drooling drunk sleeping off his drink farther down the counter turned Deilo's stomach.

After a moment, one of three barkeeps managed to peel free of current activity, and came over to where Deilo was. "What can we get you, today?" She asked, her long flowing fur shining in the light, it was so silky.

"Er – I was wondering if you knew who might be needing help, around here. My friends and I are looking for work." Deilo said. "Ma'am."

At first she frowned, at the direction he was going, but the 'ma'am' put a smile back on her face. "Well, sir, there *are* a few landholders looking for competent hands out on their ranches, but what sort of work were you inquiring after?"

"Ranch work is fine." Deilo said. "What else do you know of, ma'am?"

"Ah, well ... I can't say as I know of anyone here in town in need of aid ... except old Girtu, maybe. He runs the stable down the road ... you can't miss it. Big doors are always open in the daytime." She replied.

"Ok, thanks. Can you give me some names of who is looking for help, out on the ranches?" Deilo asked.

"Ah." She pulled a pad of tissue-thin paper out of a pocket on her apron, and scribbled on it. Tearing the sheet off, she handed it to him. "Won't do you much good, though. Folks are hard to find, around these parts, especially if'n yer an outsider. You want to know the best way to get their attention?"

"What's that?" Deilo asked.

"You put your name up on that there board over there, and where you can be found ... as well as how long you'll be in town before moving on if no one comes for you." She pointed to a board by the door that was covered in tag end of pieces of parchment, most of it illegible.

Deilo looked at it a moment. "Ok. Well, Ma'am, I have a little problem ... I don't speak the local language, and I don't write it, either."

She smiled. "I can write it for you, if you want."

"I'd be much obliged if you would ... also, could you put down that we'll be needing language lessons too?" Deilo asked, as she produced a fresh piece of parchment from under the bar. She smoothed it out on the counter, produced a charcoal writing stick, and proceeded to write across it in a large, flowing script. Deilo watched, but couldn't make heads or tails of what exactly she'd just written.

"Do you have any special skills?" She asked, as she wrote.

"Well ... I'm good at whatever I turn my hand to ... though I will need a learning curve. But my friends already have experience handling animals and their care." Deilo gestured at Horus.

She looked up at Horus, then nodded. "How many of you are there?"

"Three, looking for work." Deilo said.

"Does that mean there are others?"

"Just one other ... but she's not liable to be able to get work on a ranch."

"What are her skills?"

"Varied, but there's only so much someone four inches tall can do."

"I heard that!" Lillia said, from Horus' forelock.

Noticing Lillia for the first time, the barkeep's eyes went wide. "She's so small!"

"Not as small as you think." Lillia grumped.

Horus clapped a hand over her, to shut her up.

Deilo only shrugged. "We'll be taking care of her ourselves."

"Ok." She wrote quickly, adding to what she had. "And where will you be?"

"Um ... I don't know. Around. I don't think we have any money to be spending at the inn." Deilo said.

"Ok." She finished the page off, and gave it to him. Deilo looked at it, impressed. It looked very professional, and he wished he could read that writing. "Just tack it up there. Don't worry if it covers something else up."

"Thank you, ma'am." Deilo did as she instructed, and then looked around the tavern. There were a few people here and there, most of them taking lunch and minding their own business. There were men, Dtri, tall furred folk, and one fellow who looked sort of like a Centaurii, except his other half wasn't equine ... it was bovine. He looked very bulky and un-wieldy, not prone to much movement of any speed. There were a few Races there that Deilo had never seen before, and had no idea what they were like. After a moment, he nodded to Horus and headed out.

"Well?" Mutsgae asked, as Horus followed Deilo out, releasing Lillia.

"You -!" Lillia puffed, irritated. But she said nothing else, straightening her dress and sitting down again, cheeks all red.

"Maybe. The waitress -?- in there drew us up a flier, saying we are looking for work." Deilo said, unsure if she was actually a waitress as he sat down on a hitching rail. Farther down, two heavy reptilian draft animals were snuffling at the dirt, tied to the same beam. Deilo watched them, and decided that the beam wouldn't even slow those two down, if they decided to bolt. It was a good thing they appeared to be docile and good-natured. One of them had a large, smooth crest fanning up to cover its neck, while the other only sported a blunted horn growing out of its snout. Both sported clubbed tails that were currently were resting on the ground. Their wide, flat feet suggested that they didn't move very fast, and their wide, flat mouths said they were plant-eating monsters, rather than carnivorous ones.

"Maybe we'll get lucky, then." Mutsgae said.

"Yeah, but we really need to learn the language." Deilo said. "In a real hurry."

"We seem to haven't had any problems communicating thus far." Horus said.

"Well, I've had some. And in case you haven't noticed, we never left the shadow of the mountains, either. Apparently just enough people cross back and forth for folks to learn the languages on either side. And we've gotten lucky. I really would like to not depend so much on luck. If we're going to live here, we need the language." Deilo said, watching as one of the draft animals yawned immensely.

"Let's go see what the town looks like, while we wait, ok?" Lillia asked. "If this is the best we're going to get as far as town goes, let's learn what all is here."

Horus bobbed his head, making her squeal, and then loped off down the street. "I feel like nothing more than a riding beast."

"At least I don't weigh much, hm?" Lillia countered.

"At least. Though I think you are beginning to put on some weight ..." He jibbed.

Lillia swatted at him, but he barely noticed ... it was little more than if a fly had tried to swat him. Horus laughed, and bobbed his head again.

They toured the main drag seven times, making each lap in about two minutes, until Horus tired of trotting up and down the small street, and simply plopped in the dirt near where the other two were sitting ... Deilo was actually sitting on Mutsgae, who didn't seem to notice at all. Deilo looked up at Horus, and then went back to picking idly at a bump on Mutsgae's back.

"You know, you'd make a right fancy pair of boots ..."

Mutsgae rumbled heavily in reply, making Deilo laugh.

Three idle, boring days later, the small group was approached by a tall furred person, who simply watched while the group settled down from chasing each other around and around in a spot of grass. Deilo noticed him first, and slowed abruptly. Horus had to swerve sharply to avoid running him over – landing a foot square on Mutsgae's head as Mutsgae shot past.

"OW!" Mutsgae stopped, and when released, rubbed his head with both front paws.

"Be ye the ones who posted the paper at the tavern?" The furred creature asked, once they had all slowed down some.

"We had a paper posted there, yes." Deilo said.

"What skills have ye?"

"We all worked at an inn, a while back. I worked the kitchens, Horus and Muts worked the livestock, and Lillia did everything she was big enough to do." Deilo gestured to each member in turn.

"Is that all?"

"It was the only job we have ever held." Deilo said. "But we can learn new skills easily."

The fellow eyed Mutsgae for a moment. "Is your herding creature well trained?"

"I am not a herding creature." Mutsgae replied. "Nor am I trained."

"What are ye, then?"

"I am Lizard." Mutsgae replied. "My mother was a fierce mercenary warrior."
"And what are ye?"
"I worked at an inn, after I grew up."
"Not a warrior, then?"
"I never had the training, no." Mutsgae replied.
"You look like a wild animal."
"Alas, this is so. Many treat me as such."
The fellow looked then all over, then turned to Horus. "You have skills with animals and can move quickly?"
"Yes, sir." Horus said.
"And you can cook?" He asked, of Deilo.
"Yes, sir. As well as other things. I do some repair work on iron and steel, and I can also mend clothing articles."
"You do a woman's work?"
"No, sir. I do anything I set my hands to. At the inn, those were things that simply needed done." Deilo said.
The fellow grunted. "What sort of work are you looking for?"
"Any." Deilo replied. "We merely want to live."
"You certainly seem to have plenty of energy." He gestured at the grassy patch they had been running around on.
"Yes, sir."
"We may have a use for you, then." He said. "Do any of you have any skills with majick rods?"
"No, sir." Deilo replied. "Why?"
"The ranch is sometimes raided, and you may need to defend yourselves and it."
"I have had some instruction with a short blade, sir." Deilo said.
"I need no weapon." Mutsgae said.
"I imagine you don't." The fellow said, to Mutsgae, before turning to the others. "You are willing to learn?"
"Yes, sir."
"Then come with me." He turned, and walked back towards the main road of the little town. The four followed, Lillia getting scooped up by Horus and being deposited on his shoulder. "You will be given room and board, until you become skilled enough to earn payment. Will that suffice?"
"Yes, sir."
"We will be headed back out to the ranch at the end of the day. Be in or near the wagon when we leave, or you will be left behind." He showed them a large, already half-loaded six-wheeled wagon that had a six-hitch team dozing before it. The draft animals were all large, tall, and sported horns on their furry heads. They were muscular creatures that looked like they could

move a sizable load at a good pace. They were built for speed as well as power, and their long, silky fur coats shimmered in the light breeze, all the way down to their feet, where the hair became both shorter and matted by road mud. Their noses were large, soft, and quite expressive along with their big, round black eyes.

Each of the animals were a different color, making for quite the striking team. One was strawberry red, one was black, one was a soft brown, one was white, one was a shimmering blue, and the last one was a soft mouse grey.

"What a set of creatures!" Horus said, walking around them. "What are they?"

"Those are ridali. Fast, strong, and hardy. They are primarily what we raise and sell. They are even good eating." The fellow said. "We also raise some cattle, but mostly these."

"I don't believe I have ever seen one, before." Horus said. "And I've seen a lot of different animals."

The fellow nodded, obviously proud of the magnificent animals.

"What is your name?" Deilo asked.

"You may call me Mar-kai." He replied. "I am the foreman at the Floating H ranch." He gestured at the wagon. "Do not be late." And then he walked away, across the street and into a store.

"Well!" Lillia said. "A foreman! What exactly is that, anyway?"

"I have no idea. But I think it means he's someone important ... probably the boss." Deilo said.

"Probably." Horus said, reaching out to touch one of the six ridali. The reaction was instant – and would have been fatal had he not been used to dodging sudden movements on the parts of animals. The ridali swung its head around on its long neck, and nearly gored him with one of the four wide-arcing horns. "Whoa!" he said, as he jumped back. He caught Lillia as she tumbled off his shoulder, and hung onto her.

"You idiot!" she exclaimed. "What did you do that for?!"

"I didn't know it would do that. They're in harness ... they ought to be used to being touched!" Horus defended.

"Obviously not by you, at any rate." Deilo said, glad he wasn't the one who had done that ... he would have been skewered, if he had.

Horus glared at him, and then backed away from the animals warily. They moved a lot faster than he had thought they would.

Mutsgae grunted, and hunkered by a back wheel of the wagon, waiting.

"What do we do while we wait?" Deilo asked.

"Well, we should go terminate our place of lodgings, gather up our few things, and then wait right here. We don't need to be late."

"Alright." Deilo headed that way, and Horus followed. Mutsgae watched them go, but stayed put.

A few hours passed, and the others came back, with a few satchels on their shoulders.

"Where did you get all that?" Mutsgae asked. "We didn't have that much stuff."

"No, we didn't." Deilo agreed. "We decided to spend what we had left on some things before we leave town."

"Like what?" Mutsgae asked.

"More arrows." Deilo said. "Some changes of clothing that will hold up to some abuse. Some soap. We managed to find some materials to make shoes for Horus. We bought some things for Lillia – they're not liable to have anything in her size at all. So we got her a bed, dishes, clothing, bedding, that sort of stuff."

"It was all dolly stuff. Nobody here had anything at all for a real person. But I suppose it will have to do." Lillia said.

"And who is going to carry all that, an unknown distance?" Mutsgae asked.

"I was hoping we would be able to stash it on the wagon." Deilo admitted.

"Good luck."

"What? You think they won't let us put it on there?"

"I doubt it. We're in for another long walk, carrying everything." Mutsgae said. "You wait and see."

Deilo grunted. "Pessimist." He set his burden down near the wagon, and looked around. "How long do we have?"

"A little while yet." Mutsgae said.

A few moments later, though, the foreman came striding up on his long legs, and bounded up into the wagon, taking up the reins that were lying there. "You all might want to move." He warned, disengaging the brake on the wagon.

The little group snatched up their belongings, and moved away from the wagon, watching.

The foreman nodded, and clicked to the ridali. The great animals grunted, and moved to one side, stepping in unison. Soon, the wagon was turned around, and they leaned into their harnesses to get it moving forward. Deilo glanced at the others, and then followed the slow moving wagon.

The wagon rolled clear to the end of town, and around behind a building, before being stopped there. There was a team of people there, waiting next to a large heap of bags. Once the wagon stopped, half of them hopped up onto the wagon, and started catching the heavy bags that were thrown up to them from the people below.

In a very short time, the wagon was heaped up with the bags, and the team of people left, back into the building. The foreman walked around the wagon, inspecting the load, and making sure nothing would slide off. Then he stopped, and looked at the little group watching.

"Well, are you ready to head out?" he asked.

"Yes, sir." Deilo replied. "May we put our things on the wagon?" he ventured.

Mar-kai nodded, once. "Go ahead and climb on, yourselves, if you feel so inclined. But do it now ... the wagon will not be stopping between here and our destination."

Deilo didn't waste any time, tossing the bundles onto the wagon, and making sure they were secure, as Mutsgae clambered up on top of the great heap. "Will they be able to do ok, with the extra weight?" he asked, from his vantage point.

"Sure. They've moved far heavier loads the same distance. They are quite capable." Mar-kai said, bounding up to his seat on the front of the wagon.

Deilo clambered up the heap, too, and then took Lillia from Horus. "Careful, now. Don't get squished." He told her, setting her down on the heap.

"I have no intention of doing so." She replied, walking across a sack and sitting down there. "Sure is high, up here."

Horus looked up at them, then around.

Mar-kai clicked to the ridali, and the team moved out again, leaning into their harnesses again. The wagon started forward, slower than it had been before. The wagon was turned, and then started out of the last part of town. Once they were out again, Mar-kai called to the animals, and they lunged into their harnesses, making the wagon roll faster. Startled, Horus moved into a trot to keep up with the wagon that was suddenly steadily gaining speed. Very soon, he found he was having to gallop hard to keep up with the wagon. The wagon was heavily loaded enough to keep from jouncing around too much on the worn track that passed for a road, and made for an interesting ride across the landscape.

The road wound through the grassy plains, through another small patch of woods, across two rivers ... or maybe the same one twice, they couldn't tell ... and around a large butte of rock that jutted jaggedly out of the landscape. It looked like a side of the nearby mountains had fallen off and come to rest in the plains. The ridali pounded along before the wagon, as if they were pulling next to nothing, shimmering in the evening light. Deilo spent a great deal of time watching them, as well as the land, fascinated that such a large creature could move so gracefully, and fast, despite the heavy wagon.

They sped around the base of the butte, up over a low rise, and then plunged down the abrupt hillside that was there. The butte and the rise had hidden a large valley that was significantly greener than the rest of the plains, and was dotted all over with more ridali, some of the animals shimmering in fantastic colors. There were tall fences everywhere, dividing the land up into pastures that were miles across. Down in the bottom of the bowl was a cluster of buildings, enough to make up a small village.

Mar-kai turned the wagon off the main road, as it were, and onto a better-maintained road that led down into the heart of the bowl. As if spurred on by unseen forces, the ridali jumped forward, hitting their harnesses again.

Horus began to be left behind by the speeding wagon, and he wondered how fast the ridali would go if they weren't hitched to a wagon. In a last desperate attempt to keep up, he lunged for the wagon, and held on with both hands. Then he began an odd bounding stride ... he simply tried to keep his feet under him, as he was towed along behind the wagon. Deilo saw him, and laughed. "Having fun?"

Horus frowned at him, too out of breath to reply.

"You can never slow them, when they are on the home stretch ... they love coming home." Mar-kai said, glancing back at his passengers.

"How can they go so fast, with this wagon?"

"They are far stronger than they appear. Legend has it that the ridali are three parts animal, one part magic."

"Magic?" Deilo asked. "What's that?"

"Some ancient form of majick, is my nearest guess." Mar-kai shrugged. "Though I have seen nothing of magic or majick in these animals ... they are simple remarkable animals. At one time, they were used as war steeds ... can you imagine a cavalry unit made up of these?" he gestured at the pastures, where the ridali there were speeding towards the road, to run alongside the returning members. Deilo looked out at the animals, and was quite impressed, and knew that would be a formidable cavalry indeed ... if the riders could stay on.

"How would one ride such a creature?" Deilo asked.

"Very carefully." Mar-kai said. "I believe that is why they are not still used today ... they may be fast, they may be strong, but they're bloody hard to ride and stay on. That coat of theirs is very slick ... only a special saddle will stay on top, and even then ... it's not easy."

"Interesting." Mutsgae said, head resting on his hands as he watched the animals run alongside the rocking wagon.

"I'm flying!" Horus managed to shout, at one point, making a jump into the air.

Mar-kai laughed out loud. "Indeed!"

Horus was very glad when the wagon began to slow, and when it slowed enough, he let go entirely, and trotted to a stop long before the wagon reached its destination. Horus heaved a sigh in the middle of breathing hard, and just stood there for a time. After a moment had passed, he trotted out again at an easy speed, and followed the still traveling wagon. Those creatures were incredible, he knew. When he arrived by the wagon, it was already nearly half unloaded already. There were lots of people of several different Races swarming over the wagon. The animals had been unhitched from the wagon and were in the process of having their harnesses removed while others were throwing the payload down to those on the ground. Once one had a bundle of goods, they turned and handed it to the next person, who handed it on. The bundles moved quickly across a small opening and into the large open door of what looked like a large barn that could be completely closed up. Once the wagon was emptied and the harnesses were carried off, the six ridali were led to a different barn that was obviously used strictly for the ridali. Tied to a metal rail that ran the length of the long side of the barn, the animals stood on the sloped ground while they were washed. After they were washed and cooled, they were fed what looked like a soft mash before being turned out into various paddocks. Deilo watched all this from a slight distance, amazed at it all. He had never seen the like before, having spent all his life inside a town before the journey to Gnaria. Even the husbandry that had happened at the inn had been nothing like what went on at this place.

Once all was taken care of and most of the people moved on to tend to other tasks, Mar-kai turned up at Deilo's side as he leaned on a fence post watching the animals. Mar-kai watched him in silence for a long moment, and then nodded, leaning on another post. "What do you think?"

"They're incredible. And not just the animals, either ... everyone here. It's amazing. I never knew the like existed. And it all flows! Like, everyone knows exactly what they are doing, how to do it, and when to do it. It really blows the mind." Deilo said. "This place is incredible."

Mar-kai laughed. "Delov will be pleased to hear you like his place."

"Delov?"

"Yes. This is his place, and he wants to see you. He has already seen the others."

"And?"

"You will see." Mar-kai said.

"Where do I find him?" Deilo asked.

"Follow me." Mar-kai straightened, and walked back into the cluster of buildings. In some places the breezes were blocked and it was very hot in the lee of the buildings, and in other places the breezes were funneled into brisk winds, and it was considerably cooler. Each hot or cool place was used to it's full potential, for what ever could take advantage of the varying conditions. Thus far, the breezes that blew through the bowl prairie seemed to be a steady, constant thing. In the heart of the cluster was an open area that appeared to be used as a training area for the animals. There wasn't anything going on there at the moment, but there were complicated circles, paths, and patterns pounded into the dirt where they regularly walked – or ran. Mar-kai continued on across the area, and between two more barns on the other side. These two had many windows, some large, and some not, as well as some expanses of wall that had no windows at all. Deilo soaked it all in as he walked on, trying to not miss a thing. On the far side of the cluster of buildings, Mar-kai stopped before a sprawling structure that appeared to be a house of some sort ... only the windows were primarily high and small. And the doors were huge, and always hung in pairs.

Mar-kai looked at him, and gestured at the doors. "Go in. Tolus will take you to Delov."

"Um... okay." Deilo walked up to the doors, and looked at where the latch was situated ... at eye level. He considered what that might mean, and then reached for it. Before his hand reached the latch, it fired and the door swung inwards. Deilo stood there with one hand in the air as he stared up at who he guessed was Tolus ... Tolus was a huge troll of a suited creature, who would obviously need the doors that big. " ... hi." Deilo managed, lowering his hand.

Tolus nodded, and gestured that he come in. Deilo hesitated a moment, then walked in, onto a tiled marble floor that appeared to be a mosaic. In the moment he had to look at it, Deilo failed to see what the picture was of. Tolus ushered him through the house, through a room, down a hall, and into another room. Everywhere they went, there was a light breeze that kept the place cool, and colorful tapestries hung the walls, usually depicting the ridali more often than not.

At a door in the room, Tolus paused, and opened it, indicating that Deilo go in. Deilo glanced in, then walked past the troll into the room. Tolus gently closed the door behind him, remaining outside.

Deilo paused there, as the room was rather dark compared to the rest of the house, and he couldn't see a thing.

"Good afternoon." Said a low voice from the darkness. "How are you?"

Deilo got chills as he listened to the sound, not knowing why. The tone was friendly, and he sensed no malice, but the sound made him wary. "I am alright. A bit blind at the moment ... it's dark in here." He added, not wanting to make it seem he was actually *blind*-blind.

The voice laughed, and as Deilo's vision adjusted, he could see a more or less humanoid form walk towards him. "To most, it is." He said. "I cannot tolerate the level of brightness most enjoy."

"...might I ask why?" Deilo asked.

"Maybe another day. Today, you are here for me to decide whether or not you are fit to work on my land." He said. "I am Delov, owner and operator. And you are?"

"Deilo."

"Deilo? That is it? No other name? Where are you from?"

"Deilo is the only name I know I have. I started out in Yelm, before it was razed. Then I was taken to Paratora with my friends, where we grew up, working at an Inn."

The man seemed to nod. "And why did you leave there?"

"The inn was destroyed in a war." Deilo said.

Delov turned and walked to a chair, where he sat down. "I do not think any such cities exist in Gnaria."

"They are both outside the mountains." Deilo said. "We only just arrived in Gnaria."

"Oh? And how did you get here?"

"Over the mountains."

"All by yourselves?"

"No. We were guided through."

"By whom?"

"A pair of SwordDancers."

"SwordDancers? They are not your typical guides. They are mercenaries, not guides. You must have paid a pretty penny for that."

"We didn't ... they thought they owed it to us."

"Why?"

"They were the ones that put us in that city to start with."

"SwordDancers are odd creatures at times, I think. So ... you started out in the lands beyond Gnaria, and were escorted here by SwordDancers whom you never paid?"

"Yes, sir."

"Odd, to say the least. So the two places you have lived have been demolished. It seems to me that bad luck follows you wherever you go." He remarked.

"I wouldn't say that, sir. That is simply the normal way of things, in those lands. I have never heard of a time that was not war torn, short of the era of Wizards, and that was a very long time ago." Deilo said.

"True." Delov said, with a nod. "And why, do you think, should I hire you?"

"I don't know, sir. But we need jobs, to earn a living, to survive. We are all hard workers, even Lillia. We all learn quickly, too ... we can do a lot."

Delov laughed. " 'I don't know' won't get you hired any place you ply that in your interview, son."

Deilo sighed. "I've never done this before, sir. Before, it was the SwordDancer that got us our jobs."

"Indeed?"

"Yes, sir."

"Interesting. And what do you think of this place?"

"Fascinating, sir. Beautiful. Incredible. Everything is ... it's ... I've never seen anything like it, sir." Deilo finished.

Delov sat in silence, as if thinking for a time. "Tell me ... what can you do?"

"At the inn I worked the kitchens, worked the tavern, and at times, helped Horus and Muts in the yards. I can learn other things, too. What do you need done?"

Delov nodded. "You can cook?"

"Yes, sir."

"Good. Not very many here, can, and we do have a lot of people to feed several times a day."

Deilo nodded, not arguing. He had been hoping to be outside where he could see and maybe work with the incredible animals, but he'd take any job he could get.

"You do not enjoy cooking?" Delov asked.

"Ah ... I have not really found anything that I particularly enjoy or dislike, sir." Deilo said.

"Hm. Be that as it may. Do you wish to work here, now that you have seen it?"

"Yes." Deilo said, after a moment.

"But?"

"I ... I don't want to stay, if my friends leave." Deilo admitted.

"I see." After a moment, Delov waved a hand. "That is all, for now. You may go."

"Sir." Deilo turned, and reached for the door. Once again, it opened before he touched it, and Tolus was there. Deilo looked up at the massive troll again, then walked out past him. Tolus re-closed the door, and led Deilo back out of the house, to where Mar-kai was standing. With him were the others from Deilo's group, waiting.

"Well?" Horus asked.

"I don't know." Deilo said.

Mar-kai nodded. "I'll show you all to your rooms for the night."

"Night?" Deilo asked. "Is it already that late?"

"Night comes quickly here. And you do not want to be out when night falls. Always be indoors *before* nightfall, and never go out in the darkness. Ever." Mar-kai said, before turning and walking away. The others looked at each other, before following the tall foreman across the way.

Maybe being here wasn't such a good idea after all.

"May we ask why?" Lillia asked, from atop Horus' head.

Mar-kai glanced at her. "Dangerous things lurk in the darkness, here."

"Like what, things?" Lillia asked.

Mar-kai shook his head, without replying.

"This all seems a bit odd." Lillia remarked. "Do you not know what?"

"Look, miss ... those who go out at night, or do not make it in before night ... they're usually found the next morning dead, and usually in pieces. Is that incentive enough to stay indoors?" Mar-kai asked.

"I would suppose so." Lillia said. "But do you know why?"

Mar-kai just looked at her for a moment, before silently opening a door to one of the large barn-like buildings. He gestured for them to go in, and after they passed, he followed them in. "These are the hand quarters. You will stay here, and if you are hired, live here. The others can show you around." Mar-kai nodded, and then promptly left again, sprinting for another building as the sun flared at the edge of the bowl.

A Dtri promptly barred the door with a heavy beam, and nodded to them. "Afternoon."

Deilo looked around, then, a tad bit alarmed. "What, exactly, happens after dark?"

"Well ... most of the time, nothing. Most of the time. But then, most of the time, no one goes outside after dark, either. When someone does ... they're found the next morning, cold and stiff." The Dtri said.

"Cold and stiff?" Horus asked.

"Yeah. As in, dead?" the Dtri said. "There's something out there, we don't even know what it is, that roams this place at night, and it rips the hearts out of whoever is out and about. It eats the hearts, we think – it's never there – and then sucks the body dry of blood ... no matter the color or flavor thereof." It gestured at the room in general. "This is the common room ... we gather here for meals, and during leisure time. That over there is the kitchen." The Dtri pointed at a room through a doorway in the corner where there was a fire stove surrounded by counters and cabinets. Off to one side was a small sink. "After dinner, I'll show you to your spaces."

The Dtri then ushered them to a long, lower than usual table, and sat them down – all but Horus, who was left to stand, or kneel, as he saw fit. There was no chair or bench that could hold him. He eventually settled for kneeling down at the table, resting his hindquarters on the floor.

"The ridali aren't bothered by this thing?" Deilo asked, as dinnerware was set on the table.

"Not in the slightest. They're never attacked, or even disturbed." A thick-set froggy looking fellow said.

"Never?"

"Never."

"How weird." Deilo said. "Do you think that maybe whatever it is, can't take down something as big as the ridali?" he asked, as he was given an oval plate. He looked at it, as the furry thing that had given it to him passed out similar plates to the others. The plate was a shiny blue in color, and was almost translucent. The thing looked incredibly fragile ... and expensive.

"No. Some of the creatures that have worked here have been either as big, or bigger than, the ridali. And they are attacked just like the rest of us." The furry thing said, it's voice sounding like it was run through a grain-grinder and mixed with shards of glass.

"That doesn't make any sense." Horus said, also inspecting his plate with interest.

Lillia was walking across hers in elongated strides, measuring it. "This is big enough to feed me a thousand times over!" she stated.

"Size doesn't seem to matter. The bigger people don't even have a fighting chance, it seems. They die just as fast, with the same sort of yell ... if they yell at all. The ridali ... no one really knows what goes on there. There has to be something about the ridali that keeps them from harm. Most of them stay out all the time, much less at night." The Dtri said, resting feathered elbows on the table's edge as it inspected the backs of its scaly hands. The left hand, Deilo noted, was missing two fingers.

"Do you think that it is the ridali that do that?" Horus asked, alarmed.

"A fellow once swore up and down that it was ... but that's been disproved time and again. The ridali have nothing to

Restoration of Numar

do that kind of damage, in that fashion, and show no inclination to eat anything other than the grasses. There are cases even where people sleep in the same room as the more prized ridali." The frog-looking fellow said.

"Oh." Lillia said, sitting down on the edge of her plate, dangling her shins toward the table.

Mutsgae heaved himself upwards enough to prop his chin on the edge of the table, and eyed where 'his' green-tinted plate had been set. It was still empty, and even if it had been full, it was situated where he couldn't get to it without wrecking something. Heaving a sigh, he slid backwards, and rested on the floor. "What then? No one has set up majick devices to try to catch it? Or even see it?"

"Nope. The boss says he'll get something like that just as soon as he can afford to ... those things are mighty expensive, around these parts, and they eat up tons of majick, too ... to *maybe* see something. Some speculate that we might actually have an *Elf* on the loose, here." The Dtri said, putting his hands down.

"An *Elf*?" Lillia asked, her voice high and squeaky. On top of the normally high and squeaky sound she had, it made her nearly inaudibly incoherent to the others.

"What's an Elf?" Horus asked, curiously.

"Don't let Huteri here scare you like that. The Elves left this world a very long time ago, and probably will never return. In fact, the *only* proof there is that they ever actually existed are the Helves, and no one can really prove that that's what they are. Really." The big furry thing said, sitting down at the other end of the table, making the small chair it sat on groan. "As for what is an Elf? The legends have it that they were beings of darkness, down right evil things. They were mostly indistinct, and when they were seen, they were described as a wispy cloud of darkness, with small horns and sharp claws being the only distinct things on 'em. The eyes always glowed, and every tale reports a different color for the eyes." It said, shaking its head. "It is said that things got a lot better in this world, when the Elves left, taking their chaos with them. But they left behind their half-breed progeny, the Helves. Every Helf you'll ever meet is a nasty bugger. Most folks, if they don't get killed in the process, will either kill a Helf on sight, or will trap it, and keep it caged, as a more or less guard dog. They go completely bonkers every time they see anybody, or any living thing for that matter. Bloodthirsty creatures. Anyway ... Elves could not be killed, it was said, and their Helf offspring are bloody hard to kill. And they seem to live forever, the Helves do. No one has seen one die of old age ... only of mortal wounding, and that's rather hard to do."

Horus shivered. "I'm glad they're not real, then ... or at least not here anymore."

A tall, multi-legged creature sauntered into the room through a doorway, wielding a pot that it would have taken two or three or more others to move. It slung it around as if it didn't weigh anything, the contents splashing about inside it. "Hallo, everybody! Dinner will be shortly." It announced, setting the gigantic pot down with a bang on the stove, and starting the fire roaring underneath. It then turned about on itself, stepping back over its own back end, slowly straightening back out as it moved over to the table, where it promptly collapsed, all twenty or so legs folding up at once. It rested four elbows on the table, and propped its triangular head on top of four balled up fists. "Whew! Boy, am I tired!" It looked the four newcomers over. "And who might this be? I didn't know we were having guests ... I'd have fixed more."

"Wh ... what are you?" Deilo asked, unable to keep from staring.

"Me? Ah, I'm the cook, currently, as I'm the best there is at the moment. And I spend most of my time doing just that. Cooking. Or preparing to, at any rate. I just got through finishing off the meals in the house." It said, waving an arm that it wasn't currently resting on, for emphasis.

"But what *are* you?" Deilo asked. "I've never seen anybody like you before."

"Ah ... you probably won't, ever again, either." It said. "I'm something of a mix of a few races, and as a result ... I don't have a word to call what I am. Beyond ... ah ... what did they call me in town??"

"'Mutt'." The furry thing ground out.

"Ah, yes. I'm a mutt." It said. "You can call me Ton."

"Ton?" Horus asked. "Is that really your name?"

"No, but then, no one on this ranch can *make* the sounds that comprise my name." Ton said, shrugging in a ripple effect all the way down.

Deilo cleared his throat, after watching that. "Uh ... why are you called Ton, then?"

"'Cause he's got a ton o' legs." The froggy-looking fellow said, hiccupping.

Horus wrinkled up his long face. "Okay."

"Doesn't matter to me what I get called, so long as it's consistent." Ton said.

"I smell something!" Another tall, furred creature entered the room, ducking the top of the doorway as it entered. This one sported four arms, and low-curling horns on its head. It stomped over to the table, and more or less collapsed at the table, apparently barely landing on the floor next to it, rather than on the table itself.

"It's not done cooking yet." Ton said, making a rather strange face at the new arrival. Ton then looked at the others again. "And who might you all be?"

"I'm Deilo, this is Horus, Lillia's on the plate, and down there is Mutsgae." Deilo said, pointing to the others in turn.

Ton lifted its head and rose up slightly to look past the far edge of the table, down at where Mutsgae was standing. "Ah! A Lizard!" it jerked backwards as if stung. "I hope it is well trained!!"

"To do what?" Deilo asked, confused.

"Don't mind Ton ... he's got this phobia about Lizards, ever since an insane Lizard warrior ate two of his legs off one day, before dieing from the poisonous reaction to Ton's blood." Huteri said. "He's been shy of all Lizards ever since then."

"Figures." Mutsgae said, before sniffing the air for a few moments. He then sighed. "Stew. Again." He grumped to the floor.

Horus looked down at him, then at Ton. "Do you have anything that Muts can eat? He's not really fond of stew."

"Stew?" Ton asked. "Neither am I. We're not having stew ... and it will suit his particulars as well as the rest of us ... assuming you four all eat some flesh."

"We do, to varying degrees." Deilo said.

"Then the meal should suit you all quite well." Ton said. "It may be a short time before it is done cooking, though."

"In the mean time, we can have a round or two, eh?" The furred fellow with only two arms suggested.

"Sounds like a grand idea!" the other one with four arms announced. "I'll go get them." And with that he pushed to his feet and wandered out, ducking the doorframe.

"A round of what?" Deilo asked, uncertainly.

"Say, where are you from, anyway?" Ton asked, getting off the table and curling over backwards to more or less hold what he used as a torso up.

"Er ... Originally, we're from Yelm, in King Cerin's land. From there we went to a larger city, Paratora, and from there we came here." Deilo said. "Why?"

"King Cerin?" Ton asked, looking over at the froggy-looking fellow uncertainly.

"They must be from over the mountains." He responded.

"Outside!" Huteri started. "You're from *outside*??" he asked. "How in the world did you get into Gnaria??"

"A couple of SwordDancers showed us the way." Horus said, simply, as if that was a fairly normal thing.

"*SwordDancers*??" Ton asked. "My lands. You certainly have come a long way. It sounds like it would be an interesting tale to hear, too."

"I'd really rather not. It wasn't exactly pleasant, at any point." Deilo said.

"In time, maybe. For now ... we're going to have some fun." Ton said, rising up to his feet again and walking around the long table. Other creatures were starting to arrive, attracted both by the smells from the cook pot and the noises of conversation. Then the four-armed fellow returned, carrying a large object under each arm, followed by several other fairly large creatures also carrying strange looking objects.

To the quartet's surprise, many of the others grabbed a hold of the table, and moved it clear to the side of the room, rotating it out of the way, clearing a large area of floor space. Lillia merely hung onto her plate as the table was moved, afraid she might fall off and get stomped. The space was not clear for very long, as it was filled with bodies, working on assembling something. Soon, most left again, standing back to watch as a few select persons climbed into the middle of the mess. The four-armed fellow was dead in the middle of it, and he started pulling on various things. The contraption he was in the middle of started to make the strangest noises, horrible sounds indeed.

Mutsgae groaned, and covered his head with both hands.

After a few apologies, the four-armed fellow stopped, as several others climbed in along side him, pulling and shoving on things, rearranging again.

"You'd think they'd have it down by now." Ton said, shaking his head. "It's not like it's complicated."

"Easy for you to say!" The four armed fellow said. "You who can manage that many limbs at the same time ..." he grumped. After a time, half the number crawled back out, and the four-armed fellow started again. This time, the contraption around him practically sang. He stopped, and tried that again, then nodded to the others. They too started pulling and shoving and whacking, making the loudest racket. Then the four-armed fellow started again, and the racket transformed into a wonderful sounding song.

After a short time, all the other hands there started stomping or singing along, and even though the range was extreme, they apparently all knew the song well and it sounded rather good, their voices blending together into something no one singer could have managed. Then, from the back, the two-armed furry fellow opened his throat and sang. For having such an awful sounding speaking voice, he had an incredible singing voice, and apparently was singing the lead part. The four from outside the mountains just sat and listened and watched, fascinated. They had no idea what the song was about, as it was in the native Gnarian language. After several verses of that song, everyone suddenly fell silent, even as the strange instrument continued to play, the people inside it working up a heavy sweat working it. Gradually the tempo changed, and a new sound was added, but that sound did not come from the instrument. After a bit of looking around, Deilo noticed that it was Ton making the new sound, all his many feet tapping off the floor, creating an interesting counter-sound that fit right in. And then the hands all started singing again, this time a different song, many of them dancing about in the cleared area that was left over from the instrument. The dance was incredibly disjointed, as no two creatures were even capable of the same movements.

There were a few more songs, and then the players let the instrument slowly grind to a halt, huffing and puffing as they climbed out.

"Your turn." The four-armed fellow told Ton.

"Mine?" Ton asked, acting surprised.

"Yes you." He said, plopping down into a seat.

"Ah, come now, Torj, is that all you've got?" Ton teased, moving towards the large instrument. Everyone got out of his way to let him past, then simply waited as he wormed his long, tall self into the middle of it all, curling up into a weird-looking coil. Lifting better than half his appendages, he grabbed a hold of the instrument, and started working it. Apparently a lot stronger than Torj and the others had been, he made it all look easy, and was able to work it with a speed and grace the others had not been capable of. The songs he belted out were fast and cheery, keeping everybody hopping as they attempted to dance to it, singing at the top of their lungs.

Deilo couldn't understand what any of it meant, but he certainly enjoyed watching and listening, grinning.

After a long session in the instrument, Ton stopped it from playing, instead of simply letting it grind to a halt. "Somebody go stir that pot." He said, pointing at the giant cook pot. "I can smell it, it's fixing to start burning."

Since he was the closest, and one of the few not worn out from all the fun, Deilo got to his feet, and drug a chair over to the pot. Getting up on the chair, he grabbed a hold of a spoon he could have killed someone with, and attempted to stir the giant pot. After a moment, he got some help from Horus, who was not only taller, but better braced on the floor.

"I think," Deilo managed, "That lots of smaller pots would make this job easier to stir, and faster to cook."

"Oh, probably." Horus said, plunking a hoof on Deilo's chair as it started to go over, keeping Deilo from falling into the pot. "Careful."

"There. I think that's it." Deilo said, dragging the spoon back out of the pot. "Gee. I think now I know what Lillia feels like, when faced with a regular bowl and spoon."

Horus only laughed. "That Ton fellow must be massively strong, eh?"

"Must."

Deilo set the spoon down with a thud, and then climbed back down off the chair. Horus picked it up and carried it back to the table, as Deilo followed along behind. By the time they were done with the pot, they rest had gotten started on yet another lively song.

At the end of that song, Ton left the instrument, and moved through the crowd to the pot, to stir it himself. After watching it intently for a moment, using four arms to force the spoon around and around in the pot, he pulled the spoon out and announced that it was ready. The others were a flurry of motion again, as the instrument was disassembled, moved out, and the table returned to its original position, chairs and cushions being brought back to it. A larger cushion was furnished by one of the hands for Horus to sit on, so he could be comfortable.

Once everyone was returned, they formed a line and walked past the pot and Ton, who filled their plates to brimming with large hunks of meat, whole tubers, chunks of other vegetables that Deilo couldn't readily identify, and soft blobs of what looked like might have been dumplings.

Horus came back with a full plate, and set it down next to Lillia. "Take what you want." He told her. "Don't burn yourself, though." He warned.

"Thanks." She said, climbing up onto the edge of the plate to reach the food there, and start worrying small pieces out of it with her little knife.

Deilo sat down with two plates, one of which was full of nothing but meat. That he set down on the floor under the table for Mutsgae. "There you go."

"Thanks." Mutsgae said, surprised. He hadn't even bothered to go through the line, as he had no way to carry the plate without smashing it, and walk too.

The meal was more or less silent as everyone found a place to sit and worked on putting massive amounts of food away. Each of the hands went back for thirds and fourths, cleaning their plate every time. Ton stayed by the pot, serving out ladle after ladle full to each. Once everyone was satisfied, Ton grabbed up the mostly empty pot, and carried it off.

"Doesn't Ton eat anything?" Deilo asked, tearing a miniature loaf of bread in half to slather it with some of the intensely yellow butter that was on the table.

"Oh, sure. He'll clean that pot out ... he always eats last, and always eats *the* last scrap. Nothing wasted." Torj said, breaking a round, full-sized loaf into quarters. He passed one quarter to Huteri with one hand as the other three hands worked at drowning the remaining bread in the butter. Huteri accepted the bread without even looking, as if that was standard procedure, and ate it dry.

"Well, that was delicious ... where can I get a drink?" Horus asked, dusting breadcrumbs out of the fur on his chin.

"Through that door." Huteri said, pointing at one of the many doors. "There's a drinking fountain."

"Okay, thanks."

"Just place your used bowl to the left of the fountain." Torj said, before stuffing an entire quarter loaf into his massive mouth.

"Okay." Horus got to his feet, and went through the indicated door. The room was apparently not used for much that he could see. There was a small fountain in one corner running continuously into its basin with crystal clear water, and in the opposite corner was stashed the many complicated parts of the huge instrument. Horus walked over to the fountain, and looked at it. It was an ornate piece, looking like it was made of several different kinds of stone and glass, with decorative vine work crawling up the main structure in spirals. To the right of the fountain was a sizable cabinet attached to the wall, and to the left was a table with a large tub on top of it. In the tub was a small stack of ceramic bowls, all of them looking wet. Horus looked over at the cabinet, and pulled one of the doors open. Inside it was stacks upon stacks of clean bowls, more than Horus cared to try and count. Hundreds, probably more. And they were neatly sorted into various piles of different sized bowls. There were some that were downright huge, others were merely cup sized, along with every size in between.

"Weird." Horus said, before taking a bowl that he could easily dip his snout into. Closing the cabinet, he stuck the bowl under the falling water, and waited for the bowl to fill. Once it did, he drained it completely, before refilling it again halfway. This he also drank, before leaving the bowl in the tub on the table and returning to the other room, wiping his chin dry.

"Did you find it?" Deilo asked, when Horus sat down.

Horus nodded. "Wasn't hard."

"Alright." Deilo got to his feet, and went to get a drink, also. When he returned, he sat down looking rather satisfied.
"Now, I could sleep for a week." He said, feeling rather stuffed.
"Can't do that here." Torj laughed. "Here, there's work to be done."
"Oh, I know that. We used to work at an Inn." Deilo said. "I imagine this place is even more intensive."
"An Inn, eh?" Ton asked, making his way back into the room. "Say ... do any of you know how to make any of your native dishes?"
"Sure!" Horus said. "Deilo, here, can cook up lots of things. He used to help the cooks out from time to time."
"Really! That's grand! You'll have to show me." Ton said, coiling up and folding all his many long legs into the coils, resting his front end on the top of the coils. Basically, he made his chair out of his own self. It all looked rather awkward to Deilo, unable to imagine ever even trying to do that with his own body. But Ton made it look easy, graceful, and completely comfy.

Deilo jumped when there was suddenly a loud racket coming from outside. It sounded distinctly as if there was a giant pack of huge wolves out there, all barking and howling and snarling at once. "What is that??" Deilo asked, noting that the whites of Horus' eyes were showing.

"Them'd be the Mnar." Torj said. "Another good reason to stay inside at night."

"Mnar?" Mutsgae asked. "As in, Mnarag?" he asked.

"Good heavens, no. We wouldn't have any stock left if we had those things running around. The Mnar are indeed little cousins to the Mnarag, but they're not the same. For one, the Mnar don't have any weird majickal tendencies, and are lots smaller. Still bigger than your typical wolf, but that's all they really are. Wild dogs ... wolves. They don't bother anything, and actually help with keeping the pests at bay. It's a bloody mess when a deer or something gets into the grain stores." Huteri said. "But they'll eat you just as quick as a deer, so stay inside."

"If I might ask, how do you know it's not the Mnar that do the other things, too?" Lillia asked, sitting on the tabletop.

"Because, with us staying inside, that thing out there preys on the Mnar instead. Makes quite a racket."

"That doesn't mean anything." Deilo pointed out. "There are lots of creatures that will prey on their own kind, if there's nothing else."

Huteri shook his head. "What ever it is that's out there, it is *not* a Mnar. Mnar eat the whole body. Not just the hearts and blood."

"Something that the thing has killed, the Mnar won't even touch. They won't touch a body that's been sucked dry at all." Torj said.

"Weird." Horus said.

The rest of the evening passed in more or less silence, as the group listened to the Mnar outside while most finished up what they were doing. The hands were all listening intently, wondering if the creature was going to strike again this night. The small group of friends, however, were all wondering if the Mnar were actually going to stay outside.

Slowly, the dinner group broke up, going through the two doors at either end of the room that led to the sleeping quarters. Ton stayed put, almost completely still, as Huteri led the four friends through a door. They found themselves in a long, wide hall that was completely barren, lit only by a few low-profile majick-powered lights in the ceiling. He led them to a vacant room that was of considerable size.

"We usually bunk down four or six to a room. If you have no objections, you all can stay in here together."

"That'll be fine." Deilo said. "Is there something that we can rig up for Lillia to stay in? A small cupboard or something will do."

Huteri considered Lillia for a moment, where she was sitting on top of Horus' head. After a moment, he spoke again. "I'll see what I can find. The closet over there has a selection of blankets and pillows and things. Use what ever you need." He gestured at the closet door, and then left.

Mutsgae walked into the room, looked around, and walked to the middle of the room where there was a heavy rug. This he seized in his jaws, and drug over to beside the door. Dropping it, he pushed it around with his hands and snout until it was quite wrinkled up, and then plopped down in the middle of it, stretched out.

Deilo just watched that, and then laughed. "Okay. But, do you realize, that behavior just exactly like that is what makes lots of people think of Lizards as animals?"

"Who cares?" Mustgae said. "I'm not sleeping on one of those beds."

"Alright." Deilo went to the closet and opened it. There was indeed a selection ... it was jam packed with items. There were pillows of every size, blankets of every size, and in two different weights. Some were heavy, and others were light. Deilo selected an appropriately sized pillow, and a light blanket of similar proportions. He carried them over to a bed, where he dropped them both. Horus walked over to the open closet, and considered it. After a moment, he randomly selected a blanket, and carried it over to the other floor-level bed. He grabbed one corner, and threw the blanket at the bed. It unfurled, landing in a wrinkled mess of a heap on the bed. He then walked back to the closet, and pushed it closed until it latched.

"Must be quite a chore, furnishing this place with enough stuff for such a wide variety of people." Deilo said, sitting down on the bed and removing his boots.

"Certainly expensive." Horus said. "And it's not even like they simply went with the cheap stuff. The dishes are all expensive looking, the fountain ... and even these blankets ... they're not the homespun type. They're all quite fine." Horus said, contemplating his dirty hooves.

Huteri returned suddenly, bearing a big box. "Will this do?"

"Well enough." Deilo said, standing to take the box. "Thank you."

Huteri nodded, and left again, going down the hall to another door.

Deilo set the box on the floor in a corner, and pulled a knife out of his pocket. He worked on the box until it had a few holes in it. One carved big enough for a door, and a few for ventilation. Then he opened the top, and put some very small bundles from his pocket inside. "Okay, Lillia. All set for you to move in."

Horus walked over, and set Lillia down on the floor in front of the box. She looked up at it for a few moments, and then walked in through the rough doorway. Inside, she started untying her bundles that Deilo had carried in his pockets. One was a rolled-up mattress complete with bed sheets, and another bundle contained all her clothes. All in all, it all could have fit inside a coin-purse with plenty of room to spare, and Deilo had never noticed carrying it at all. But it was the sort of thing that most places did not tend to have.

"Okay. Thank you!" She called, after making sure the bundles were complete.

Deilo went back to his chosen bed, and made ready for the night. Mutsgae already appeared to be zonked on his rug. Horus, on the other hand, was trying to wipe most of the dirt off his feet, before trying to figure out the best way to get into the bed. He would have preferred a pile of good straw on the floor, but was not about to sleep on the bare floor. Even Mutsgae had secured a bed of sorts ... the only rug in the room. After a few tries, Horus just dumped over onto the bed, making it groan in protest at the landing. Tucking his feet up under him, Horus heaved a sigh, pulling part of the huge blanket he had up over him. "Good night."

"Good night." Deilo said, before crawling under his own blanket.

* * *

In the middle of the night, the Mnar suddenly grew very quiet, and the absence of the constant noise woke everyone in the quarters building. Everyone lay awake, and quite still. The regular hands knew that it meant that something else was out there, but the four friends hadn't the slightest idea what was going on. For a time that seemed like forever in the darkness, there was nothing but silence and the sounds of companions breathing in the room. But then there was a strange sound that wasn't quite loud enough to determine what it was, and then everyone in the building heard the distinctive sound of a wolf squealing in terror and pain. There was a sudden roar of noise as what sounded like the entire pack going into war mode, snarling and barking. A few strangled screams later, and it sounded like the entire pack took off in flight, out into the countryside.

After that was complete and utter silence. An uneasy silence that kept all four companions awake.

The hands all went back to sleep, however. They knew that what was going to happen had already happened. Nothing more would occur.

And there was work to be done in the morning.

A banging on the door early in the morning made everyone in the room jump. Deilo sucked in a breath of air, and then answered the door.

"Breakfast. Hurry." Torj said, before walking away, down the hall.

"Breakfast?" Deilo asked. He then closed the door and hurried to dress. He then went to the box, and retrieved Lillia. Horus, having managed to get out of the bed somehow, took her from him, and set her on his shoulder while Deilo helped Mutsgae get out of the rug without ripping it to shreds in the process. His talons had become entangled in the fibers of the rug, and as a result, Mutsgae was thoroughly stuck to the rug. Eventually, Deilo got him free of it, and the four headed out the door into the hallway. They made their way back to the dining room, where it was already packed and bustling. Ton was standing by a long, wheeled table, dishing out food to everybody.

"You can wash in there." Ton said, as they arrived, pointing to the room where the fountain was. Deilo went that way, followed by the others, and found a large washing basin had been set up in a corner that had been otherwise unoccupied before.

Deilo took Lillia and set her on the edge where there was a wide lip, and then started washing. Lillia knelt down and dipped her hands into the water to scoop out some for her own washing.

Once they were done, Horus scooped up a towel, soaked it, and dropped it on Mutsgae, before washing his own hands and muzzle.

Mutsgae clawed at the towel until he got it off the top of his head, and then sat back on his haunches in a rather awkward-looking manner, using the towel to more or less wipe off.

The four then returned to the dining room together, and were given heaping plates of food again. This time, it was a huge pile of soft scrambled eggs with cheese bits mixed in, and a pile of link sausages along with all the rolls and butter they cared to eat. After they had eaten that, they were given a huge pile of fried tubers and onions.

"Goodness. No wonder that wagon was piled so high." Deilo said, as he waited for Lillia to take what she wanted.

"Most of our foodstuffs don't come from town." Torj said. "That trip is merely for things that we don't make, here. Like cloth, dishes, some of the more complicated tools. And sometimes, we get lucky and get some things that we don't really need, but like to have around."

"Like, candy." Huteri said, grinning.

"They also get the store of majick, in town. We don't make majick here, though we do use quite a bit of it." Torj said.

"What happened, last night?" Deilo asked.

"The thing made a meal of a few wolves, is all." Torj said. "Nothing unusual. It was expected. Things will be quiet for a few days ... the wolves won't come back until then."

"Oh. What keeps the thing outside?"

"Apparently, it can't open doors. We know it knows we're here." Huteri said.

"That's why there aren't any windows." Torj said.

"How can you stand to live in a place that is haunted like this?" Horus asked.

"As long as you take the proper precautions, there's nothing wrong with it." Huteri said. "Besides, here there's work. Food. A living to be made. Despite the problems that we have here, they're simply a trade off for the things we *don't* have."

"Like what?" Lillia asked.

"Well," Torj said. "We're not prone to drought, here. Or flood. Or sea-storms. Or tornados. We aren't prone to earthquakes, volcanoes, or even dragons. Except for the wolves, and what ever that other thing is, this is an ideal spot."

"Weird." Deilo said.

"I have to ask ... how did anyone stay here long enough to build these buildings, without getting killed?" Horus asked.

"Well ... wolves are easy enough to keep at bay, with enough people and watch-fires. They probably even had some sort of guard animal ... probably big dogs or the like. The other thing ... is actually a new addition. It showed up some twenty years ago, and hasn't ever bothered to move on. This facility has been here for, oh ... easily eighty years. Maybe longer."

"Oh." Horus said. "It's been around that long, and still no one knows what it is?"

"Well ... no one knows what it is. But Tolus has seen it once. Scared the shit out of him, too." Torj said. "And that's hard to do."

"Tolus?" Deilo asked. "The butler?"

"Yeah. Him."

"How'd be manage that?" Lillia asked.

"Well ... he says he couldn't get back to the house in time, and it got dark on him. As he was approaching the complex, he saw something – he doesn't know how to describe it beyond 'a bloody fast shadow with teeth'. He says he made like a wall, and it went on the other direction, around the building. Once it was gone, he continued on to the house. Where he didn't come outside again for at *least* a year." Torj said.

"Made like a wall??" Horus asked.

"Well, if anyone can make like a wall, it's him." Huteri said. "He practically *is* a wall." The Dtri pointed out. "He's huge."

Ton took the table out of the room as the hands started cleaning up the table. Deilo hurriedly cleaned off the last of his food, and then added his plate to the pile.

"Alright." Mar-kai said, coming in through the door from outside, where a blush of dawn was showing on the edge of the bowl. "Deilo, you're to work with Ton ... Delov wants to see what you can come up with for today's meals. Torj, you take the Lizard, and show him the rounds. Fohrel, take the Centaurii with you, today. See what he can do." Fohrel, the two-armed, tall furry fellow with the strange voice nodded, crossing his arms across his chest.

Deilo watched them for a moment, noticing how much alike the two were. He thought they might be the same Race, and maybe even related. But there was no way he could really tell.

"Where is the Gnome?" Mar-kai asked, before spotting Lillia on the table, waving at him. "Alright. You come with me." He said, stepping over and holding out one massive hand for her to step onto. "Delov says he hasn't got a spot out here for someone as small as you, but wants to know how good you are with numbers and things."

"Quite, I believe." Lillia said, putting one hand on Markai's thumb to steady herself.

"We shall see." He said, before leaving, carrying her away in his hand.

The hands all left, leaving the dishes piled on the table in neat stacks. Deilo stayed put, not knowing where Ton had gotten off too. He sat down after a time, waiting. He didn't have long to wait, as Ton shortly returned, pushing a different cart.

"Well! What are you still doing here?" Ton asked, transferring the piles to the cart quickly.

"I'm supposed to help you cook, or something." Deilo said. "I guess the owner wants something new to taste."

"Oh, probably. My cooking skills are somewhat limited. But it keeps everybody going. And while the others may know some different things, I'm the only one that can prepare that much food fast enough to feed everybody."

"Probably helps that you can move that huge pot all by yourself." Deilo said, pushing the stacks closer to Ton.

Ton only laughed. "Probably. Having me be the cooking team frees up everyone else to go do other things." He said.

"Well, come along, then. Let's see what you've got." Ton turned around, and headed out, pushing the cart ahead of him as he went. Deilo followed along, through the fountain room and into a very extensive kitchen. Here there were multiple stoves, multiple counters, and several dozen ovens. Apparently, Ton only used the small kitchen near the dinner room when he had a one-pot meal for the hands.

"Wow." Deilo said, looking around as Ton shifted all the dishes into a long sink. He then pushed the cart aside, and reached over to a leather bound book and opened it. "These are the things I ... we ... have to work with. What all do you know to do?" Ton asked, as a half dozen limbs on his far side started washing and drying the dishes. Deilo just stared at that for a moment, before walking over to the book to look at it.

"Goodness." He said, looking down the list.

"I must ask, can you read, or are you pretending?" Ton asked.

"Oh, I can read ... but not this. I don't know this script. Some of the symbols I know ... like this one here." Deilo pointed one out. "I also don't know the local language, spoken."

"Well, we'll have to remedy that, first, won't we?" Ton asked, pulling the book over to the edge of the table. "We'll start with this ... seems like a good place to start..." Ton said, running a finger down the page. "Can't say as I've taught anyone to read or speak, before, so forgive me if I hit a few stalls somewhere..."

"Okay." Deilo said.

Horus followed Fohrel out to one of the huge barns, where several Dtri were working on harnessing a ridali to a large cart. The beast looked like it was standing there asleep, not caring in the slightest what the Dtri were up to. Fohrel climbed up into the cart, and walked to the back end. "Alright! Bring down the sacks!" he looked at Horus. "Can you catch a thrown sack?"

"Maybe?" Horus said, uncertainly. "How big a sack, and of what?" He jumped nearly clear out of his skin when a large sack impacted the ground right next to him, sending up a cloud of dust. After a moment, Horus looked up, and a stout four-legged creature waved from a loft, before chunking another sack down to land next to the first. Horus scurried out of the way.

"Don't just stand there! Get those sacks up here!" Fohrel said, waving his arm at Horus to get him going.

Horus scooted real fast to the first sack, and bent to pick it up. It wasn't as heavy as it had looked, though it was nearly as big as the equine half of his body. He tossed it up to Fohrel, who caught it and transferred it to the front of the cart.

"What is it?" Horus asked.

"Feed, for the animals out in the fields." Fohrel said, catching the second sack that Horus tossed to him.

"Oh."

Seeing that Horus had moved the two sacks that had already been tossed, the creature in the loft whistled before tossing another sack. Horus looked up just in time to get smacked in the chest by the sack. All the air came rushing out of him as he sort of managed to catch the sack. He gasped for a moment, and adjusted his grip to toss it to Fohrel. "Why isn't it tossed straight to the cart?" Horus asked.

"Can't do that." Fohrel said. "From that high up, having that much feed land in the cart over and over ... it hurts the ridali after awhile, leaving him crippled."

"And what about me, catching it?!" Horus asked.

"You're not catching it in the middle of your back in a very localized area." Fohrel said. "And you'll be switching out with him up there halfway through."

"Oh." Horus said, as he attempted to catch another sack that was thrown at him. He dropped many, missed many, and some of the ones he tossed missed their mark, landing short of the cart. As he went, he only got worse, as his arms and body grew tired. It was still only morning, and the cart wasn't even half loaded yet.

For his part Fohrel was encouraging, if disappointed.

Finally, the cart was half-loaded, and the fellow up in the loft came down backwards down a ladder, using only his back feet and hands. His front legs he kept tucked to his chest as he descended. Horus watched that, gasping, astounded. How did something built so similarly to himself manage that? Once down, the fellow said something, but it was completely unintelligible to Horus.

"Huh??" Horus asked.

"He said, you can go up, now." Fohrel said. "Get on up there."

"Er ..." Horus went to the ladder and contemplated it. After a moment, he attempted to get up it. He nearly fell off several times, and got tangled in the rungs a couple times ... not using his front legs was something that took a great deal of thought and concentration ... and not having them to guide where his back feet went was even harder. After the ordeal of getting up there was over, Horus looked around at the loft. It was stuffed with sacks, some of them marked with different colors. Finding some that looked identical to the ones he had been catching, he pulled one of those out of a stack. Walking to the edge, he looked down.

There was nothing there but a floor, and a few Dtri working on what looked like harnesses.

Horus frowned. Where had they gone? Then he heard Fohrel's distinctive grinding-glass voice from behind him. He turned around and walked to the other edge of the loft, and looked down. There, parked right where it should be, was the ridali and cart, with Fohrel in the back, and the other quadruped on the floor behind, waiting.

Heaving a sigh, Horus heaved the bag over the edge.

It landed far short of the fellow waiting to catch it. He just looked at it a moment, then back up at Horus, and said something.

"You're supposed to toss it this way, not just drop it!" Fohrel shouted, translating.

"Sorry!" Horus looked around, and spotted a stack that was much closer to the edge. Taking one, he carried it to the edge again, and heaved it with all his might. It, too, landed far short.

Fohrel said something to the other one, and backed the ridali and the cart up, the other quadruped also moving closer, to about where Horus was getting the bags to land.

Horus heaved a sigh. This was a lot harder than they made it look.

By the time they got the cart loaded, Horus felt like jelly. And he still had to get back down the ladder! When he tried it, he missed completely, and tumbled all the way down to the ground floor. He landed with a terrible thud, and just lay there for a moment, one leg stuck through the ladder.

Fohrel walked over to him, and looked at him for a moment. "Are you alright?"

"Do I *look* like I'm alright!!" Horus grumped, pinned down by the leg that was stuck through the ladder.

Fohrel shook his head. "If you can yell like that, you're just fine." He stepped over Horus' body, grabbed a hold of the offending leg, and pulled it free. Then he rolled Horus upright. "It's a trick that will take a little time to learn." He said, helping Horus back to his feet. "You'll get the hang of it. Get in the cart."

Horus groaned, and made his way over to the cart, feeling like a huge bruised sack of jelly. He managed to get on the back end of the cart, and lay there, one leg dangling off the back end.

Fohrel walked up, and lifted the leg up into the cart. "Never let limbs dangle off, unless you wish them removed. Ridali travel very quickly, and if your leg hits something passing under the cart..." he moved to the front of the cart, and climbed up on top of the feed, taking up the lines. Shortly, the cart was rolling out of the barn, and down a well-worn track towards the fields. "I'm going to need you to open and close all the gates, and when we're in the field, to start pouring the feed out of the sacks off the back end. I'll tell you how many sacks for which field."

"Okay." Horus said, glad to be sitting still at the moment.

The sun was already a hand span's width into the sky ... and quite warm to boot. Fohrel drove a ways down the track, before stopping at a gate to one side. "Okay, get the gate. Be quick, the stock already see we're coming."

Horus jumped off the back, and hurried to get the gate. But he discovered he couldn't figure out how in the world the latching mechanism worked. "How do I open it?!" Horus called, frustrated. The ridali in the field were fast approaching, eager to get their breakfast, which was already considerably late.

Fohrel got down off the cart, and showed Horus how to open the gate, then got back on the cart. Horus held the gate open as the cart went through, and then quickly shut it again behind, just before the ridali herd arrived.

"Get back in the cart, quick!" Fohrel said.

Horus squeaked, jumping aside as a ridali nearly stuck him, and launched off the ground to land in the cart – hopefully where he would be safer.

"Alright. I'm going to drive in a big circle. You rip open seven of those bags right now. And as I drive, you pour them off the back just as fast as you can. Stuff the empty bags into that box on the side." Fohrel pointed. After a moment, he asked, "Do you know how those bags open?"

Horus looked at the bags. "No."

Fohrel climbed to the back, and showed Horus how to open the bags.
"Okay. Thanks."
"Open seven, for this field. We'll be going pretty quick, I hope you have a good balance." Fohrel climbed back to the front as Horus opened seven bags.
"Okay." Horus said, picking up one bag in preparation. Pouring feed was easy. He could do that.
"Off we go, then." Fohrel said, smacking the lines off the harnessed ridali. The beast lunged forwards, hitting the harness hard and sending the cart rolling forward over the uneven ground. Horus yelled as he toppled over the back end of the cart, impacting the ground. The bag he had a hold of spilled its contents into a large heap, and all the surrounding hungry ridali mugged him, fighting and shoving for the feed. Horus squealed in pain as he was stepped on and jabbed with the weird horns as the animals jostled for position.
Fohrel pulled his ridali to a stop, launched over to the back of the cart, grabbed up two bags of feed, and jumped off the back end of the cart. Feed poured out of both sacks as Fohrel sprinted for the herd, yelling at the top of his lungs. When the sacks were empty, he stashed them both under one arm, and started smacking the rumps of the animals. They moved out, moving along the line of feed, eating. Gradually, Fohrel managed to extract Horus from the animals, and took him back to the cart, along with the third sack. Stashing the bags in the box, he looked Horus over.
"You're lucky you're not dead." Fohrel said, shaking his head.
Horus only groaned, sporting many more bruises on his aching body.
"Let's try that again ... this time, *don't fall off.*" Fohrel said, climbing back on the front, as Horus managed to get into the back. He pulled a sack over, and hung onto the cart as Fohrel got it started moving. Once he was sure he was going to stay on, he started pouring feed, while lying down in the back of the cart. Once the last sack was empty, he yelled at Fohrel to let him know. Fohrel waved an arm to signal that he heard, and drove quickly back to the gate.
Horus groaned as he got off the cart and made his way to open the gate. Fohrel drove out and stopped in the lane, waiting for Horus to close the gate and get back on.
"It was easier crossing the stinking mountains than it is to do the chores around here!" Horus grumped, getting back on the wagon.

"Was it, now?" Fohrel asked. "Don't worry, you'll get the hang of it." He pointed off to the opposite field, where a similar team was feeding. One person was driving the cart at top speed in a big circle in the field, all the stock chasing it around. In the back on the cart a Centauroid was *standing* while pouring feed out as fast as he could grab the sacks up.

"Yikes." Horus said, as the cart started rolling down the lane again.

"We don't tend to put anyone but folk like you in the back ... having four legs helps you stay upright while riding over that kind of terrain." Fohrel said.

"It didn't seem to do *me* much good." Horus said, feeling rather beat up.

"You'll get the hang of it."

Mutsgae was resting on the ground just outside the fence of a really heavy-duty corral, as Torj and several other big fellows jostled some stock into the pens. All the animals shied away from where Mutsgae was sitting, avoiding his proximity entirely despite all the excitement going on. Torj yelled something at one of the others, and someone suddenly jumped from the top of the fence to land on the back of a ridali. He then jumped from there to the next, running across the top of the herd to the far side, where he worked the latches on a huge gate. The gate swung open, and the herd pounded through. Once they were through, he pulled the gate shut again, and fastened it, even as the next herd came pounding into the first section of the corral.

Mutsgae just watched as pen after pen was filled with animals. All the satellite pens that stuck out from the edges were left empty, however. Once all the main pens were full, the entrance to the corral was closed off, and people started sprinting across the tops of the herds, all of them headed to new destinations.

"What do you think?" Torj asked, landing on the ground next to Mutsgae.

"What's the point?" Mutsgae asked.

"We're going to sort out all the babies." Torj said. "Weaning time."

"Babies?" Mutsgae said. "I don't see any babies."

"Of course not. They're still inside their mothers." Torj said. "They always hide there when they get scared."

"*Inside?*" Mutsgae asked, astounded.

"Sure. Just watch for the first round ... then I'm going to need you to start cutting animals out for us. You're low enough you won't get gored. They can't get their horns that low. But you do need to watch out for their feet. How fast are you?"

"Over short spans, very. I can't run very far, though." Mutsgae said.

"Okay. That should do." Torj said. "We're going to start in this pen." He waved three arms at someone, pointed two arms upward, one down, and one to the side. The other ranch hand waved one arm in return, and started running along the fence towards a gate.

Mutsgae only then noticed that each pen in the corral had two satellite pens coming off of it. One was connected to the side of a narrow chute, and the other connected to the end of the chute. The first gate was opened, and from sheer pressure from the herd, one animal was pushed into the chute. The gate was slammed shut behind it, even as it pedaled backwards, trying to get back out. When that didn't work, it slammed into the side with all the force it could summon, making the whole contraption rock alarmingly.

"Why isn't the chute attached to the ground??" Mutsgae asked.

"Because, if it was, it would get destroyed. Those animals are so big, and so strong, the key to restraining them is not rigidity, but rather, flexibility. The chute rocks, absorbing all the impact, rather than getting busted off and smashed to bits."

"Oh."

The ridali was shoved forwards by a floating panel operated by a majick-powered piston, and then was fastened into place. The sides of the chute then pushed inwards, locking onto the ridail's horns. The beast bellowed suddenly, the very first sound Mutsgae had heard any of them make, as it kicked out in all directions. Someone yelled, and scrambled away from the chute, dodging the dangerous feet.

"Okay, we've got her." Torj then jumped up to the top of the chute, and slid down behind the beast, inside. He crouched, wormed his way forward, and stood up. He completely disappeared inside the long flowing hair under the animal.

The ridali suddenly went very still, standing with its legs thrown out to all four corners. After a moment, a strange cry was heard, and Torj emerged from the fur of the ridali, carrying a miniature ridali in his arms. It was struggling to get free, its own fur gleaming in the sunlight. Torj scooted through the side gate into the side satellite pen, and turned the baby free. It shot out across the pen, hit the far side, spun around, and came right back. Torj quickly jumped out of the way and scaled the fence to get out of the way.

"Make no mistake." He gasped, landing on the far side. "The babies are *just* as dangerous as the adults."

The ridali in the pen bellowed again as the young one continued to batter at the gate, squalling. The gate in front of the adult was opened, and the enraged mother shot out of the chute just as soon as her horns were turned loose. She shot around the pen so fast they almost didn't get the gate shut again in time. One hand jumped from the fence near the gate just as the beast hit the fence right there full-tilt. The entire pen shivered, but held.

"Yikes." Mutsgae said, as the young ridali trotted up and down the side of the pen that was nearest to its mother, squalling.

The team just sat there for a moment, as if waiting. Then as if by magic, the two ridali that had been separated both went quiet, and ignored each other.

"What just happened?" Mutsgae asked.

"Weaning." Torj said. "Mother and baby ridali are never more than mere feet apart. *Never.* Once they are separated father than those few feet, they completely forget about each other. Well, not completely. They'd still recognize each other if they met up again, but the severe bond will still have been broken. They don't *need* each other anymore."

"That's so weird." Mutsgae said. "That's not even normal."

"For Ridali it is. If we don't wean them like this, they never get weaned until the little family unit gets so stinking big, they get forced apart by sheer numbers. That can take a very long time, and isn't very good on the pastures. It's awful hard to train an animal that is an adult and still glued to its mother."

"That doesn't make any sense. How do they work, in the wild?"

"They don't. There's no such thing as a wild ridali herd. They were rather drastically majickally created. But that's where the majick ends ... they're just animals. Who ever made them wanted something strong, patient, fast, and not liable to lose its young to predators all the time. Thus ... the ridali." Torj said. "A lot of people don't like messing with them ... they're too big, and too strong, and take a certain amount of understanding. So, ridali are rather rare. When they sell, they sell high."

"It is all very weird."

"Of course. Anything involving majick always is." Torj said, gesturing at the animals. "They got a very strange critter that is darn hard to wean. But at least it doesn't take long."

"There are some pretty massive herds here ... rare is not the word I would use. Haw many do you expect to sell?" Mutsgae asked, as another animal was shoved by its herd-mates into the chute. That one was allowed to pass straight through, as it apparently did not have a young ridali to extract.

"About half the young will be sold, half will be kept. Of the half that is kept, half of them will be returned into the herds, and the other half will be raised, trained, and *then* sold, for a much higher premium." Torj said.

"Ah."

Torj climbed the fence again, approaching the chute as another animal was restrained therein. He slipped down expertly under the creature, and extracted another young animal, repeating the process all over again. That young one nearly got him, though, before he could get away up the fence.

"Whew!" Torj said, landing on his feet. "That one's quick ... we might keep that one."

"Are you always the one to retrieve the infants?" Mutsgae asked.

"They're not infants. They're a full two years old, at this stage. But yes ... in this group, I am. I can do the work of two, in this case. Having an extra set of arms on most everyone else is very helpful, here. Normally, it takes two people to hang onto a young ridali, and move it to the pen. Me, I can hang onto it all by myself." Torj flexed all four arms. "Quite handy, that."

"I can imagine."

"Teams have to be really well co-ordinated, or they could get each other killed, doing that right there." Torj said, more seriously. He gestured over at one of the other corral pens, where similar efforts were underway ...indeed it was taking two people to wrestle each young ridali to the pen. There were only two other instances where there was only one, and in each case, they were either quite stout, or multi-limbed like Torj, though not as big.

The group working the pens were flying through the animals as fast as they were getting weaned – they did not dare open the gates for a new animal as long as the last ones were still thundering about. When the herd was half done, Torj called on Mutsgae to start cutting animals into the chute. The pens were empty enough that they weren't going in anymore. Mutsgae slipped under the lowest railing, and shot into the herd, his short legs propelling him quickly over the ground. He twisted and turned under the animals, zipping through the silky curtains of hair as he selected one to cut. He lunged upwards towards its lowered eye, and snapped his massive jaws at it. It shied in the other direction, moving to avoid him. Mutsgae then zipped around behind it and to the other side, snapping at it from there, too. It swung its head at him, but was too high to even be dangerous to him. Mutsgae lunged again, making sure it knew that, and then herded it right into the chute, against its wishes. He then scooted out of the corral, as a larger animal was coming at him with the obvious intent of stomping him to mash.

"That was pretty slick, there!" Torj said, after having retrieved the young ridali. "You're a natural."

"I'm of a predator Race. It's what predators do." Mutsgae said. "I can't say how often I can do that, though."

"We shall see." Torj said, quite pleased. "Soon as you get toned up, you'll be quite the asset."

"Thanks." Mutsgae said, resting while the weaning was happening.

Once they were ready for another animal, Mutsgae went back out into the herd. This time he had to dodge through the herd a few times, to try and lose the one animal that was intent on murdering him. Cutting another animal from the pack, he drove it towards the chute. He had to abandon it half way there, and scoot under the fence again, as the one particular animal had found him again.

"What's with that one??" Mutsgae asked.

"That's the buck." Torj said. "The herd always has three of them, and that's the king buck. He's very protective of his herd. You might want to cut him first, so we can get him out of the way." Torj suggested.

"I don't think I'll have to cut him at all." Mutsgae said, before turning and going back under the fence that the king buck was busy trying to tear down. Mutsgae shot between the buck's feet and out the back, heading towards the chute at top speed. Head lowered, the buck spun about as if gravity did not apply to it, and charged after him, intent on his prey. Mutsgae shot into the chute, and out under a side railing. The buck hit the fence there full-tilt, and it looked like it might not hold for a moment. But the chute eventually rocked back upright again, as the gate slammed shut behind the buck. The front gate was opened quickly, and the hands prodded him out of the chute and into the processed herd.

"That worked rather well. He really hates you, doesn't he?" Torj laughed.

"Apparently." Mutsgae remarked, contemplating the herd again. After a moment's thought, he headed back out into the herd. Almost without any catches, he managed to get that one to go into the chute rather quickly. Then he slid back under the rail and rested while the others worked on extracting the young. Torj joined him, after the two animals were released into the pens for weaning.

"Whew." Torj said. "It's been too long since I did this."

"You *enjoy* doing this?" Mutsgae asked.

"Not really. But it does take a certain amount of quickness. And practice makes it all go smoother. I'm saying I'm out of practice. That one nearly got me, too."

"Maybe you're just getting old."

Torj just stared down at him for a moment, before he realized that the Lizard had been making a joke. Then he laughed heartily. "Maybe, indeed."

Mutsgae rested his chin on the ground, completely relaxed. Over the course of the day, Torj got better and better at avoiding the animals he worked with, showing that practice did indeed help a lot. However, the team on the chute was getting longer and longer breaks as it was taking Mutsgae longer and longer to get the animals to go where they needed to be. He was getting slower as he grew more tired, and as a result, it was taking even more time and effort in subsequent efforts.

After an animal managed to get clean away from Mutsgae, Torj called him out. "You sit here and rest for a bit, okay? You look rather beat. We can get them in here for a while." Torj said, hopping down off the fence with a short pole in one hand. He was followed by nearly half of the chute team, and they managed to cut one animal and get it into the chute. They continued with the operations, processing five more animals before one of the team members got hung by the adult ridali charging out of the far end of the chute. The animal threw its head up, as the hand screamed in pain, hung quite thoroughly on the horn.

Torj yelled something, trying to get rid of the young ridali so he could get over there to help. He ended up having to fight the young animal off, though, as the others started climbing fences and jumping gates, trying to get to the enraged adult.

Mutsgae, unhindered by fences and gates, shot through underneath it all, and latched onto the beast's soft nose with his teeth, snarling. The animals uttered a surprised squall, and jumped backwards, jerking its horn free of the ranch hand in the process. Mutsgae released the soft nose, opened his jaws all the way, and roared loudly as he lunged at its face. It backed off again, swinging its head uncertainly, until it bolted at the fence, and around, to join its herd mates. Mutsgae grabbed a hold of the ranch hand's odd clothing with his teeth, and drug him out of the corral even as the others were only just coming over the last barrier. Once he had him clear of any new dangers, Mutsgae let him go, unable to do anything more.

The hand merely groaned in pain, lying there on the ground as the others came to his aid.

Finally getting free of the young animal, Torj made it up the fence and over, joining the others around the wounded hand. After a few quiet words, three of them set off to carry him back to the complex.

"That was incredible." Torj said, to Mutsgae. "I've never seen anyone move so fast ... and I thought you were fast when you were doing the cutting." He said. "Thank you."

"I only did what I would want to happen, if it were me in trouble." Mutsgae said. "I could, so I did." He said, sagging to the ground, now even more exhausted than he had thought he had been, before. "Will he be alright?"

"Maybe, if they can get him back to the complex in time. But he has that chance because you got there so fast. How did you know to do what you did?"

Mutsgae thought about that for a moment. "I didn't. It was an instinctive mark."

"Oh. Well ... thanks anyway." Torj said, before going on to announce to the rest of the team that they were going to break for a while. Everyone could use the break, before anyone else got injured. And maybe an early lunch was in order.

At that, everyone working the corrals quit, and loaded into the wagons that they had ridden there on, and sat down. Mutsgae walked up to the back of one, considered it for a moment, then just sighed. He didn't feel he had the energy it would take to jump that high, anymore. Then he stiffened when something big grabbed him, and set him in the wagon.

"There you go." Torj said, patting him on the head, grinning.

Mutsgae just looked at him for a moment, and then just sat on the bottom of the wagon as others continued to load in around him. Once the wagons were all full, the drivers started the paired ridali teams moving out towards the barns at a quick but easy pace. When they reached the quarters, the teams were tied to hitching rails, and everybody filed into the building.

"Hey." Horus said, looking up when the others came in. He wasn't about to get up or move, though. He was in more pain than he knew he could feel, at the moment.

"You look horrible." Mutsgae said, walking up and slumping next to him.

"I *feel* horrible." Horus agreed. "I've had a rather rough morning."

"Looks like it." Mutsgae agreed. "Lunch time?"

"Apparently." Horus said. "We finished feeding, and Fohrel said I could come in and rest a little bit, before we started something else."

"What would that be?" Mutsgae asked.

"I have no idea. What have you been doing?"

"We were sorting young animals from the adult herd, weaning them. That is, until someone managed to get caught on a horn. Word has it he might live."

Horus thought about that, and then winced. He'd had his own share of close encounters, and was quite glad his had not ended in that fashion. "Have you seen Deilo anywhere?"
"Nope. I only just got in from the corrals." Mutsgae said. "I'm tired."
"Me, too. I never would have thought a simple feeding chore could be so brutal."
"You were only feeding?" Mutsgae managed to suppress a laugh. "I see. Not as practiced as you thought you were, eh?"
"There's a big difference between an Inn's yard and a ranch, I'll have you know." Horus said. "For one thing, the number of uncontrolled animals."
"Ah-huh." Mutsgae said, sniffing the air. "I don't smell any food."
"Neither do I." Horus said. "I'm just glad to be seated."
They both looked over when Ton appeared partially through a door, and looked at the crowd gathering in the dining room. "Ahh ... might I ask why everyone is here so early?" he asked.
"There was an accident at the corrals." Torj said, from the outer doorway. "We're taking a break ... and maybe hoping for a snack."
"Snack?" Ton asked. "Humph!" He backed back out of the doorway, and disappeared once more.
"He didn't sound too pleased." Horus noted.
"Um ... even a 'snack' for so many would be a big undertaking." Mutsgae pointed out. "I doubt anyone would be pleased, faced with that."
"There are worse things." Horus said.
"Sure."
"Have you seen Lillia?"
"I just told you ... I just got in from the corrals." Mutsgae said. "Would Lillia be out there?"
Horus shrugged. "In this place? Who knows who would be where."
Mutsgae only grunted. "No, I haven't seen her."
"Oh." Horus said, falling into silence.

*   *   *

Lillia stood on the sheet of paper, studying the numbers written on it. When they had asked about math, they were serious about math, she had discovered. There were some serious numbers on that sheet ... she had been reading numbers off of similar papers all day.

Apparently the problem lay in that the farm dealt with a *lot* of money going in and out, along with the numbers pertaining to supplies going in and out. The owner of the ranch was good at numbers, but there was so much he was continually falling behind. And the butler, for all that he was a very good butler, was almost illiterate when it came to numbers and couldn't work them very well at all. On top of that, he had trouble with the small print the numbers were always in.

It was all quite huge to Lillia, but it had to be, as others had to be able to read it, too. It didn't bother her much ... she had been accustomed to helping the maids out with various things, and that included writing and numbers. She could haul a pen about on paper in a very neat fashion, writing big enough for the larger people to read.

Lillia shook her head, and walked to the edge of the paper to sit and rest. Her head was pounding from all the numbers she was putting through it. After a moment, she got up again, went to the teacup sitting nearby, and dipped some tea out of it to drink. It was the smallest thing that Tolus could find to give her something to drink in, and it was indeed a tiny, delicate thing. But it was still large enough for Lillia to bathe in.

"Ah, how are you faring?" Delov asked, walking up to the table.

"I'm getting it done, sir ... but at the moment I am taking a short break. My head is starting to hurt from it all." Lillia said, dropping a quick curtsey.

Delov nodded. "I can understand that." He said, reading the paper she had been working on. "You wrote this?" he asked, indicating the script on the next page over.

"Yes, sir." Lillia said.

"Amazing. You write better than most larger people ever do. Alas ... I can read these numbers, but I do not understand the words you have written ... even the characters are unfamiliar to me."

Lillia walked over to the page and looked at it. "I am afraid I cannot speak your tongue, much less write it." Lillia said.

"You will have to learn it." Delov said.

"I suppose I will. Who can I get lessons from?" Lillia asked.

"I have heard that Ton is teaching Deilo the language, so that he can use the cookbooks and supply books ... I don't see why you can't join in." Delov said. "You can spend the evenings over there learning that, and the mornings working the numbers. I'll have to sort things for you, so that you will not have to write any script until you have it learned."

"Thank you, sir."

Delov nodded. "Good work. All the numbers appear to be in order ..." he said, running a finger down the row of calculations. "Do you use an assist?"

"Sir? I know not what you're referring to."

Delov looked at her for a moment, then pulled a drawer out of the desk that Lillia had been working on the surface of. After a moment of sorting things around, he came up with a small cube-shaped thing that had the stink of majick about it. Lillia could smell it plainly, though she knew that the larger peoples could not smell the aroma that majick gave off. Delov set it down on the table's surface, and touched the top of it. It unfolded slightly, revealing a string of raised buttons. "This."

"I don't know what that is." Lillia said. "What does it do?"

"It calculates numbers ... a lot of people use these. Sometimes when they don't know how to work numbers, or if they simply don't want to. Tolus uses this one often."

"I'm afraid I wouldn't even know how to use it. Is it accurate?"

Delov laughed. "Of course. It wouldn't be much good if it wasn't accurate."

"Oh." Lillia leaned on the edge of it, stretching to see the surface of it. "I think I would be better off just doing the work myself."

"Possibly." Delov said. "If you wish."

Lillia nodded. "I think I will stick with what I know how to use, for the time being. I have a great deal to learn, already."

"That, you do." Delov said. "Dinner is only a few hours away. After you eat, you may go with Ton, and learn the language."

"Yes, sir."

Delov nodded again. "Keep up the good work." He then turned, and walked away again, back the way he had come.

Lillia shivered, glad to be out of his gaze. His strangely colored eyes always unsettled her, their weird red color always making him look like he was fixing to explode or something. That and the lights in the place always went really dim when he entered a room, making it awfully hard for her to see much of anything clearly. When he left the room, the lighting automatically readjusted to normal brightness.

Other than looking rather strange, Lillia thought the owner of the ranch was a rather nice person, as she had gotten the chance to speak with him several times over the course of the day.

Heaving a sigh, she walked back over to the page with all the numbers on it, and started crunching numbers in her head again. For the most part she was left to herself, to do as she saw fit to get the job done. When dinnertime arrived, Tolus showed up and took her from the desk to the front door, where Mar-kai took her all the way over to the quarters building, to join everyone else at the lunch table. All the hands were there, getting ready and waiting for the meal to arrive.

Ton always took the meals for Delov and Tolus to the main house first, and then worked on delivering the prepared meal to the hands in the quarters building. After everyone had eaten a very hearty meal, they dispersed once more to attend to the work of the evening. It tended to be lighter work than the morning had been, with the exception of the seasonal corral work. The corral workers returned to processing and weaning the animals in the pens, with extra help along. Everyone else spent the afternoon hours in the various barns doing work in the shade thereof. Cleaning, sorting, repairing, generally anything and everything that needed to be done. A very few, select group of people were in the square area inside the ring of barns, working in full sun, training some new ridali to the harness work they were expected to do. They were split into two teams, one working while the other rested in the cool shade, trading out often, to keep the animals working.

Once the animals were hot and tired, they learned quickly, figuring out what was expected of them in the hopes that once they got it done, they would be allowed to stop and rest. But getting them tired at all was the trick, indeed, as they had a very high endurance level.

At the end of the day, the last feeding was done in a big hurry, while everyone else cleaned everything up and stowed every last thing that wasn't planted in the ground, closing up and locking all the barns. As the sun started to touch the horizon, everyone raced for the Quarters building, hurrying to be inside before the last bit of sun disappeared.

The door was locked and barred from the inside, as everyone set to cleaning up. Everyone bathed once they were in, cleaning and washing in the various fashions each had. Once that was done, they started rearranging the dining room again, to set up the instrument.

The work of the day was over, and now they could play. After supper was over and everything was cleaned up, everyone vanished off to their beds, tired after a long day of work.

As time passed, each of the friends grew better at their assigned jobs, until they excelled at it. Lillia and Deilo learned the language quickly, and became fluent in it. Deilo went on to cook meals that he was familiar with, teaching the techniques to Ton, who found the new dishes interesting. Delov also liked the new variety in the diet, and made sure that Mar-kai fetched in whatever ingredients Deilo needed to keep the food coming. Lillia learned how the assist worked, and discovered that it did indeed speed things up, and sometimes appeared to be dancing some exotic dance as she jumped from button to button, racing back and forth across the desk top as she did her work both in her head, on paper, and with the assist, churning out neatly written, accurate pages for Delov. When she wasn't busy with that she got around better, as Delov had acquired a bird for her, trained by other Gnomes for riding. With the little bird, she could travel anywhere on the farm at her own discretion, with no danger of being trod on.

Mutsgae grew accustomed to playing predator to move stock around quickly and effectively, and also slowly got to where he could race about like that all day long, instead of only in short bursts. He was also found to be quite useful in other areas, delighting in digging up and wrestling with the wolves that plagued the place. A few of the other hands found this to be great fun, as well, and would join with him to rout out a whole pack.

Horus got to where he could ride the ridali drawn carts with the best of them, becoming stronger than most Centaurii ever became, throwing and catching feed in the mornings, and ultimately, helping to train the ridali. He became fast enough on his feet that few other hands could keep up with him when he lit out at full speed. No one ever got as fast as the ridali were, but that wasn't going to stop a lot of them from trying.

They all gained new friends, and had great fun on the ranch, enjoying life to the fullest, knowing that they weren't going to be routed out by war again. The peace and rhythm of the place did great things to heal over the wounds the wars had created.

But they were always careful to be indoors before darkness fell.

Until one day, darkness happened in the middle of the day, catching everyone off guard. Every hand on the ranch stopped what they were doing, and looked up. It appeared that the sun had gone fuzzy, and was fast fading as the sky darkened.

"Ah, hell." Torj said, where he was working with Horus.
"What is that?" Horus asked.
"That is dirt in the air, way up high. It only happens when there is a quake outside the Gnarian valley. Not very often. It will take nearly a week or so to clear. Get to the Quarters, as fast as you can. *Go*, and don't come back out!" Torj said, before following his own advice, sprinting for the barns, even though they were a very long ways away.

Elsewhere on the ranch, everyone else was doing the exact same thing. Some were driving ridali, but most were on foot. Everyone dropped what they were doing, and sped for the safety of the Quarters building.

Some paused long enough to close up all the barns, some long enough to unharness and release the ridali. But most did not stop on their headlong plunge for safety.

Even as the last person made it inside, the door was closed and barred.

"Now what?" Horus asked. "Are we going to have to stay in here until it is gone?"

"Yes. This darkness lends the same results as a true darkness. If we're lucky, it won't be a complete darkness. Maybe it'll only get dim." Huteri said. "If it does get dark-dark, Delov and Tolus are going to get *really* thin."

"We'll get food over there to them somehow." Torj said. "Tolus could probably make it, but I don't think Delov could go that long without food."

Ton came through a doorway, and looked at everyone. "Now what?" he asked.

"Quake shadow." Fohrel said.

Ton just stood there in silence for a moment, and then sighed. "Drat. Not again."

Deilo came out, behind him, and looked at everybody, looking like he had been standing too close to an oven for too long. "A what?"

"Quake shadow." Ton said. "We're going to have to operate as if night lasts all week. It's now dangerous to go out, even during the day."

"Uh ... that can't be good." Deilo said. "What do we do?"

"For the most part, sit tight." Ton said. "It's all we can do." He turned, and went back into the kitchens. After a moment, Deilo followed.

The mood was very quiet and dull, as everyone said not a word for a very long time. At the very end of the day Ton made a quick trip to the main house to deliver some food. He then hurried back, moving very quickly, every leg he owned propelling him faster and faster.

In the main house was where Lillia stayed. It was where she had been when the quake shadow had arrived, and where she could still continue her work, with the lights on. So there she stayed, hoping the others would stay safe.

In the middle of the week she happened to be standing in a windowsill looking out, when a moving shape off to the right, near the corner of the house caught her attention. It was not big enough to be Ton, and in the wrong direction. The darkness made it very hard to see anything, but she could see it was small, and fast. Small, in comparison to the likes of Tolus and Torj and the rest. It was thousands of times her own size.

It seemed to be moving in a random fashion, not tending to any one course or destination, and Lillia just stood there and watched, nearly invisible in her perch, and completely unnoticeable. For a very long time she stood there, partially terrified, and mostly curious.

Maybe she could see what it was!

Around the corner of the Quarters building came Ton, completely oblivious to the thing out there with him, hurrying across the stretch between buildings. The thing noticed him, however, and started in his direction, obviously stalking. Ton was a fast thing to stalk, however, and it started trying to keep up with him. Then something else made an appearance. The greatly diminished wolf pack came tumbling and yipping around one of the barns, playfully bounding around in circles in and out of itself. They were obviously well fed on some deer or other animal they had managed to catch.

Ton ignored the noisy animals, bent on reaching the house quickly.

The other thing, however, slowed, apparently having realized that there was no way it was going to be able to catch Ton easily. It stopped, and turned back, this time moving in on the wolves. A wolf would be much easier to catch, though it would have to fight all the wolves to get one. However, there were far fewer wolves than there had been, and that would make it easier.

Lillia stood there in horror as she watched the thing rip into the wolf pack, and eventually kill one, running all the others off. She knew then that it was indeed the thing the hands had spoken of, as it first sucked the body dry, and then ripped the heart out and ate that, too. It left the carcass where it lay, and resumed wandering.

Ton, having reached the house safely, and then heard the wolf-pack's fight, had wisely decided to stay put for the time being in the main house. He found Lillia in the window, staring out of it like a transfixed statue.

"Lillia?" Ton asked, moving the curtain aside and looking out, too. He did not see anything of interest that could keep her so captivated, having just missed the thing disappearing around the barn. He looked down at her curiously. "Lillia?" he asked, again.

"It's out there..." she said, pointing at the barn.

"I know. I heard it." Ton said, looking where she pointed.

"I saw it." Lillia said. "I've been watching it for a very long time."

"You have??" Ton asked, still not seeing anything.
"What was it?"
"I don't know. It's too dark out there, too bright in here, and it's too far away for me to see clearly." Lillia said.

Ton looked around the room, then left the window to go turn the lights out. Then he returned to the window to look out. Maybe it would come back around, and he, too, could see it.

He felt very lucky, at the moment, to have made it to the house alive.

"You're faster than it likes to go." Lillia informed him. "It was chasing you for awhile, before it spotted the wolves. I guess they're easier."

Ton did not say a thing, now feeling *very* lucky to have made it to the house alive. He hadn't known it was there, and frankly, hadn't wanted to know. That was scary.

"There! See?" Lillia pointed, as it appeared around the other end of the barn. But it was so far away neither of them could see anything but a vague size about it. There was no distinct shape to be seen.

"It's too far to be seen." Ton said, finally.

"I know."

They stood there in the window for a long time, both of them invisible in the darkness now that the lights were out. Right when Ton was thinking that maybe it had left and now he could go back, they saw it again. This time, it was right next to the house again, approaching the front porch. It paused several times, as if looking around cautiously. Then it froze, as if stung, plainly watching the Quarters building. Lillia and Ton both looked that direction as one, to see what had drawn its attention. Around the corner of the Quarters building, a long, low shape was moving in the darkness, also slow and stealthy, searching and watching.

"Muts." Lillia said, recognizing the profile.

"The idiot. He's going to get killed." Ton said, quietly.

"He's probably looking for you, since you didn't go back." Lillia said. "Go back." She continued, speaking to Mutsgae, who could not in any way hear her. Then she turned and jumped down off the sill. "I have to go out there and warn him!" She said, calling her bird down.

"Are you crazy?" Ton asked. "You'll get eaten too!"

"No, I won't." she said, climbing aboard her bird. "I'm too small, and will be airborne. Please, open the window."

Ton just looked at her for a moment, and then shook his head, opening the window slowly, holding the curtain aside. Lillia urged her bird on, and it took off, flying quickly out the window. Once outside, she looked down to see again what was happening.

She saw that the thing was moving towards Mutsgae, who was apparently unwittingly moving towards it.

She dove at Mutsgae, zipping past his head once to get his attention, then circling back again once he looked up to see her flying. Lillia landed on his shoulders. "It's out here, Muts! Get back inside! It's coming this way."

"Where's Ton?"

"He's in the house. Now get inside!" Lillia said, before taking off again. She looked back down, to see Mutsgae turning to hurry back to the Quarters building. And behind him, the thing was stalking him, swiftly catching up. Lillia dove down again, and let loose with a warning cry just as the thing leapt forward, trying to catch Mutsgae before he got to the door, and safety.

Mutsgae turned at the cry, snapping his jaws open as he spun, in instinctual reaction. The thing impacted Mutsgae's toothy maw rather than his back and recoiled in shock, it's surprise attack spoiled. But it was too late, as Mutsgae's jaws snapped shut automatically on it upon impact. It screamed a scream that would haunt many a person's dreams for years to come, and then attacked Mutsgae's face, trying to get free. Flailing and thrashing, it tore at Mutsgae's scaly hide, striking at his eyes and nose and anything else it could reach.

Mutsgae, for his part, was terrified out of his wits. But at the same time, he knew instinctively that he had it good, and letting go would be a *very* bad thing to do. Trying to dislodge it from its attack, Mutsgae started thrashing himself, slinging his head back and forth, shaking his attacker vigorously while squinting his eyes closed. Things snapped and cracked and broke, crunching audibly as the two fought each other.

The noise from their battle had the attention of everyone inside, but nobody opened the door, and nobody came outside.

Unable to help at all, Lillia just circled overhead, wishing that she could help in some way. All she could do was fly, and shout, and yell.

Finally, the thing started to slow, and then stop, apparently having taken too much damage from the bite and shaking to continue on. Long after it quit moving, Mustgae opened his eyes to look at what he had in his mouth that tasted so horrible. His face was completely torn up, and hurt incredibly. When it did not move, he opened his jaws, and released it, backing away warily. When it continued to not move, he turned, and fled the rest of the way back to the Quarters, followed closely by Lillia on her bird.

With a lot of thudding and yelling, they got someone to unbar the door, and let them inside. Lillia flew in, and landed on the table, where she got off the bird, running back to the edge of the table to look at Mutsgae.

Bleeding with scraps of his hide hanging off all over his face and shoulders, Mutsgae was a horrible sight to see. The other hands quickly re-locked the door, cleared an area, and fetched supplies to take care of Mutsgae's wounds.

After the shock of the fight, and the pain of the wounds, Mutsgae just sat completely still, as if turned to stone, though he was quite conscious and aware. Several of the Dtri hands started working on him, cleaning and bandaging him as best as they could.

"What did he tangle with?" Torj asked, of nobody. "It sounded like the thing that eats people, but ... if that was so, how did he live?"

"It was the thing you speak of." Lillia said, tears of relief running down her face. "And he did win. I warned him, and its attack landed it in his mouth, rather than his back. I saw it all. It was horrible. It screamed, and attacked him, trying to get free, and he just sat there, shaking it back and forth, back and forth. Oh, Muts! Are you okay??" Lillia asked, desperately.

"He'll be fine. Scarred, but fine." A Dtri said. "Physically, anyway. You're lucky you kept both of your eyeballs intact." It told him.

Mutsgae did not reply in any way, completely still, though the pain from their ministrations was exploding inside his head. He closed his eyes, resisting the normally automatic reaction to bite them all. It all hurt a lot.

"Is it still out there?" Torj asked.

"Yes. It might be dead, but I don't know." Lillia said.

Torj considered that for a moment, then took up a lantern, lit it, and headed out. Fohrel followed him out, carrying a stout, long stick. It was the best item they had in the Quarters, as far as possible weapons went. The two large fellows walked along the wall of the building, Torj holding the lantern high, looking for a body. They came to where the fight had been, and knew it by all the blood soaking the ground. Both colors stained there, the color of Mutsgae's blood, and that of the other thing. It was obvious to them that Mutsgae had indeed wounded it severely, just by the amount of soaking. They looked around the immediate area, and saw nothing. The creature itself was gone. Fohrel crouched near the spot while Torj held the lantern, inspecting the area to try and see which way it went. They were both very wary, as it was quite obvious that it was not at all dead yet. In just that much time, it had gotten up and left.

Fohrel opened his mouth to say something, when he froze, looking past Torj's knees. Torj, seeing the expression, turned, then spun completely to the side as a blood-soaked body hurtled past him, screaming in fury. It was the same thing that Mutsgae had tangled with, as it was severely wounded ... and very angry. It had been thwarted for the second time, that night, and that made it all the madder. It landed and spun about, preparing to attack once more. Fohrel rolled to the side, coming up again facing the thing. It sprang at Torj again, who spun out of the way again, smashing the lantern on what he hoped was its head as it went past him. The fire lit its fuel as it spilled everywhere, lighting both the thing and Torj's thigh. Torj flung the remnants of the lantern aside, useless now, and slapped a broad lower hand over the fire on his thigh, squelching it. Fohrel tossed the stick to Torj, and then sprinted for the nearest barn, where he knew he could find a better weapon.

    Torj caught the stick in one lower hand, and transferred it to a cross-handed hold, one upper, one lower hand, as he turned to face the thing again. It had moved, but it was not hard to spot. Still on fire, and apparently not caring, it was on the rooftop, screaming at Torj in its ultimate fury. Never before had it been thwarted, much less three times in the same night, twice by the same individual!

    "Well, come on, then!" Torj roared at it, throwing his two empty hands wide. "Give it your best shot!"

    It screamed at him again, and launched off the rooftop at him. Torj stepped to one side, straightening his staff. He grasped it in all four hands to steady it, as he butted the one end on the ground, aiming the other end at the creature.

    Seeing that, it tried to turn aside, but it was committed to the trajectory by that point, smacking into the stick broad-side in its attempts to avoid it. With a sickening crunch, the stick plunged through the thing's body, exiting the other side. Torj stepped aside, reflexively letting the stick go. But a split second later he had a quad-hold on it again, even as the thing screamed in pain. He heaved it over his head, and swung the stick downwards to the ground, bouncing the thing off the ground as hard as he could. It hit with a meaty thud, then was on its feet again, yanking the stick out of Torj's grasp in the process.

    It snarled at him, drawing the stick out of its own side in one quick movement and flinging it aside.

    "Ah, hell." Torj said, now crossing both sets of arms in front of his torso. Now he had nothing but his own hands to fight it off with. "Fohrel, *hurry!*"

    Crouching, the thing snarled again, its intent to rip Torj limb from limb quite clear. It moved to spring, as Torj crouched suddenly, hoping to dodge the attack once more.

Its middle exploded in a brilliant blue-purple pyrotechnic display mid-leap, and landed heavily on Torj in nearly two pieces. It screamed in pain again, and shot to the side as Torj rolled the other way and got to his feet.

"What does it take to kill this thing?!" Torj exclaimed, as he saw Fohrel take aim again with the majick-powered staff.

The purple-blue swirling sphere on the end of it glowed briefly, and a bright white blast erupted from it, streaking even faster than the creature to impact it once again, sending it rolling. This time, it lay still, with not a sound coming from it. Fohrel walked towards it. Out of the Quarters building came Huteri with another lantern, and Mar-kai appeared out of the main house, also bearing a lantern and majick-rod.

The three parties reached the body at the same time, and under the twin lanterns they looked at it. It was a weird looking thing, being chewed, skewered, bitten, and half blown to bits. But it was definitely dead. It looked like it might have been something darkly colored and vastly dangerous, but it was in a state of flux, the dead body working on changing its form.

Fohrel aimed his staff at it, just in case that was how it repaired and reanimated itself. He wasn't going to take any chances.

"Oh, Gods above." Huteri said, crouching nearer to the thing. "It's ..."

The other two stared at it, as well, as Torj approached just as it finished shifting. "Holy Hells!" Torj exclaimed, looking down at the destroyed body of Delov.

"Incredible." Mar-kai said.

"What, exactly...?" Torj asked, confused.

"This, Torj, is the stuff of myths." Mar-kai said, as Fohrel nodded in agreement.

"It appears that our employer was one and the same as our predator. A were-vampire." Fohrel said.

"Now that makes some sense out of why he was so light-intolerant." Mar-kai said.

"No dang wonder he was so reluctant to get something to find out what was eating the hands!" Huteri said. "It was *him*, all along!"

"This is incredible." Torj said, shaking his head.

"Now what?" Fohrel asked.

"We continue on." Mar-kai said, as the other three looked at him.

"What?" Torj asked.

"Delov had no heirs, and no family. Which also makes sense now. He had long outlived any family he ever had. And we do have a remarkably well-run facility, here. We continue on. No one has to know Delov is dead. He never came out, anyway." Mar-kai said. "Would you rather have to send everybody away with no jobs, no place to go, and abandon this place, simply because there's no one to inherit it? The locals don't need to know there was a were-vampire here, anyway. That would really hurt any business. He's dead, now."

Fohrel just looked at him. "And the hands?"

"We can tell them that the creature is dead. They, too, don't need to know that it was Delov. He is dead, now, and cannot harm anyone. They don't need the crush to moral that this would create ... not to mention the distrust it would make in everyone's hearts, no longer being sure who is what they appear to be." Mar-kai said. "We'll just leave it at that, and keep going. We have a very good business here, and most of the people here have no where else to go."

The others considered that for a very long time, contemplating the corpse of their former employer.

"Well, at least it's safe out, at night, now." Huteri said.

"Tolus would know." Fohrel said. "He spent a lot of time with Delov. And the Gnome?"

"Tolus we'll have to tell. The Gnome ... she's very good at her job, and until I get caught up on things, we can't afford to lose her work. With her, we can simply say that Delov is sick, for a time. Then once we're set, we can move her to other things, if we must."

"And Ton?" Huteri asked.

"Ton already knows." Ton said from behind Torj, having walked up. "Interesting turn of events, that." He remarked.

The other four turned and looked at him, in silence.

"Sounds like the best idea at the moment." Ton said. "Go for it. Let me know if you need help." He gestured loosely. "Though I think they ought to know he's dead ... even if you don't tell them that he and the thing are the same."

The other four considered that for a moment.

"There were certainly enough of us out here ... and it is dark ..." Fohrel said.

"Why not stick with the truth?" Ton asked. "The thing killed him. And it did." He gestured at the body. "Being the creature is what got him killed."

"You're a bloody good shot, by the way." Torj said, to Fohrel.

"Thanks."

"I'll take care of the body. We'll have a funeral in the morning." Ton said, stooping to pick up the body.

"Alright." Mar-kai said. "Let's go to the Quarters and tell them." He gestured for the rest to move out. They returned to the rest, as Ton carried the body away. Ton stayed missing for the rest of the day and night, while Tolus was summoned from the house. When everyone was assembled in the dining room of the Quarters building, Mar-kai called for everyone's attention.

"I have some good news, and some bad news." Mar-kai said, pausing for a moment to make sure he had every one's attention. "The creature that had plagued us for so long has been killed, this day. Its reign of terror is at an end, and we may now travel about safely at night once more, as in the old days." He paused, as the hands all cheered. Loudest of all was Tolus, in the back with his booming voice. When the cheers died down, Markkai waited a moment to continue. "Alas, but our esteemed employer has also died this night." He said, the announcement falling into the silence that followed. "He did not survive, being too close to the creature." Mar-kai said, slowly. "Ton is preparing his body for a funeral in the morning. I wish you all to attend, if you would." He paused for a moment to compose carefully what he said next. "We will not make anyone leave ... you may go if you wish, but you all are welcome to stay on in your current capacity. Delov had no family or heirs, and there is no one to hand the ranch to. We are here, and here we can stay. We have a very good set up, we know what we are doing. We can continue on, the same, though it will be trickier, without Delov's guidance. Thankfully, Lillia has been learning in the end that Delov worked, and she can help us get back on our feet." Mar-kai gestured to Lillia. "If you would."

Lillia only nodded, in silence.

"This, we hope, will allow us to continue on in Delov's absence. We will inherit the ranch, and we will keep it on, in his memory. We will continue his legacy of the incredible ridali." He stopped, and bowed his head as a low, heavy thrum came from the gathered hands. The heart of the sound came from the Dtri, a sound of mourning and reverence. The others carried along with it in the best fashion that they could, adding their own emotion to the sound.

The next morning, lit by many lanterns in the still complete darkness, Mar-kai found Ton working next to two coffins.

"What is this?" Mar-kai asked, looking in the longer one. It held Delov, cleaned up and dressed in new clothing. He actually looked more or less intact, rigged up like that, in proper funeral style.

"Funeral." Ton said, lifting the lid of the second coffin. "You need a bad guy in full light for this to work, you know."

Mar-kai moved over to the other coffin, and looked in. A terribly mutilated, gruesome looking monster lay therein, and Mar-kai initially cringed from it. "What *is* that?"
"It used to be a wolf that Delov had snacked on. A bit of majick, and it was transformed from wolf to ...that. Something suitably dangerous and horrible looking." Ton said.
"Sometimes, Ton," Mar-kai said, closing the lid. "... your brilliance is scary."
"You're welcome." Ton replied. "Is everyone up?" he asked, picking up and situating Delov's coffin suitably for the funeral. "I know Tolus is ... he's digging the graves."
"They're up. They're also eating. Apparently, Deilo is rather good in the kitchen, even by himself. It's a thin meal ... but even that isn't being entirely eaten." Mar-kai said.
"At least they're eating." Ton said. "I think it's time to bring them all out." He said, walking around the area and hanging lanterns on a series of poles that Mar-kai had not previously noticed. The lanterns burned brightly, making the morning seem more like morning, despite the darkness imposed upon it.
Mar-kai watched for a moment, before going to fetch everybody.
The hands of the ranch assembled on the hilltop where Ton had set things up, and the funeral was held in more or less silence. Each Race had its own way of doing funerals, and it would be impossible to fit each one into the same event, and thus it was left as a silent paying of respect. No one knew what the customs for Delov's people were, and thus could not do him in his own fashion, either.
After an appropriate time had passed, Ton spoke up. "Rest in peace." He said, simply, before he and Tolus carefully moved the coffin over to where the grave had been dug. They set it down in the hole, and with one gigantic hand, Tolus buried him one handful at a time.
The funeral over, the hands all gathered around to take a look at the 'monster' that had done their employer in. Many took one look, and walked away, disgusted. Others stood and stared in disbelief. Others still just looked, in utter fascination.
"What *is* that thing??" One of them asked.
"I haven't the slightest idea." Another answered. "I've never heard of such a creature."
When interest waned, Ton and Tolus buried that coffin, too, though not on the hilltop where Delov was buried. That would have been improper and would have caused a major uproar. Instead, they took it to the bottom of the hill, and buried it there.
The hands all went to take care of their daily chores and work, then, working hard to make the ranch go on. Mar-kai went

to the main house, and spent the next several weeks struggling through everything that Delov had managed before. He was very grateful for Lillia's help, though she did not know everything.
There was going to be a long period of trial and error. Thankfully, no one would go hungry. The ranch supplied its own foods for worker and beast alike. However, the other things that were brought from town might have to be done without, now and again, until the little nuances of running a massive ranch were figured out.

Time passed slowly, as the ranch got back up to speed, everyone working hard to make sure they did all they could do to help. The dust in the skies cleared one week to the day after the funeral, allowing work to be done as normal once more. The people that came to the ranch looking to purchase never noticed a difference in operations, as they had rarely ever seen Delov himself, anyway. They placed their orders for various animals – sometimes in specific colors – with Mar-kai, who then had Torj round up a team to go get animals to fill the order.

Eventually, things settled out into a smooth rhythm again, and progress was made once more.

On one bright sunny morning, Mutsgae and Horus were surprised by a visit from Deilo out at the pens, where cattle were being branded and sorted.

"Hoy." Horus said. "What are you doing out here?" he asked.

"Ton gave me the morning off." Deilo said, leaning on the corral railing.

"Why?" Mutsgae asked.

"He's a sentimental sort, I guess." Deilo said, with a shrug.

"What is that supposed to mean?" Horus asked.

"Do you know what day today is, Horus?" Deilo asked, looking at him.

Horus thought about it for a long moment. Unable to think of anything specific about the day, he shook his head. "No."

"It's the 14th, Jousdy." Mutsgae said, very practically.

Deilo only laughed. "Very good, Muts. It's the one year mark from when we first arrived here. It doesn't seem like that long ago, does it?"

"One year?" Horus asked, thoughtfully. "That's not right. We haven't had winter yet."

Deilo shrugged. "According to Ton, winter doesn't happen here like it did in Paratora. No snow. Barely gets any cooler. Winter happened ... we just never noticed it."

"Incredible." Mutsgae said. "Winter with no snow?"

"Yeah. Blows the mind, doesn't it?"
"Yeah." Horus said. "Bummer. I liked snow."
"Not me." Mutsgae said. "I always got lost in it."
　　Horus only grinned, and thunked Mutsgae's head lightly with a hoof. Mutsgae opened his jaws slightly, letting out a low, throbbing rumble. Horus only laughed, and set his foot down on the ground again. "Well, does that mean you're going to help us out, here, or what?"
　　"Maybe." Deilo said, setting one foot on the railing.

Chapter Four

The Dragon's Army

Far away, in the wide range of mountains that bordered the far northern edge of Gnaria, Senior Mage William walked out of a large wide tent that housed him and the rest of his Troop ... one other Mage, and a Dragon. He nodded to another Mage he passed, walking up the row of tents to a crossroad, also lined with more large tents.

It was there that his counterpart, Junior Mage Timothy, met him. "Hey. I got here as soon as I could. What's going on?" Timothy asked.

"I don't know yet, but we've been summoned to Building 6 just as soon as Guiran gets here." William answered, pulling a pair of grey fleece-lined gloves on. He and Timothy both wore the same garb as every other Human around them, in the Dragon's Army base. They wore heavy weight loose brown breeches, loose grey shirts, and a short, heavy tan traveling type cape. It was all designed to keep them warm in the high reaches of the sky, and were somewhat uncomfortably warm on the ground.

A large blue Dragon walked past them, carefully not stepping on any of the Humans in its path, large powerful wings held up high on its back, out of the way. It was a large, powerful creature, sleek and streamlined, with a solid crest adorning the head. The wings attached to the back just behind the shoulders, and only at the joint. The membrane of the wing spread out from there, supported on strong wing fingers. The tail tapered gracefully to a fine end, with no spade of any kind. The front feet doubled as hands, having a full set of fully mobile fingers and opposable thumbs. The back feet were far simpler in contrast, meant only for walking, and launching into the sky. The massive thighs of the Dragon were built specifically for that purpose ...getting the creature and its payload into the sky quickly.

Timothy waved at the Dragon, who nodded in reply.
"Where *is* Guiran, anyway?"
"Out feeding. Or, he was. He should be back soon."
"Ah."

Timothy was no younger ... and not technically junior to William. The two were in most cases equals, their denoting rank simply signifying who rode in which position on the Dragon's back.

A large black hole opened in the sky, high above the teeming Base, and a brilliant yellow-tinted green Dragon flew out of it. The hole itself closed up just as soon as the Dragon was clear of it, leaving not a trace in the sky to betray it had ever been there. The Dragon looked around, gliding for a time, before starting a fast descent in a tight circular pattern. Opening his wings fully just above the ground, he set down gently, reaching down with his back legs before settling fully to the ground.

"Ah." Timothy said.
"Greetings, Guiran." William said. "How far, exactly, did you go?"
"Not far." Guiran said, folding his wings atop his back. "Your message just caught me in the middle of a carcass, is all. I thought I might as well finish the meal, since I had gone to all the trouble of catching it."
"In most cases, that is fine. But we've been summoned by the Council."
"Ah. I imagine Bahran gave them another mission to delegate out?" Guiran asked, as the three started walking down the adjoining pathway.
"I have no idea." William said. "Maybe, maybe not. Bahran stays pretty busy, himself."
"Yes, that he does." Guiran said, with a nod, following along behind his Mages after stepping to one side to allow another Dragon to pass, going the other way.

The three walked in silence to the designated building. There, they were surprised to find one of the Council Mages standing outside the building. "Ah, there you are." He said. The Mage was old enough to have retired more or less from active duty, since he had survived long enough to get that old. Having more experience than most Mages ever acquired before their time came, he was one of the Council, a group of Mages who talked things over with the leader of the Army, the Dragon Bahran.

Often times, the Council's ideas and strategies saved many a life in the ongoing battle for balance in the world.

Most of the men in the Army were the original Mages from Earth, when that war had been won, and the entire Army had been shifted over to this world, where the previous group of Dragons had failed miserably in regaining the balance. Very few of them were the Humaniod 'men' of this world. The two species looked a lot alike, although they were by no means the same race.

"Here we are." William said. "What's going on?"

"Oh, just the usual. Chaos beyond all hope of repair." The Council member laughed. "Anyway ... we still, more or less, have no idea where the heart of the problem lies."

"We know that." William interrupted. "Get to the point."

"I was getting there." He said, holding up a hand. "It has been discovered that this world is falling apart around us."

Timothy sighed. "We know that, *too*."

The Council Mage frowned at him. "I mean *literally*." He said. "It is falling *apart*. As in, great earthquakes, fit to swallow entire countries. As in, massive volcanoes blowing their tops sky high. As in, this little globe we're sitting on is *coming apart at the seams*."

"That's not good. What caused that?" William asked.

"Well ... at the heart of it all probably lies the chaos, evil malice, and imbalance, yadda yadda." He said, as the two nodded. "But the most prominent symptom is the drain the people are having on the world. Ever since magic was lost, they created and started using majick. That creation and use is killing the planet. We have reached tolerance. Anything more will destroy the whole world, turn it all into floating gobs of rock."

"And how are we going to fix *that*?" William asked. "We can't very well convince everyone to stop using majick."

"No, we can't." the Council Mage agreed. "However, we just *might* be able to restore the magic."

"How in hell are we going to pull that off? That takes an understanding of this world that we don't yet have!" Timothy exclaimed.

"You're right. We don't have that."

"It will also take gobs of energy. Probably everything the Army's got, if that will be enough." William said.

"There, you are also right. We have a plan, after a fashion." The Council member said.

"And?" Guiran asked, after contemplating the shining blue sky. Over the two Army Bases were the only places that the sky was blue. Everywhere else it was the odd purple hue from having had too much majick drained out of it.

"We're going to send you three to speak to the Wizard. He owes us a few ... maybe he can provide the understanding of the world that we need to pull this off."

"You're building a plan around a *maybe*?" William asked, doubtfully.

"It's the best we've got at the moment. For now, we've got three Troops working on finding some way to give our energy a boost." The Council Mage said. "Go to the tower, or wherever that fishy guy is hiding now, and talk to him. Maybe he even knows how to give us a boost."

Timothy shook his head. "You really think he knows that much?"

"We're *hoping* he knows that much. If he doesn't ... we're in deep shit."

"No kidding."

"Be on your way, then. And safe flying." With that, he turned and walked back into the building.

"The world is really bad off." Guiran said, following the two Mages back towards their tent, where the flying harness was stashed.

"Apparently, worse off than we thought it was." William said. "Hopefully, if this does work, it will give us the time we need to get this mess back on the road to recovery, so we don't have to do it again."

"They haven't even figured out which plane the imbalance is on, have they?" Timothy asked.

"No, we haven't. For that matter, we don't even know *who*, or *what* is pushing this little world along the path to destruction. Frankly, I think we were lucky, last time. After all ... who'd have thought that the being trying to destroy Earth was hiding as a *rosebush*??" William asked, walking into the tent.

"We were lucky, indeed." Guiran said, stopping outside. For now, he did not need to go inside. "It is no wonder that the Dragons that were sent here ended up so off course and killed all the Wizards but the one. Maybe we shall fare better yet again."

"What makes you think that?" William asked, coming back out of the tent with Guiran's harness. He tossed part of it to Timothy, who helped him get the massive thing on Guiran, who crouched low to aid their efforts.

"Well, we did it once and won. We have you men, the Sikes, and the Nymphs. Those are all things that the original Dragons did not have. They were only just themselves. We have your help, and you are all capable of so much more than we."

"You're just blowing our horns, like usual." Timothy laughed, finishing up the last sturdy buckle.

"Hey, *someone's* gotta do it. Or you'd all get so down that we wouldn't get anywhere." Guiran remarked, straightening. "I don't think we need the spear launcher, for this trip."

"I agree." William concurred, regarding the ballista-type device that was sitting next to the tent. It was designed to attach to the harness where it would sit across a Dragon's hips, to be fired by the Junior Mage, who always rode backwards. He turned, and jumped at Guiran. Giving himself a telekinetic boost, he sailed all the way up, to land on his feet atop Guiran's back. He slipped down, straddling the Dragon and slipping into his harness. He tightened the various straps that would keep him aboard through most any maneuver Guiran could accomplish. Before he was finished, Timothy was seated back to back with him, also strapping in.

"Okay. All ready back here." Timothy said. "Let's go."

"And we're off." Guiran crouched as if to launch into the sky. But then he paused, and straightened, to merely amble off down the lane.

"That was really weird." Timothy remarked.

Guiran walked out of the area that held all the tents, and climbed farther up the mountainside a short ways, pulling himself up onto a flat chunk of rock that jutted out over the Base. It was a favorite spot to go for sunning for some of the Dragons ... and made an excellent launching base for those who bothered to walk to it, first. Guiran paused for a moment to look down at the Base. At its center were the six Buildings that housed various essentials to the Base, and surrounding it was rows upon rows of the large white tents. The trees that grew everywhere overshadowed the rows of tents. The Army had left them unmolested when they had moved into the area. Around the exterior of the Base, however, had been cleared enough to allow a long track to be operable. Even as Guiran watched for the moment, a Dragon appeared through a hole, towing a winged cart behind him. The Dragon coasted around, and released the cart from his grip, allowing it to glide down on its own and land neatly on the track. It rolled most of the way around the Base, even as another cart was taking off from a short, steeply-rising track. A Dragon flew over it, grasped the pole that reached out ahead of the cart, and towed it up the slanted track and into the air, where the stiff wings kept it aloft behind the Dragon.

Looking up, Guiran waited until there was sufficient space in the busy sky to allow him to take off. When he saw a clear area, he launched up into the air with his powerful rear legs, snapping his great wings open at the apex of the leap. He hung there for a split second, before a second strong beat carried him higher into the air. Once he had gained enough altitude, Guiran leveled off and coasted for a short ways, before a dark hole appeared in the sky ahead of him. He flew straight into it, unblinking.

Over a luckily vacant field near the sprawling city of Kentalic, an identical hole appeared in the sky, and Guiran flew out, not a whole second after he had entered the first one. In almost no time, they had traversed halfway across the vast Gnarian valley. Guiran landed quickly, before he was seen, and hunkered down low. Both of the Mages stripped out of the harness and quickly slid off.

"I'll wait here." Guiran said, before disappearing as his hide quickly changed colors. He went from looking like a large Dragon to looking like a heap of hay with bushes growing around the base. If anyone took the time to look closely, they might be able to tell that it was merely a chameleon effect, and that he was really a Dragon. But most people never looked that closely at hay piles.

"Alright. Let's go, then." William said, striking out for the nearby road. Timothy followed close behind him, occasionally stopping to pull a burr out of his pant legs.

The Dragon's Army was more or less a secret from the world in general ... only select individuals knew of them. The population at large only knew of dragons as the strange looking beasts that lived in untamed wilderness, chasing ybexi and other wild animals around ... not to mention any unlucky travelers. A big, intelligent Dragon capable of sustaining flight for long periods was unheard of. The Mages also were secret from most, not wanting to get embroiled in anyone's feud or war. They were not there to fight kings for kings, or anything else ridiculous like that. They were there to run far scarier things out, and restore balance and peace, where death came only in due time, rather than in mass extinctions of areas. Usually, their fight happened on the same world, but on a different plane of existence.

The two Mages looked like nothing more than two men walking into the city to most, and that was how they liked it. They walked all the way to the city, and up through the heart of it to the massively tall, twisting Tower that stood at the very center.

The Tower had been destroyed completely by a chaos-formed storm, in an attempt to kill the last remaining Wizard the world had. The storm had failed utterly due to the Army having rescued him from the structure. Later on they had rebuilt the Tower for him. The new Tower was now storm-proof. The mind that had originally sent the storm to destroy it apparently was aware of that fact, as no repeat storms had been sent.

At the main entrance to the Tower, the guards stopped the pair.

"No one may enter here unless invited." A guard informed them.

William looked at Timothy, who shrugged. They turned, and walked away. "That was new." Timothy said. "It wasn't that way, before, was it?"

"I had heard that it was ... I was hoping to be able to walk in, but it doesn't look like we can." William paused in the street, and looked at the top of the tower ... where the Wizard's main work chambers were. He closed his eyes while letting his mind explore the upper reaches of the tower. He could feel every wall, every corridor ... and at a deeper inspection, every being that occupied the area. After a moment he looked at Timothy. "Let's go inside." He decided, gesturing to a nearby building. The two walked inside, and paused in a more or less unoccupied corner. "I'm going to 'port in ...are you going to want to come along?"

"Sure, why not." Timothy said. "Should I look, or are you going to let me follow you?"

"You can follow." William said, before opening his mind to greater reaches.

The pair vanished suddenly from the corner, leaving not a trace behind. When William completed the teleportation, they were standing in a corridor far overhead. Just as soon as they arrived he fell against the stone wall, and drew a deep breath.

"Are you alright?" Timothy asked.

"I ... I'll be fine." William answered, waving him off. "I wasn't expecting the wards ... those are new. I had to fight them, mid-'port, to get us in here."

Timothy looked at him for a while, a concerned expression on his face.

After a moment's rest William pushed off the wall, and walked over to the window. "We're really high up." he noted, before turning, and heading down the hall. Timothy followed in silence, well aware of exactly how high up they were. The two walked down the corridor until they came to a majickally locked door.

Timothy held an open hand over the lock, and worked a magic spell in his mind. The majick, being only a fraction as strong as true magic, gave out without much resistance, and Timothy laid a hand on the latch to open it. It took a tad more effort than he had expected to push the door open, though. Once it was open far enough to permit his head, Timothy peeked in to see what the problem was.

There was a heavy table blocking the doorway, completely covered in heavy, dusty tomes. It looked like the Wizard was in the middle of something big. Timothy put his shoulder to the door, shoving it farther open with a grunt. The table moved grudgingly, and once it was far enough, Timothy slid in, and around the table. He grabbed the end of it, and lifted it to move it aside, allowing to door to open farther with next to no resistance.

William pushed it open the rest of the way and walked in, looking around.

"Busy fish." Timothy remarked, pushing the door closed again.

"Apparently, we came in by a door not used anymore." William noted, glancing at the tomes. The pages were covered in a script that he couldn't read, and as such it did not hold his attention.

"Apparently." Timothy answered as he moved the table back to its original position.

William pulled his gloves off, and tucked them under his belt, as he walked around the cluttered room, looking at various items. At one table, he paused, and looked back. "Timothy. Look at this." He pointed at the tabletop.

Timothy walked over, and took a look. The top of the table was formed as a hard map of the land of Gnaria, and a great deal of the territory surrounding it. Cities marked out in miniscule detail. Timothy squinted, bending over to take a closer look. "Surely he's not planning on extending his area of influence, is he?"

"I don't think so." William said, running a finger along a crack in the table. "I think this is what he's concentrating on ... keeping Gnaria safe from the natural disasters."

"That has to take a lot of energy, considering the state of things." Timothy said, straightening.

"It might be why we felt the majickal spells on the mountains weakening, awhile back." William said. "He can't keep the guard spells active *and* do this."

"I imagine not."

They both turned around when they heard a door at the far end of the room swing open. Through a loosely filled bookrack, they saw the Wizard seemingly float into the room. Taller than either of them, the Wizard appeared to be a fish-like being in a long robe. And his movements made him look like he floated across the floor, rather then stepped. Many a Mage suspected that he possessed no legs at all, under that robe, and was actually really floating.

The Wizard pushed the door closed again, round protruding eyes rolling around until he had seen the entire room ... and the Mages in it.

"What are you doing here?" he asked, moving away from the door and folding his arms across his chest.

"We came to talk to you."

"I won't even bother to ask you how you got in here. I can't seem to keep you people out. What do you want now?"

Timothy waved a hand at the table. "We see you are aware of the disasters going on."

The Wizard just looked at him for a long silent moment, his wide mouth drawing a straight line across his face. After a moment, he sighed, and let his arms down. "Indeed." He said, moving over to where the table stood. He looked at it for a moment, and shook his head slightly. "I fear I cannot keep Gnaria safe for much longer."

"We fear for the entire planet." William said, leaning on a nearby bookcase casually. "The whole world is coming apart, and we were hoping we could get you to help us stop it."

The Wizard looked at him in silence for a moment. "What do you think I could possibly do for the whole world, when keeping *Gnaria* safe is killing me?"

"The reason why the world is coming apart is still eluding us." William said, ignoring the rolling of the Wizard's eyes. "However, until we find the cause, we believe we can treat this symptom, and hold it together until we *do* find the cause."

"So, what's holding you up?" The Wizard asked. "Go ahead and do it, then."

"We don't know how." Timothy answered. "We don't know this world that well, yet."

"Ah." The Wizard said, moving away, back across the room. "There's always a catch."

"We were hoping you could supply that input." William said, pointedly.

"I can't. If I take any of my attention away from my current task, there won't be a Gnaria left." The Wizard said.

"We need that knowledge." Timothy protested. "Or there won't be a *world* left!"

The Wizard only frowned at him.

"He's right." William said. "There won't. We're not entirely sure that this will work completely, but it would help a lot."

"What, exactly, are you planning, anyway?" The Wizard asked.

"The reason the world is coming apart, symptomatically, is because too much majick has been stolen from the world. It has reached a critical point. We *might* have the energy to re-infuse the world with magic, and get it enough back to balance so that we can figure out what the underlying cause is. Because majick use, all by itself, won't do this. Not in this time frame, at any rate." William said. "But, to do that, we need intimate knowledge of the world, and how it works."

The Wizard sighed. "I can't help you."

Timothy opened his mouth to say something, but stopped, when the Wizard held up a hand.

"I can't help you ... I am too tied up, too tired, and don't really know all that you need to know. *However*, I know of somebody who can help you not only in your quest for knowledge, he can also help you exponentially expand your magic casting." The Wizard said.

William's brows shot up. "Who might this be?"

"His name..." The Wizard moved across the room again, picking up a small statue and carrying it back. "Is Malici." He set the small statue on the table's corner. Timothy looked down at it, to see a small form of a square-standing winged horse with, apparently, and extra set of ears on his forehead.

"A four eared Pegasus?" Timothy asked.

"No. Two of those are horns ... I apologize, they are broken off... The statue did not survive unharmed when the storm hit." The Wizard said. "A formidable warrior, in his day."

William just looked at the statue for a moment. "Why do you have a statue of somebody?"

"Malici has been missing from society for hundreds of years." The Wizard answered. "He has gone from fact, to legend. Soon he will fade to myth. The SwordDancers know a great deal about him ... indeed it was he who *made* the SwordDancers who they are today."

"Hundreds of years ago." Timothy looked at the Wizard. "Isn't he dead, then?"

"By no means. He is akin to me ... he does not age. He tired of society, the endless feuding, and he left. Off to his little hidey hole."

"And where is that?" William asked.

"I am not entirely sure. We were not exactly on speaking terms when he left. I can make an educated guess, however ... and if I am right, then neither you nor I can get there."

"Why is that?" Timothy asked, growing more concerned for William ... he looked a little paler than he ought to.

"Because there are guards on the area. No one with any magical, or majickal ability or tendencies may enter there. If they do, they die immediately. I know not all of your power stems from magic, but simply that you have a hold on magic will do you in. Only those with no magic or majick can enter. And even then ... the one entry way is heavily booby trapped." The Wizard said. "I do not recommend going there."

William looked at Timothy, who looked back in silence. *We have those who haven't finished training yet ... magic is the last course at the Cathedral.* Timothy suggested in silence.

I wouldn't trust a Mage who isn't fully trained ... much less with this sort of mission. For one thing, they have no experience. William replied.

"I wish you two would not think at each other." The Wizard said. "If you want me to help you, you will have to be honest."

William looked at him. "We were merely going over possibilities ... thought is faster than speech."

"Indeed. And what have you come up with?" The Wizard asked.

"Nothing. Timothy suggested a Mage that wasn't trained to magic yet ... but that would be a bad idea, I think." William answered.

The Wizard nodded slightly. "I agree. I could hire someone qualified to go in and fetch him out?"

"Would that work?"

"I don't know. And I won't, until it is tried." The Wizard confessed.

"Finding someone who has never messed with majick will be rather difficult." Timothy pointed out. "And to send them where they are more than likely to get killed just getting there? Who would do that?"

"There are people who would do anything, for enough money." The Wizard said, waving one webbed hand dismissively. "As for majick ... I think, that so long as it was long enough ago ... one could get through. Majick traces do wear off after awhile."

"How long a while?" Timothy asked.

"Depends on the heaviness of the use. Could be anywhere from a year, to a lifetime." The Wizard said.

"Does such a person exist in this warped land?" Timothy asked.

The Wizard frowned at him. "Be careful what you say, little man. This is my land you speak of." He moved to a large window, where a large mirror lay on a table, reflecting light at the ceiling, where it was caught by more mirrors and redirected to various locations throughout the room. The two mages followed him over, curiously. "This is a scrying mirror ... the only one that is this big. It is potent enough to see anything I want it to show me ... provided I supply it with enough majick." The Wizard looked at William. "Unfortunately, I have none to spare for such a task."

William looked over at Timothy, who nodded. "I can supply magic, for a time." Timothy volunteered.

"Alright, then." The Wizard stretched both hands flat out over the mirror, and began to hum almost inaudibly. The mirror came to life, the image flickering and wobbling. "Now." The Wizard said.

Timothy held one hand out, palm up, with his other hand palm forward over his wrist. He worked a complex spell through his mind, and released the flow that came to him to the mirror. William watched for a moment, and then reached over to make slight adjustments to Timothy's hands, making the flow easier on Timothy.

The image in the mirror flew quickly, showing a series of pictures all too fast to follow in the slightest, until it started to slow. It stopped on a grassy plain.

"I have found what you seek." The Wizard said. "I will send for someone to fetch them here."

"How soon will they arrive?" William asked.

"I can dispatch a message to a rider near there. They can be there today. As for the return trip ... that could take awhile."

"We don't have awhile." William said.

"I can't speed their journey without employing majick." The Wizard said, letting the mirror sleep. Timothy was glad it was over, letting his arms down. The amount of magic he had just channeled made him weary.

"If we supplied more energy, could you extend your hold on the land?" William asked. "Even once they are here, they will have to set out to go find this Malici."

"True. I will see." The Wizard moved across the room again. He touched a few items, and a tall object sitting on the table there flashed brilliantly. "The message has been sent. They will be on their way by tonight."

"What makes you think they'll come, just like that?" William asked.

The Wizard looked at him. "When I summon, my people come. Always."

Timothy grunted. "Okay." He looked around. "And the land?"

"Give me a while." The Wizard moved over to the table loaded with tomes, and started looking through them. After a long period of nothing to do, Timothy wandered over to watch. "It looks like it might. If you can somehow supply magic into the spell ... I wouldn't have to change it at all, and the area covered would expand by twelve times." The Wizard said, looking at them. "It will take a lot, however ... a great deal more than was used for the mirror. Can you do that?"

"That would take several Dragons." William said. "But I think we can."

"I have no where to put several Dragons." The Wizard pointed out.

"That is not a problem. Dragons can channel from anywhere." William said. "Or so I have been told."

"We shall see, then." The Wizard said. "Go, then, and tell your Dragons." He waved a hand.

Timothy looked to William, then jumped forward in alarm as William crumpled to the floor unconscious. "William!" He stopped short, and then looked at the Wizard. "What, exactly, sort of wards did you have on this place?" he asked.

The Wizard just stared at William for a moment. "Only the usual."

"How many?"

"Thirteen."

"Oh, dear God."

Under the cover of night, Guiran climbed the tower, until he was able to look into the window of the room where William had been placed. "He doesn't look good." The Dragon observed.

"No, he doesn't. That 'port taxed him more than even he knew. But it looks like enough rest and he'll be right as rain. However ... I am not feeling so well, myself. I spent a lot, to find the people I told you about earlier."

"What can I do, then?"

"I have already spoken to the Council ... that took some energy, too. They say that we two are to stay put for the time being, and rest. We're to be here when those people get here. You, however, they want you to watch over the traveling party. We can't afford them to have serious mishaps along the way." Timothy said. "Good luck."

"That I can do. How do I find them?"

Timothy reached out, and let go of a small green disk that just floated in mid-air, in Timothy's telekinetic grasp. "The Wizard says this will lead you to them. It's keyed in to the messenger, actually."

Guiran reached up and took it out of the air with his own massive hand. "Alright. You take care, and take care of William. Trying to counter wards *while* 'porting sometimes kills people."

"I am aware of that." Timothy said. He then moved away from the window to watch over William's sleeping form.

Guiran let go of the tower, twisting backwards away from it. Once he was back upright in the flip, he opened his wings, and flew away, out into the inky black sky.

Chapter Five

The Tower

A human man on a brilliant blood bay horse rode up the lane to the main house on the Floating H ranch, and dismounted there, holding the reins as he walked up to the porch. Tolus watched him approach without comment.

"Where can I find the person who runs this place?" The man asked.

"Down at the barns, most likely." Tolus answered. "His name's Mar-kai."

"Thank you." He turned and walked towards the group of large barns, wondering which barn was the right one. When he reached the edge of the nearest barn, he just stopped and watched in amazement as a group of individuals of many races were working and training one of the huge ridali. Almost immediately he was spotted and Mar-kai walked over to him.

"How can I help you?" Mar-kai asked.

"I'm looking for Mar-kai."

"That'd be me." Mar-kai answered.

The man looked up at Mar-kai's towering furred form, and blinked. "Oh. Um ... I'm here with a summons for a few people that are here."

"Summons?" Mar-kai asked, blindsided. He had expected that this man was someone looking for animals. "From who?"

"The Wizard." The man said, pulling a scroll out of his saddlebag and handing it to Mar-kai. "The individuals listed therein are summoned to the city of Kentalic, to the Wizard's Tower, to meet with the Wizard himself." He said, as quickly as possible, expecting to be interrupted.

    Mar-kai heard him out, though he was frowning the whole while. He knew as well as anyone that those who were summoned to the Tower generally never came back out again. After a moment of frowning at the man, waiting for him to go on, Mar-kai decided that he wasn't going to keep talking after all. He lifted the scroll, and popped the seal on it, to see whom it was he was going to be robbed of.

    The very short list of names on it surprised him.

    "Why these?" Mar-kai asked.

    "I have no idea. I am only the messenger. But they're to report with all haste."

    "I can imagine." Mar-kai said, striding across the training grounds to the far barn. He spoke briefly with a hand there, who promptly turned and galloped off out toward the fields. Mar-kai then sent someone else to go get the others.

    When Deilo arrived, Ton came with him. "What is going on?" Ton asked, rather irritated.

    "They've been summoned to the Tower." Mar-kai said, handing Ton the scroll. Ton opened the scroll in silence, and read the few words scrawled on it with a frown.

    "Why?" Ton asked.

    Mar-kai only shrugged. He spoke briefly to another hand that approached him, and they too hurried away into the nearer barn.

    The messenger just started openly at Ton.

    Lillia arrived next, astride her bird. She landed on Deilo's shoulder, and stayed there. "What's going on?" she asked.

    "Seems we're fixing to go on a trip." Deilo said.

    "Oh. To where?"

    Mar-kai turned to the messenger. "Go wait by the house."

    The man nodded hastily, and led his horse back over to the house, as a ridali and cart pulled into the training area. Training had already come to a halt as everyone watched the unusual happenings. Out of the cart came Horus and Mutsgae both, and they walked over to where the others were gathered.

    "Now, you four. Listen up. It appears that the Wizard has heard of you – odd as that is – and wants you to come to the Tower in which he resides. That's in Kentalic, a city a good bit to the north of here." Mar-kai said, once they were all together. "I will not send you off blind ... I have never heard of anyone ever coming back out of that Tower, dead or alive. Ever. I doubt anyone else has."

To that Ton only nodded.

"Why the Wizard is interested in you is anybody's guess ... I can only wish you the best of luck." Mar-kai said, as a second ridali and cart came out of the nearest barn. The driver brought it over to where they were all standing, and stopped the cart.

"Horus, I trust you have learned to drive?"

"Yes." Horus answered.

"Good. Here is a beast and cart to carry you on your way."

"Why should we go, if no one ever comes out?" Deilo asked. "Why not just head out, away?"

"You can't. The Wizard can see you at any time, and wields the power to drop you dead anywhere in Gnaria if you tick him off. You'll never make it through the mountains, much less over the border." Mar-kai said. "Since he has summoned you, you can count on his watching your progress to the Tower, to make sure you go."

"That stinks. What did we ever do??" Deilo asked.

"I don't know." Mar-kai said. "This ridali will allow you to travel fast enough to be safe from any sort of bandits ... you should be able to use the cart all the way to the city. But if not, there is a saddle stored under the cart. It can carry you all, should you need it."

"Thank you." Lillia said.

"Good luck to you all." Mar-kai said.

The four all climbed into the wagon, and found that it was well stocked for a long journey with bags and barrels of food, water, and other supplies. The hand gave the lines to Horus, and hopped down out of the wagon.

"Here." Ton said, lifting more than the usual bit of himself free of the ground to reach over the side of the wagon. He extended a hand to Deilo, and dropped a small but heavy sack into Deilo's hands.

"What is this?" Deilo asked.

"Money. In case you should need anything." Ton said. "Spend it wisely."

"Thank you."

"Safe journey, what ever awaits you." Ton said, backing away from the wagon.

"The messenger waits for you at the house." Mar-kai said.

Horus urged the ridali forward, and discovered that this particular animal was one of the well-trained ones. They pulled up to the house, and the man by his horse looked at the wagon doubtfully.

"How quick can you travel like that?" he asked.

"As quick as you like." Horus replied. "Lead on."

The man shook his head, but climbed back into the saddle. Once he was set, he kneed his animal forward into a quick trot. Horus let him get a short ways before starting the wagon moving, not wanting to terrify the horse too badly. The ridali eased along after the horse, not even trotting yet, itself, but easily keeping up.

Once he had reached the end of the good road that was the ranch lane, the rider stopped to look back and see how far behind the wagon was. He was startled to find it swerving sharply to avoid running him over. He shook his head, and kneed his mount on once more, headed down the poor track that served for a road. Horus guided his ridali after him, headed up the rise towards the butte that jutted out of the land there.

It had been just more than a year since they had last seen that land mark. They had gone into the ranch, and then never came back out again, always busy. Mar-kai was the only one to leave the ranch, and only at intervals to fetch certain supplies from town.

Traveling at the slow speed that the horseman was setting, it took them nearly a half-day to reach the small town, and there they stopped. The messenger waved them off the wagon.

"We stop here for a meal." He said.

Horus tied the ridali to a rail though it wouldn't even begin to stop it should it take a notion. The foursome then followed the messenger into a low building that passed for the town's inn. In the front room, they sat down and had a hot meal on coin that the messenger furnished. Little was said over the meal, beyond finding out that the messenger's name was Lianel.

After they had eaten, they all went back outside again, and the foursome all climbed back into the wagon. Lianel considered their wagon and ridali, and then instructed them to wait there. He rode to the edge of town, where he gave his horse to someone there. They led the animal away as Lianel walked back to the wagon.

"Would you mind terribly if I rode with you?" he asked.

"No. We can travel faster, without the horse." Deilo said, making room.

Lianel thought that was an odd statement, but did not say anything about it as he climbed into the wagon, throwing his saddlebags down next to a pair of water barrels.

"Ready?" Horus asked.

"Yeah." Deilo said.

Horus turned the wagon, and had the ridali walk out of town. When they reached the end of town, Horus stopped and looked back. "Where are we going from here?" he asked.

Lianel got up, and moved up to the front of the wagon. "That way. Just follow the road." He said. "Until we reach the next village up."

"Okay. You might want to hang on."

Lianel gave him a strange look, but placed a hand on the edge of the wagon to hang on.

Horus shook his head, and slapped the lines across the ridali's back, calling for it to move out briskly.

The ridali lunged forward like it had been waiting for that call, hitting the harness hard. The wagon lurched forward, being towed along like it weighed nothing. Not having been hanging on adequately for such a maneuver, Lianel came free and tumbles to the back of the wagon. He came to a stop half off the back of the wagon, where Mutsgae had seized his leg in his jaws. Lianel gasped in shock at the ground whizzing past his head, and then curled back up again, grabbing for anything solid.

"He did say hang on." Deilo laughed, securely holding onto the side of the wagon, himself.

"Indeed!" Lianel said. "What *is* that thing? Is it possessed?"

"Not at all. It's a ridali. That's how ridali are." Deilo answered, as Mutsgae released Lianel's leg.

Lianel rubbed his leg, but was happy that there weren't any holes punched in it. "How did you tame that thing, much less train it like that?" he asked, referring to Mutsgae.

Deilo only laughed, before Mutsgae replied; "I'm not an animal."

"...oh. Apologies. Thanks for stopping me before I fell out."

Mutsgae only grunted, resting his chin on his front feet as the wagon sailed along fast enough to make most of the bumps miniscule.

"Is this as fast as it goes, and how long can it do this?" Lianel asked.

"What?" Horus asked, nearly deafened by the wind.

"This is akin to an easy trot, for your horse." Deilo answered. "It can do this all day long, and go even faster, if need be. But with a wagon on board ... that can be dangerous."

"I can imagine!" Lianel said.

They reached the next village by the end of the next day, the ridali 'trotting' the whole way, through the night. At the village they stopped for a full day to let it rest. It had been impossible to stop it at nightfall while on the road, as it had wanted to keep going. It was not often that it was allowed to just *go*, and keep going. The animal was enjoying itself thoroughly.

When they left the village, they struck out cross-country, heading away from the mountains. Deilo just sat in the back and watched them recede, remembering when they had come down out of those mountains into that village. It seemed like so long ago, and yet just yesterday, too.

This time, Horus worked on the beast until he got it stopped, and thereafter made it stop every night as they traveled across the country. Through open plains, over rolling hills, skirting clumps of forest, and working their way around a large marsh that took them two days to get past.

All the while Mutsgae sat in the bottom of the wagon, looking up. There was something up there that he could see, but he couldn't tell what it was, or why it appeared to be following them. It didn't really, as it was sometimes going the other way. But yet it was always there. When he had asked Deilo about it, Deilo had been unable to see it at all.

Far higher than even Mutsgae suspected, Guiran circled endlessly, watching the little wagon travel across the country. He could see everyone in it clearly, and everything that they were going to encounter. He had to keep circling, lest he leave the little wagon far behind. He glided on the stiff upper air currents, almost never beating his massive wings, just hanging there all day and all night, for days on end. He was beginning to grow weary, but he could –and would– stay there for much longer.

Thankfully, that strange little creature they had tied into the wagon was traveling at a decent pace. He had feared that the group might travel on horses or saurians, or worse yet, on foot. But they weren't. He also noted that the only things that seemed to have any majick about them were the messenger, and the animal in the harness. And the animal had it only as a part of its being ... apparently it was a creation, rather than a naturally evolved animal. Guiran tilted his wings, to begin yet another broad circle, watching as they forded the Drefi river just before dusk.

A week into their trip, they were nearly half way to the outskirts of Kentalic when they started being able to see the very top of the twisting Wizard's Tower. Deilo stood up in the back of the wagon, hanging onto the side. "What happens once we get there?" he asked.

Lianel only shrugged. "Depends on what the Wizard wants to see you for."

Deilo looked down at him. "Are we going to get to go back home?"

"Depends on what the Wizard wants."

"Can you say anything else?"

"Sure. What do you want me to say? I'm only the messenger, I don't know why he wants to see you. I have only ever been to Kentalic twice before, myself."

"Do people come back out of the Tower, once they've been in to see the Wizard?"

"Sure. But like I said, it all depends on what the Wizard wants to see you for."

"That's not very encouraging." Deilo said, sitting down. He pulled the bag next to him open, and pulled out a loaf of waybread. It was sweeter than any other variety he had eaten in previous travels. And he liked it better, too. It had more flavor, and wasn't as hard, though just as dry. He closed the pack again, and started pulling chunks off the loaf to eat. When Mutsgae suddenly opened his jaws wide, Deilo looked at him for a moment. Then he laughed, and tossed a chunk into Mutsgae's mouth. Mutsgae chewed on it for a moment, thoughtfully, then swallowed. "What do you think?" Deilo asked.

"I don't want any more." Mutsgae said, simply.

"Okay! More for me." Deilo said, munching happily.

"Uh, guys?" Horus asked, as Deilo gave a crumb to Lillia.

"What?" Deilo asked, before stuffing another bite in his mouth.

"I can't see the Tower any more." Horus said. "The sky is getting black."

"Rain?" Deilo asked, before getting one knee under him, one hand on the wagon edge to steady himself as the wagon hit a particularly rough patch.

"No. It's not a cloud. It's just ... dark."

"Weird. It's not near dark yet." Deilo managed to get to his feet, and Lianel stood next to him, as they both looked forward.

The sky was indeed getting black, and streaky. It looked down right sick. And it wasn't just the sky. The land in front of them was starting to get rather bad looking, morphing before their eyes. Plants withered and died, turning to dust. Animals started slinking away, looking dull and ill.

Horus started pulling on the ridali, trying to get it to stop before they ventured into the sickening area. "What is going on?!" He asked, pulling harder, even as the ridali was fighting to slow the wagon.

"I don't know." Lianel said. "I've never seen the like."

The wagon slowly came to a halt, and they all just stood there and watched as it got worse and worse. Then the ground began to cave in, collapsing as a large rift opened up. A few hundred yards in front of them, something very dark and indistinct crawled up out of the rift, stopping to rest on the edge as it looked around. Large, sharp horns sprouted from its head, narrow eyes glowing a fiery red. The only other thing that could be clearly seen were the razor sharp claws that it had climbed out with.

Lianel sucked in a sharp breath. "I don't believe it ... an *Elf!*" he hissed. "Turn us around, get us out of here!" he said, reaching for Horus.

"Sit down!" Horus commanded, pulling on the lines to get just that going. The ridali did not protest, spooked by the apparition before it.

As the wagon was turning, the group in the wagon heard the oddest deep hiccupping sound they had ever heard, as well as a sound that might have been heard when strong winds were rounding a sail. But there were no sails, and there was no wind to speak of.

Deilo sat down hard as Lianel collapsed atop him after losing his balance. Shoving Lianel off, Deilo got back up to his knees to look back at where the Elf was, even as the wagon started moving away. He saw three large *things* come flying out of the sky, each one splashing into the ground around the Elf. One of them glanced the Elf, and upon impact, the Elf was partially iced over, as well as all the other areas that had been hit. Deilo looked upwards, just in time to see Guiran come crashing out of the sky, jaws wide open, wings tucked tight, talons spread wide.

The Elf, also seeing the Dragon hurtling out of the sky, roared its fury, and tried to break the ice that held it captive.

The wagon topped a hill just as Guiran impacted the Elf heavily, and the both of them tumbled off the edge into the rift, slashing and tearing at each other. The last of Guiran's tail vanished a split instant before the entire rift disappeared from view, the wagon having gone down the far side of the hill.

Deilo turned to look at Lianel. "Did you see that?!" He asked.

Lianel didn't respond, his face stuck in an expression of pure shock and terror.

Deilo took that to mean he had seen it, too. "Muts?" He asked, looking for the Lizard.

"I saw it." Mutsgae answered quietly, as the wagon thundered its way back the way it had come earlier in the day. "It was the biggest honking flying lizard I have ever seen."

"No kidding!" Deilo said. "I would say it was a dragon, but it looked nothing like the dragons we saw in the mountains."

"What's this, now?" Horus asked, concentrating on keeping the ridali from hitting anything with the wheels that might overturn the speeding wagon.

"Something came down out of the sky and attacked that Elf-thing!" Deilo said, excitedly, even as a thunderous clap sounded from the other side of the hill. Deilo slapped both hands over his ears, to protect his hearing. But Horus could only fold his ears down flat. Lianel never moved a muscle, still staring.

"I think he's in shock!" Lillia shouted, looking at Lianel, even as she covered her own small ears.

Mutsgae also covered his head in general with both front feet, groaning in misery.

The ridali topped the next hill, then suddenly swerved to one side, squalling in terror. The wagon tipped dangerously as it followed the ridali around. Deilo saw what had caused the animal to shy ... there was a pack of large cats sitting there, where they hadn't been before, surrounding a fresh kill. The cats looked up at the swerving ridali and wagon, then scattered in all directions that were generally away from the large animal.

The ridali squalled as the wagon pulled on it in awkward directions, the big animals' sides between the shafts being the only thing keeping the wagon from tipping over completely, at the moment, as it charged along down the hillside. Horus pulled hard on the lines again, trying to get the animal to slow down somewhat, as well as direct it to smoother ground, before the wagon completely lost it. The ridali arced its short neck, but turned anyway, and as it did, the wagon crashed back down onto all four wheels, bounced a few times, and then settled down to merely rolling along at breakneck speeds behind the terrified ridali.

Horus kept working the lines until the beast slowed considerably, before it wore itself out completely. "Alright ... now that we're not fixing to dash ourselves to pieces ... *now* what do we do?" he asked, as the ridali trotted along at a decent pace.

Deilo glanced up at him, from trying to get Lianel to snap out of it. "I don't know. What do you think we should do?"

"I really don't know. I thought Elves were mythic." Horus said. "As in, non-existent? What *else* does this land have, besides a Wizard?" he asked.

"I don't know. I've only seen as much of this place as you have." Deilo said.

"What was that thing that came out of the sky, anyway? It was unlike anything I've ever seen." Lillia asked. "Granted, it bore similarities to a dragon, but that's like comparing a cow to a ridali."

"I don't know!" Deilo said, frustrated. "If Lianel would come around, maybe *he* could tell you."

"It was a dragon." Mutsgae said, simply. "A flying one."

"What makes you say that?" Lillia asked.

"That's what it looked like, is why." Mutsgae said. "Why over complicate things?"

"Things can be far different from what they appear, Muts." Deilo said. "You know that. For all we know, that wasn't even really a lizard."

Mutsgae grunted.

"Alright, barring that our original route is now barred by a new wasteland with a rift and a couple warring *things* ... what are we going to do? Are we still going towards the Tower? Do we return home?" Horus asked.

Deilo sighed, as sat back on his heels, grabbing at the edge of the wagon with a hand to steady himself. "I don't know."

"I ... I think we should find a new way around. Maybe the Wizard will know what is going on." Lillia said. "We'll just have to be careful."

"We're just going to find a safe place to camp, for today, and leave it at that." Horus said. "After all that excitement and running pell-mell ... I think our ridali has about had it as for traveling today."

"That sounds like a good idea." Deilo said. "Except ... where is possibly 'safe', anymore? You saw just like I did. That ground started out normal. It just *died*, and then *fell in*. That could happen anywhere!" he exclaimed, gesturing broadly.

Horus considered that, and then nodded. "Point taken. Alright, then. Let's just get a little more distance away, and then we'll camp wherever looks good."

"Are you sure the ridali can't keep going? The first day out it went two days, non stop." Deilo pointed out.

"Yes, it did. But then, it was fresh. Now, it's been at this work for a week now, with virtually no time for grazing." Horus said. "If we expect to get there with the ridali still alive, much less in any kind of condition, we are going to have to make allowances."

Deilo grunted, and turned back to Lianel. "Lianel! Snap out of it!" When he got no reply, he slapped the man's face. He winced, and shook his stinging hand, before rubbing his palm with his other hand.

Lianel blinked, before working his jaw. " ... wh-?"

"Lianel. How long are we allowed, to get to the Tower, before we get into major trouble?" Deilo asked.

"Uh ... as long as you're making a pointed effort, as long as it takes. The Wizard sees and knows all." Lianel said. "Why?"

"We're going to stop for camp early." Deilo said. "Tonight."

"Why?"

"Our ridali needs a break after all the running it just did." Deilo said.

"Running?" Lianel asked.

"Yes! You were here! Don't you remember all the ...?" Deilo slowed to a halt, as he realized Lianel's blank expression mean that the man had not only gone into shock, but into denial. He honestly didn't remember anything. Deilo sighed. "Never mind."

Lianel got to his knees, and looked out of the wagon, hanging onto the side for balance. "We're going the wrong way. Why are we turned around?"

"We just got a little lost, that's all. We'll make camp, and in the morning we'll try again, by another road. The one we were on is impassable." Horus said. "I haven't the foggiest idea where the road is, anymore, by the way." He added, to Deilo, having come to the same conclusion about Lianel.

"That figures." Deilo looked at Lianel again. "How well do you know the area?"

"I don't. I don't leave the area of my home very often ... and I only knew the one road to Kentalic." Lianel said. "You say it's impassable?"

"Yes. There's a massive chunk of land missing ... and it's infested with nasty creatures." Deilo said.

Mutsgae grunted, from the bottom of the wagon.

"We couldn't just go around the missing chunk of road?" Lianel asked.

"No, I'm afraid not." Deilo said. "I've never seen anything like it, and I've seen a lot of places."

"You have?"

"Yes. All four of us are from the Kingdoms." Deilo said, crossing his legs as he settled in the bottom of the wagon.

"Oh." Lianel said. "I suppose you would know."

The group rode in silence for the next hour, as Horus concerned himself with the ridali and finding a suitable spot to stop, as Lianel wondered what exactly had been going on, and the other three worried over the events they had witnessed.

What did it all mean?

When they stopped Lillia approached Lianel while Horus was taking care of the ridali and Deilo was setting up the camp in a small, dense cluster of trees. "How often do people see Elves?" she asked.

Lianel looked down at her with a strange look, and then he laughed. "Nobody sees Elves, little lady. They're just myths. Granted, they're scary myths, but they're just myths."

"Oh." She said.

Deilo looked over at them both, after setting the cook pot on the ground near where the fire would be. Lillia looked back at him, meeting his gaze. After a moment, she looked up at Lianel again.

"How often do patches of the land just up and die?" Lianel gave her a rather strange look. "I am afraid I don't know what you are talking about, miss."

Lillia looked at Deilo again, who was still watching them.

Lianel looked at her closely. "What have you been eating?"

"Excuse me?" Lillia asked, shocked.

"Are you having hallucinations?" Lianel asked. "Why the strange, outlandish questions?"

Lillia gave him a worried look, and then walked over to where Deilo was. He put a hand down for her to step into, then he lifted her to his shoulder, waiting until she had a hold on his shirt before he resumed his chores.

"I fear he remembers nothing, and that speaks volumes more than his statements do." Lillia said.

Deilo merely nodded, without comment.

"I fear the events we witnessed today are far from ordinary ... something strange is going on here." Lillia said. "And I do not know what to do about it."

Deilo waited until he was a little farther away from Lianel, before he replied. "For now, I think the best course is to continue on to the Tower. Find out why the Wizard wants us. And we'll tell him what we've seen. If anyone would know, if anyone could do anything about it, it'd be him." Deilo said.

"I hope you're right." Lillia said. "I don't hold much faith in him, though ... those who go in don't come out? That is rather sinister, right there."

"That's what the folks back home said, and they're far removed from the Tower." Deilo pointed out. "Lianel said it all depends on what the Wizard wants. That means some do come out again. Maybe he just randomly calls in people to do things for him."

"I find that highly unlikely. And why us? We aren't special in any way. We're as ordinary as they come." Lillia said.

Deilo shrugged only slightly, avoiding knocking her off. "I really don't know, Lil. I really don't. I can only guess. Whatever the Wizard intends with us ... I still think we should tell him about what we've seen today."

"Assuming we live long enough to get there." She said, grimly.

"Keep a happy face on." Horus said, unexpectedly, from beside Deilo. "All's well that ends well."

Deilo and Lillia both looked over at him, and he smiled in return.

"I'm glad you're feeling alright." Deilo told him, glumly. "I'm rather worried ... and more than a little alarmed."

"Oh, I know. So am I." Horus said. "But we're still here. Take it one day at a time, one moment at a time." He held a hand out to Deilo's shoulder, and Lillia stepped over into his hand before he deposited her in his forelock. She grasped the long hairs there, and settled down.

"Are you done with the beast?" Deilo asked.

"For the time being. I staked it out so it could eat what little grass there is." Horus said.

"There's grass over there." Deilo pointed beyond the edge of the grove of trees they had stopped in.

"I know. But I don't want it that far away from camp ... who knows who all comes around here?" Horus said. "Ridali are expensive animals, and currently, the only one here that can pull that wagon." He gestured at the heavy wooden creation.

Deilo nodded. "Do you think we ought to post watches?"

Horus considered that. Before he could answer, Mutsgae walked over, head swinging slowly from side to side.

"I think someone should be up at all times." He said, pointedly. "I'll watch."

Deilo looked down at the Lizard. "You do?"

"Yes. I don't like the smell of this place." Mutsgae said. "I'll watch."

"Okay ... we'll set watches ... and I guess Muts can have first watch." Deilo said, looking around.

"No. I said I'll watch. You all get some sleep. I can sleep through the day." Mutsgae said. "No big deal ... I can see better in the dark than any of you can, anyway."

The others regarded him in silence for a moment, and then they nodded.

"Alright." Horus said. "You got the job."

Mutsgae walked away again, slipping under the belly of the wagon.

Deilo watched him go, and then looked at Horus. "Well?"

Horus clapped his hands, and then rubbed them. "Well! What's for dinner?"

"Oh, right." Deilo said, having completely forgotten the food items he had been holding. He poked a few under his arm, and selected a few other items from the wagon before walking back over to the cook pot. Lianel already had a nice fire burning, and had moved the big pot to the edge of the fire, starting it heating. Deilo sat down near the pot, arraying the items in his lap before starting to prepare the evening meal.

Horus retrieved a chunk of salted meat from the wagon, and threw it under the wagon. It never hit the ground, Mutsgae's toothy snout snapping around to catch it mid air. The Lizard shivered convulsively at the sudden drench of salt in his mouth, but did not drop the meat. He worried at it until it was small enough to swallow, glad that it was not dried.

Mutsgae stayed under the wagon, watching the others as well as the surrounding area. When the meal was over and the things washed and stashed, the fire was put out with dirt before the others all turned in for the night. Deilo and Lianel bedded down in the wagon, while Horus folded up next to the side of it. Lillia was in the wagon as well, nested down in some of the softer bundles to the front of the wagon.

Mutsgae said nary a word as everything stilled, listening to the ripping and chewing the ridali was doing, not far off.

There was no road anywhere nearby, so travelers were unlikely. But that didn't mean there wouldn't be any. Bandits never traveled on the roads ... they just raided off of them.

Halfway through the quiet night, Mutsgae left the shadow of the wagon slowly, pausing every few steps to smell the air and watch for movement. When he was a few dozen yards away, he paused, and tilted his head to the side to look up.

The stars far overhead twinkled merrily, as if there was nothing wrong in the world. Here and there small, wispy clouds blurred them. But there was one spot directly overhead that concerned him. There, a select few stars were blinking out, and a split moment later, blinked back in. As if there was something up there.

Like there had been for the entire trip.

Something really big, and really high.

Something that was obviously following them. Watching them.

For the time being, it was still up there, doing nothing. Mutsgae looked at the area around the camp again, and then made his way back towards the wagon in the same fashion that he had left it, ever wary.

When dawn came, it came bright and early, with not a cloud in the sky. Mutsgae ignored the normal morning proceedings as the others got ready to set out once more. He ventured to an open spot again, and looked up.

It took him a long moment to spot it, but he did find it again. It was very hard to see in the daytime ... as if it was sky colored. But it was still there, still slowly circling. It was still very high, and almost invisible. Mutsgae returned to the wagon when Deilo called, and clambered up into the back. Deilo closed the tailgate once Mutsgae was in before climbing in after him.

"We're ready." Deilo said.

"Alright." Horus said, before urging the ridali onward.

The wagon groaned into motion, and then silenced as the wagon shifted out of its rest state. Mutsgae blinked wearily, and closed his eyes.

Deilo shook out a blanket, and draped it lightly over Mutsgae, to help block the light out so he could rest easier.

Lianel leaned on the side, and looked around.

"Any idea which way is best to go?" Horus asked of him, glancing back.

"Well ... there are villages to both the east and the west, and either one might have a road towards Kentalic." Lianel said. "The eastern village is probably closer."

"Alright." Horus said, turning the ridali.

They rode in relative silence for hours, no one saying much of anything. Deilo fixed them a cold lunch while they traveled, and took the lines from Horus so he could eat. When they found a small brook after lunch, they watered the ridali and refilled the water barrels that needed it. They crossed the brook fairly easily, as it had a gravel bottom and was not very deep. The ridali strained only slightly to get the wagon started up the soft bank on the far side. Once over the obstacle, the beast started out once again at an easy trot.

As the afternoon turned into evening, they encountered a road that wandered in the general direction they wanted, and they turned onto it, headed north once more. They glided along it, compared to the rough cross-country ride they had just taken.

Under the blanket, Mutsgae heaved a weary sigh.

*

As the friends turned onto the road, a band of furred people rode into the grove the friends had slept in, and dismounted, gathering around the obvious campfire. They looked at each other, then out at the land around them.

"Some one has been here." One growled, obviously.

"They not only were here, they *camped* here. It looks like we've got rustlers again." Another pointed out.

"Nay." A third said, looking down at the ground as it walked around. "There are marks here of wheels. Four wheels." It pointed at the marks. "Rustlers don't travel with wagons."

"Then what? Thieves?"

"I don't think so. Why would they have a wagon? Thieves travel fast. They have to."

"I hope we don't have a new band in the area using this place as a staging ground. They could very well have met here with the wagon, to put their loot in."

"There was a robbery lately ... there were a lot of items taken ..." another pointed out.

"We had better track them down."

"I see hoof tracks." Another said. "Along with something much larger ... I don't recognize the track."

"Probably the beast they harnessed to the wagon ... and an escort rider?"

"There are saurian tracks, as well."

"This sounds ominous."

"I see, possibly three ... maybe four man-tracks." Another said.

"Are you sure? I only see two distinct sets."

"Never you mind!" Another called. "Let us be on our way ... with a wagon, they can't have gone far. We may yet catch them before dark ..." he waved an arm, and vaulted up onto his mount's back.

The others all followed suit, and the group of saurian-mounted people sped out, strung out in a single line. The one in front rode bent nearly double, keeping an eye on the wagon track they followed.

Come dark, they encountered the brook, and contemplated the deep ruts that climbed the far side.

"That was a heavy wagon." One remarked, finally.

"And they went across this like it was nothing." Another said.

"They must be traveling faster than we thought ... I still see no wagon ahead. Just a winding track."

"We'll catch them in the morning. Make camp."

A long ways off, down the road, the friends were all making camp as well, in the company of another wagon. The wagon had come upon them from the other way, and had stopped, for the night. The goblin family that rode in it behind a little draft pony were all too happy to stay and talk. The friends learned from them that the road did indeed travel to a town where they could get on a much better road that would take them all the way to Kentalic.

That night, before going to bed, Deilo wandered out to where he saw Mutsgae sitting, and stopped next to him, looking northward at the Tower. It was still a very long ways off, and glowed ever so slightly with the majick it contained.

"Any bad smells tonight?" he asked.

"Just those goblins. I think they haven't bathed in months." Mutsgae said.

"You're a fine one to talk." Deilo jibed, lightly. "But no ... as far as I am aware, goblins *never* bathe. They're hydrophobic."

"Pitiful state to be in."

"I know." Deilo said.

"I think we'll be okay tonight." Mutsgae said, before looking upwards again.

"You sure spend a lot of time looking up." Deilo noted, before looking up, himself. "What are you looking at? I never see anything."

"I am not sure. I can barely tell there's something up there, myself. But it is definitely following us. And after yesterday ... I have to wonder."

"Are you referring to the flying dragon?"

"Yes." Mutsgae said. "If the sky can hide something that big ... I can only wonder what it is that is watching us."

Deilo shrugged, still not seeing anything up there. He turned, and walked back to the wagon.

Near noon the next day, the group of riders reached the road, and contemplated the turning tracks that vanished onto the road.

"Do you think we will find them, now?"

"Maybe. Half of us will pursue, the other half will return."

The band split in half, some speeding away the way they had come, and the rest racing down the road, as fast as they could make their mounts go.

It was not until nearly night that they managed to catch up to the ridali-drawn wagon, even as it sped along at its own rate down the road.

"Damn. Look at that thing go. No wonder we had such a hard time following it!" One of the riders said, before they spurred their mounts on, to catch the wagon.

The friends watched the riders come on, amazed at the speed at which they moved.

"That's fast." Deilo remarked.

"They look like they're trying to catch something." Lillia said, from her perch.

Horus looked back, worried. "I hope it's not us they're after."

Lianel looked at them, then at Horus. "Do not worry – I do not think they are bandits. And we are on a mission for the Wizard. They will not detain us."

"Says *you*." Deilo said.

Lianel gave him an indignant look. "This is Gnaria, not some backward Kingdom!"

"Yeah, whatever." Deilo said. "Muts."

"I'm awake." Mutsgae said.

"We might have trouble." Deilo said, quietly, as the riders overtook the wagon, surrounding it.

"Stop the wagon!" One of the furred riders called, gesturing with one arm.

"Why? Who are you?" Horus asked, as two riders closed in, in front of the ridali.

"Stop the wagon!" The demand was repeated.

The riders in front began to slow, but not for long, as the ridali put its head down, and poked the saurians in their rumps with its four splayed horns. The saurian mounts squealed and leapt forwards.

"I don't recommend you do that!" Horus called. "Ridali don't hesitate to run folk over." He warned.

"Stop the wagon, before we force you to!"

"Why? Give me one reason why I should." Horus said, as Deilo climbed up front next to him.

"You transport stolen goods!"

"Preposterous!" Horus replied, after he'd gotten over the shock of the accusation.

"Stop the wagon!" The demand was repeated, as a rider came up side of one of the spinning wheels with a stout stick.

"Can they really jam that stick in a wheel spinning that fast?" Deilo asked, knowing that if they did succeed, that wheel would break and shatter.

Lianel got to his feet, though a bit unsteadily. "If you hinder the progress of this wagon, you will deal with the Wizard's wrath!" he bellowed, palming a silver medallion. "We are on a most urgent mission, and we carry no stolen goods." Lianel said.

The rider looked at Lianel, and then at the medallion. They gestured dismissal. "Apologies." A shout later, and all the riders peeled away, before stopping completely.

Lianel toppled over into the bottom of the wagon when a wheel jounced over a fist-sized rock. "Ah!"

"Thanks." Deilo said. "I wasn't sure if they were bandits, or not."

"No, they weren't. That was a posse, I believe." Lianel said, righting himself as he stashed the medallion inside his clothes.

"To answer your question ... it is possible to jam a wheel, at the current speed, but it would be very difficult." Horus said. "If it had looked like they were going to try, I would have gone faster. Then it would have been nearly impossible."

"Ah." Deilo said, clambering back down into the back of the wagon. "Drink?"

"Please." Horus replied.

Deilo carefully poured drinks for everyone, and passed them out. The water was handled carefully, lest it should spill on the dry goods.

"How far are we from Kentalic?" Deilo asked.

Lianel looked up at the growing apparition. "I don't know. Maybe four days." He said. "When we start to see lower buildings at the base, we will be a day out."

"Ah."

Far above the traveling wagon, Guiran circled again, flying despite the tattered wings and bloody chunks hanging off his hide. The Elf had given him a run for his money ... if he'd had his Mages, it would have been no match. But by himself, the creature of mayhem had been difficult to subdue. He was almost certain he had not killed it ... but he had most certainly put a kink in its plans. He had left it badly mangled and coated in a thick layer of ice at the bottom of that chasm, before he had expended a lot of magical energy to close the rift. That done, he had pulled on the Life force of the area to patch up the dead area, starting seeds growing in repair.

Guiran was glad all he had to do at the moment was glide ... anything else was more torturous than he cared to admit. He had watched the band of riders following and then catching up to the wagon closely, fearing he might have to come down again, to defend the wagon. But the group in the wagon apparently had it all well in hand, as the riders had backed off, and then retreated the way they had come.

Thankfully.

He circled again, tilting his wings ever so slightly. They would be at the Tower in a matter of days, and when he got there, William or Timothy could heal him, put him back together again.

He was also aware that the crocodile in the back of the wagon knew he was there ... it kept looking up at him repeatedly. That alone piqued Guiran's curiosity. Was it indeed and alligator? Or something else? Whatever the case was, it had some incredible vision ... far exceeding that of a typical crocodile.

The creature seemed to be a guard dog or guardian of the group, he noted, as it was usually the one appearing to stand guard, doing naught much else. The others in the wagon all had things they did as a matter of rote, but not that one.

Guiran continued to puzzle out what might actually be the case, wondering what exactly the Wizard had in mind, and which one of those down there was the one actually sent for.

Three days later on, the group of friends had made good time on the well-maintained road, and were driving up to the outer wall surrounding Kentalic. The Tower was a vast spire stretching high up into the sky before flaring outward again at the very top, beneath the conical roof that was capped off by a large sphere. The city closest to the Tower was made up of taller buildings than most of the rest of the city, though by no means anywhere near the height of the Tower itself. The Tower dwarfed everything.

Toward the great outer stonewall, the buildings progressively got lower and wider. Outside the wall were merely houses and shops, dwarfed in the shadow of the wall. Off to the west could be seen the teeming docks and sailing ships at the Kentalic river, a wide and swiftly-flowing watercourse essential to trade.

"This is like *nothing* I've ever seen before." Deilo said, sitting almost on the edge of the wagon even as he hung onto the sides with both hands, looking out at everything.

"I know what you mean." Lianel said, also looking out at everything. "It all changes from one visit to the next ... yet it's all the same. Kantalic is almost the biggest city in Gnaria."

"What do you mean by 'almost'?" Lillia asked, from Horus' forelock.

"Well, above ground, it is the largest city, period. But if you count things that go below ground ... Mukil is far larger. It is twice as large under the surface as it is above." Lianel said. "I've never been there ... that's a city on the farthest northern border, on the Viget river."

"Ah." Deilo said, looking up at the Tower. "What will you do, when we get there?"

Chapter Six

To the East

"Report to the Wizard, with you. If he has nothing more for me, I will go home again, afterwards." Lianel said. "Hopefully, he will allow me a mount."

"Ah."

Horus slowed the ridali to a more sedate pace, as they became mired in traffic. There were many other wagons on the road, along with foot traffic and mounted traffic. But none of the animals drawing the carts were ridali ... they were all slower beasts, most looking rather scruffy. Other, smaller wagons were towed here and there by Centaurii ... and those gave the ridali and Horus a rather strange look.

A Centaurii *riding in a wagon* ... and driving a sort of creature not found in the central region surrounding Kentalic was a rather unusual sight.

The ridali all by itself got them a lot of attention, ranging from interested looks to strange-sounding shouts of foreign tongue.

"Do they still speak the same language here?" Deilo asked, of Lianel.

"Yes. But not everyone speaks *just* Gnarian. There are dialects, as well as scraps of other languages. This is a trading city, as well as the Wizard's home. You'll hear almost anything here. Most use Gnarian as a matter of courtesy ... and to ensure everyone can understand everyone else." Lianel said. "The accents get me, sometimes."

Deilo looked around at everything again, amazed and awed. He looked up at the Tower again, and wondered what was going to happen next.

The journey through the city to the Tower took them a whole other day, just to get through the traffic in the jam-packed streets. By the time they got there, the ridali was rather restless, at having been trapped to a slow walk the whole way, also irritated at all the jostling that had been going on.

Once they reached the inner wall, they stopped at the gate. There was a street circling completely around it, and it appeared that all the gates through it were closed and guarded. Lianel hopped out of the wagon and walked up to the guards, to speak to them in low tones and show them his medallion.

The guards nodded, and started working on opening the iron latticework gates as Lianel walked back to the wagon.

"I wonder if we ought to get one of those medallion thingies." Horus mused.

Deilo laughed, as Lianel climbed into the wagon. "No thanks."

"What is this, now?" Lianel asked.

"Nothing." Horus said, driving through the opened gates. The guards closed the gates behind them, securing them against all other traffic. Though the path ahead was perfectly clear, Horus held the ridali back to a sedate walk even yet. "Where to, now?" Horus asked.

"Up to the door." Lianel said. "Staff will be there to take the wagon elsewhere."

"Ah ... that might not be a good idea." Deilo said. "Ridali are rather touchy about their handlers."

"We'll figure something out." Lianel assured them.

The path was cobbled, all the way up to the Tower, winding through patches that looked like manicured gardens, and patches that looked like chunks out of a wild jungle. Birds and creatures included.

At the base of the Tower the area was completely cobbled over, the wear on the stones indicating why – it was a high traffic area. If it hadn't been cobbled, it'd likely be a mud hole or a dust bowl.

Horus drove right up to a set of wide, tall doors banded in metal, and stopped there. The guards on either side of the doors looked at them strangely, but never moved or spoke.

Lianel hopped out again, and walked up the length of the wagon, as a pair of Dtri showed up, one taking either side of the ridali's head. Amazingly enough, the ridali never protested.

"We will take the animal." One of the Dtri said.

"Take good care, we will." The other said.

Lianel nodded to the friends. "That indeed they will. Leave everything here ... and follow me."

The friends looked at each other for a moment, not sure if they wanted to travel this next bit at all. Behind those doors was an unknown unlike anything else they had ever encountered ... and it was doubtful they would ever come out of there again.

But they eventually started moving, Horus unfolding from where he was, preparing to jump down out of the wagon, as Deilo moved to the back to undo the tailgate. Lillia grabbed a hold of a large tuft of hair and held on tight as Horus jumped down, landing with a clatter on the cobbles. Deilo slid out the back onto his feet, and right behind him Mutsgae dumped out, almost landing on his nose.

Both guards jumped, and froze for a moment, not knowing what to do, obviously considering lowering their ceremonial pikes at Mutsgae. One guard's hand twitched towards the rod at his belt – a very real majickal weapon that could blow any of them to bits and pieces.

"It's alright." Lianel said, hastily holding up his hands to forestall them. "Don't worry about anything."

Deilo looked at the guards for a moment, before closing the tailgate and walking over to where Horus was. Mutsgae followed at a sedate pace, knowing better than to make any sudden movements.

"Well ... we're here." Deilo said, softly.

Horus heaved a sigh. "My hooves are dead." He commented.

Deilo gave him a strange look, and then laughed. "Okay."

"This way." Lianel waved, and started up towards the massive doors. The friends followed, with Deilo walking in the rear, to make sure Mutsgae was not waylaid.

Lianel pushed one of the doors open when he reached the top of the low stairs, and stood there as he watched them come through the entrance. Once everyone was in, he shoved the door closed again. The door swung readily enough, but it was still a massive weight to be moving.

The entrance hallway was massive, the ceiling far over their heads. And though it was decorated in darker colors, it was far from being a dark place. The air moved from one side to the other as if there were windows hidden in alcoves to either side, even though no windows had been seen from outside at this level. The air was fresh and clear, the place didn't seem to have a speck of dust in it ... barring what they had carried in from off the road. The high walls were decorated with colored tapestries, some being pictorial, some being geometrical in design.

Lianel led them down the massive entryway, towards the other end of the hall. To either side could be seen alcoves, partially lit. Some had doorways tucked into them, others had airshafts in them, overhead. Many were sparsely decorated in the nature of the hall itself. As they drew nearer to the far end of the hall, it became apparent there was a set of doors there, and to either side, a steeply rising staircase that looked little used, though impeccably clean.

"This place is down right weird." Deilo said, under the cover of Horus' loudly echoing metal-shod footsteps.

"I know it." Horus said.

Lianel came to an unexpected halt, twenty paces off the doors and stairs. He held up a hand, and the others stopped as well, arranged higgledy-piggledy behind him. There they all stood silently, waiting for what might happen.

After an excruciating moment, the doors slid open to either side, vanishing into the walls. The Wizard himself emerged from beyond them, and seemed to glide across the polished floor towards them, hands folded together within his sleeves.

"The Wizard is a *fish*?" Deilo hissed.

Horus didn't dare reply.

The Wizard stopped ten paces from them, his large eyes taking in everything about them. "You are certainly an odd group ... and certainly not what I expected, considering your natures." He said, finally.

"They are all four that you asked for, my lord." Lianel said, stepping aside and gesturing at the four.

It was clear that the Wizard indeed knew that four stood there, though Lillia was nearly obscured in Horus' forelock. He looked them over again, and grunted. "You may return to your steading, Lianel. Excellent work ... and in good time, as well. Take this to the saddlery, and give it to the headmaster." The Wizard flicked one hand around to clear it of the sleeve, and extended a small object to Lianel, who stepped forward and took it with a curt bow.

"Yes, my lord." Lianel looked at the others, and then hurried out, the way he had come.

The Wizard folded his hands together again, the sleeves falling back down to obscure them. "And what have you four to say for yourselves?" he asked, after the massive door had shut.

"Why are we here?" Deilo asked, bluntly.

"Because I have something I wish you to do for me." The Wizard said.

"Why should we do anything, and why us?" Deilo asked.

"Do you speak for the whole group?" the Wizard asked.

The friends looked at each other, and Horus nodded ever so slightly. Deilo looked at the Wizard again, and nodded. "It appears so."

"Ah." The Wizard said, gliding closer to them, and looking at Deilo with his intent gaze. Deilo held his ground even though he wanted most to turn and flee for his life. The Wizard's pupils slitted, as his eyes closed slightly. Deilo looked back at him, up into the strangely fishy looking face with what he hoped was defiance. After a tense moment, the edges of the Wizard's wide mouth edged upwards, and he turned to look at Horus, before moving back to his previous place. "Good." He turned, and looked at them again. "Why I sent for you? I need you to go to a place most cannot. You can. Otherwise you would not be here." He said, simply. "You have no majickal tendencies, and yet you seem to have a fluency for survival in the oddest circumstances."

Deilo frowned. "I don't like the sounds of this."

"I imagine you don't. But in reality, all I need you four to do, is to go to a place, and retrieve a person for me." The Wizard said. "It is imperative that you do so in all haste. Much resides on this person getting here in time."

"Why couldn't you send someone like Lianel to fetch someone, like you did us?" Deilo countered.

"I told you, did you not hear me? Not many can go where I want you to go. There are majickal wards. Those who use majick cannot go there. You, none of you, use majick." He pointed at each in turn. "Otherwise the mirror would not have pointed to you. Also, there will be other wards ... I am confidant that you will survive thus, as well. You are skilled in the art of surviving ... and remarkably, more or less intact." The Wizard said, folding his long fingers back together again as his sleeves fell over them.

Deilo sighed, and looked at Horus, then at Mutsgae. He looked at the Wizard again. "Do we have a choice?" he asked, simply.

"Not really. I will tell you a few things, but first you must swear that you will not breathe a word of it to anyone else, besides the one to whom you are to bring to me." The Wizard said. "I cannot majickally induce your silence, either ... that would defeat the whole purpose of fetching you out of your hole."

Deilo considered that, and he nodded. That meant the Wizard could do *nothing* majickal to them ... and considering he was a *Wizard*, that was his strongest suit. Interesting.

"Give me your word. All of you." The Wizard said.

There was a moment's hesitation as they each thought it over, and then they all gave their word.

The Wizard nodded, then. "Excellent. The world as a whole is coming apart ... it is destroying itself in its agony. Do you know what this means? This means that we will *all* die very, very shortly. Do you understand?"

The friends just stared at the Wizard, as if he were completely insane. After a moment, Deilo nodded, dumbly. How could the world do that??

"The reason for this is majickal. It is too complicated to explain to you well enough that you understand it at all, as you have no affluence in majick. So I will leave it at that for the time being. Now, if you aid me, there is a slim chance the world can be repaired enough to hold together long enough to find and cure the root cause. If you do not help me ... you and I will all die, along with every other living thing in this world. Do you understand me?" The Wizard asked. It was not a demand, but an honest query.

After a moment, Deilo nodded again. "I understand."

"Good. Will you go on this mission? I will not lie ... it is liable to be perilous. Dangerous, even. But I will not send you in blind *or* ill-equipped." The Wizard said. "You will have whatever you think you'll need, and what ever we think you need. Barring anything majickal."

Deilo considered that, and then looked at the others. They just looked back at him, silent as ever. "Come on, say something." He said, finally. "I can't speak for you on this."

The others said nothing for a long moment, until finally Horus spoke up. "You're the smartest one, Deilo. You know it and we know it. We're also your friends. You decide, we follow." He said.

Deilo frowned slightly, only then realizing that the others always *had* turned to him with problems, with questions. And he was oldest, as well. He looked at Lillia and Mutsgae, who also nodded, in their own fashions. He sighed, and looked at Horus again, looking for help.

Finding none, he looked at the Wizard again. "Are there any others who could do this mission for you?"

The Wizard considered the question for a moment. "Doubtful, but possible. I was unable to locate any more, when I was searching ... I did not intend to place all my intent on just one slim hope that you would accept. But you four are the only ones I could find, within the borders of my land ... and as such the only ones I could send for. Anyone else is too far for me to find, much less get here in any reasonable amount of time. To get there, and back again."

Deilo sighed, and looked at the others, hoping he was fixing to say the right thing. After a moment, he nodded, and looked at the Wizard again. "I guess we have to, then."

"I did not expect much more enthusiasm, especially considering you do not yet know where you are going." The Wizard assured them. "Come with me, and I will show you." He turned, and moved towards the open doors he had entered through. The four friends followed him, at a short distance. But they were forced into close proximity by the nature of the little room they entered. Mutsgae stopped in the doorway, considering the situation. "You must come all the way into the room, Master Lizard." The Wizard said.

Mutsgae looked at the Wizard warily, but moved into the room, taking care to curl his tail to the side to make sure it did not get caught in that bewitched door.

The doors did indeed reappear out of the walls, sliding shut once more, enclosing everyone in the small room. But a mere breath later, the doors were opening again, onto a new room.

"Hey ... how did the room change like that?" Horus asked.

"It didn't change." The Wizard said. "This is a different room, much higher in the Tower." He glided out of the little room, and the friends all gratefully spilled out of it, into the much roomier chamber. It was vaguely circular, with tall bookshelves along one wall, and a large table in the center of the floor. Two large windows in the opposite wall looked out on a crystal clear violet sky, over the city. The Wizard moved to the table, and rested his palms on it, long skinny fingers spread wide over its surface as the others gathered around the edges.

Mutsgae stood next to Horus, unable to see the surface of the table from where he was, but made no comment. The Wizard noted that, and made a slight lifting motion with one long, spindly-fingered hand. The floor under Mutsgae heaved upwards, until he was high enough to see the tabletop. Mutsgae only hunkered down as the floor lifted, slightly alarmed. Then he lifted up again, and peered forwards at the table, then at the Wizard.

"Better?" The Wizard asked.

"Thank you." Mutsage answered.

Deilo looked at the chunk of floor, and marveled at what kind of powers the Wizard must have, to be able to manipulate matter like that with no obvious majick and no spell-chanting. He jumped away from the table when its surface began to ripple and wrinkle, becoming three-dimensional. "Wh-?" he asked, looking at it.

"It is only a map." The Wizard said, patiently. "Have no fear."

Even as the Wizard spoke, the surface settled down into a miniature three-dimensional representation of the entire Gnarian Valley. Deilo's eyebrows went up, and he bent over to look at it. It was unlike the few maps he had seen – those were crudely drawn by comparison, and always had strange blank spaces. This map – if it was to be called a map, was utterly complete, down to miniscule buildings, tiny rivers ... no detail lost. Not a 'blank' spot to be seen.

"Whoa." Deilo said, even as Horus and Mutsgae looked at it in awe. Lillia shrieked, tumbling off Horus' head, landing smack in the middle of a miniature forest that was carpet-deep to her. She rolled over, and got to her feet, looking around at the map she stood in the middle of.

"Interesting." She squatted down, looking at details that the others probably couldn't see.

"This, as I am sure you know, is the entirety of my realm. This, is Gnaria, as she truly stands today." The Wizard gestured over the table. "This is where you were." He placed a finger on a spot very near the southern range, his small fingertip veritably covering far more than the entirety of the Floating H Ranch. "And this is where we are now." He pointed at the small Tower sticking up like a needle out of the middle of the miniature Kentalic.

"Amazing!" Deilo said. "Oh!" He said, remembering. He pointed to a spot on the map. "About here ... I am not sure, exactly." He started.

"We saw something rather frightening." Horus added.

The Wizard looked at them, then at the map.

"The ground there died, while we watched, and everything left, the plants turned to dust. Then the ground fell in, making a big, ragged hole. And something black and smoky or cloudy or ... *something* ... crawled out of it, with fiery eyes." Deilo said. "Naturally, we ran."

The Wizard looked at him. Deilo couldn't tell if that was a non-expression expression, or if that was a very concerned look. "Did it follow you?" he asked, simply.

"No ... while we were running from the area, something *else* came out of the sky so fast ... it was big, with wings." Deilo gestured uselessly. "It looked like it was attacking the other thing, and they both fell into the hole."

The Wizard nodded slightly. "I see."

"I don't know what happened after that." Deilo admitted. "Do you know what that was?"

"I have an idea ... I will look into it. Do not concern yourselves over this matter." He waved a hand dismissively, turning back to the table. "This area, here, is where you are going." He pointed to the far east, where the valley tapered off to a crooked point ... pointing out a very small area that was, oddly enough, *not* detailed. It was the only place on the map like that. "I have no idea what that area looks like, as it is blocked from my view by the very majick wards I spoke of earlier." The Wizard said.

"That's a very long ways away." Deilo said. "We're not from here, you must realize ... we don't know our way around this country."

"I am aware of that." The Wizard said. "You will be supplied with a guide. For as far as that guide can go. They will have to leave you before you cross this barrier ... they won't be able to go with you."

"Huh."

"But who are we going after?" Horus asked.

"I don't know if you will know who I speak of, or not." The Wizard said, as the map rippled and shifted, zooming in on the mountainous region that had a blank, flat spot in it. Lillia shrieked, tumbling over as she lost her footing. "His name is Malici."

A strange expression crossed Deilo's face, but he said nothing.

"Malici is not a person as you are used to." The Wizard touched the table, and made a lifting gesture. The table under his hand warped and lifted, forming a new shape. An accurate image of Malici rose up out of the table, showing a better form than the broken statue that sat elsewhere in the Tower.

"Hey! I've seen a statue of a creature like that before!" Horus said, pointing. "Uh ... I don't remember where."

Deilo looked at him, crossing his arms over his chest as he looked at the Wizard again. "On a pavilion, in the town where we first met Roan." He said. "Malici is a *myth*." He told the Wizard pointedly.

"Not so much, not anymore than a great deal of other very old things. If I had pulled out of society as he had, you would probably call me a myth, too." The Wizard said, matter-of-factly. "Malici is not only very real, he is very much alive. And he is there." The Wizard pointed at the blank, flat area. "He is also the only one that I know of that can help us get out of the mess we are all in."

Deilo watched the Wizard carefully, suspicious. "You're sending us on a phantom goose chase?"

"Not at all." The Wizard said, patiently, placing both long hands on the table's surface. "You must understand. Malici is very real. He is very old, and he is very alive. And probably the most dangerous being walking this world." He gestured slightly at the place on the map. "The most powerful single entity. More so than myself, even. And we need him. He withdrew from society a very long time ago, having tired of the whims of short-lived folk. And over the centuries, he has mostly faded from memory. Only a few know of him, and even fewer know anything about him." The Wizard pointed out. "Now, we need him desperately. And I think he will come."

Deilo sighed, and looked at the others. They only looked back without a word. Lillia was seated now, not risking the tabletop moving again. Deilo looked at the Wizard again, wondering what he should say or do. After a moment, he shifted his feet, and looked at the map and the miniature representation. "How do you expect us to convince him to come back with us?" he asked.

The Wizard regarded him with what could have been a thoughtful look. "Tell the truth, of course. I have told you a great deal, already. Any of which he might already know. Only there is one more thing that you should know. Malici and I were not on such good terms the last time we met ... I do not know if he will still be in that state of mind, regarding me. There is something you should tell him; it is not I, per se, who wishes to meet with him, but others. Others who have the power, but not the knowledge, to repair the world. You be sure to tell him this."

"Others? Who? What others?" Deilo asked. "Aren't you the only Wizard?"

The Wizard nodded slightly. "I am. I am the last. However, there is another group, who are greatly powerful in their own right, and there are lots *of* them, all working together. Together, they amass an amazing force to be reckoned with. But they are new to this world and do not know all its little intricacies." The Wizard said. "While I do not have the faculties to tell them what they want to know so they *can* repair the world, Malici does. I believe Malici may also know of a way to multiply the repair upon itself, thus making it more effective. It is they who wish to meet with him."

"But who are they?"

"They call themselves the Dragon's Army." The Wizard said. "And that is all."

"Dragon's Army?" Deilo asked. "As in, belonging to a dragon, or that they *use* dragons?"

The Wizard considered the question. "I do not truly know that much about them. Other than that at times they are useful folk to know, and at times they are the most annoying creatures I have ever come across."

Deilo considered that for a moment, before heaving a sigh. "I suppose we ought to be on our way, then. What do we do, first?"

The Wizard nodded, satisfied finally that they would go. He moved over to a strange looking statue that looked to be a dead tree covered in a flowering vine. He touched one of the blooms closest to the base of the tree, picked up a quill, wrote quickly with no ink onto the flat base of the creation, and then touched the flower again. It glowed ever so briefly. He turned about again, to face them. "I have arranged that your wagon be cleaned and re-equipped, for your journey. Your remarkable animal will aid in your haste to get there, I believe. I must warn you ... use no majick what so ever at all, or you will perish when you step through the wards on the area." He gestured at the map. "I have sent for a guide to take you there ... but your animal and the guide both will not be able to enter the area. You must leave them outside."

Deilo nodded. "Alright."

"You will leave today, as soon as your wagon is ready." The Wizard picked up a palm-sized sphere, and handed it to Deilo. "If you encounter some problem along the way that you cannot overcome, drop this into a bowl of water. It will send a signal I will receive here in this Tower, and I will look in on the matter. Understood?"

Deilo looked at the sphere as it sat in his palm, wondering at the smooth dark grey surface. "Understood." He said, simply. He tossed it to Horus, who caught it deftly, tucking it into a pouch at his waist. Only then did Deilo see the grimace the Wizard had. "What?" Deilo asked.

"That device is *fragile*." The Wizard managed to grind out. "And I expect it back, *in one piece*."

"Oh." Deilo said. "I thought it was a rock."

The Wizard heaved a weary sigh. "No." He gestured to the small room they had arrived in. "You may go."

Deilo looked at the others, and then picked Lillia up before following Horus to the small room. Mutsgae looked around, and then simply dumped off the raised chunk of floor to follow, a split moment before the floor had started to re-acquaint itself with the rest of the floor. Mutsgae scrambled after the other two, not wanting to be left behind. Once again, he took great care that his tail was inside, before the doors shut.

A moment later, the doors reopened, onto the hall they had walked into. Only now it was quite crowded with people of many Races hurrying back and forth, in and out of the many recessed doors. Some bore burdens, while others hurried about with none.

"Whoa." Deilo said, looking out at that. The group left the little room, looking around at the busy commotion.

"Looks like this place just came alive. Or awake, or something." Horus said, as the folk gave them all a wide berth, watching Mutsgae warily.

"Well ... let's get going, then." Deilo said, with a sigh. "I really don't want to go wandering off on a 'mission' like this ..." he said.

"Neither do I, but the Wizard didn't exactly give us much choice, now did he?" Horus asked.

Deilo looked at him, as they walked towards the large doors. "He seemed to be willing to let us not go."

"Not so ... as long as it was possible we might accept his mission he was being nice ... that's the way of things." Horus said. "If you had said flat out no at any point ... he might have simply vaporized us, having no reason to keep us alive."

Deilo just stared at him for a moment. "You know ... that never occurred to me, but I believe you might be right."

Horus looked back at him, and his ears flicked back, and then up again. "At least we are all still alive, and still together. Fetching a person can't be all that bad."

"We'll see. This all smacks of things great and dangerous." Deilo answered, pulling the door open.

The others filed through, and stopped on the steps outside, while Deilo pulled the door shut again behind them. There was nothing there but an empty courtyard, and the two guards at the door.

"Where is our wagon?" Horus asked of one, but didn't get a reply, just a look. Horus sighed, and clattered down the stairs. He stopped on the courtyard, and looked around. "Where's our wagon? He said he'd give it back to us."

Deilo walked down the stairs over to him, and set a hand on his higher shoulder. "Maybe it's taking some time to supply the wagon, like he said he would do."

Horus looked at him. "I don't want to walk all that way, Deilo, and I sure don't want to lose that ridali."

Deilo only nodded.

"Hey, D? Can I go over to Horus?" Lillia asked, from his shoulder.

"Sure." Deilo said, before transferring her over. Horus lifted her up to his head, where she settled back into his forelock, where she could more easily stay put than on Deilo's shoulder.

Mutsgae slithered down the steps, and stopped on the cobbles. "I hear wagon wheels." He said. "And hoof beats. Someone is coming swiftly."

Horus pricked his ears, but heard nothing. "I don't hear it."

Deilo turned, as the said hoof beats became audible. "I do." He pointed, and as he did so, some one went blasting past on horseback, headed for the gate. "And there they go." He said, turning to watch. "I wonder where they're off to, in such a hurry?"

"I don't know." Deilo said. He turned around again, as the sound of wagon wheels came to greet them. "Maybe this is our ridali."

Horus turned, shoes clattering on the stones, and watched as two Dtri – possibly the same two Dtri – led the ridali around the base of the Tower to them. Behind the ridali rolled the wagon, filled to brimming with supplies.

"We have brought your wagon and animal back to you." One of the Dtri said.

"Thank you." Horus said, taking the lead rope. The Dtri both turned, and left again, back around the Tower from whence they came. "Well." He gestured at the others, and then at the wagon.

Deilo went to the back, and looked at the tailgate ... if he opened it, it was quite possible he wouldn't be able to get it shut again. "Uh ..." he looked down at Mutsgae. "We've got a little problem."

Mutsgae looked up at him, and then around at the area. "Back it up to the stairs."

Horus turned the ridali, and started it backing the wagon up, slowly. He eased it back, until the back wheels just bumped the bottom stair. Then he stopped it.

"Alright." Deilo said, gesturing to Mutsgae. "Give it a try."

Mutsgae crawled up the stairs, and turned around, gauging the still considerable leap to the back of the wagon. He rushed forward, and jumped up as high as he could. He impacted the sacks in the back of the wagon, and scrambled, trying to keep from sliding back off, his blunt claws pulling on the material of the sacks. Deilo stepped up, and gave Mutsgae a push from behind, helping him get up on top of the heap. He them climbed up after him.

"Quite a climb, huh?" Deilo asked, sitting down next to the Lizard.

Mutsgae only grunted, as a man ran up to the wagon with a sack in his hand.

"Here." He said, handing it up to Deilo, who took the sack.

"What's this?" Deilo asked.

"Coin. To buy any additional supplies you may need when you run low." The man said, before walking away again.

Deilo looked at Mutsgae, then pulled the top of the sack open and looked inside. He reached in, and pulled out a handful of small coins. "Well ... it is coin." He put it back, and closed the sack before stowing the sack in the wagon.

"It seems that even here in the center of Gnaria they think they have to carry everything they will need for a trip." Mutsgae said. "We may do well to invest in hunting gear ... most of the territory we are to cross looked to be wild. Very few small towns."

"That might be a good idea." Deilo nodded, while Horus checked the ridali and its harness over, making sure everything was the way it was supposed to be. And then he double-checked everything in the hitching.

"I think we are ready to head out." Horus said, moving towards the wagon after securing the lead rope and retrieving the lines.

"The Wizard said something about a guide." Mutsgae said. "I think it would be prudent to wait for the guide ... we would get lost too quickly without one."

Horus looked up at the others, and then nodded, before taking Lillia from his head and setting her on a sack in the wagon. "Take care ... I do not know how well they packed everything." He told her as she clambered over the sack farther into the wagon.

They did not have long to wait ... the rider that had sped out into the city rode back in, this time accompanied by a green and yellow Centaurii. The rider turned and said something to the Centaurii, before riding away, around the Tower. The Centaurii stopped, and looked over at the wagon, and his ears folded back. After a moment they pricked forwards again, and he walked over towards them.

"So." He said, stopping off the near wheel.

Deilo looked over at him, and his eyebrows went up. "*M'lar?*" he asked.

The Centaurii looked up at him. "And who are you?"

"Deilo." He said, before gesturing to Horus. "Horus."

M'lar looked at Horus, and then at Deilo, and then past Deilo, at the low ridge that was visible of Mutsgae's back. "Huh." He said. "Well, I'll be. What in the Gods' names are you doing *here*?"

"Ah ... well ... apparently, we've been drafted into doing something for the Wizard." Deilo said.

"You don't sound too happy about it." M'lar said, scratching one ear thoughtfully.

"Would you be? To be yanked up out of your home for the umpteenth time, for reasons you have no control over?" Deilo asked.

M'lar shrugged. "My home is wherever I am. But ... I, too, have been ... 'drafted', as you say. But seeing that you are my charges makes me feel a lot better about the issue. They could have done worse. Much worse." He said, before looking at the ridali. "What sort of creature is this?"

"That's a ridali." Horus said.

"No kidding! I've only heard of them ... the Wizard gave it to you?"

"No. We brought it with us, when we came to the Tower." Deilo said.

M'lar considered the wagon. "Can it pull that load? That wagon's a tad heavy, you ask me."

"It can ... but we won't be going very quickly." Deilo said.

M'lar considered that. "We can fix that. I was told this was a mission where speed was imperative, no?"

"We were told the same."

"Alright. We can definitely fix that." M'lar said. "Follow me." He turned, and headed back towards the gate. Horus considered the wagon, and then passed the lines up to Deilo.

"There's no way I'm getting up there and staying there." He said. "I'll follow. Just be careful with those lines." He said. "I can coach you from down here."

Deilo nodded, moving closer to the front of the wagon.

Horus walked beside the wagon, as Deilo drove it out of the Tower yard, and back into the city proper. They followed M'lar, who blazed a path for them through the traffic, which was considerably lighter than it had been when they had come in.

M'lar led them to a yard behind a building, where they promptly unloaded every last thing on the wagon, and sorted through it into two piles. Things they definitely needed, and things they could do without. The things they could do without – all the huge amounts of food and such – were loaded back onto the wagon, and M'lar took Horus and the wagon out to the market, where they sold all of it. They brought the wagon back, and they loaded all the rest back into the wagon – a considerably lighter load. And then they went back to the market again, this time with Deilo along. They purchased gear they could hunt with, and a few other items M'lar thought they might need on this particular journey.

For the most part, the Wizard's people had covered everything, so there was very little to get. A skinning knife, a whetstone, a short bow, and several quivers of arrows. The

Wizard had already supplied them with two short swords, and a long bow with three quivers of long arrows to go with.

"He sure has a lot of confidence in your ridali." M'lar commented, as they headed out of the city. Both Centaurii walked along behind the wagon, M'lar occasionally shouting instructions up to Deilo on which way to go.

"How did we end up with you, on this trip?" Horus asked, out of curiosity. "That's a really interesting coincidence."

"Same from here ... how did I get so lucky to get you four as a group? You four travel in a very efficient manner – if slowly. And with this ridali ... maybe not so slowly." M'lar said. "After I left you where you wished to go, I picked up a pair that wished to go to Julski, but did not know the way. From Julski I went on to Mukil, through Unmukil, and back out through Mukil again, taking all sorts of folk all sorts of places. I then went to Coche, and from there to here. I had just turned into the guild and had spent two days resting when a rider from the Tower turned up, looking for someone who knew the eastern region of the land. At the moment, I was the only one who had the slightest idea about the eastern regions. So I was drafted, as it were. Copious amounts of money were involved, of course. Not that I could have refused ... no one refuses the Wizard anything, unless they've got a wish to vanish suddenly. Or so the rumor goes." M'lar realized then, that all his detailing of his travels had gone completely over Horus' head, as Horus had no idea where any of those places were. "Anyway ... here we are. I was dreading what I might find that I was to guide ... much relieved was I when I realized it was your little group. Some people are such idiots, when it comes to long travel."

"Oh." Horus said. "Do you know the way we're going?"

"I was told you wanted to go as far east as the mountains would allow. That's easy enough ... we just head east until we see mountains, and follow them until there is nothing but mountains." M'lar said. "Never been that far, personally, but then ... no one has, in the whole guild. At least ... no one in the guild has mapped the area in question."

"Even the Wizard did not have a map of the area." Horus said. "What guild?"

M'lar gave him a strange look. "The Cartography Guild, which else? I'm a guide, a mapper."

"Oh." Horus said, simply.

"For being a Centaurii, you sure don't know very much about anything." M'lar said.

"I lost my mother when I was less than a year old." Horus remarked. "Since then, I have been with my friends. I rarely met any Centaurii while I was growing up at the inn. And those I did see did not speak to me. I was busy in the yard, tending the animals."

"Huh. Odd. No wonder you seem strange to me." M'lar said. "Who named you?"

"My mother." Horus said. "Why?"

"Horus isn't a usual Centaurii name. It is very strange." M'lar said. "That is all. I thought maybe someone else had named you, since you lost your mother at such a young age."

"No. I was old enough to know my name."

"Huh. Well ... you've certainly grown out in the last year ... look a lot better than you did when I last saw you, too."

"When you last saw me, I had been traveling for a long time. Now ... I rode here in the wagon, and at the ranch I had plenty of time to rest and eat." Horus said.

"I see. So you found work?" M'lar asked. "On a ranch?"

"Yes. We all did. The Floating H Ranch. They raise and train ridali, and raise some cattle." Horus said.

"Really! Well, no wonder you have one, here." M'lar said. "That answers that question. I had wondered how you had come to own such a magnificent animal."

"We don't ... it's on loan. It belongs to the ranch, still." Horus said.

"I see."

"Where now?" Deilo called, from up top.

M'lar took a quick look ahead. "To the left. From there it should be a straight shot out the eastern gate."

"Okay."

Mutsgae poked his nose over the tailgate. "You're a nosy sort, aren't you?" he rumbled.

M'lar only laughed. "Just curious." He said.

A thought occurred to Horus, and he ducked down real quick to look under the wagon. He saw what he wanted to see ... the saddle was still under there, where Mar-kai had said it would be. Apparently, no one at the Tower had removed it.

"Hey!" M'lar said, catching Horus' arm. "Are you alright?" he asked, pulling him back up. "What'd you do, trip?"

"Uh ... yeah." Horus said. "Thanks." He walked along in silence then, watching the city go by.

Night fell before they left the city, and it lit up like noon in the middle of the night. No stars at all could be seen overhead due to all the streets being lit up, along with the interiors of nearly all the buildings. However, after dark, the traffic almost vanished from the road they were on, and they made better time than they had made all day. A few hours after dark they passed through the gates of the city, just before the city guards started closing the gates. They were not very far away when they heard the sound of the metal gratings fall into place.

"We might as well stop here." M'lar said. "Let your animal rest a bit. Tomorrow will be a long day."

The friends said nothing at all, following his lead. There was no point in having a guide if they weren't going to listen to what he told them. Since they had taken the time to go through everything they had while in Kentalic, they knew exactly what they had, how much, and where it was stowed.

In a matter of minutes they had a large tent set up, and the ridali staked just outside, where they could hear it, and sometimes see it through the fabric. Deilo made them all a cold dinner, and they ate in perfect silence before turning in. They all had plenty of blankets to sleep on or under, as each saw fit. Lillia slept inside her own little blanket that had come all the way from the ranch, on top of a fat sack of clothing, so no one would squish her in the night.

M'lar got them all up and moving before the sun came up. The sky was just starting to show color to the east when they finished packing everything up. They moved out in similar silence, having nothing at all to say. Horus took the time to double check the harness again, just to make sure everything was good. M'lar stood to one side and watched him with great interest. And then they set out, down the road once more. The road's surface was quite good, and they made excellent time, passing many people going in both directions, to and from the city. Just before noon, they came upon two men in grey and brown garb standing on the side of the road. As they drew abreast, one of them called out to them.

"Wait!"

Deilo looked over at them, but neglected to pull on the lines ... the ridali kept right on going. Horus stayed with the wagon, following it on, but M'lar stopped.

"Who are you?" M'lar asked. "And what do you want?" he didn't call after the others, knowing they would not leave the road without his direction ... also knowing that stopping a wagon just because someone called to them was a bad idea. Even this close to the city.

"My name is William." He said. "You are bound for eastern Gnaria?"

M'lar gave him a suspicious look. "What's it to you?"

"We just wished to see you off. That is all. And greatest of luck to you all." William said, easily.

M'lar noted that William was completely and totally relaxed ... it didn't feel like a trap. But then, some bandits were very good at what they did.

"We're not bandits, if that's what you're thinking." William said.

M'lar gave him a suspicious look. "Oh? And what would convince me otherwise?"

William shrugged. "You'll just have to trust me, I suppose." He looked over at where the wagon was still rolling away. He looked at M'lar again. "You take good care of them, you hear? Do not lead them astray. They will have to move on without you, when you all get to where you are going. But do not leave ... they will return to you, and you will bring them back here, to Kentalic."

M'lar crossed his arms over his chest, ears flat back. "How do you know these things?"

"I have great interest in that you are successful." William said. "That is all. If I could, I would even try to aid you. But that is beyond my powers. Unless ... wait. I think I know of something. Let me see your map."

M'lar's nostrils pinched shut in displeasure. "Are you aware of what you're asking?"

"Yes. Quite."

"Then you know quite well that I am not going to show you my map." M'lar stated, coldly.

"Why not?" he looked over at the other man, suddenly, and then nodded.

M'lar tensed, then, ready to gallop away at top speed, glad the wagon was farther on. Men on foot couldn't hope to catch a galloping Centaurii ... much less that wagon with the head start it had. That ridali was in incredible creature indeed.

The other man simply stepped up, as non-threatening as he could possibly be. He pulled a scroll out of his tunic, and handed it to William. William took it, and held it out to M'lar. "Here. As a token of good will."

M'lar looked at it for a moment, and then cautiously took it. "And what is this?"

"*Our* map. I hope you find it helpful." William said. "You may keep it, for the time being."

M'lar's ears lifted slightly – but only slightly. He looked down at the scroll, and then turned it over. He popped the wax seal with his thumb, and pulled it open. It unrolled easily, the fiber quite supple. It was a far cry better than the stiff material most maps were scrawled on. Most maps one had to physically hold open. This one simply unrolled in his hands. He lifted it, and looked at it. His nostrils flared in surprise at the detail. What he knew matched the map, and there was a considerable bit that he never knew ... even details on the Saren hills ... no one went to the Saren hills! Those hills were a big blank area on *all* maps.

"How did you come across this information?" M'lar asked, suspiciously.

"Easily. We looked, and we drew." William said, gesturing at it. "Keep it, for this trip."

"How will I find you to give it back?" M'lar asked.

"We'll find you, have no worries. And if we don't come for it ... keep it." William said. "It's quite accurate, I assure you. If it is drawn, there it is."

M'lar looked at the map again, and noted that it even extended outside Gnaria in places. It was quite extensive, though by no means a complete map. There were great swaths outside Gnaria that were blank. But each and every mountain was drawn in great detail. "Well ... assuming this is truly the gift it appears to be ... many thanks to you." M'lar said, dipping his snout in a perfunctory bow.

"You're quite welcome. But be careful. There are things about, these days ... that are none too kind." William said.

"Such as?" M'lar asked, glancing down the road at where the wagon was ... and noticed that it was stopped ... He turned, and looked that way, to see if he could see why. It looked almost as if the Lizard had fallen out of the wagon. Idiots.

"The usual. Plus a few things." William also looked that way, and also gained a look of surprise. "What are they doing?"

"Gods if I know." M'lar said, as Mutsgae took off at right angles to the road, headed out across a small field towards a large hay pile. "That crazy Lizard!" M'lar said, taking off down the road at top speed to get to the wagon.

Mutsgae, rather intent on his target, slowed, his eyes searching out every detail of the haystack. He slowed considerably, and crouched low, slinking through the grass towards it, sucking in great breaths of air to get every scent he could. Something was not right at all.

He started to circle it, but stopped, and went back around to the side closest to the road. There, he stopped, and stared up at the massive heap. Mutsgae lifted his head slightly, upper lip lifting slightly, almost as if he were considering growling.

A small part of the stack moved, then, and Mutsgae nearly came unglued, jumping up and back, landing at full extension, as tall as he could make himself on all four legs. He squinted at that little spot – though it was not so little. It was small, compared to the heap, only. And it did not look like hay. It looked instead like some majickal gem, colors swirling around in its depths. It shrank slightly, becoming oval rather than round.

Sniffing the air but coming up with nothing, Mutsgae crept closer only slightly. Only to jump away again when more of the pile moved, towards him. But it only moved slightly – but by far enough to let Mutsgae know that was no pile of hay he was looking at. It was massive!

You are a perceptive little lizard.

Mutsgae jumped again, and looked around, then at the heap again. "What are you?" he asked, quietly, just in case he was hearing things. He didn't want the others to think him a complete lunatic.

I am a Dragon. Do not alert the others to my presence, if you would be so kind. I am trying to hide.

Mutsgae shook his head, at the voice sounding between his ears. It was too weird. But it definitely looked like a giant lizard, the part of it he could profile ... that head that had moved oh so slightly was *huge*, big enough to swallow him without a single thought. "Why are you hiding?"

I prefer if most do not know I exist.

"Uh. Why?"

It would complicate things greatly.

"What are you doing, out here?"

Watching. Waiting.

"For?"

You.

"Me?!"

Yes. I have been watching you for a long time, now. I have seen you watching me, as well.

"You were that thing in the sky?" Mutsgae asked.

Yes.

"Oh. Why are you watching?"

To keep you and your friends safe. You cannot do what you need to do, if you do not arrive at your destinations in one piece.

Mutsgae considered that. A massive flying lizard that could talk was looking out for them. What a concept! "Uh ..." He looked back at the wagon, where he could see M'lar arriving at a dead gallop, sliding on the road as he attempted to stop.

You should go. Do not tell them of me.

Mutsgae looked at the pile, and then simply turned and headed back to the wagon. He was not one to argue with a predator that big. He wouldn't stand a chance.

"What, by all the Gods, are you *doing*?" M'lar demanded, hotly.

"I thought I saw something." Mutsgae said. "That is all." He attempted to climb back into the wagon, and Horus gave him an assisting boost.

"You idiot! You do *not* stop on these roads! It's a good way to get murdered!"

"So let us be on our way." Mutsgae said.

M'lar glared at him. "Do not do that again." And then he glanced over at the haystack, before moving on. Idiot Lizard.

The wagon started forwards again, with not a word from Deilo, who glanced back at Mutsgae with a concerned look. Mutsgae simply sat where he was, silent, thinking. That he had seen that Dragon in the air was a minor miracle. It was huge ... and had to have been very far overhead to appear as small as it had. That it was not contemplating eating them was another minor miracle. But, that it had seen *him*, had seen him *looking* at it ... that Dragon had eyesight like nothing he'd ever heard of!

William and Timothy both walked up to Guiran, in his hay pile guise. "What was that?" William asked.

Guiran opened one eye again, to look at them. "The little Lizard saw me ... again. It has seen me throughout their trip. He is quite attentive."

"And?" Timothy asked.

"I spoke to him, briefly. Told him not to tell the others." Guiran said.

"Why?"

"Why what? Why speak to him? Couldn't exactly not, he knew I was here. He saw through my attempt to hide. I did not want him raising the alarm. So I would not worry him to death. He's got other things to do than worry about me. Why tell him not to tell the others? You should know the answer to that."

William nodded. "Alright. It had to be done, I suppose. We'll be heading back to the Tower later today. You find a better guise than that ... maybe find a heap of rocks to expand. If one saw you, others are liable to. And we don't need the excitement your discovery would bring."

"I will make an effort. As soon as dark falls, I will head out, and watch them go east. It is a shame I cannot simply *take* them where they need to go. It would be much faster, even if I had to fly direct." Guiran said.

"Unfortunately, you generate too much magic, according to the Wizard ... you would infuse them with too much to get through the wards." Timothy said.

Guiran snorted. "Darn stupid, to set up wards against *magic*. It's part of life."

"Not much we can do about that." William said. "Take it easy. Try not to get so torn up next time you encounter an Elf, alright?"

"So that was an Elf?" Guiran asked.

"According to the Wizard, yes. It was." Timothy said. "A far cry from Earth's Elves, eh?"

"Yes. I wonder if they started out the same, millennia back, and diverged somewhere along the way in ideals." Guiran said.

"I doubt it. They're too different. Our Elves did not have horns or claws, or glowing eyes." William said. "Too bad they couldn't come with us when we came to this world."

"They were not part of the Army." Guiran said, simply. "You should be on your way ... help the Wizard keep it together until our little band gets back with Malici."

William nodded, and looked over at Timothy. "Let's not 'port straight in this time, eh? Maybe he'll open the door for us."

"I hope. If not, he's a worse fool that I thought." Timothy said. And with that remark, both of them vanished in teleportation back to the foot of the Tower.

*

The wagon rolled along the road easily, bumping and jiggling over every little discrepancy in the road. Both Centaurii walked along behind the wagon even still, every member of the group lost in their own thoughts.

M'lar carried the new map in his hand, thinking over the odd encounter with the men, and wondering just how accurate the map was. He intended to go over it in every smallest detail, comparing it to his own. Even if that much matched up well, he couldn't help but be suspicious of the rest ... who were they? What were their interests? How did they know of the mission?

Deilo thought about Mutsgae, and worried over the Lizard's actions. What had prompted such strange behavior? Suddenly ditching out of the wagon with no warning what so ever was unheard of, for Mutsgae. Landing from the wagon with the tailgate down was sometimes a wrench ... why leap from a moving wagon, atop a load? It seemed insane. All to run out across a random field to stare at a haystack? To what end? Deilo feared for his friend's mind.

Lillia however, was not so concerned over it. All the members of the little group did some of the darndest things, to her thinking. Much of what they did seemed to make no sense to her. She merely poked seeds into the little cage that housed her bird, occasionally petting it on the head and murmuring little words of encouragement.

Horus spent most of his time worrying over Deilo and the lines ... Deilo didn't seem to be paying very much attention to the ridali at all. He was grateful the beast was well trained, and not prone to sudden wild maneuvers just to see if its driver was paying attention to it.

Mutsgae sat in his own thoughts, well aware that Deilo was concerned over his mental faculties. He figured he'd have to come up with something he could tell Deilo. He had been told not to tell them about the Dragon ... but what could he do? Trust was a big thing between the friends, and he did not want to be the one to break that. He could see no way out, except to maybe hope it would all blow over if he held his silence and did nothing else that could be construed as weird or crazy.

The day's travel wound on until dusk, when they stopped once more. All the preparations were done in silence, until over the evening meal, Deilo asked, "Where are we going?"

M'lar looked over at him. "I assume you mean the first leg?"

Deilo nodded. "To where are we headed?"

"First, we're going to Tekma. It's a little town on a river that more or less follows the mountain range. There, we will hire a tug that will take us, and your wagon, upstream towards the east. The route is actually northeast ... but then the border of Gnaria goes northeast. Gnaria is a wedge-shape, see." He took out his map and pushed it open, on the ground between his knees. He used each knee to hold the sides open, as one hand was occupied with his dinner. With his other hand, he pointed out places on the map. "This my map of Gnaria ... this triangular shape is the entire valley. We are here." He pointed to a spot just off the blot that was Kentalic. "Gnaria isn't really all that big ... especially compared to the Kingdoms outside. Tekma is here." He pointed to a little dot on a river that carved a wobbly line to the northeast, before abruptly ending. "I don't know how far that river goes ... I will see as well as you will. But travel on the river will be far faster and safer than trying to hoof it." A finger traced a circle around a patch of the river that went past an area marked *dry lands*. "This area here is notorious for bandits. I want to stay on the river at least until after there. I would like to stay on the river as long as possible, though. There is a city, out there in the east, somewhere. I have never been there, myself. Nor do I know what it is called. I have heard it is entirely underground ... I hope the river goes that far. I have personally never been any farther east in the Gnarian valley than Isifer, here." He pointed at a little blot just north of Takmetak. "This area on the highland cleft I was told about, and I copied it off another map. All guides in the Valley are warned about that spot. It can be deadly."

Deilo leaned over and looked at the map. "You don't know very much about the east at all, do you?"

"No, I don't. But I was the only one who had been *that* far east. And the most experienced one, who was there at the time. I imagine there is some nut, *somewhere* who went all the way east that he could, just to see what was out there. Almost no one goes out there. I don't know why. Probably because it's more prone to flash floods and all that. The snowmelt off the mountains is pretty ferocious out there." M'lar said. "At least, that's what I've heard, from folks who moved west out of that area." He lifted one knee, and then the other, allowing the map to roll back up. He picked it up, and set it aside before pulling out the map he had been given. "I was given this map today, by those men who tried to stop the wagon ... or didn't, as the case might be. I don't know who they were or what they wanted ... but ... they gave me this map. I didn't get a chance to really inspect our route, at the time. Let's see what it has to say." He set it down, and unrolled it with one hand, the map lying flat as he did so, completely pliable. He looked down at it, chewing on a bite of his dinner as he traced a finger over the surface. The river he had spoken of was on the map, and showed that it went east for a ways before curling up northwards, where it forked, and one branch headed east again, just before becoming a lake. The lake had two inlets on the north and east. The eastern one curled back southward again, where it met up with what looked like it might be a small village, if it weren't for the weird shading all around it. "This *might* be the underground city." M'lar said. "Nothing on this map is labeled. It's as if who ever drew it didn't have the foggiest idea what anything was called." He mused, before tracing the river onwards. It left the little village-town-city, and forked several times more, one of the root streams ending quite close to the far eastern edge of Gnaria. "I don't know what the condition of this river is. We might be able to go this far in a boat, but I doubt it. Least wise ... no boat that could take our wagon. But at least we'll have a landmark we can follow reliably to this point. After this point here, we'll have to strike out on our own, cross country and hope we end up in the right place." M'lar looked over at the others. "Why are you all going out there, anyway?" he asked. "There's nothing out there."

"Someone lives out there, supposedly. And if he's still there, and still alive, the Wizard wants us to bring him in." Deilo said. "That's it."

"Huh. I wonder why he yanked ya'll up for that. He could just as easily have sent one of his cavalry men out there."

"Something about a ward on the area." Deilo said. "We're apparently going to have to leave you and the ridali behind, to get through the ward."

M'lar sat up a little straighter, frowning. "Odd. What sort of ward?"

Deilo shrugged. "Can't say, really."

M'lar shrugged, as well. "I guess the Wizard knows what he's doing, if he goes this far out of his way to do this."

"I hope he knows what he's doing." Deilo said, quietly, tucking one knee up to his chest to lean on. He reached over to his plate, and picked up his last biscuit and dipped it in the gravy that puddled on one edge.

"This is all very weird." M'lar said. "Hopefully it will be uneventful."

"I hope." Deilo said. "The last thing we need is excitement. We'd get lost all too quickly."

"I know." M'lar said, quietly, studying the map. He wondered again why nothing was labeled. It was obviously a map of Gnaria ... but it was not labeled as such, and not even the main cities were labeled. Even rural folk knew the name of Kentalic!

Mutsgae came inside the tent, having finished eating his own dinner. He stopped there, and looked at everyone, well knowing what was happening ... the tent was far from soundproof. He walked around everyone, and slumped in the back of the tent, resting his snout on crossed forelegs.

M'lar glanced over at him. "And?"

"Nothing to be seen but grass. I'm too short." Mutsgae said.

"I'll take a look before I bed down." Deilo promised.

Horus shifted his weight, getting one hind leg out from under his prone equine body. "What will we do, if we do get lost?" he asked.

"The area appears to be riddled with rivers." M'lar said. "If we manage to find a river, we'll follow it downstream until we find known territory, and then head back up again, following the branches we need." He said. "Should be fairly simple, so long as we don't lose this map. It looks like the region *is* prone to flooding."

"Can I look at that?" Horus asked.

"Sure." M'lar picked up the map, and handed it over to Horus, who handled it as if it were gossamer. He studied it intensely. He couldn't read Gnarian very well, yet, though he could more or less speak and understand it. Thankfully, this particular map didn't need reading skills. He looked at the area they would be traveling for a long time, trying to commit the image to memory, following every line of the various rivers, and their proximity to other things. Mountain ranges, lakes, the big blot of forest ...

"It's kind of hard to get a sense so scale on that thing." Deilo said, leaning on Horus' lower shoulder to look at the map, too.

"Not so much." M'lar said. "You just have to have traveled enough to know about how far you can go in one day. This, of course, is throwing me for a slight loop ... that big animal of yours is throwing new numbers into the equation. Wagons just simply don't travel that fast. But yours travels quite fast ... faster still if it weren't held back by us on foot."

"Hey ... if you feel like running the whole way, I can let it go." Deilo said.

M'lar wrinkled his snout. "Running is all fine and dandy ... right up until you have to do it all day, day in and day out."

Horus dropped the map slightly, and looked at M'lar. "I can run all day." He said, simply.

M'lar looked at him. "I doubt it. It takes a lot of endurance to do that sort of thing."

"I know. It was my job, at the ranch." Horus said. "I can run all day. So can Mutsgae, now." He nodded to the Lizard that appeared to be sleeping in the back.

M'lar considered Horus for a moment, then looked over at Mutsgae. With legs that short, M'lar found it hard to believe him running *anywhere*, much less all day. He looked back at Horus. "Alright. We'll give it a shot, then."

"Alright. But when you get tired, you let us know. We don't need you straining yourself into injury." Horus warned.

M'lar just looked at Horus again. All of a sudden it seemed like the tables had turned ... Horus, a rather young Centaurii, telling M'lar what and how to do. M'lar thought about it for a moment, then looked at Horus again. If the youngster could indeed run all day ... he had to be massively strong to go with all that endurance. "What kind of shoes are you wearing?" M'lar asked, suddenly.

Horus blinked at the unexpected question. "Metal."

"*Metal?*" M'lar asked. "Not wood? Not leather?"

"Metal." Horus confirmed, before rolling to one side to bring one foreleg out from under him. He stretched it out ahead, so M'lar could see the metal contraption that was fastened to his hoof with a series of clamps.

M'lar bent to look at it closely. "Huh. I've never seen the like, before."

"Huteri and Torj made them for me. They got tired of my always needing new shoes." Horus said.

"I wonder if I could get a set made like that." M'lar said. "I wear wooden shoes ... they tie on the leg." He too rolled to one side for a moment, to bring a foreleg forward. On his hoof was a wooden cog, with leather ties circling his pastern to hold it on.

Horus shook his head. "Too bulky for fast work. And when thinned down, they were too fragile for running. Especially over uneven ground." He said. "But even before the ranch, I always wore metal shoes. They were hideously expensive, but they didn't wear out like wood or leather. And they certainly didn't twist and sprain the leg. But those weren't designed for the work these here were." He reached down and fiddled with the front of the shoe, and the clamp popped open, allowing the shoe to drop off. He picked it up, and handed it to M'lar.

M'lar looked it over, fiddling with every little bit of it. "Interesting. They're certainly sturdy." He nodded. "If we do this running thing ... I may need a set."

"Would Tekma have a smithy?" Deilo asked.

"Should. Might be hard to find ... Tekma is just a village." M'lar said, handing the shoe back to Horus, who clamped it back on his foot before folding the leg back up under his chest.

M'lar folded his leg up, as well, thinking. Those metal shoes were not only less bulky, but they also weighed less. Interesting.

"Maybe we can get some made." Deilo said. "Maybe."

"If we make good time, we'll look into it." M'lar said.

Deilo got to his feet, and started collecting the dishes up. Once he had them all stacked up, he carried them outside, where he cleaned and stowed them back in the wagon. He paused there, to look around at the landscape surrounding them. They were still in farm country, this close to Kentalic, and there was little to see that wasn't normal for farms. There was an occasional building here or there, some animals here and there, in clumps and clusters. A lot of grass, far more crops. Occasionally an odd tree in strategic locations. Heaving a sigh, Deilo went back into the tent, and found himself a good spot to start arranging his bedding. Lillia was already atop the clothing sack, her bed made underneath her. She watched him without a word, still listening to everything that was said.

In the morning they were a jovial bunch, poking fun and cracking jokes as they prepared to get going that day. Horus tripped over Mutsgae twice, when entering and leaving the tent, which evoked some yelling and some laughter. Lillia stowed her little bundle of things, and then saddled up her bird.

"Where are you going?" Deilo asked, setting the tent bundle in the back of the wagon.

"I'm going to do some flying. He's getting restless, always being caged ... and me too. I can see farther from higher, so maybe I can do some good." She said, running the lines to the little saddle.

"Alright. But you be very careful. We don't need to be rescuing you from a hawk."

"I'll keep an eye out." She promised, before climbing aboard, and taking off into the sky.

Deilo watched her go for a time, and then shook his head before returning to his packing. Horus walked up, leading the harnessed ridali to the wagon. He maneuvered it into the shafts, and started hitching it up.

"Do you ever forget some of that?" M'lar asked, walking up with another bundle.

"Sometimes. That's why I check it so often before we head out. If I get something wrong or forget something ... it could be disastrous." Horus said.

"How long did it take you to learn all the ins and outs of that rig?" M'lar asked.

"About a week. There are different rigs, though ..." Horus said. "You should see a six-ridali hitching. Now *that* can move a wagon."

"I can't imagine that many stuck to the same wagon." M'lar said, honestly. "Just one seems amazing."

"There's this giant wagon that the foreman always took to town." Deilo said. "He always hitched six to it. They put several tons of stuff in that wagon, and they'd *run* with it, all the way back to the ranch." He said, tightening a rope that held their things secure.

"I'd like to see that some day." M'lar said, before helping Horus get Mutsgae up onto the wagon.

"I think we might need to build some sort of ramp for you, Muts. This is getting old." Horus said.

"Hey. I can climb your tail, if you like?" Mutsgae said.

Horus frowned at the lizard, as Deilo laughed.

"Those two don't like each other, do they?" M'lar asked of Deilo, as Deilo climbed up into the front of the wagon.

"To the contrary. Those two are the closest of us." Deilo said. "They just don't show it very well."

"Hum." M'lar said. "Where is the little lady?"

"She's riding her bird, for now." Deilo said, as Horus handed him the lines. "As soon as you two are ready, we can go."

M'lar nodded, and double checked that his own shoes were well secured. He did not want to suffer a sprain while traveling that fast.

"I'm ready." Horus announced, from the other side of the wagon. "I made sure our fire was good and out, too."

"Alright." Deilo said. "Anything I should know, before I attempt to drive at that kind of speed?"

"Keep a very light touch on the lines ... a heavy one could wreck the cart. Stay engaged, too ... you don't want the ridali wandering where ever it feels like going. It's not as easy as it looks, I assure you." Horus warned.

"Okay. I'll give it my best shot."

M'lar heaved a sigh. Now or never, he supposed. But then Horus started talking again.

Restoration of Numar

"We'll go along in front, and you follow. That should make it easier. Also it'll keep you from leaving us way behind. If you have a problem, yell. Okay?" Horus suggested.

M'lar cocked one ear. These kids were nothing like they had been, when he'd first met them. They had enough confidence in themselves now to be giving orders here and there like they really knew what they were doing.

"Okay." Deilo said. "Whenever you're ready."

"M'lar?" Horus asked. "Are you ready?"

"Sure. Why not? Let's go." M'lar said, before heading out down the road at an easy trot. Horus caught up to him quickly, and they could both hear the wagon start rolling behind them, getting back on the road while Deilo talked to and encouraged the ridali.

"I'll match you." Horus said, simply.

"Alright." M'lar said.

They trotted out in tandem for the first mile, before M'lar stepped up the pace again, having warmed up sufficiently, switching over to a canter. Horus matched him, stride for stride, with never a comment.

It was not long before M'lar felt like his lungs were going to turn inside out from the exertion, not being used to lengthy bouts of speed. He glanced over at Horus to see how the young Centaurii was doing, and noticed that Horus seemed to be breathing normally, slow and regular ... and very, very deep. M'lar wondered at that for a moment, almost to the point of gasping for air. He kept pounding away at the road, listening to the ridali hot on their tails as it towed that heavy wagon. He hoped he wasn't going to suddenly pass out and fall ... that beast wouldn't have the time to get that wagon stopped before it all ran right over him.

Horus looked over at M'lar, noticing the unusual amount of difficulty he was having. "What are you doing??" Horus asked. "Trying to kill yourself? Breathe! Use your other lungs!" He said, slapping M'lar's lower shoulder.

M'lar had an epiphany, then, suddenly realizing how Horus was managing to breathe so easy. Not being used to running or hard labor, M'lar – like most Centaurii – had never learned to use his larger equine lungs that were deeper in his body. He set to concentrating on using them for the first time in his life, and it made a profound difference. His vision cleared up as if it had been in a fog, and it became a lot easier to maintain the canter.

"Much better!" Horus said, not really understanding the problem M'lar had been having. Unlike most Centaurii, he had never learned to *not* use all his lung capacity. He had always been a busy little person, always hard at work when not traveling cross-country.

As he practiced breathing deep, M'lar found stores of energy he never knew he had, and once he got the hang of it so he didn't have to concentrate on it, he leapt forward again to an even faster pace. Now, he could do it. Now, he *wanted* to do it. Especially since if they made good enough time, they could stop and get some of those strange shoes made for *his* feet.

Horus was behind him only in the split second of the initial jump, but quickly matched him up again. Behind them, they could hear Deilo calling to the ridali, who was sounding like it was having the time of its life, blasting down the road at speeds that a wagon really ought not go.

Travelers who saw them coming quickly vacated the road entirely, standing far off to the sides to watch the odd procession go tearing past as if their tails were on fire. However – there was not a hint of terror or fear in any of them. Instead, they looked like they were simply enjoying themselves.

Horus turned his head to the side to glance back when he heard the ridali honk and bellow suddenly. He grinned, and surged ahead again to catch back up with M'lar as the ridali shook its massive four-horned head, pounding along behind them, getting into the spirit.

They traveled a very long ways down the road by the time the sun reached the crest of its westward journey ... and it took a lot of convincing to get the ridali to slow down and eventually stop so they could break for lunch. Horus unhitched the beast so it could graze while they ate ... they had plenty of time.

"How far are we from Tekma?" Deilo asked, as he worked on making the meal.

"I really can't say. I haven't traveled that fast, before." M'lar said, before taking a small drink of water. He and Horus were both hot enough that anything more might be dangerous for them. He passed the water bag over to Horus, who also only took a small drink.

Lillia zoomed in on her bird, and landed nearby. "You boys are insane!" She practically yelled at them, storming over towards the group. If they hadn't really known her, her small self storming over and yelling at them would have been only comical. "I am *really* glad that I was not on that wagon! Have you no brains between you?!" She yelled, waving her arms in frustration once she'd reached them. "You could have easily wrecked the wagon! Killed yourselves!"

"Lil, you worry too much." Deilo said.

"No, I don't!" She said, stomping a foot. "You're being reckless!"

"We were fine." Deilo said. "And we made good time, to boot."

"Made good time! Made good *time*?" She crossed her arms, frowning at them all. "And what exactly would making good time do us, if you suddenly wreck the wagon, and we have to *walk* all the way across the valley? Huh? Seems like you'd *lose* time, to me! And wouldn't it be *prudent* to get there and back again still *alive*? Huh? Did that occur to any of you? At all?" She gestured widely. "You're *not* doing that again!! Do you hear me! You do *not* do that again!"

Deilo sighed, and nodded. "Alright."

M'lar watched all this silently, wondering.

"Looks like we're stuck at a trot, guys. Hope you enjoyed your run." Deilo said, going back to working on lunch.

M'lar only nodded, and unrolled his map, to try and figure out where they were, and how much distance they had gained. When the meal was ready, Deilo passed out the bowls, making sure everyone got plenty to eat. M'lar and Horus both ate plenty, and then chased it all down with a considerable amount of water.

"We're going to have to refill our barrels soon, you two keep drinking like that." Deilo said, as Horus took a bucket of water to the ridali.

"We'll be at a river shortly. Having enough water will be the least of our worries." M'lar said, still studying the map and looking around at the countryside.

"Any idea where we are?" Deilo asked.

"Somewhere on this road." M'lar said, pointing. "But you knew that."

"Yes. I did." Deilo said. "I take it that means you don't know."

"Nope. I haven't a clue." M'lar said, rolling the stiff map back up and stowing it.

"Boy, it's a good thing you're one of the best guides." Deilo said, sarcastically.

M'lar pulled a face, and then wandered over to the road, to look towards their destination. On the very edge of the horizon the tips of the southern mountain range were visible. He turned around, and walked back to the wagon, unrolling the other map. "Deilo. Come show me where you are going." He bid.

Deilo stood up and walked over to the wagon, where M'lar had spread the pliable thing. He looked at it briefly, and plunked a finger down on the spot that had been blank in the Wizard's map. "There." It was almost dead on the border, in the far point of the country, deep in the mountains.

"*There?*" M'lar asked. "What insane fool would live there?"

Deilo shrugged. "I find it interesting that this map has that place mapped in, on the forms of the mountains. Even the Wizard's own map did not have anything written there ... he couldn't see it."

M'lar pulled on his lower lip. "Interesting indeed."

"Who exactly was it that gave this map to you?" Deilo asked.

M'lar shrugged. "All he said was that his name was William – odd name, that – and that he had interest in us getting there successfully."

Deilo considered that. "Huh."

"This is all so weird. But at least the weird stuff has been in our favor so far ... except for your location that you're going to. That's a perilous journey right there, and you may be awhile just getting through the mountains." M'lar said. "And I can't go with you."

"I know."

"If you'll notice, the river we'll be on dips southward, on this map, then comes back up almost right to the spot you're headed to. That's a long ways to be in the mountains ... but you wouldn't get lost. Even if it was just a stream ... you couldn't lose a stream. However, we could cut across country here." He drew a line with a finger, leaving the river and going across the valley again, directly towards the point Deilo had picked out. "Go through the mountains here until you found the river again, and *then* follow it. But I don't know how well you navigate. I'd have to leave you at the mountains. I suppose it's easy enough – keep your face to the rising sun."

"We'll cross that bridge when we get there." Deilo said. "We still have to get *to* the river." He pointed out.

"Quite right." M'lar said, before rolling the map up.

Deilo nodded and went back to his work, cleaning up after the meal and repacking the supplies. Horus had listened to all that was said, as he re-hitched the ridali to the wagon.

"Lil, are you going to ride with us this time?" Deilo asked, setting a bowl of water in the wagon so Mutsgae could drink – he'd never left the wagon, to forestall having to get *in* the wagon.

"I'm going to have to, now aren't I?" She asked. "To keep and eye on you boys."

"Hey, now. We're a tad old to be boys anymore." Deilo chided.

"You don't act it!" She shot back.

"Alright! Alright. Calm down, okay? It's not the end of the world." Deilo said, setting her and her bird in the wagon. "Secure your bird, alright? We'll take care of the rest." He reached over and took the empty bowl from Mutsgae, and stowed it.

"If what the Wizard said was true, and you do something stupid and kill yourself, it *will* be the end of the world." Lillia led her bird over to the cage, and inside, where she unsaddled it and fed it, before leaving the cage and locking the door. By the time she was done, Deilo was climbing back onto the wagon, and the group was setting out once more. Horus and M'lar trotted behind the wagon again, following the wagon down the road. It was not long before the sky began to darken as clouds moved in from the west, off the sea. M'lar watched it with concern, but did not say anything at all. Horus also took notice, but he was thinking more along the lines of how to keep the dry goods dry. It took M'lar a moment to realize Horus was talking to him as they trotted.

"What?" M'lar asked.

"Do we have a tarp?" Horus asked again.

"A what?" M'lar asked.

"A tarp! To cover the wagon." Horus gestured at the wagon. "If it rains."

"No. We don't have a tarp. But we do have the tent ... it should be waterproof." M'lar said.

"Okay. At least we have that." Horus said. "In case it rains."

"Oh, it'll rain alright." M'lar said.

"How can you be that sure?" Horus asked.

"Because of the way Gnaria is laid out. It's a triangular wedge, from west to east. And when moisture blows into that wedge from off the sea, it gets compressed between the mountain ranges as it goes east ... the farther east it goes, the nastier the storm gets. That's *part* of why the eastern reaches flood so badly! The moisture gets pounded down their throats. During the summer that's no big deal ... it runs off as fast as it gets there. But in the winter it turns to snow and ice, and stays. And builds up. And then in the spring, all that melts, and floods the whole area."

"Oh." Horus looked up at the gathering storm.

"We're still far enough west, I don't think we'll have much of a problem." M'lar said. "But it'll definitely be worse than what you experienced on the ranch."

"Should we stop and cover the wagon now?"

"Might be a good idea." M'lar said, before opening up and passing the wagon. He pulled up even with Deilo. "Stop the wagon!"

Deilo glanced at him, said something to Lillia who sat next to him, and then started working on stopping the wagon as

Lillia found a safe spot to stay while the ridali started trying to slow the heavy weight.

Once the wagon was stopped, Deilo turned around in his seat to look back at the two Centaurii as they started poking about in the wagon's bed. "What's going on?" he asked.

"We're going to cover the wagon." Horus said. "Where's the tent?"

"Over there." Deilo pointed at one of the back corners, before looking up at the sky. He made his way into the wagon himself, to aid in the covering. He also extracted a jacket to wear, to keep himself dry when it started raining. Taking a corner of the tent material, he draped it over the birds cage, after Lillia went in. "Take it easy in there, alright?" Deilo asked.

"I will." She said. "Don't do anything crazy."

Deilo laughed. "I won't." He tucked the tent around the cage snugly, to keep water out as the other two tucked the edges of the tent down around the rest of the load. "Are we ready?" he asked, once they were done.

"Yeah. Let's get going." M'lar said.

Deilo nodded, and made his way carefully to the front again, apologizing when one lump under the tent growled at him when he stood on it. "Sorry, Muts."

Mutsgae sat still under the tent, hoping he wouldn't smother once it all got wet. The wagon started on down the road again, with the road all to itself as the inclement weather continued to build as it caught up to them.

"Are we going to be able to keep going, in the weather?" Horus asked, as they trotted along.

"Should. I don't see why not. The road is still paved ... we should be fine." M'lar said, before reminding himself to breathe deep. He watched Horus with growing admiration as they traveled, and the time slipped by. His own muscles were burning with the exertion he had been putting on them all day, but Horus seemed to be powering along just like he had in the morning, showing no signs of lagging responses, tiring legs, or missed beats. It made him feel bad after a fashion, that he couldn't hold up to that kind of endurance.

Horus didn't say much as they traveled, watching the weather warily. It continued to get darker, as the winds started kicking up their heels. "Keep a tight hand on those lines, Deilo!" he called.

"I am!"

"Good!"

Bits of foliage blew across the road, skittering ahead of the winds that pushed them into activity, swirling madly about the pounding feet that carried the group forward. After a time it became apparent that not all of the darkening of the skies was due to the storm ... it was getting late enough that the sun was starting to go down.

"Let's keep going!" M'lar said. "Maybe we can find some shelter for the night!"

Deilo nodded, without comment.

"Are you sure you're up to that?" Horus asked.

"I'm fine." M'lar insisted. "Let's keep going."

"Okay." Horus said, without conviction.

The clouds roiled overhead, but kept to themselves even yet, the wind gusting and tugging at every thing it could, tearing at their clothing and wagon, making the tent billow and pop.

"We can't keep going like this!" Deilo said, when it started getting too dark to see the road. "We have to stop!"

"Let's find a hilltop." M'lar suggested. "We don't need wet bedding."

"Bedding!" Horus said. "Hah!"

M'lar didn't know what Horus meant by that remark, until after they had stopped and gotten the tent set up and staked down securely. Horus promptly had the ridali back the wagon into the tent, taking up nearly the entirety of the inside area. M'lar watched this with some concern. "And where are we going to stay?" he asked, once the ridali was staked out and the harness carried in.

"Inside." Horus said, simply.

"There's no room."

"Sure there is. Walk in down the side of the wagon, lie down, and roll under. Deilo can stay on the wagon, with Lillia and Mutsgae. I'll be on the other side." Horus said. "With the tent set up, we can't leave the wagon out, uncovered."

M'lar heaved a sigh, but did as was suggested. It was far from comfortable, but they were at least sure of being dry. Deilo sat in the wagon next to Mutsgae, and made them all a cold dinner, working mostly by feel.

Then there was an audible pop, as M'lar rapped a small sphere against his own shoulder. The sphere glowed softly, shedding light on the interior of the tent.

"Hey. What's that?" Deilo asked.

"Majick." M'lar said, holding the sphere up. "Flame-less light. I didn't want you inadvertently poisoning us ... or making dinner inedible with the wrong ingredients."

"Ah, I couldn't do either." Deilo said. "But it *might* become distasteful."

"That won't do well." M'lar said, as Horus laughed.

"I just hope that thing isn't going to put majick on *me*." Deilo said. "I don't want to die when I try to cross that ward."

M'lar looked at him strangely, and *then* remembered that part. "*Oh*. I forgot. Well ... it shouldn't. The majick is locked inside the sphere. But just in case, I'll hang onto it myself."

Deilo nodded, working swiftly to make and hand out dinner. Once it was all wolfed down, M'lar popped the sphere again, making the light go out. He tucked it away into a pocket on his harness, and then laid down next to the wagon. He ooched over sideways so he was partly under the wagon, and away from the tent wall. On the other side, he heard Horus do the same thing. The wagon overhead creaked slightly as those in it moved around, settling in.

They were all awakened in the middle of the night as the howling wind suddenly stopped. Shortly thereafter, the rain came, pouring down hard enough to make the entire tent shiver on its poles.

"That's a lot of rain." Horus said, quietly.

"Aye." M'lar said. "It is, indeed. I'm glad we have the tent."

"Me, too."

The wagon creaked slightly, when Deilo sat up, listening to the rain come down. After a few minutes he laid down again, and the group tried to go back to sleep. A mere hour later, however, Horus was awakened by a rather rude, cold touch. He yelped, coming out of his sleep in a hurry, jerking up. He smacked into the bottom of the wagon, and fell back down again, groaning as he held his new bruises.

M'lar rolled over, waking. "What-?"

"Ouuuuuw." Horus groaned. "It's *wet* over here! There's water coming inside!" He said, getting up again – this time careful of the wagon.

M'lar moved, then, also getting up with a yawn. "It won't kill you."

"No ... but it's a rude bedfellow."

M'lar's yawn was interrupted with a laugh. "I have to agree with you, there."

"It's still raining." Deilo said, sleepily.

"Yes, it is." Horus said, grumpily.

"Looks like we'll have to sleep on our feet." M'lar said, pushing the tent wall away from his side. It was cold, and *felt* wet.

Horus grumbled unhappily.

"Hey ... we can rearrange things here, and you two can climb in. The wagon's big enough. It's not like we're gonna try to move it with ya'll in it." Deilo suggested, as Mutsgae crawled to the front.

"That sounds like an idea." Horus said, starting to move the things in the wagon that he could reach. Deilo started stacking stuff up. It would never ride like that, but they weren't moving, so it was no big deal. Once enough space was cleared, the two Centaurii climbed into the wagon and laid down again. Deilo passed out blankets, and everyone went back to sleep again, waiting out the storm.

The rain continued until a few hours after dawn, when it abruptly quit, leaving behind a partly cloudy purple sky. The group worked quickly to re-arrange the wagon again, and take the tent down. During the rain they had eaten, so no time was taken for that. In a very short order, they were off again, the ridali working hard to get the wagon to the road once more. The patch the tent had covered was wet, but still fairly firm. But between the tent and the road was downright mushy. The two Centaurii pushed on the wagon from behind, and the three of them managed to get the wagon to roll up onto the paved road. That done, they moved out at a trot again.

M'lar didn't say anything, but he knew that what little time they'd gained the day before, they had already lost, in their late start this morning. That meant that there would be no time to stop for metal shoes.

Oh well.

Before noon arrived, though, they pulled into the little town of Tekma – far sooner than M'lar had expected. Deilo found a spot to park the wagon, and then threw a small sack to Horus, who caught it despite not having a warning. "We'll wait here. Go get him some shoes." Deilo said.

"Do we have time for that?" M'lar protested.

"Do we have time for you to wear out a shoe, or come up lame?" Deilo countered.

M'lar conceded the point, and headed out, Horus following along behind. They asked a few people, and found the blacksmith fairly quickly. But to get him to make a set of the complex shoes that Horus wore took a pretty chink indeed. It was well after lunch before they got back to the wagon, M'lar carrying the new set of shoes made especially for his own hooves.

"You're not going to wear them?" Deilo asked, as M'lar tied them to the tailgate, dangling down.

"No. They're still too warm to be comfortable. They fit, I'm willing to wait. Thank you, by the way." M'lar said. "Let's find a boat, and be on our way." He led the way down to the river, where a small fleet of small boats were bobbing. Some were leaving, some arriving, and a few just sitting there, tied off. M'lar wandered the docks, looking for a boat big enough to take on the wagon – he wasn't even going to consider leaving it behind. In the end they had to wait until dark, when the biggest boat of the lot came in. M'lar managed to hire the boat, but again it took a lot of coins. The boats were used to ferrying *downstream*, to Kentalic. Not upstream, into the wilderness.

That night, they loaded the wagon and ridali onto the boat. It was a tricky process, and the boat wouldn't sit still for the transfer, trying to wiggle its way out from under the wagon as it rolled onto the deck. Once they were all on the boat, it rode rather low in the water. They unhitched the ridali and took it to the bow, where they tied it securely. Then they secured the wagon with every scrap of rope they could dig up. By the time they were done, the wagon never moved despite the swaying of the deck. The group then all turned in, finding a spot on the deck to bed down as the captain of the boat started it going upstream. The engine sputtered and growled as it started its heavy load up the river, against the current.

The captain of the boat sat up the entire night, guiding the boat along its way, while everyone else slept the night through. In the morning, the only other crewman on the boat took over, while the captain turned in. The friends all stayed quiet and out of the way, watching the land glide by. There was not much of anything to do, anymore.

M'lar leaned over the side, lying on the deck, and dropped his new shoes into the river water, holding on to the rope he had them all tied together with. Even after the cool night, they were still too warm to wear. He had to wonder what in the world they were made of. But after an hour or so in the river itself, they were cooled off sufficiently. He took his old, wooden shoes off, and put the new ones on, clamping them securely in place. They felt very funny, grabbing onto his hoof like that. But they never moved, quite secure in their placement. He got to his feet and walked around a bit in them, then sat down again, out of the way.

Horus stayed in the front of the boat with the ridali, keeping it calm and occupied, brushing out its long coat and getting all the travel-wear out of it. After the second day, the animal's coat verily shined in brilliance, not a speck to be seen.

They rode the river for a week in peace, a long, boring peace. Three more storms like the first caught up with them, each one a little meaner than the last.

"Surely this isn't just the valley narrowing in." Deilo said, after the third one let up finally. They had been working hard for about an hour, slicking all the water off the deck to keep the boat above water.

"No. It's just the season is changing. We're coming into the winter season, and as we do, the storms will become more frequent and ugly." M'lar said. "Though I only know this through hearsay. I've never been this far east, myself."

Deilo thought about that. "I hope we get in and out before it starts snowing."

"We have a good month, before that starts to happen." M'lar assured him. "Though it might not be that long, in the mountains."

"How far are we?"

"I don't know. The only landmarks I'll have are the forks in the river. Not even the captain knows where we are on the river. Some days we make good time, other days we've barely made *any* progress. It's really hard to tell, when this area is as little traveled as it is."

Deilo sighed.

"Don't worry. I'll let you know the moment I know where we are." M'lar said.

"I'm sure you will. But this is a very bad time to get lost."

"We can't get lost. We're on a river, for crying out loud. There's only one way to go." He pointed upstream. "That way."

Deilo looked at him for a moment, then wandered off.

M'lar only shrugged, and then pulled out the map that had the river on it ... he was glad that strange fellow had given him the map, whatever his motives were.

That evening, an alarm was raised, as the boat stopped moving upstream entirely, working only to hold its position and not float back downstream. Everybody stopped whatever they were doing – even if it was nothing – and looked ahead.

There was a heavy chain strung across the river, from one bank to the other, each end tethered to a stout tree.

"This doesn't look good." Deilo remarked.

"Indeed!" The crewman said. "That's how bandits stop boats to raid them."

"Then where are the bandits?" M'lar asked, looking around?"

"Boats don't *go* upstream." The crewman said, as the captain got his wits about him after having been awakened. "We're on the wrong side. They're probably as surprised to see us, as we are the chain."

"What's this, now?" The captain asked, stumping around. "A chain??"

"Yes." The crewman said. "But I don't see any bandits."

"That's because they're not there." The captain said, rubbing his palms.

"Why?" M'lar asked.

"Seeing how we're headed upstream, they probably thought we were authorities sent out to deal with them." The captain. "They saw us coming, and fled the area. Let's get that chain aboard."

The crewman started the boat moving again, though slowly. Once they reached the chain, the boat was stopped again, and the captain grabbed a hold of it, and went along it, hand-over-hand to the shore, getting thoroughly soaked. Once ashore, he undid the tether, and pulled himself back up the length of the chain to the boat. Climbing aboard, he fastened the chain to the boat, and then repeated the process to the other side. Once he was back again, he pulled all the chain up into the boat, and they started upstream again.

"Scored a right fine chain, just then." The captain said, smugly, grinning as he looked at the heap of metal. "Must be an easy thousand chinks worth of chain right there."

"Uh, well ... congratulations." M'lar said.

Deilo just stared at the captain, confused. "What are you going to do with it?"

"Oh, make me a few tethers out of it. Imagine! Me! With a chain, rather than a tatty old rope to tie my boat. Only rich folk can afford chain. Much less chain like that. The rest ... I might find a use for it, or I might sell it, get some upgrades going. I don't know yet." The captain said. "Right piece of luck, getting that."

"Right piece of luck we didn't get *raided*!" Deilo said.

"Oh, well, yes. That, too." The captain said, before gathering up the chain and hauling it below decks, whistling a merry little tune.

"Happy sort, eh?" M'lar said.

"Crazy sort, you ask me." Horus said.

"Opportunist is the word you're looking for." Lillia said. "That's all he is. Opportunistic."

"I suppose that's one way to get ahead." Deilo mused. "Awful dangerous game to play, though. Thieving from the thieves."

"At least we won't be here when he goes back the other way." M'lar said. "Not our problem."

"Why would he have problems going the other way?" Deilo asked. "He's got their chain."

"Yeah ... but if they can afford that hunk of chain ... you know they're bound to have a spare." M'lar pointed out. "Bandits about these parts are no small cheese."

" ... oh." Deilo said. "Then how are we going to get back, if we don't retain the boat?"

"We can't afford to retain the boat." M'lar said. "Regardless. It took a lot just to *hire* the boat. We're going to have to go it on foot."

"Oh, fun." Deilo remarked.

"At least we missed that snare." M'lar said.

"At least." Horus said. "Lil?"

"Yeah?" She asked, from his forelock.
"Care to do some flying? I promise, we'll be good."
She thought about that. "Why?"
"Well ... if there are traps out there, a forewarning would be very nice, indeed." Horus pointed out.
"Point taken. I'll see what I can see." She said. "Take me to the cage?"

Horus turned, and walked back to the wagon, where the bird was caged. He took Lillia down from his head, and set her there. "Be very careful." He said, before rejoining the others.

Lillia prepared to ride the little bird, and then climbed up onto its back and took to the air. She flew first to the side, and then upwards, until she could see a lot, following the river's course to see what was ahead.

She returned to the boat when the wind started being too troublesome, as another storm front was building. That evening they were battening down the hatches again, preparing for another night of fighting the rain off the deck.

After the storm broke, the next four days were nothing but sunshine, and they made excellent time getting up the rain-swollen river despite the faster rate of flow. On the sixteenth day out of Tekma they reached their first fork in the river.

"I know where we are, now." M'lar said. "But it looks like it's going to be quite cold, long before we get there." He said, pointing the fork out on the map, even as the captain and crewman both fought the river to get the boat headed up the chosen fork.

"We've come that far, in almost three weeks ... that's a good distance, right?" Deilo asked.

"Well ... all things considered, yes. But to be honest I had hoped to be farther along than this. It has been almost three weeks since we left Kentalic, as you pointed out. I had hoped to be *here* by now." He pointed at a spot farther up the river.

"I guess we take what we can get." Deilo said. "We are, after all, going *up* stream."

"Very true. And we are making a safer trip, on the water." M'lar said. "This shows a forest ... we might be able to see it day after tomorrow. And then we'll be skirting its edge all the way up to and through this lake, here. At the lake we may have to leave the boat ... that all depends on what that inlet river is like." He pointed out the inlet that went the way they wanted to go.

Deilo considered the map in silence. This trip was taking a very long time ... it was already the longest trip they'd ever taken. Not in distance, but in time. The SwordDancers had taken them farther ... but they'd used majick to do it.

"I'm getting tired of this trip, already." Deilo griped, finally. "If we get out of this alive ... I don't think I'll ever travel again."

"Don't say that." M'lar patted his shoulder kindly. "Travel grows on a body."

"Not mine!" Deilo said, getting to his feet and wandering off.

"He seems awful short, today." M'lar mused.

"I think it's the boat, rather than the travel." Horus said, simply. "I have to admit ... I'm getting rather itchy, too. We're out and about, but we're in a little cage doing it."

M'lar only nodded in silence.

The forest showed up as a fuzzy green blur on the horizon the very next morning, as they followed the river between hills headed northwards. They spent most of the day fishing off the prow, dragging in fresh meat for a small feast. They ate all they could stand, and Mutsgae ate all the rest that was left afterwards, too, chewing the heads off the fish very carefully. When they reached the next fork, they took the eastern branch, following it along the southern edge of the forest. Two slow days later, they pulled in at a dock on the edge of the river. The dock was very small, with only one little fishing boat tied to it. The furred folk standing on the small pier were quite surprised to see the big boat come powering up the river and pull in.

The captain told the group to stay put rather firmly, before he left the boat, headed up the dock to talk to one of the people standing there. They turned, and led him away, towards the forest that wasn't all that far away.

"I wonder what's going on?" the crewman asked.

"My map shows a very small town just in the edge of that forest. I bet he's going to see about fresh supplies." M'lar said, for the benefit of everyone around him.

"I haven't seen people like this, before." Deilo said. "They're even weirder than Torj or Fohrel."

M'lar glanced at him. "I don't know who or what you're referring to ... but it's probably due to these people being so isolated." He said. "I've seen one or two of their race, before ... but it was nowhere near *here*."

"Well ... obviously. You've never been here before." Lillia said, astride her bird on the boat's railing.

"Quite true." Deilo said.

"Lillia ... go keep an eye on the good captain, will you? But don't be seen." Mutsgae said. "I've got a bad feeling, all of a sudden."

Lillia looked over at the others at that request. When they nodded assent, she took to the air and flew away, out towards the forest. It was not long before she came speeding back. "Break dock!" She yelled, as her bird came in for a hard landing.

"Why?" The crewman asked.

"Just do it!" M'lar said, already attacking the knots that held the boat fast.

"But why? What about the captain?" the crewman persisted.

"He's dead!" Lillia said. "Get us out of here!"

At that proclamation, the crewman launched into motion, setting the boat free from the dock. They just managed to get out into the river again when a whole group of the furred people came running down towards the dock, shouting and waving their arms.

The people there on the dock started moving excitedly, piling into the one boat they had, also casting off.

The crewman got the engine running, and poured all the power it had into getting them going upstream.

"The captain apparently managed to insult the people here ... I don't know if it was intentional or not." Lillia said. "But a fight started, and they cut him down where he stood." She looked back at the other boat.

"I don't think they intend to let us go, either." Deilo said, watching the other boat make chase.

At first it gained on them quickly, the people manning the oars intent upon their work. But as the trip wore on, the oar-powered boat began to lose ground to the engine-powered boat, as the oarsmen grew weary.

"Nothing quite like a good workout to dull an angry bent, eh?" M'lar said, once the boat started turning back, trying to alleviate the tension on their own boat.

"Eh. But what now? The captain's dead." The crewman said.

"Well ... first you get us to where we're going ... or as close as you can. After that ... it's entirely up to you." M'lar said. "If the fellow had any heirs, turn the boat over to them. If not ... I guess it's yours."

The crewman seemed to perk up at the idea of having his own boat.

"Now, don't go getting any ideas and just take it." M'lar cautioned. "You'll get yourself more trouble than you'll ever care to see."

The crewman merely nodded, slowing the engine down some to conserve the fuel.

M'lar continued to watch the local boat until it vanished from view. "You might want to be careful when you come back this way ... maybe try to go by there in the night ... you don't want that bunch chasing you while you're alone."

The crewman only nodded again. "I'll keep that in mind."

The group slowly relaxed again, but they spent more time helping out with the workings of the boat, as the boat's crew had been halved in one fell swoop. Horus ended up learning far more about boats than he ever cared to learn ... he couldn't wait to get off the thing.

Between M'lar and Horus, though, the boat continued on smoothly. They were big enough to have the weight to manipulate a lot of the ship's workings. Deilo could do some, but often times had to call on the crewman to help him. The boat had been built by a big race, with a big race in mind for operation. The crewman was one such, just as the captain had been.

Mutsgae just stayed out of the way, watching out ahead and to either side for any sign of danger. On the rare occasion he looked upwards, to see what he could see. Often times, all he could see was clouds. There was another storm front moving in, though slower than the ones before.

Three days more brought them into a large lake that took them a whole day to get to the other end of.

"So far, the map is holding out true. I'm really impressed. Who ever drew this thing really knew their stuff ... even the ratios are right." M'lar said. "We want the southern inlet." He told the crewman.

"There isn't a southern inlet." The crewman said. They're both to the east."

"I know that." M'lar said, patiently. "We want the *southern* one. The one on the right, yes?"

"Oh! Okay. Sure. We can go that way." The crewman said, guiding the boat along the shore towards the indicated inlet. It was only a half a day later when they started hearing a grinding noise coming from the whole boat.

"What is that?" Horus asked, alarmed.

"That ... I don't know what that is." M'lar said, before turning to the crewman.

"We're scrubbing bottom." The crewman said, simply. "We have to stop here. There's a fork, up ahead. That might tell you where you are. But I have to go back, now."

"Alright. I was afraid of that." M'lar said. "Take the boat to the shore, then, so we can get the wagon off."

The crewman nodded, and did the best that he could. The low-riding boat couldn't get very close to shore at all. They had to rig up a ramp between the boats deck and the shore. But before they attempted to cross the ramp, they tied the other side of the boat to the far shore, to keep it from tipping clean over when the entire weight of the wagon rested on the one edge. Once that was secure, that started carefully maneuvering the heavy wagon off the boat.

True to character, the boat started wiggling all over the place, trying to get out from under the wagon completely. Seeing the boat starting to slide back into the river, Deilo smacked the ridali with the lines, to get it moving faster. The ridali lunged forwards, taking the wagon with it, even as the boat went the other direction, sliding right out from under the ramp, ripping the fastened ends out of the deck. The ramps dropped sickeningly into the river, even as the ridali got a foothold on solid ground. M'lar and Horus both jumped into the shallow river, swimming for the rear of the wagon that was, oddly enough, floating. The wheels spun uselessly, but the bottom of the wagon box was just barely below the surface of the water. M'lar reached the wagon first, and then Horus, and they both reached downward into the mucky bottom of the river with their hind feet, seeking purchase to push on the wagon with. Up in front, the ridali strained against the weight that pulled against it, trying to get the wagon up the bank.

Mutsgae slipped off the boat's deck, plopping down into the water with a mighty splash. But he swam like a fish, speeding towards the wagon. He plowed powerfully into the tailgate, shoving the wagon suddenly forwards just a little bit. He then tucked his head under the wagon, bracing his muscular shoulders against the wagon bed as he churned the water madly with his long body and thick tail.

The wagon inched forward, until the ridali managed to get its back feet on solid ground. Deilo called encouragement to everyone involved, especially the ridali, as the ridali started the wagon rolling up out of the water onto the bank. Once the wagon was far enough out for the two Centaurii to get a foothold, the wagon gained a little more momentum as it headed up onto dry ground, running water out of all the cracks.

"So much for keeping everything dry." Horus remarked tiredly, once the wagon was safe.

"Aye." M'lar said. "We'll have to unpack everything and let it dry, before it molds."

"Yeah." Horus agreed, before collapsing to the ground. "That sucker is *heavy*."

Mutsgae crawled up the bank after them, and then slumped there, not quite as tired as the others.

"Hey. Neat trick back there." M'lar said. "I'd hate to meet you on a bad day in the water."

Mutsgae grinned toothily and M'lar laughed at the expression.

"Is everyone okay?" Deilo asked, climbing down off the wagon.

"Yeah. I think so." Horus said. "We're going to have to be careful with the ridali, though ... that was a lot of strain it was under, just then. Oh!" He reached over, and hauled the saddle out of the bottom of the wagon.

"What by all the Gods is that contraption?" M'lar asked, as Horus attempted to sop water out of the padding on its underside.

"It's a saddle. For the ridali ... just in case we had to ditch the wagon." Horus said.

"The boat is leaving." Mutsgae said. "No one left anything behind, did they?"

"Where's Lillia?" Deilo asked.

"I'm here." She said, as her bird landed on the tailgate of the dripping wagon.

"Oh, good." Deilo said.

"That thing can *wear* a saddle?" M'lar asked, amazed.

"Sure. It's tricky, but it can be done. That fur makes it really hard to make the saddle stick." Horus said. "I hope the dunking didn't ruin it."

"I shouldn't think so, so long as it gets oiled ... just like the harness." Deilo said. "Do we have any oil?"

"No." Horus said. "I doubt Mar-kai thought we'd be using everything this long."

"Huh." Deilo grunted.

"Oil?" M'lar asked.

"You wouldn't just happen to have any, would you?" Horus asked.

"Uh ... only some that I use on my hooves now and again, for dry travel. I don't know if it would do a saddle any good. *My* harness is woven. It doesn't need oiling."

"Huh." Horus said. "What kind of oil is it?"

"I have no idea. Hoof oil." M'lar said, fishing the tiny can out of a pocket.

Horus looked at it, but the label had been worn off entirely. "Well ... there's not enough of it to do any good, anyway. I hope it'll be okay."

"I hope. It was just a dunking ..." M'lar offered, as he tucked the can away again.

The group got busy, then setting to unpacking and spreading out every last thing they had on the grasses around the wagon, so it would hopefully dry before the next storm system. Horus staked the ridali out so it could fill its belly on the grass, while they waited.

Deilo found a few packages of dried foods that had been soaked, and set about using those packages in making dinner – there was no point in letting it go to waste. That night they ate well, seated around a crackling fire under the open sky ... even the tent was spread out to dry.

Most of them slept through the night, the best sleep they'd gotten in weeks, being on solid ground again. Mutsgae stayed awake, though, wary now that they were on land again ... no telling what all was out there.

Just before dawn the camp was found by a pack of scavenging wildlife, and everyone was awakened rudely when the first one died loudly in Mutsgae's powerful jaws. He dropped it to the side, twitching, and rushed at another one, jaws thrown all the way open in a very pointed threat. The rest of the pack dispersed into the darkness quickly, fleeing before the Lizard. Mutsgae walked around in a large circle around the scattered objects, to make sure all had gone.

M'lar walked over to the dead thing, holding his majick light. "What is *that*?" he asked, nudging it with a fore hoof.

"I don't know." Deilo said, yawning. "But it doesn't look too friendly."

"No, it doesn't." M'lar bent down to inspect it closer, holding the light nearer. It was roughly scaled, yet had retracting claws like a big cat, and jutting tushes. It twitched convulsively, and M'lar jumped away from it, on edge. "Are we sure it's dead?"

"Yes." Mutsgae said. "It's dead." He walked up to it, and sniffed it. "Doesn't taste like much, but it's definitely dead." He rolled it over with his snout, revealing that it had a pair of spiny protuberances coming out of its spine, gobs of loose skin hanging from them. "Looks like it can glide, too, by the looks of it."

Deilo shivered. "A relative of the mountain dragon?" he asked.

"No, I don't think so." M'lar said. "They're too different."

"But just as scary looking." Horus said.

"And they come in packs." Mutsgae pointed out. "We'll have to be very careful."

"Aye." M'lar agreed.

After that, no one could go back to sleep, so they all found make-work to do as they waited for the sun to rise, and start drying their things again.

The next morning enough stuff was dry to start repacking the wagon, and what wasn't dry was spread out on top, some of it dangling off the sides and back to air-dry as they traveled. Having had a novel idea, Horus moved the saddle into the back of the wagon, so Mutsgae could ride in the compartment underneath – something he could get in and out of with ease.

And there he rode as they moved out at a trot across the country, following the river back towards the south again. When they happened across grasslands they made fairly good time, following the water along. But on occasion they encountered thick stands of brush that went on for miles. At times they could hack their way through with the swords they had, and at other times they were driven far out of their way to get around the thicker stands that couldn't be blazed. They did fairly well despite it all, however, with Lillia spending most of her time in the air scouting out ahead for easier ways through.

Another two weeks into their journey and they were all wearing jackets and blankets to stay comfortable, not having made much progress at all following the river. The brush slowed them considerably, and the farther along they went the worse it seemed to get. On the thirteenth day in the brush, they stumbled into a clearing. Glad to be out of the brush, they stowed the dinged up swords in the wagon and continued on at an easier pace. A few hundred yards on a Dtri stopped them, appearing as if out of nowhere.

"Halt!" it called.

Surprised, they stopped. "Who are you?" M'lar asked.

"Who are *you*? You're the ones trespassing!"

"Uh ... sorry about that. We're just passing through."

"Travelers? Travelers don't come this way." The Dtri countered.

"We did?" Deilo pointed out, helpfully.

The Dtri looked at the two Centaurii, and then at Deilo and the ridali. Apparently deciding that they weren't bandits after all, it spoke again in a kinder tone. "Then welcome to Turoun."

"Turoun?" M'lar asked.

"The city." The Dtri said, helpfully.

"I'll be! We finally made it that far. Okay. Thanks. Any chance we could buy some supplies so we can continue on?" M'lar asked.

"Certainly." The Dtri replied. "This way." It turned, and lead them onward, through the cleared area to a drop in the ground, at the bottom of which was a gated entrance to a tunnel. It spoke to the two tall, furred guards there. The guards looked like they were of the same Race as Fohrel and Mar-kai, though their fur was a completely different pattern of colors.

The two opened the gates, and the whole wagon was permitted to enter. The Dtri led them downward, through a rather dark tunnel for a short ways. The tunnel opened out into a larger well-lit tunnel after only a short span.

"Welcome to Turoun." The Dtri said, again. "Doesn't look like much ... but then you can't see the whole city from one spot, either. It's a complex of tunnels from place to place, instead of roads. I can get you a guide?"

"Another guide." Deilo muttered.

"Hey. I've done good so far." M'lar protested, before nodding to the Dtri.

The lizard-avian Dtri turned and sprinted away, off down a small side tunnel.

"I know. But soon we'll have more guides than members of the party, is my point." Deilo said, helping Lillia get her bird into its cage before it flew away in a fright.

"Thanks." Lillia said, gratefully.

"No problem." Deilo said. "Stay over here, where you won't get squished ... it's a little harder to see in here."

"Alright." Lillia said, sitting where he indicated, on top of a box.

"Don't fall." Deilo warned.

"I won't."

The Dtri returned, with a short goblin girl. "Here's your guide." He said, before flitting off back towards the gate.

M'lar frowned at the goblin, but she didn't seem to notice. "Where do you wish to go?" she asked.

"First, we need some dried foods." M'lar said. "A waterproof tarp. Some oil. Some caulk." He said.

"Then you want the market hall." She answered. "May I ride in the wagon?"

"Sure, why not?" Deilo said. "Don't crush anything." He warned.

M'lar picked up the diminutive form, and set her on the wagon. "You heard him."

"Of course." She replied, before pointing out the way.

Despite M'lar's initial misgivings about the goblin, she proved very productive to have around, leading them to all the right places, where they managed to get some fairly good deals on new supplies – and more warm clothing, as well. The city was a massive maze, though well lit and well marked. The shops and homes and such places were all hollowed out of the ground, rather than built in a cavern. Everything had a distinct spherical flair, even the styles of decoration. Most of the occupants of the city seemed to be the underground sort, though ... either goblin or one of two other underground-type species that none of the group had ever seen before. On rare occasion they saw one of the type of creature that had guarded the smuggling tunnel so long ago.

The goblin girl then directed them to an exit out of the city to the southeast, leaving them at the gate and refusing any payment at all. "It is far easier to give guides to the few travelers that come through, than to have to haul your stinking carcasses out of the tunnels when you get lost and die there." She said, before scurrying away.

"Huh. Nice of them." Deilo said. "Well, on we go."

That gate was guarded similarly to the first, two tall furred folk, one holding a majick rod, and one bearing a halberd.

M'lar stopped to talk to one, once the wagon was past the gates and headed up the ramp. He soon caught up with the wagon, however. "He said there is a path ... says there is a path all along the river. Apparently we missed it, the first time." He said, happily. "If we're lucky, that means no more hacking!"

"Yay." Horus remarked, tiredly.

They stopped long enough to add a few layers of clothing to what they already wore. The clouds had moved in again and they were sitting rather low, threatening ominously. Once everyone was bundled up warmly, they set out again, M'lar leading the whole group. He walked straight towards the wall of brush, at an area that looked thicker than all the rest of it. As they approached it became apparent that there was indeed a well-maintained path there, though just barely wide enough to permit the wagon. They traveled easily, compared to their earlier jaunt through the brush, making excellent progress along the way. As they traveled they could hear the gurgling of the river not very far away to their left. On occasion M'lar and Horus made trips through the brush to the river, where they filled empty water barrels to carry back to the wagon. On such pauses in travel, Deilo spent his time sharpening the swords they had abused so badly, trying to get the nicks and dings out of them. Where it had taken them two weeks to get to Turoun from the edge of the brush, it only took them four days to get to the next fork in the river. In following the paths that kept them closest to the river, Lillia spent much of her time in the air again, to see where the paths all went. She managed to find one that allowed them to cross the southern fork, leading down to a spot that had been altered to allow easy fording.

They crossed the river in ease, but on the other side they were reduced back to hacking their own trail in most places.

Three more days of hard work brought them out of the brush and into the clear once again. They were all quite happy to see open grasslands sprawling before them, though the ground there was mushy in places. Twice the first day they had to extract the wagon from a soft spot.

The ridali worked hard, getting the wagon back out of those places, but it never gave up on them, always hauling on the wagon with everything it had.

"I'm getting sick of this." Deilo said, that evening over dinner.

"I know what you mean." Horus said. "If we ever get back to where there are real roads ... I don't think I'll ever leave." He said, wistfully.

"Real roads!" M'lar said. "Are you aware of how much of the world has no roads at all?" he asked. "Very little of it. Very, *very* little of it." He said. "I don't know if I want it to warm back up again, or to get colder. I imagine it will get colder, and when it does, all this mushy business will clear right up."

"You mean, when it gets cold enough for the ground to freeze?" Deilo asked, dejectedly.

"Yeah." M'lar said. "It's plenty cold already, though."

"Tell me about it!" Deilo griped. "You at least have a fur coat on, under all that extra stuff." He said. "And enough mass to be of any good. Think of Lillia ... She has to stay in my coat pocket to stay warm!"

"It's mighty linty in here, too." Lillia's muffled voice came from inside his coat. "But at least I'm not frozen."

"Unless I'm mistaken, that sky looks like snow, tonight." M'lar said. "We may want to pitch the tent over the wagon again." He suggested.

"Oh, why not. Why weren't we equipped with a heater of some sort?" Deilo asked.

"We are. You're sitting next to it. You just can't build a fire inside the tent and still have a tent afterwards." M'lar said, poking the said campfire with a twig, before dropping said twig in the fire to burn.

"I meant for in the tent." Deilo said. "I'm tired of a cold blanket."

"You sure do complain a lot."

"We're going to have to hunt, tomorrow." Mutsgae said. "We've exhausted all our dried meat supplies."

"Well, that was dumb." M'lar said.

"What?" Deilo asked. "Why?"

"Well ... we already used up the dry stuff." M'lar said.

"We know that. Why was it dumb?" Deilo asked.

"Animals go to ground in the cold, kid. They don't keep wandering about, being easy to hunt in the winter." M'lar said. "We should have saved the dry stuff for the cold spell, and hunted while it was warmer."

"Nice of you to say something ahead of time!" Deilo growled.

"Hey, cool it, okay?" M'lar said. "I know you're uncomfortable ... we all are. That's no reason to bite people's heads off."

"*Now* what are we going to do?" Horus asked, doing his level best to not lose *his* temper. It was all too easy to get angry at every little thing.

"Hunt." M'lar answered. "It's all we *can* do. I doubt any of us can convince Mutsgae there to go herbivore ... and I don't want to be around when he decides we're all fair game."

"I wouldn't." Mutsgae said, rather offended at the idea.

"That's what you say *now*. Just wait until you've been starving for a week or so." M'lar said. "Just trust me, okay? I've been out in worse weather than this before, and I've seen how all kinds of people react to similar situations."

"Similar situations?" Deilo asked. "I thought you didn't travel light."

"I don't tend to. But everyone has a learning curve. Even I had to discover things, and learn to set my own rules. And then there are always those things you can't plan for ... like getting stuck on the wrong side of a flooding river. Or the mountain pass that was there a month ago is now a rockslide a mile long. Things like that. And some people are just pigs ... they eat cause they've got it. Which means that before the journey is over they're out of food ... and getting hungry." M'lar said. "I was rather impressed with how you all traveled, the *last* time I took you somewhere. You were frugal with what you had, only consuming what wouldn't keep – from when you hunted. Which is a rather unusual trait, I might add. No one I had ever met before hunted. And you've done rather well on this journey, too ... but I take it none of you have ever traveled in the winter before?"

"Never. We only ever traveled when we had to. Thankfully, it always had been in warm weather. And we learned hunting in travel from the SwordDancers." Deilo said. "In both journeys they were there to guide us. The first journey wasn't very long, not compared to this. The second journey was long in miles ... but not all that long, either. We used majick to cross a great deal of it."

"You did?" M'lar asked, amazed. "Tell me about this."

"There's not much to tell." Horus said. "Deilo had picked up and kept a phial of some kind of majick in our original home."

"Yelm." Deilo interjected. "It was sky majick."

"And he gave it to Till, one of the SwordDancers, and she cast a huge spell that took us all the distant way to the Gnarian border." Horus continued. "Left us all feeling more than a little strangled."

M'lar looked at Horus for a moment, then laughed quietly. "Didn't quite have enough majick, vial full or not. I've done that. Knocks the wind right out of you when you get there. But that is a very expensive way to travel." He said. "You must have been a very long ways off, to use that much majick, and *still* come out gasping."

"Um ... I think that's why they considered it. It was going to take a very long time to get here." Deilo said. "I think."

"Seems like you have all been around a bit. A lot more than most folks." M'lar said. "But yes ... winter travel is a whole other game than summer travel." He shrugged. "And hunting will be a big challenge." He looked over at Mutsgae, and shrugged. "Maybe you'll be indispensable in that regard."

"Maybe." Mutsgae said. "I haven't done much of anything else." He noted.

"Not true. Not very many thieves will poke their hands into a wagon that's got the likes of you sitting in it, looking back at them." M'lar said. "Most folks don't know that you're a rational being."

"I noticed that." Mutsgae said, dryly.

Deilo reached over, and pulled the pot out of the fire with a stick, and served out the last of the meal. They ate it all quickly, before it had a chance to get cold again. Once the last bite was eaten, Deilo poured water into the pot and let it sit there for a while, to warm, before he used it to wash all the dishes and do other things that required water. Tossing the water out, he packed it all away again. By the time he was done, M'lar and Horus both had the tent set up again over the wagon. Deilo climbed up into the wagon and arranged the contents so that everyone could get up into it and off the ground. Once everyone was in and settled, a pair of heavy blankets was spread out over the top.

Deilo was careful how he moved, to avoid crushing Lillia in his pocket, and even more careful how he settled in. Between the two large bodies of the two Centaurii, he was quite cozy and warm, under the blanket. Mutsgae lay on Horus' other side, his scaly hide more resistant to the cold and keeping Horus comfortably warm. M'lar simply applied an extra blanket to his own exposed side, and all settled in for a relatively warm night.

The next morning they were all quite stiff, but well rested. Deilo moved to leave the tent to start preparing a warm breakfast only to stumble into knee-deep snow. Startled out of his morning stupor, he yelled, and jumped back inside, into the warmer confines of the tent, smacking the white cold off his knees.

"What?" Horus asked, blearily. "What?"

"Snow." M'lar said, slightly more coherent, stretching.

"No kidding!" Deilo said, stomping his feet. He went back to the wagon and fished out another layer to put on. "I don't think I'll be making a fire out in that."

"Probably not. But we can pack snow into the water barrels." M'lar said. "How is the ridali?"

"I have no idea. I didn't get that far." Deilo said.

"Will the ridali handle snow alright?" M'lar asked.

"Probably." Horus said. "It's got an incredible coat on, and will be doing a lot of work ... making any kind of time at all will be an issue, though." He pointed out.

"Huh." M'lar grunted. "Once we get the tent down and the wagon moved, you can build a fire right here." He said. "No snow."

"Is it still snowing, right now?" Lillia asked.

"I don't think so, but it might yet snow again." Deilo said. "Awful dark."

M'lar moved to the door, and took a look out, careful to not let too much of their warmth out. "It's not a lot of snow. Just a foot or so. Deeper in the drifts. The ground seems to have frozen over night." He noted. "Not deep enough to hinder the wagon ... Horus and I can break the pack ahead to make it easier on the ridali itself ... we'll have to take care of hidden missteps."

"No kidding." Deilo said.

"But at least we won't be digging the wagon out anymore. Not today, at any rate." M'lar said, shrugging.

"You're a rather cheerful sort, this morning." Deilo observed.

"No point in complaining about what can't be changed." M'lar answered. "Let's start getting this tent down, and use it to cover the wagon ... just in case."

The group went to work doing just that, leaving the water barrels exposed for the time being. Once the tent was down, Horus hitched up the ridali, and moved the wagon. He and M'lar both started filling the barrels with snow while Deilo started a fire in the snow-free area, cobbling together a hot meal. By the time he was done, the barrels were full and well wrapped to melt the snow in any warmth the sun might happen to bestow.

They stuffed the meal into their bellies in a very short order, to keep the warmth as well as the food itself. The dishes were scrubbed out with more of the snow, and then packed back into the wagon in the first convenient spot before Deilo scrambled aboard and they started out once more. Mutsgae rode in the underneath again, watching the world recede from his perspective, as the two Centaurii blazed a path through the snow ahead of the wagon.

"Careful!" Lillia cried, getting squished somewhat as Deilo piled a few things on either side of him to block the slight breeze, and help withhold his own heat. Not doing anything but riding made him rather cold all over, especially his fingers, toes, and nose. But there wasn't much he could do about those extremities.

After a few hours the clouds broke up letting the sun shine down on the brilliant white wilderness they had created. Other than being particularly cold the day was marvelously beautiful, everything sparkling like it possessed a thousand facets.

Near noon time, when they stopped the wagon to water the ridali and fix up a quick lunch, Mutsgae left the group, hunting. He wasn't gone very long, having found nothing of interest. Each time they stopped, for whatever reason, Mutsgae made forays out into the snow, looking to see what could be found. For several days they progressed as such, the snow slowly melting under the sun's gentle touch. When there was almost no snow left, Mutsgae managed to find another hunter. The two fought viciously, the one because it was hungry, and the other for the territory.

The others were not in the slightest bit interested in eating the creature once Mutsgae had killed it, so he ate it all by himself, right there on the spot, feeling rather starved. He cracked the bones in his powerful jaws, and ate them as well, leaving not a scrap behind.

That night it snowed again, and in the morning Mutsgae struck out once more as the others broke camp. He returned empty handed, but with news that he had found a track of some sort. Deilo snatched up his bow and quiver, vaulting off the wagon onto Horus' back as the Centaurii jumped past the wagon to follow Mutsgae. Horus trotted along behind Mutsgae's fairly swift pace, until they reached the track. Mutsgae stopped there, not really able to see anything from his low point of view.

"Go back to the wagon." Horus said. "We'll be back."

Mutsgae nodded, and returned, as Horus leapt out at a gallop, following the track. Judging by the track, it looked like the daintily-hoofed animal was taking its time moving, stopping to nibble here, watch there. It was not very long at all before they found the animal itself, frozen in caution with big ears aloft as it listened to Horus' approach.

Horus sounded to it like another herbivore, but why he might be running like that had it spooked. Realizing this, Horus slowed to a trot, and then a walk as he went around it, looking for a better vantage. Deilo rode silently, as still as he could be, also watching with an arrow knocked on the string. Finding a good spot, Horus stopped completely and turned sideways. The animal was still watching him, but less warily, eventually turning its attention back to nibbling on little twigs here and there.

Deilo moved ever so slowly, raising the bow and hauling back on the string. Once he had it drawn, he waited a moment to be sure of his aim, and then let fly. The arrow flew true, sinking up to the fletching in the animal's side. It squalled and bounded away, the arrow sticking out of both sides of its ribcage. Horus exploded into action too swiftly for Deilo, taking off after the wounded animal. Deilo rolled backwards right off Horus' rump and landed softly in the snow. He picked himself up, and dusted the snow off himself as he watched Horus pursue the animal. He had hoped to make a clean kill ... an animal that ran never tasted as good as those that didn't.

Horus caught up to the flagging animal in short order, kicking up snow in a spectacular show as the two ran. Catching it by the head, Horus gave it a wrenching twist, ending the animal's run abruptly. Picking it up, he turned and trotted back to Deilo, who climbed back aboard again.

"Sorry about that." Horus said.

"'Tis alright." Deilo said, before settling in for the swift ride back to the wagon. They strung the animal out and cleaned it, leaving the hide on. They then tied it along the back of the wagon, where it could chill and tenderize as they traveled. It was plenty cold enough, the meat wouldn't even begin to spoil before they finished eating it at leisure.

Even though they now had a kill, Mutsgae continued the hunt at every stop, sometimes returning with something, sometimes returning with news of something in the area. If Horus wasn't too tired from a day's traveling, he and Deilo would go out to see if they could find and shoot it.

They brought in just enough meat to keep them all satisfied food-wise, if they rationed out the meat rather than gorged on it. Being just the beginning of winter, all the animals had put on a good layer of fat, and were quite tasty once cooked.

Horus and M'lar both ate more of the meat than they ordinarily would have, as they did not have the quantities of vegetation they would otherwise have consumed. What vegetables they had were being stretched, along with the meat, to make it all last. What they had along was also being shared with the ridali, in place of the grasses it could only rarely find under the snow.

Another snowfall and nearly another week of travel, and they reached the end of the river, which was nothing more than a low spot that occasionally carried water. They could see the mountains clearly, in all but one direction. To the west was open land.

"Well ... does anyone know how far it is that I can go?" M'lar asked, that next morning, consulting the map.

"No." Deilo said, looking at it, too.

"Then I suggest I stop here. I can take care of the ridali and watch over the wagon. We'll be here when you come back." M'lar assured them.

"Alright. Better safe than sorry." Deilo said. "Can we take the map, though?"

"Rather a silly thing to not." M'lar said, rolling it up. "Be careful out there. I won't be there to warn you of things."

"Like what things?" Deilo asked. "Are there liable to be dragons in this part of the ranges?" he asked.

"Oh, highly likely. Not to mention big cats, or other such predators. And steep drops with rocky stops. It's snowing ... so try to take the lower passes. You really don't want to get stuck in snow, or drop off an edge or into a hole that the snow concealed." M'lar said. "For that matter, it might be a good idea to tie one another together. Have Mutsgae go first ... he'd be less liable to pitch off of something, going ahead. Have Horus in back. He's big enough to haul both of you back up, *should* you fall." M'lar said. "Okay?"

"Uh ... okay. I'm beginning to wonder about the wisdom of this journey." Deilo said. "Sounds like suicide."

"Only if you're not careful. Run, if you see a dragon. Find a nook to hide in."

"Ah ... actually ..." Deilo said.

"What?" M'lar asked. "Don't tell me you're one of those that freeze when spooked."

"No ... but Roan ... he found out that the best thing to do is to *not* run, when you see a dragon ... we even got a chance to test the theory. That's how the subject came up. Dragons can't see you as prey if you don't move. He said you're no different to them than a rock you sat on. He said he learned it from the mountain goats. By accident." Deilo said.

"Who is this Roan?"

"A SwordDancer that brought us in." Deilo said.

M'lar thought on that. "SwordDancers aren't known for being crazy ... but if it works ... then do that."

"Okay." Deilo said. "Any other bits of sage advice?"

M'lar looked at him for a moment, and then burst out laughing. "Okay."

Deilo just waited, not seeing what was so funny.

"Just ... be careful, okay? Use your head." M'lar said. "And good luck to you."

Deilo nodded. M'lar helped them rig up packs for Deilo and Horus, leaving Mutsgae free of burden to make it easier to scout ahead any maybe come to their defense should he have to. Once they were loaded with whatever they might need, Deilo set

Lillia back in a pocket, and off they went, leaving M'lar and the wagon behind.

M'lar looked at the ridali, and heaved a sigh. "Well, it looks like it's just you and me, now. I hope you like me, after all this time."

The group of friends trekked eastward as accurately as they could manage, heading up into a band of foothills after the third day. Four days of the growing hills got them into the mountains, and there things got trickier. The snow was deeper there than it had been down in the flatlands, and took a deal of wading to get through in some places. Mutsgae was very picky and careful in where he went, often times scooting about ahead of them on his belly, leaving rather strange tracks behind him as he used his forelimbs and chin to test out the snow ahead. Sometimes he simply doubled back without any explanation what so ever, to retry the eastern journey in a different place. Once he went so far as to go back a whole mountain's worth, to try again in a different valley. Deilo and Horus tried to not say anything along the lines of a complaint, knowing that their friend was doing his best to keep everyone safe.

As the days wore on the snow only got deeper, snowing every night until even Horus found it easier to scoot around on top of the snow, on his belly, than to try and force his way through it. Once they started traveling that way, they were in a rather precarious spot indeed, as every so often they ended up sliding downhill, until Horus managed to get his front legs embedded into the snow enough to haul everyone to a complete stop.

Frequently this action left him bruised all over his lower chest and forelegs, but he never complained about it, the cold of the snow keeping most of the pain out.

*

Back towards the west, a pair of big cats happened across the odd set of tracks that the friends had left, and sniffed about them, trying to decide if they were worth tracking down. Eventually deciding that they were, after all, edible, they started bounding along the track on their wide-splayed feet, with a fleetness none of the friends could hope to match ... except for maybe when they were sliding downhill.

Perched on a rocky ledge that had been swept clean of snow, a lone dragon watched the cats bound along past it, below it on the slope. It stretched out with both front legs in a leisurely motion, and yawned, before getting to its feet. It had just finished digging a new section of tunnel in its underground nest, and wasn't in too much of a hurry to do much of anything else. But it *was* hungry. Scratching between its twirled horns with a jutting chunk of mountainside, it nearly crumbled the chunk to bits before it was satisfied. Then it slid down the slope on its belly, and landed with a plop in the snow, obliterating the tracks the friends and the cats both had made. Then it turned, and ambled along at an easy gait behind them, wrinkled gliding-wings tucked up close to its body to avoid losing too much heat.

*

Fining another impassable spot, Mutsgae turned around again, and started back, past Deilo once more.

"Oh, come on. Isn't there a single way through this mess?" Deilo asked, tiredly.

"I'm sure there is." Lillia said, conciliatorily. "We just have to keep looking until we find it. Too bad I left my bird back at the wagon."

"You'd only get eaten." Deilo said, poking her back into the pocket before she let too much cold into his coat. "And you couldn't see anything but more snow, anyway." He turned, to follow Mutsgae back around again, when he stopped, looking past Mutsgae's still form. Sitting beside Horus on the snow, Mutsgae was staring down a pair of big cats that were creeping towards them, large fangs showing though they made no sound what so ever.

Horus, seeing Deilo's expression, turned his trunk to look back the way Mutsgae was looking. He yelped, and leapt up out of the snow, performing a turn in mid air before coming back down into the snow, now facing the cats.

Deilo scrambled forward, knowing that his bow and quiver were on Horus' harness. He carried his sword, but there was no way he wanted to get that close to those cats.

Mutsgae opened his jaws, and made a small lunge at the cats, roaring.

The cats only gave a moments pause, before advancing again, snarling.

A larger, heavier roar echoed through the valley they were in, and both Deilo and Horus looked at Mutsgae, startled.

"That was *not* me." He stated, as the cats both stopped completely.

"Uh-oh." Deilo said, hunkering down, now that he had reached Horus' back.

Mutsgae also flattened himself, as the dragon's head appeared around the last bend. It marched right through the snow as if it was not there, straight at the cats who had now half-turned, and were snarling and hissing at the approaching dragon, trying to warn it off.

The dragon didn't even hesitate, lowering its head down to their level, opening its maw once more to let out a reply roar, identical to the one they had heard before.

The two cats turned, and leaped off to the side, headed up the slope as fast as they could propel themselves up it. The dragon dove after them, snow flying in all directions as it waded up the slope, jaws snapping. The cats yowled in distress, and leapt higher. The dragon managed to catch one by its tail, and snapped its big, armored head around, yanking the cat back down to its level. The cat wailed appropriately, and attacked the face of the dragon, desperate to free itself from those jaws. The dragon closed both eyes and nostrils, the only vulnerable places on its face, and released the tail, trying for a better grab, both front feet occupied with not letting it fall down into the valley.

The cat made a leap for it, once it was free, but didn't get very far. The dragon had scored a leg, and yanked it back again. The cat howled its fury, attacking the dragon's face again. Levering itself to one side, the dragon freed one foot, slamming the cat down onto the rocks with its snout. Planting the free foot down on the cat, it readjusted its hold on the cat, and ripped it in half. The cat howled one last time, before it was silent, and swallowed in halves. The dragon looked up a short cliff at the second cat, which was screaming its indignities down at it, at the murder of its mate. The dragon lunged upwards though it couldn't hope to make it up that cliff. Taking the hint, the cat vanished past the rim, and wasn't seen again.

After spending a few moments looking to see if there was a way up that rather steep cliff, the dragon turned around, and slid back down the slope, towards the group of friends that were still holding quite still.

It sniffed the snow all the way up to where the two cats had gotten, and then beyond, catching their scent. It paused, and looked at them, then beyond them. It looked at them again, lowering its head like it intended to pounce on them and eat them as well.

Instead, it roared once more, trying to spook them into moving. Horus' muscles twitched, but otherwise didn't move.

The dragon stared at them for a long time, evidently trying to decide whether or not they were really there. Just as it decided that they weren't there, Deilo's precarious perch on Horus' back slipped, and he landed almost soundlessly in the snow, arms sunk all the way down into it after having tried to catch himself.

The dragon hesitated, and then looked their way again, having seen the abrupt motion. But none of them moved again, Deilo holding very still in his new position. Undeterred, the dragon started to move forward again, growling ominously.

When it got too close, close enough to feel the warmth of its breath, Mutsgae made a suicidal move, launching himself at the dragon's face, roaring his own challenge as he attacked. The rope that trailed after him snagged on a rock, and broke with a loud pop, not having slowed Mutsgae's assault but only a fraction.

Not having expected *that* move, the dragon was taken aback for a moment, but unhurt. Then it hollered when Mutsgae clamped his teeth on the dragon's open nostrils, drawing blood.

It slung its head around, and swatted at its own face with both front feet, trying to scrape Mutsgae off. The dragon's nostrils tore, and Mutsgae came free, tumbling through the snow as the dragon turned to face him, roaring again.

Deilo jumped out of the snow, reaching for his bow, though he didn't know what good he could possibly do with it.

Mutsgae rolled over right side up again, as the dragon approached, and jumped forward again, jaws wide, roaring once more.

But this time the roar echoed throughout the valley with a deafening tone that set the dragon back several paces. It looked at Mutsgae warily, second-guessing its decision.

Mutsgae leapt forward again, slinging his tail around to the side to make himself look bigger, hissing menacingly.

Deciding its nose hurt a terrible lot and that the cat was enough, after all, the dragon beat a hasty retreat down the valley, leaving them be.

Deilo sat up, on Horus' back again, and watched it go, an arrow knocked. "Uh?"

Mutsgae more or less swam through the churned snow, towards them, where Deilo tied the rope back together.

"How did you *do* that?" Horus asked. "That was one heck of a sound, to come out of little old you."

"He ain't so little. But, yeah ... you sounded bigger than the dragon." Deilo agreed.

Mutsgae only shrugged, not saying anything. He knew it hadn't been him. He had also seen the shadow of giant wings speeding through the valley, as Guiran had sailed past overhead, lending *his* voice to Mutsgae's bluff.

But the big Dragon was nowhere to be seen again, having vanished over a nearby ridge before anyone's attention had left the retreating hunting dragon.

Mutsgae felt glad that the strange Dragon had been there to aid ... as little as it had taken. He definitely wouldn't have won, without it. It also made him feel better about their overall situation, knowing they had a benefactor like that watching out for them, moment to moment.

If his friends believed it had been them, he couldn't dissuade them from that belief ... he had been told to not tell them about Guiran.

Once everyone's nerves settled enough that they could move in a coherent fashion, they resumed their trek once more, slipping and sliding through the snow. They were rather impatient to get out of that valley, and away from that hungry dragon.

That encounter seemed to be the turning point in their luck, as they had to make far fewer turn-abouts, making more miles to the east than they had been scoring, before.

Mutsgae continued to test out the immediate path ahead of them, but he had learned to navigate by another means altogether. He was watching the sky as he felt his way along, taking cues from the Dragon that apparently only he could see.

Far overhead, almost far enough up to be completely invisible to most eyes, Guiran was pleased to see that the little lizard down there seemed to be paying attention, and listening when he offered advice on an easier route through the mountains, guiding them through lower passes and less snow-choked valleys.

He didn't know for sure where exactly the destination was, but he had a pretty good idea where, from what he'd been told by William, who had learned it from the Wizard. He could see the entire area of the range ... that was not a problem. But figuring out where exactly was the person in question ... that was a lot harder.

"Muts ... do you have any idea which mountain we're on?" Deilo asked, finally, unrolling the map.

"Nope." Mutsgae said, simply. "Just going east."

"We can't just go east." Deilo protested. "We're looking for a specific area, here. We keep just heading east, and we could easily pass it right up."

"Trust me, we're in no danger of *that* yet." Horus said. "Stinking mountains go on forever."

"Not so." Deilo said. He pointed to the spot that had been blank on the Wizard's map. "This is where we're going."

Mutsgae gave it a cursory look, and then nodded. "I know." He said, before tilting his head so he could look up with one eye. He saw Guiran dip suddenly, coming startlingly low, color-changing to match the sky even closer, to avoid detection. Mutsgae wondered what the Dragon was doing, then ... it didn't seem to be a warning of immanent danger...

He couldn't even begin to guess that Guiran was concentrating on reading the map in Deilo's lap, from way up there, noting where it was Deilo had pointed to. Once he was reasonably sure that had been the destination rather than where they thought they were, he ascended again, and pulled his wings into odd contortions, to give cues to Mutsgae, whom he knew was watching him again.

"We'll get there." Mutsgae said. "Eventually." He said. "Let's go."

"I don't want to get lost, and wander out here until we die of cold and starvation!" Deilo protested.

"We won't." Mutsgae assured him. "Let's go."

"D, we haven't exactly got time to sit and argue. Muts seems to know where he's going." Lillia said. "Let's go."

Deilo sighed, wearily, and got to his feet again. Horus grabbed his arm, and helped him up, steadying him until he got his balance in the snow. "Thanks." Deilo said.

"No prob." Horus said. "Come on. Every step gets us closer, at this point."

"I hope. I'm really gonna ask for a lot of pay-back, when we get back to that stinking Tower. This trip is misery."

"I know, I know. But it's gotta be done."

Mutsgae led them on, once more, again taking cues from Guiran in the sky, hoping that the Dragon knew where it was leading them ... he certainly seemed to be leading them, rather than making random gestures that Mutsgae simply pretended was guidance. Their trip had certainly gotten a lot easier, since Mutsgae had noticed those strange signs.

He had to wonder, though, how something could stay in the air for that kind of duration. What was the Dragon eating? Air?

Three days later, Horus yelled as something near him exploded. He started jumping around in the snow, slapping at his chest, and then started shedding his harness quick enough to tear it in many places, still yelling like it was eating him. Both Mutsgae and Deilo stopped, looking back at him.

"Horus?" Deilo asked. "What's wrong?"

"That stinking sphere the Wizard gave me just exploded and set me on fire!" Horus yelled, piling snow on his harness once he had it off.

"The-?" Deilo asked.

"The emergency device." Mutsgae reminded him. "It was probably majick."

"Oh, dear god. The idiot." Deilo said. "Are you alright, Horus?"

"Yeah ... I think so." Horus said, drawing a deep breath.

"Well, that tells us two things." Deilo said.

"Two?" Mutsgae asked.

"Like what?" Horus asked.

"Well ... we reached the warded zone, obviously. It blew up, did it not?" Deilo asked.

"Well ... it was supposed to be majick-free." Horus said. "Wasn't it?"

"Obviously not. Most technology does incorporate majick, you know." Deilo said. "Apparently the Wizard thought that piece was clean enough ... and the ward said otherwise. Thank goodness it was supposedly majick free ... imagine what something *majickal* would have done to you." Deilo said.

"Oh, dear gods." Horus said, watching the snow rapidly melt as the harness continued to burn with no apparent inclination to stop.

"Looks like that piece is shot. There wasn't anything on it, was there?"

"Not that piece, no." Horus said. "When we had it, I had been carrying spare food bags on that part."

"Well ... no great loss, then. At least, not at the moment. Now we need to find this Malici." Deilo said. "Any ideas?" he asked, rubbing his arms to warm them up again now that they were standing still.

"Keep wandering. If he lives here, he'll find us." Mutsgae said.

"That's a mighty big if, Muts." Deilo said.

"Not so ... the wards are here, obviously. That's a note to the positive."

"I think he has a point." Horus said.

Deilo nodded. "I agree. But wandering seems like a poor plan."

"Hey ... if the dude can do *that* to my harness, without even *seeing* it ... I think he'll know we're here." Horus said.

"Shouldn't we hold still, then?" Deilo asked.

"I really don't want to hold still, in this, D. It's too cold for that." Horus said.

"And it's not like you're leaving a trail that's hard to miss." Lillia said, her head poking up out of the pocket again, one small hand pointing back the way they'd come.

The others turned to look at it, and then had to agree the point. They finally got to moving again, just to keep warm, hoping they'd eventually stumble across the legend. Preferably before they froze to death.

Chapter Seven

Malici

A small white bird sat on a barren twig, watching the group pass by within inches, as it never moved from its place. Sitting completely still, hunched down, it looked a lot like a small heap of snow itself, unless one knew to look closely. When it saw all that there was to see, it flitted from its branch to one higher up, startling Horus into a sideways stumble with the surprise of the movement.

"Hey! Look at that! A little bird!" Horus exclaimed, as it flitted away across the valley, heading southward. "Looked just like the snow, until it moved. Amazing!"

"What bird?" Deilo asked, glancing back in the moment that Mutsgae spent poking about in the snow, testing the footing.

The little bird flew straight and true, only dipping and rising with the ambient temperatures of the air, headed for the opposite ridge. Rising as it neared the other mountain, the little bird put more effort into its flight to get over that ridge. Closing its wings after it topped that last obstacle, it zoomed ever faster down the far side of the mountain, only occasionally flitting one wing or the other to dodge obstacles in its path.

Reaching the valley, it spread its wings wide and rose upwards suddenly, to land in the top of an evergreen tree. There, it ruffled all its little feathers, and sang at the top of its little voice, notes trilling higher and lower in a spectacular song.

Out from a stand of smaller evergreens a much larger being emerged, alerted by the song, to look up at the little bird.

Malici listened with both ears pricked all the way forward to the news the little bird brought him. He had known something majickal had tried to cross his wards, and had been waiting for just such a messenger. He carried his feathered wings close to his sides, much like the little bird did, keeping his own body quite warm. This also had the effect of making him look a lot like a normal horse from any kind of distance. He listened to the extent of the song, and then watched in silence as the little bird flew away again, back the way it had come.

Shining white, himself, he moved through the snow with an ease that not even the mountain cats could rival. Though he appeared similar to a horse in basic form, he was far larger than any horse ever born got to be. Massive, yet fine, there was little that he could not do. He started up the mountainside with ease, pushing through the lower branches of the sleeping trees, making his own path through the sparse underbrush. The bushes simply leaned aside, and then returned to their original position after his passing. Other than the snow having been shaken off their branches, there was nothing to betray that the legend had passed ... his own tail obscured his tracks in the snow.

It took no little time for him to reach the crest of the mountain ridge, and there he stopped, to look across the valley at the little group that was leaving a starkly obvious trail along behind them. He watched them for a very long time, thinking.

Something majickal had triggered the ward ... yet there were still people over there. People that apparently had little enough to do with majick that they were unharmed by the wards. This in and of itself was of interest to him. It had been many long centuries before anyone had been able to cross the wards as such. After that, he wondered what they were doing, in these mountains, at this time of year. They couldn't possibly be trying to leave Gnaria ... not through the widest point in the range. They were taking an awfully long road through the mountains, if they were.

Eventually, he decided to investigate. He shook his head, and reached back to scratch his back with one of the very long, very sharp horns that grew from either side of his poll. That done he started down the mountainside, taking large, powerful leaps to speed his descent. Only on the rare occasion did he open his wings slightly, to break his descent when the ground dropped away too quickly for comfort. He reached the valley floor in a very short order, and started up the other side, angling back behind where the party was. As he approached, he watched them warily.

He could see the Centaurii first, being the brightest colored and the largest of the lot. He wondered what the creature was doing, in *back*, knowing that most Centaurii were guides. As he moved higher towards them, he could then see the young man, who seemed to be occupied with something ahead of his feet. Malici had to get quite close before he spotted the Lizard that was working its way ponderously with care through the snow. He could see the tether between the members, and then understood what was going on.

They hadn't the foggiest idea what the mountainside was like, and were sacrificing mileage for safety.

Malici continued up the mountainside, circling up from behind until he was above them. There, he stepped out onto a jutting ledge, shook the snow off his coat, and walked to the edge to look down on them as they passed underneath.

None of the three noticed the towering figure above them, occupied with their footing as they moved along, occasionally saying something rather odd to one another. After a short while, though, Mutsgae tilted his head over as he usually did, to look up, to see if Guiran had any advice at the moment.

He never did see Guiran as he had instead spotted Malici overhead. He stopped dead in his tracks, staring up at the giant figure.

"Muts?" Deilo asked, after noticing that he'd stopped again – and was looking up. When he got no answer, he too looked, fearing there was another dragon. Instead, he was shocked to silence at the sight.

Horus looked up quickly, and also saw. "I think we found him." He said, quietly, watching as Malici looked at each of them in turn, from his vantage point.

Malici listened to their voices, trying to decipher what they were saying. It was not even remotely the same language that had been spoken when he had left. This he had expected, and listened with more than his ears.

Him?

Had they really bothered to come all this way in this unforgiving terrain and weather … just to find him? That was a little nutty. More than a little, at that. And how in the world had they known where to look? How had they known that he was still around?

Malici moved off the side of the ledge, and moved down towards them. As he approached, the group began to realize just how big he was. They moved towards each other unconsciously, watching him in silence.

Moving up to Horus first, Malici just looked at him intently. Horus felt like those striking blue eyes were going to bore holes through him.

"Uh ... hi." Horus said, nervously. "Are ... are you ... Malici?"

Malici flicked one ear back but did not speak, thinking. Apparently, they *had* come to find him. Why? He moved in turn to look at Deilo, and then Mutsgae, dropping his head slightly to the low form. For a rather tense moment Mutsgae was silent. But then he started hissing and rumbling, backing away slightly, unnerved by the silent look.

Malici lifted his head again, and looked back at the other two, only noticing then that there was something alive in Deilo's pocket, and was poking her head out to look at him.

That is a *very* small person ...

Malici stepped back, and looked at the group as a whole. *Why are you here?* He asked, his mental voice resounding in their minds.

Deilo looked shocked, but managed to reply after a moment. "We're here to find you. If ... if you're who we think you are."

I am. Malici said, simply. *Why?*

"Your help is needed." Deilo said. "The Wizard sent us to find you, and bring you back."

The Wizard! Malici turned, and walked away.

"Wait!" Deilo said. "Don't -!"

Malici stopped, and looked back at him.

"I ... it's not the Wizard that wants you. He just knew where you were. It is others. They need your help. Something about the world falling apart." Deilo said. "Your help is *needed*."

Malici turned around again, facing Deilo squarely. *The world has been falling apart for eons, in many senses of the word.* He replied.

"I know ... but this time it's meant literally. As in ... there's not going to be a world left at all, for anyone, when it gets done. I mean ... no ground, no sky ... nothing. At all. The Wizard said so. And there's someone who wants to fix it. But they don't have time to figure out how. It's going too fast... they ... they want to fix the falling apart problem from the surface, so that they have time to fix it from the source." Deilo said, all in one rush.

Malici's ears went back for a moment, and then came forward again. *Who is this?*

"I don't know. I didn't see them. We were called in by the Wizard, to the Wizard, and he said for us to come get you, in all haste, and to bring you back to the Tower, where ... I'm guessing ... you're to meet these others. They're ... The Wizard says they are very powerful people."

Malici considered that for a moment. He could not remember a time when the Wizard had said such a thing before.

He decided that there had to be something really spectacular afoot for the Wizard himself to admit something like that to someone like Deilo. He also knew Deilo spoke the truth about the world ... he had felt it doing just that for some time, and had also felt the weakening grip the Wizard had upon the valley, trying to save it from all the crumbling.

After a moment he dipped his head slightly in ascent. *Alright. I will go.*

"Thank you." Deilo said, with relief.

This way. Malici turned, and headed down into the valley.

"But, the way back is that way." Deilo said, pointing the way they'd come, even as Mutsgae started after the legend.

I am aware of that. Malici replied, without looking back. *Follow.*

In the course of having conversed with them mentally, Malici had also listened with his ears, making the translation back and forth, that the sounds meant those thoughts, learning the language by ear.

The group did follow him, trusting that he knew where was safe to travel, and hurrying to keep up with the long strides Malici took. They traveled quickly down into the bottom of the valley, and followed it around the base of a mountain to an area that was sheltered by the shoulder of the mountain. The snow wasn't quite as deep there, and the wind was almost nonexistent. Malici led them straight up to the steep shoulder, and kept walking ... vanishing right into the rock itself.

Mutsgae stopped, staring at that, as the other two stopped behind him. "Uh..."

Are you coming, or not? Malici asked.

Hesitantly, Mutsgae moved forward, slowly, until his snout was mere inches from the rock. Closing his eyes, he stepped forward again, expecting to smash his snout on the stone. But he never encountered it. Opening his eyes in surprise, he looked around at a well-lit cavern. Behind him, Deilo and Horus both appeared through the rock.

"Whoa." Horus said.

Malici stood in the center of the circular area, watching them. Mutsgae got the distinct impression the legend was laughing at them. *Come.* He told them.

They moved across the smooth floor, towards the towering figure as Malici opened and lifted his wings partly, creating an impromptu ceiling over their heads with them. He reached down, and touched his soft nose to the floor, moving one forefoot forward. Both his horns started to glow with ethereal bioluminescence, changing the color of the lighting in the cavern.

A bright flash that left them all blinded, and then they were somewhere far warmer. Malici lowered and tucked his wings up, and looked around while the others rubbed their eyes, trying to get their vision back.

"Gods above!" M'lar yelped, jumping away from the group when he got *his* vision back, and had seen them standing there, where previously there had been nothing.

Malici just looked at him, and his nostrils flared. *That* one was so infused with the use of majick, he never would have survived the wards.

"M'lar?" Horus asked, uncertainly, looking around at the area. The wagon was there, as was the ridali, also watching everything that was going on.

They were no longer in the mountains at all ... and it was *so* much warmer ... even though there was still snow on the ground. It was far warmer than the mountains had been, and far less windy.

"Horus?" M'lar asked. "Uh ... I think you succeeded." He said.

Deilo just sat down, and drew a deep breath. "Wow."

Mutsgae shook, be ridding himself of the snow stuck to his back. "I guess now we can start back."

"*After* you eat. You three look like you've been severely rationing." M'lar said. "I was beginning to wonder how far you'd gotten. It's been quite awhile."

"Food sounds good." Deilo agreed.

M'lar nodded, and moved towards the wagon, as Malici walked in silence over towards the ridali. The animal lifted its own four-horned head, and met the gaze eye for eye, never flinching.

The two were identical in height, and almost identical in size. But far different in all other respects. They stood nose to nose for a very long moment, before Malici turned, and looked around again. It had been a very long time since he'd set foot outside his little area of the mountains.

M'lar got a hot meal slapped together in a quick fashion. He wasn't a very good cook at all, but it was warm, and it was food. It did not last long at all as they filled their bellies.

"Ohh, that feels good." Deilo said.

Malici walked over to where the group sat, and looked at them again, silently. M'lar, still on his feet, looked back at him, just as silent.

He had heard of Malici ... and had never even dreamt of seeing the legend in person. Malici was far larger than anything M'lar had ever heard. Often depicted in small statues, people just assumed that Malici was horse-sized ... a lot like the Centaurii were. Though, in all honesty, Centaurii weren't quite as big as horses, more akin to ponies.

Are you done? Malici asked, finally.

There was a scrambling, then, as people moved their weary selves, getting everything ready to move, and the ridali harnessed into the wagon.

"Okay." Horus announced, finally. "We can head out."

You intend to walk back across the country, to the Tower, when you say 'all haste'? Malici asked.

"... we don't exactly have another method of travel handy." Deilo said. "We might be able to get a boat, farther along the way."

Malici laid his ears back, and lowered his head. *By the time you would get back to the Tower, there would be nothing left of this world.*

"Then what do you suggest we do?" M'lar asked.

Malici looked around again, thinking. *Get in the wagon.* He decided.

"All of us? The ridali –" Horus started to protest.

Get in the wagon. Malici repeated, sternly.

The others looked at each other, and then simply got in the wagon, arranging themselves so that they would all fit. Once they were all settled, Malici walked up to the ridali, and touched soft nose to soft nose. The ridali stood perfectly still, as Malici's horns started to glow once more.

"Oh, cover your eyes!" Deilo warned, slapping a hand over his face, looking away.

Just as everyone moved to do just that, an even brighter flash than before lit up the entire area. When they uncovered their eyes, they could see rather well ... they could see that they were just outside the city walls of Kentalic just as the city was starting to shut down for the evening. Malici looked at the group in the wagon, lifting his head above the ridali. He turned, and headed towards the nearest city gate.

They looked around for a moment, before launching into motion. Both Horus and M'lar dived out of the wagon, even as Deilo started the wagon rolling again, back towards the city. Horus and M'lar started up the road ahead, trying to catch back up to Malici, the wagon rolling along behind them at a good clip. After the lengthy rest, the ridali was raring to go again.

As Malici approached the city gate, the guards there stopped their work of closing the gate to stare at him. Then they swiftly started reversing their own work, hauling the gates back open again to allow the legend to enter unchallenged. Behind Malici came the others, catching up quickly. Malici trotted along easily, looking around him even as he traveled towards the most prominent feature of the city: The Tower. Traffic cleared out of the streets as he arrived on them, everyone watching in complete and total silence as he trotted by, followed by the wagon.

Those who knew who he was were struck dumb by his appearance. And those who had no idea who he was were amazed, as well, though for completely different reasons. Malici trotted right up to the gates to the Tower yard, and stopped. The guards took a moment to gather their wits about them, and open the gates for him. He passed through unhindered, though the guards stopped the Centaurii and the wagon that followed them.

Malici paused, and looked back. *Allow them through.* He ordered, before continuing on. The guards hesitated, but did as they were instructed, allowing the travel-worn group into the yard. Malici moved right up to the Tower, and up the steps there, the big doors moving open even as he approached.

M'lar stopped at the base of the stairs, even as the friends all abandoned the wagon and followed Malici up into the Tower. M'lar watched them go, unwilling to enter the Tower, himself. He looked at the ridali, then. "Well, I guess it's just you and me, again."

Malici stopped in the middle of the big hall that the doors opened onto, the walls echoing his every step, even as Horus' beat a second rhythm. The group stopped in a semi circle behind him, standing in silence even as Malici looked around.

Malici remembered the hall. He had been there before. Only this one was different. It wasn't the same hall, he knew. The first one had reeked only of the Wizard. This one had a different flavor. He lowered his nose to the floor, folding his ears back. His head snapped up again, and he looked again.

The hall had a rather distinct *magic* flavor to it. Magic? There had been a lot of it, too ... the magic ran the course of every stone in the Tower, Malici could feel it.

Interesting. Very interesting.

He tested the strength of it, and found it quite strong. He also found traces in the upper levels of an even more recent magic's presence. Malici tilted his head to the side, and tried to determine the task the magic had been set to. It took him a long moment, but it did tell him what it was there for ... to Storm-proof the Tower.

Interesting.

Malici turned about, looking at the walls again, now seeing indeed that the basic parts were the same, but it was a whole new Tower. Evidently, it had been destroyed and rebuilt ... and considering the nature of the magic, had been destroyed in a massive storm that had left the city untouched.

How odd.

But the magic did not have the flavor of the Wizard ... someone *else* had rebuilt the Tower. But who?

Malici turned about in place again, as the others just watched him, more than a little confused at what he was doing. *KENTALIC!!* The mental call echoed *audibly* throughout the Tower's spaces, through the levels all the way to the very top of the Tower, where the Wizard was in discussion with William over a set of spells. The Wizard stood upright, shocked at the sounds that came to his ears. William also straightened, having heard the call.

"What in the world was that?" William asked.

"I think Malici is here." Timothy said, sliding to a stop from a hasty entrance to the room. "Guiran is back, too. He just arrived, via hole."

"Indeed. Malici is here." The Wizard said. "And I don't think he's happy with me. Still."

"Still?" William asked.

"I told you before ... we were not on the best of terms. You had better come with me to meet him." The Wizard said.

"Wait...!" Timothy said. "Why did he just yell out the name of the city??"

The Wizard turned to look at the Mage. "He didn't. Kentalic is *my* name. This city, ages ago, was known as the *city of Kentalic* ... as in, *my* city. Where I made my home. I was here, first. The city grew up around me. Over time, it became simply Kentalic."

"Ah. I see." Timothy said. "Are you averse to teleporting?"

"Not in the least." The Wizard said.

William nodded, and Timothy 'ported all three of them down, into the hall in which Malici stood. Both Mages were surprised at the sight of Malici, having expected someone a tad ... smaller.

But Malici certainly had the presence they had expected.

Kentalic simply made a courteous bow to Malici. "Greetings, old friend."

Malici looked at him, and nodded his head only slightly before looking at the Mages on either side of him. *They* were the sort of magic the Tower held. They *reeked* of magic. *Real* magic. The scent of it was almost overwhelming to Malici, who's own grasp on magic had been wasting away over the years, drained away into the starved world. They also tasted of something else ... something even more powerful than magic. Malici noted right away that while they were men, they were distinctly *not* the men of this world. They were different. Very different. *I am here.* Malici said, simply.

"Yes, thank you for coming, and in such haste." Kentalic said. "I assume that you have been appraised of the condition of Numar?"

I already knew. Malici said, simply.

"Good." Kentalic gestured first to William and then to Timothy. "These are representatives of a group that wish to repair our world. But they need your help."

A group? Malici asked. *There are more of you?*

Yes. Many, many more. William replied, in like kind.

Malici's ears pricked forward all the way, his head rising slightly. They knew their own minds well enough to *speak*! He was also interested to know that there were more like them ... to have encountered *two* was quite a shock ... those two alone were a powerful force, he knew. He could sense it. But more? No wonder Kentalic had admitted their power! He couldn't very well deny it. *What do you wish to do, and how?* He asked, after a moment.

Kentalic stood in silence, well aware that William was speaking to Malici telepathically. It annoyed him greatly when people around him spoke in such ways, as he could not hear. But things were as things were. Things needed to be said.

We need to heal the planet. But we do not have time to figure out what the root cause of this distress is ... it is falling apart too fast for that. We need to fix the surface problem. Too much has been drained from the world, and that is only making things worse. We want to replace this, to re-energize the world once more. We are hoping that you possess the knowledge we need. We have the energy, but not the knowledge to use it most efficiently. We do not know the world well enough to do a proper job. William said.

Malici considered this. *Why did you not start far sooner? Why wait until it was nearly too late? You would have been better off starting this centuries ago.*

We weren't here, centuries ago. We are from another world entirely, and have been working as fast as we know how to do. But not having an intimate knowledge of this world is setting us back rather hard. William replied.

Malici looked at him silently for a long moment. That explained his foreign nature. *Alright. What do you need to know?*

We don't think we can assimilate what we need to know, fast enough. Would you be willing to lead the effort? Guide our energy? William asked.

Malici considered that. *How many are you, really?*

William looked over at Timothy, who had been following the conversation. Timothy did a quick math problem in his head before coming up with an answer. *200,000,000, give or take a few hundred new, or a few hundred recent lost.* Timothy offered.

Malici just stared, for a long silent moment. That was a lot. Far more than he would have guessed. He had expected ten, maybe. Not two *hundred million*. After a moment, he took a deep breath. With that many people ... and with the power just these two possessed ... that was a formidable front to head. Even more formidable if you were going the wrong direction when you encountered it. That was definitely enough power to start the world healing again. After a long moment of thought, Malici dipped his head. *I will assist you. But on one condition.* He said, opening the thought up so that Kentalic could hear, as well.

"What is that?" Kentalic asked, knowing that he was the one going to have to pay the condition.

You must change the world. Stop the use of majick. Completely. Doing this repair ... with as much energy as it will cost ... will amount to no good at all, if the life is continually drained out by the generation and use of majick. Am I understood?

"Completely." Kentalic said. "But this will take some time to accomplish."

I am aware of that. But this will be your task. Change this, and I will assist.

Kentalic nodded slightly.

This includes yourself, just to make sure you know. You *will have to give up the use.* Malici said, his ears folding back flat against his head.

Kentalic made a short bow. "As soon as I can." He said. "I cannot stop just yet ... or Gnaria will be torn apart. I will start what you ask just as soon as I can shift my attention to the task ... after Numar is healed."

Malici just looked at him for a long moment, before his ears came back up slightly. *Agreeable.* He said, before looking at William again. *Where do we go, to meet up with the rest of your people?*

To the mountains. William replied. *North of here.*

Malici nodded, shifting his wings slightly. *Let us be on our way, then.*

William and Timothy both moved, towards the door. Malici turned as they passed him, and followed them out.

Deilo watched them go, then looked at the Wizard again. "Well ... we did what you asked." He said.

"Yes. Thank you. It is appreciated." The Wizard said, simply. "Is there something that you would like, in return for your efforts?"

Deilo looked at the others again, but they only looked back. Lillia was on Horus' head again, where it was cooler. The weather in Kentalic was considerably warmer than it had been back east. Here in the city, Deilo's pocket had been far too warm.

Deilo looked at the Wizard again. "All we want, really, is to be able to live in peace. No more of this crazy travel. No more catastrophes. That's all. We're tired of being rooted up all the time."

The edges of the Wizard's mouth tipped upwards. "We would all like that, wouldn't we? But that is not something I can guarantee you, I am sorry. The best that I can offer you on that count, is stay here in Gnaria. Wars do not reach here, and will not, for so long as I hold any power."

"Can we go home, then?" Deilo asked.

"Yes. But I can make you an offer beyond that. If, for any reason, you need something ... you just let me know, and I will see about it. You have done the whole world a favor."

Deilo thought about that. "Okay."

"Can we go watch Malici, though?" Horus asked. "Is that something we can do?"

The Wizard shrugged – a most odd gesture for him to make. "I do not know. You'd have to ask him, not me." He gestured at the door behind them with one long-fingered hand.

Horus looked at the others. "Let's go. Not every day you can see something like that."

Deilo considered that. "Well ... alright. We're here, already." And with that they moved to head out the door, after the Mages.

The Wizard watched them go for a moment, then turned, and moved toward the door that would lead him back up to his workrooms.

The friends found the two Mages and Malici standing outside, apparently doing nothing at all. M'lar and the wagon were both gone, nowhere to be seen. Before any of the four could open their mouth to ask what was going on, they were cast in shadow. Everyone looked up as one, as Guiran back winged, to land.

Malici watched the Dragon until he was landed, and then pricked his ears with interest. He, too, had seen Guiran over the mountains. For days he'd observed the Dragon, wondering what he was up to ... though he had not known it was a creature of this size he was looking at.

Where does one find a steed such as this? Malici asked, of William, who only laughed at the question.

One doesn't. It finds you. William answered.

Guiran also grinned, though on him it looked rather threatening. *Indeed. I found them.*

Malici looked at Guiran again, surprised.

"Greetings." Guiran said, dipping his huge, crested head low.

Malici imitated the gesture. *Greetings.*

"You can follow me. If you follow closely enough, you can travel through on my wake." Guiran said.

By what are you implying? Malici asked.

Dragons travel great distances in just one second, through portals in the sky that they generate. We call them holes, as that is what they look like. He's saying that if you ride his tail close enough, you can travel through his hole, and follow us all the way to our destination, where the Army is assembling. William informed him, as the two Mages climbed aboard Guiran's back, strapping in.

"Where are you going?" Horus asked, finally, having recovered from the shock of the Dragon's appearance.

Malici looked back at the little group of friends. *I am going to the mountains again.*

"Crud." Deilo said. "Horus ... you really don't want to do that again, do you?"

"Not really." Horus admitted. "Well ... good luck."

Malici nodded once, as Guiran took off into the air just as the last rays of the sun flashed and faded into memory. *Same to you.* Malici turned to watch the Dragon ascend for a few moments in stillness. He moved suddenly, taking off straight into a gallop across the yard as he lifted and spread his own wings. Once they were all the way open, he leapt into the air, and started beating his feathered wings strongly, climbing into the air even as his legs pulled up against his body. He spiraled upwards, catching up to the soaring Dragon. Guiran flew as slow as he knew how, waiting. Once Malici caught up with him, he started flying a straight line as Malici tucked in close behind him, flying just over his long tail.

A dark hole opened up before Guiran, blotting out a large chunk of the sky, and the Dragon flew into it, followed shortly by Malici.

Inside the northern mountains several hundred miles away, an identical hole opened in the sky over the Army Base. Guiran flew out, followed by Malici. The pair of fliers circled slowly, descending into the vast arrangement of large white tents tucked between the native trees.

Dragons stood everywhere, throughout the lanes between tents, within the tents, and dotting the mountainsides thickly. Interspersed through them all stood men, and the smaller two-legged dragons known as Sikes. Beside the Sikes stood their own partners – tall tree Nymphs. The Sikes were only big enough to carry a single rider, and more often than not that rider was a

Nymph. The two made a strange pair, as the Sike was long and streamlined, much like a similar sized predatory dinosaur. But on its arms wings grew, the last digit of the hand spanning out incredibly long to support the front edge of the sail. The Sike's head bore a crest, but it was unlike the larger Dragons' crest in that it was made up of five independently mobile petals. Most of the time they sat as a solid crest, but on occasion one could be seen with its crest spread out in excitement.

Malici looked at everything, surprised by nearly everything he saw. The very air and land here, around this collection, was healthy like nothing he'd sensed or seen for ages. He paused in his flight, coasting, and looked up. He stopped breathing for a split second, as he took in a marvelous sight indeed; the sky was a rich, healthy blue. Not the sickly purple he had gotten used to, but a true, honest blue.

He descended again, following Gurian down, soaking in the abundance of health and magic... and what ever that other essence was that he had no name for. It all felt so *good*. It also reassured his heart that these people were indeed good for the world, wherever they were from.

Malici trotted a few steps after landing, folding his wings up and tucking them along his sides once more. He looked around, from this vantage point, next to one of the large buildings. Then he looked over at Guiran again, and his dismounting Mages.

Who are you? He had to ask, once they were on the ground.

We, William said, gesturing widely with an arm. *are the Dragon's Army.*

Malici looked around, and breathed deep. *Wonderful.* He said, happily. *It's all wonderful. I haven't seen land like this, since ... I can't even recall how long it has been.*

William nodded, slightly, as the biggest Dragon of the lot approached Malici. He stopped a short distance off, and dipped his head low, his golden-tinted bronze hide gleaming in the twilight.

"Thank you for coming." The Dragon rumbled.

Malici looked at him, and then lifted his head. *Pleased.*

"I am Bahran. Something of the leader, here." The Dragon said, as another Mage walked up and stopped by his shoulder. "We would be honored, if you would lead our efforts to stabilize this world."

Malici dipped his head down. *I would be honored to participate.*

"Let us begin, then. How do you want us to start?" Bahran asked.

Malici considered it, and looked up at the sky. He couldn't have asked for a better staging ground. A remote location, where there wouldn't be any locals to interrupt ... and the land was already healthy – also a big plus. *Just feed me the energy. I will take care of the rest. Keep me supplied, until I call a halt. Can you do that?*

"Most certainly."

Malici looked around at all the ones he could see. *This will take a great deal. I realize you have a lot to you, but are you absolutely certain that you have enough? If you do not, we could all very easily die.*

"No, we are not certain. We are great, yes. There are more of us in two other locations, also ready to channel. But even so, we are not certain of what it will take." Bahran said.

In that case, I will start with a smaller casting, one to magnify what you have got. It should increase the efficiency tenfold. Malici said.

"Good." Bahran said, settling down to the ground, setting his chin on his forelegs. "Do you need anything before you begin?"

I shouldn't. Malici said. *Where is the nearest water source?*

Bahran lifted his head and pointed his snout at the building Malici stood next to. "The bathing building. There is a hot spring underneath it."

Malici looked at it, and flicked his ears. *Excellent.* He said, before he laid down on the ground, himself, resting his own soft nose in the dirt. Starting near him and rippling all the way out to the edges of the massive gathering, all the Dragons laid down on the ground, resting their heads on their forelegs, their Mages all sitting down next to them, resting their backs against the sides of the Dragons. The Sikes all stretched out similarly, only the Numphs remaining on their feet. Each one lifted her arms up to the sky, and opened her voice to the heavens.

The sound from the Nymphs was a magic unlike anything Malici had ever heard before, in all his centuries. They charged the air around everyone, as Malici closed his eyes in concentration, starting the first casting.

Toward the ocean to the west, but still in the same mountain range, all the Dragons, Mages, and Sikes all settled identically, linked in telepathically, ready to channel.

Back towards the south, at the tall structure out in the middle of an generally uninhabited plain, the Mages and two Dragons at the Cathedral settled in similarly, also connected in. The building was nothing at all like a conventional cathedral, but was an impressive thing in and of itself. It was only so named by one of the first Mages who had jokingly dubbed the schooling facility the Hokus Pokus Cathedral. To most, it was simply known as the Cathedral.

    Malici gathered up an impressive amount of magic just from the one Dragon nearest him, and cast the first spell, increasing upon the energy that was already there. The air verily crackled and sparked with the load. Even just such as it was, the area affected just by the Army's presence grew, more of the land healing and stabilizing in the influx of energy.

    Malici began drawing magic, then, even as the Nymphs raised their voices into true song, their volume growing as the energy built. Malici was more than a little overwhelmed at first. Despite the heavy draw he was pulling, it was as if he had no more than taken a glassful out of the ocean of magic and energy around him. The experience made him a tad giddy for a moment, as his own system re-energized from its own depletion. It was not something he could help ... it had to be done, first, before he even attempted to heal the world.

    Malici's grasp filled to brimming, and then he released the spell, continuing to funnel magic into it as fast as he could, making it grow. His horns glowed and burned with a light like they had never known, filling every nook and cranny in the surrounding mountains with light. There was nowhere to find a single shadow. The spell grew, gaining a momentum all on it's own even as Malici fed it the magic that was channeling into his being.

    In a growing sphere, the world began to repair and heal, the sky slowly going from purple to blue again, green plants turning a true green once more. The earth took on a darker, healthier hue, absorbing the energy it so needed. Animals became healthier, their coats taking on a new luster and shine, drained colors returning to their original brilliance.

    The edge of the sphere sped onward, through the air and across the ground and through the ground, traveling ever faster as it picked up momentum. The spell fed off of itself even as it fed off of the energy Malici poured into it, detailing everything to the world's own nature, allowing the magic to penetrate and become one again with the world. When the edge of the sphere reached the core of the world, the world ceased its troubling, and began to calm again, even as the magic swept onward. The light from Malici's horns spilled out of the mountains, and began to pour out across the land and into the air, following the spread of the magic at a much slower rate.

Standing at a northern window in his Tower, the Wizard stood very quietly, watching the sky slowly turn blue in a swiftly advancing line headed southwards overhead. And then he saw the white glow that lit the horizon like a new dawn. He smiled then, a true, and happy smile.

It had been ages since he had last seen a blue sky. It was soothing to the very soul, to gaze upon such.

Standing together once again as a group clustered about the wagon, the friends and M'lar were discussing the trip back towards the Floating H ranch, when Lillia shouted, and jumped to her feet, pointing up at the sky.

It was twilight still, but the change could still be seen clearly. Color touched the residual sunset like nothing they had ever seen, as the speeding line reached the western sky. They could stand there and *watch* the land change as the line advanced towards them. And when it reached them and swept past, they could *feel* the change it wrought, as well as see it in each other and everything else.

They did not speak, amazed beyond words at the new world that presented itself to them.

The line of magical influence sped onward, until it simply grew up out of the ground on the far side of the world, spreading out into the sky with immense power. The whole world was then healed in one last white flash, and then it all went dark again, where the sun could not see.

Chapter Eight

A New World

The sun slowly rose, bringing a new dawn that lit up the valley with a new light. It was a bright, sunny light that warmed everything to new life. The rays lit up a brilliantly blue sky that bore only a few light, puffy white clouds.

Malici opened his eyes, tiredly, and blew a soft breath outwards, clearing the dust out of his nostrils. Closing his eyes again, he heaved a soft sigh. He had never been so tired, that he could recall. Lifting his head off of his tenderly sore nose where it rested on the ground, he opened his eyes once more to look around him.

There were Dragons, Sikes, and men scattered everywhere, each and every one just as crashed out as he had been. The Nymphs, however, were still standing, walking delicately here and there as they checked on everyone else.

Pulling in a deep breath, Malici levered himself to his feet. Once up, he stretched, lifting his wings wide and high even as he arched his back and neck. Giving his wings an experimental couple of flaps, he folded them down by his sides again, and looked around again, satisfied.

Despite being tired, he felt better than he had felt in so very, very long. His heart had lost a deep woe he had carried for ages. He had the knowledge of a hope fulfilled, and a new hope for the future. There was a bright dawn on a new horizon to look forward to.

Slowly, over the next hour or two as the sun climbed up into the new sky, the Dragons and men slowly started to wake, groggy and confused.

"Ohhhh." Someone groaned from where they sat propped on the ground, as Malici inspected the building that he had been told contained water. He found a door, and pushed on it with his head. It swung open readily enough, and then re-closed itself after he had passed. There was nothing fancy about it at all. It was obviously utilitarian to the extent. The inside of the building was just as large as the exterior, all the way up to the high ceiling. The ceiling was slightly obscured from sight with all the steam that had gathered there, where it condensed and dripped back down the myriad of projections emplaced just for that purpose, falling back down into the massive stone-lined pool that took up nearly all of the floor space. Malici walked over to the edge, and touched his nose down to the water to smell it.

Water! It smelled wonderful, so far different from the energy-drained substance he had been drinking before. On top of that it was definitely spring water, sparkling clear as it reflected the light that came in the large, high windows. A few of those windows were open, but not many, retaining the warmth that the water was radiating.

Malici closed his eyes in happiness and just smelled the water for a long moment before he ever bothered to actually drink. When he did drink, he drank deep, satisfying a thirst that had been there for a very, very long time. Satisfied, he walked back out, simply pushing on the door that swung outwards now, for him. Finding that mildly interesting, he walked back and forth through the door, but it always moved ahead when he pushed on it, no matter which direction he pushed.

He moved on, to look around. Most of the Dragons and men were gone already, having left to some unknown destination. Only a few, by comparison, remained. The Base was still teeming with them, but there were by far fewer.

Bahran walked up to him, shining in the morning light. "How are you faring?"

Quite well. I feel much better than I have felt in a very long time. Malici said. *The world feels alive again. Thank you. This means a lot, to me.*

Bahran nodded, once. "And to us. Thank you, for your help. Now we can turn our attention to what caused it."

Greed. Malici said, simply. *Magic was used faster than it could replenish itself. So people turned to a new source when it was all gone, creating a weaker but still potent substance known as majick.*

Bahran nodded, again. "It is generated from the Life force of a thing, be it the sky, or the earth, or an animal or plant."

Yes, something like that. Malici said. *I never looked very closely into it, finding it disgusting.*

"I agree. However, that was not the *root* cause. That simply made the problem worse. From what we have been able to tell, this world started out with problems before that even started. Otherwise the magic would not have been so weak. Magic is generated simply by being there, simply by someone knowing it is there." Bahran said. "But something disrupted that cycle, and that is why we are here. We came to counter the imbalance this world has attained, to set it all straight again."

Malici just looked up at the Dragon for a time. *I see.*

"If we should encounter something else that we really need to know, may we come to you again, at a later date?" Bahran asked.

Malici dipped his head, flicking his ears forward. *Of course. By all means. I look forward to seeing you again.*

"Thank you. We were far better at this job on our own world, where we knew what we had to know. Here, we are grasping at straws, trying to catch up before it's too late."

I understand. Feel free to contact me for any reason. I shall make an exception in my wards so that any of you can come to me.

"That is highly appreciated." Bahran replied. "I can have a Dragon take you back to your home."

Unnecessary. I have my own methods of long-distance travel. Malici said. *Do you mind if I look around, before I go?*

"By all means, help yourself. Feel free to ask anyone anything about anything you'd like to know." Bahran said.

Malici nodded, and walked on, looking around him as he went.

Bahran watched him go, and then looked down at his Mage when he walked up next to him. "That's one thing we don't have to worry about, anymore." He said.

"Very true." The Mage said. "Now on to the next."

"Yes. On to the next."

"You know, I never dreamed to see a real Pegasus ... much less one so big as that. Though, he's got two horns on his head. So I guess he's not a Pegasus. What do you call something like that?"

"That?" Bahran asked, watching Malici move around the Base. "You call that Malici."

The Mage laughed. "Indeed."

*

The wagon sped down the lane towards the cluster of buildings down in the bottom of the bowl-shaped valley. The ridali towing it was thrilled to be home again, singing out at the top of its lungs to all the other ridali in the valley.

The herds sped towards the road, and ran along the fences, alongside the road, blowing their welcome calls to their wandering relative.

The wagon stopped near the barn, and the four friends piled out to an enthusiastic greeting from all the present hands. The ridali was swiftly unhitched from the cart and stripped of its harness, given a royal treatment of a thorough bath, and then turned out to play with the other ridali. The wagon was unloaded in mere minutes, and rolled into a receiving bay in one of the barns, everything put away nice and neat.

The hands decided that the return of four of their own from an eight-month journey at the Tower's bidding was reason enough for a massive party, and bonfires were started as Ton prepared a massive festive meal – with the help from Deilo that he had sorely missed over the months.

Once everyone settled down at the very end of the day as the last of the bonfires were burning down, everyone gathered close around under the dark, starry sky to hear the tales of their travels and all their adventures therein.

But there was one more there than had been there before. Standing off to one side and grinning his fool head off, a green-and-yellow Centaurii watched the reunion. M'lar was not a member of the group, and would not be staying long, but he was happy to watch for the time being. In the morning, he would start out on a new, much smaller adventure once again. Travel was his life.

* * *

Glossary

Base – A point of operations for the Dragon's Army, of which there are three. Each with a specific and unique purpose.
Centaurii – A pony-sized equine-like Race that sports an equine head upon a human torso over an equine body. Members of this Race are often Cartographers or Guides, outside of their home land.
dragon – A large carnivorous reptile that dwells in the mountains. Not terribly bright, but extremely good at tunneling. Can fly, but prefers not to.
Dragon – A Dragon member of the Dragon's Army. Large, chameleon dragons that are capable of instantaneous travel via wormholes.
Dragon's Army – An army of men and Dragons from Terra, devoted to the cause of restoring balance to imbalanced worlds without the knowledge of the world in general.
Dtri – An avian-reptile Race, adept at fishery.
Elf – A vicious entity that is more often than not unseen. Appearing as a collection of smoke with talons, teeth, and sometimes horns. Entirely invulnerable to normal methods of warfare.
Gnaria - A valley ruled by the last Wizard. It is the only place on the eastern continent, south of the wild forests, that is not plagued by ceaseless war.
Gnome - A very small hominid Race. Usually only a few inches tall.
Goblin – A big-eyed hominid Race, usually short and ugly, but not unfriendly. Good at navigating underground.
Helf – An Elf half-breed. Usually violent and destructive, and kept in chains when not outright slain on discovery.
Kentalic – The only remaining Wizard on Numar, or the city in which he dwells, in the Gnarian Valley.
Lizard – A reptile Race, usually assumed to be animals. They are cunning and ferocious warriors even when untrained. Appearance is akin to a crocodile.

Mage – A Human member of the Dragon's Army, trained in many mystical and usually unknown methods.

magic – a non-physical essence that is used to perform deeds without physical effort. Self-regenerating.

majick – A physical substance generated from the life force of living beings to mimic the abilities of Magic, in lieu of Magic. Not as powerful, and once used up, the creature or essence it was derived from dies.

Malici – An Immortal being of Legends from Ages gone by. Revered by the SwordDancers for his wisdom and power.

mnar – A large breed of wolf.

Mnarag – A huge, powerful species of wolf that can only be kept out of townships by gigantic stone walls.

Nymph – A tree-nurturing spirit. Most stay within their trees, but many are loyal to the Dragon's Army and fight within their ranks.

ridali – A magical mammal that no one knows the origins of, that did not evolve from any natural animal. A created species, they are excellent draft animals, fleet-footed and sure, they do not tire easily.

Sike – A small dragon that is a member of the Dragon's Army. Bipedal with wings supported by one single digit. Intelligent, usually accompanied by a Nymph rider.

shezuit – A technological marvel, powered by majick. A floating train that follows a single track and travels at blinding speeds.

SwordDancer – The term is broadly used upon an entire Race of pointy-eared hominids, though there is a sect within the Race that are actual bearers of the title SwordDancer. Swords for hire with morals, they are feared warriors.

Turoun – A town in eastern Gnarian brush country that is mostly underground.

Wizard (the) – The last remaining member of his Race, a vaguely reptilian, reclusive wielder of magic, majick, and guardian of the Gnarian Valley.

Yelm – A razed city within the lands of King Cerin's rule.

About the Author

Crystalyn Emerald Dragon lives in Southern Texas, where she trains horses to drive and raises goats on the family farm. She can often be found traveling the roads of her home county in a blue horse-cart, taking in the sights of the world as she goes. When not writing or training horses, she is usually building something new, whether that is a new cart, or a new structure. She lives off the land in a way that is mostly forgotten, needing very little at all from outside the farm. But most of all, she loves animals and spends most of her time with them.

Made in the USA
Charleston, SC
05 October 2010